I0705853

Magic Lessons

By Harlowe Frost

Copyright © 2024 Hannah Willow
All rights reserved.

The characters and events portrayed in this book are fictitious. Any similarity to real persons, living or dead, is coincidental and not intended by the author.

No part of this book may be reproduced, or stored in a retrieval system, or transmitted in any form or by any means, electronic, mechanical, photocopying, recording, or otherwise, without express written permission of the publisher.

No part of this book was created, written, or otherwise conceptualized by AI.

ISBN eBook: 978-1-959981-53-4
ISBN paperback: 978-1-959981-54-1

Editor: Weslee Imrisek
Developmental Editor: Angela Grimes
Cover Art: Getcovers.com
Formatting: Huckleberry Rahr

Books In the Magic Of The Galaxy

Series

Series 1: Viera Kor

Book 1: Galaxy Lessons

Book 2: Magic Lessons

Book 3: Conflict Lessens

Acknowledgement

I hope you enjoy this book. Book one took Viera on a trip to outer space. In this book, she'll spend most of her time on Earth. If you're hoping for more time in the great unknown, don't worry, it's coming ... just not in this book.

When my good friends Nikki Maness and Nita Maness finished this book, they were not thrilled that the last book hadn't been started. My editor had no problems finishing this book and waiting to start book three.

As always, I came up with the concept of the book, but it took my village, including Angela Grimes and Weslee Imrisek to really make it shine. My son also was a big part in the conceptualization of the world and magic.

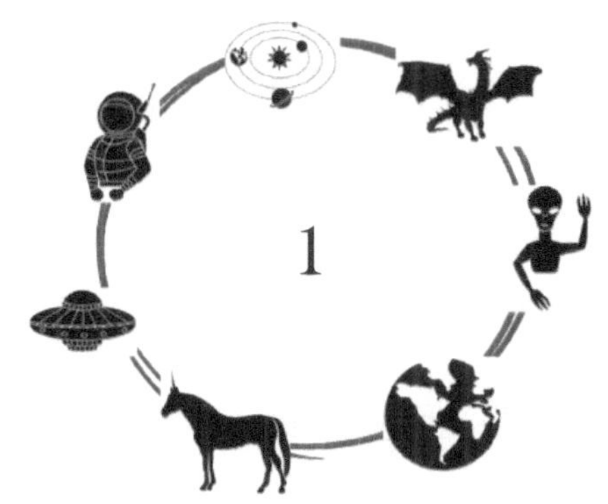

Pillar Of Humanity ... And You?

Viera

Betsy pointed an accusatory finger at Viera, then up at her ceiling, her face a mask of fury. Then the finger came back down to point at Viera's chest.

"Where the fuck did they take you?" Her voice snarled out.

Viera's mind spun a mile a minute. *What does she think happened? How much should I tell her? What do I say now? What does she know?* She stood and gaped at her friend, completely at a loss.

"Oh, close your mouth," Betsy snapped. "Did the chanzii take you up in their ship? Did you go to the summit? How long have you known about them?" She shook her head and looked disgusted. "You'd think they'd have told me." She mumbled the last as she lowered her arm and rolled her eyes.

A chill ran down Viera's spine. *Did Betsy just say 'chanzii?' What the fuck is going on? What does my friend know?*

"But how .... Wait. *You* know about the chanzii? They said no one on Earth knew. Nobody except for the pillars." Viera looked around her house. It looked just as she'd left it a week earlier on her way to her last day of school. "Why are you even here? How did you even get in? I have a security system." She waved her hand vaguely at the box on the wall near the door. The green light still glowed ... the system was on and active. *Apparently, it isn't that great, after all.*

Betsy followed her gesture. "Yeah, that's a good system, I'm just ... I dunno, I have abilities that the security industry hasn't worked into their programming yet. But let's stay on topic. I need to know what you know, Viera. This is important. What do you know about the chanzii? I've been working with them since they came to Earth. They never told me they knew you. That seems like a big oversight ... no?"

Viera took a step back, fear flooding her system. "You're not thinking of asking them to clear my memories, are you? Is that something they can do? Please don't do that. I know part of it was scary, but I want to remember."

Her friend raised her hands. "Slow down, just ... talk to me. Tell me the highlights. No one said anything about taking anything away." She took a slow, deep breath as if to model what Viera should do. "So ... you *just* learned about them?"

"Yeah ... I mean, yes. Scout, he's one of my students, an eight-year-old in my class ... but he isn't eight ... well, it's really hard to explain." Viera shook her head. "You've known about them the whole time? You know Scout? And about how old he is?"

"I know Scout and I know his real age. I already mentioned the chanzii. Don't you think if I know who they are, that means I know they age slower than the normal human? Assume for the length of your story that I know the basics. If I have a question, I'll ask." Betsy spoke slowly and calmly. She waved at the living room chairs. "Let's sit so we're comfortable as you tell your tale."

Viera sat, nodding. "Okay, right." Then she jumped up. "I need tea, do you need tea? I just ... this is so much."

"Sure, let's have some tea while we talk."

Viera ran into the kitchen and took a few minutes to let her mind battle with the fact that Betsy knew about ... well, aliens. Did she know about the dragons and unicorns, er, qynads and yonats?

When the tea was done—chamomile ... something soothing—Viera carried it on a tray to the living room. Betsy had stayed behind, obviously sensing she needed the space.

Betsy took a sip and sighed. "This is good, thank you. Can you tell me about your spring break?"

Viera let the tea warm her hands, then nodded. "I ended up on a spaceship, the Ziner."

"How? That doesn't seem like a mistake any of the chanzii or ... well, Ziner crew would make." Betsy leaned forward, resting on her knees.

"Scout had given me a mug and to thank him I gave him a hug. The timing was just ... wrong."

Her friend chuckled, shaking her head. "Okay, I can see that happening. They waited to leave until the last minute, and there was no way they could come back to drop you off. You were stuck for the trip. And what a trip. Why didn't you call or text? They have the technology."

The ridiculousness of the situation hit Viera, the last week of her life occurring to her. "It didn't occur to me to ask. I just assumed Earth phones wouldn't be chargeable. I didn't get a good charge until just before I texted you."

"And Commander Firoza was too swamped with getting prepped for the summit to think about trivialities, like your phone. I see you have an ear clip, so you could understand everyone; that's good."

Viera touched her ear and smiled. "It's like magic and not as gross as a babelfish, or any other weird creature that I've read about to help with alien translation."

Betsy chuckled. "Ah, the elephant in the room. Did they get you soaking in magic right away? Or was that another oversight?"

For a moment, Viera shut her eyes and thought about how she felt. She was back on Earth and under the blanket of magic all the creatures had talked about. She wasn't sure if she felt different, but she knew she felt better now that she was home. A smile spread on her face as she looked at Betsy. "It took until I got to the space station. Do you know Gandalf was a real person?"

"For fuck's sake, why is he always the first person?" Viera felt Betsy's annoyance pour off her. She tried not to flinch.

"You too? No one likes him? What, did you know him? The others who did seem to think he was some sort of jerk or something." Viera shrugged, not certain what they didn't like about him.

"I will tell you about grandpa Gran*dolt* as long as you don't ask to see his fucking staff. That stupid heirloom is nothing without his magic. I've tried to use it, but it's just a stick of really old wood."

Viera sat there, stunned. She opened and closed her mouth a couple of times before she blurted out. "You're a pillar? Holy shit. You can teach me."

"I can what now?" The confusion in Betsy's voice was only slightly eclipsed by that exuding from every pore of her body. Viera had dumbfounded her friend.

Lifting her hands, Viera took a calming breath. "You need to ... not be so confused. I know that doesn't make sense, but you're emitting too many emotions." After another breath, she smiled warily, then explained how the krottel took her and forced magic to awaken in her.

As the story got into the details of Viera's containment and being secured to the platform, anger radiated from her friend. Though Betsy held a blank face, her emotions seethed under her calm façade. Viera rubbed her arms, as if she could wipe away her friend's roiling emotions.

"They're bugs? The fuckers are bugs? And they bit you to read your memories and it forced magic into you?" Betsy stood, pacing the living room. "But you're okay now?"

"I am. Flower Prancer returned to Earth with us to be my trainer until another trainer could be found, but since you know magic, that can be you, right?"

Finally, a cessation from the onslaught of negative emotions. "Yes. I'd love to help you learn to use your magic. From the faces you've been making, you defin_tely have sensing. What is your elemental magic? Did the Elder figure that out?"

Viera nodded. "Yeah, energy. I can make myself go invisible!" She demonstrated, then laughed at the resulting expression on her friend's face.

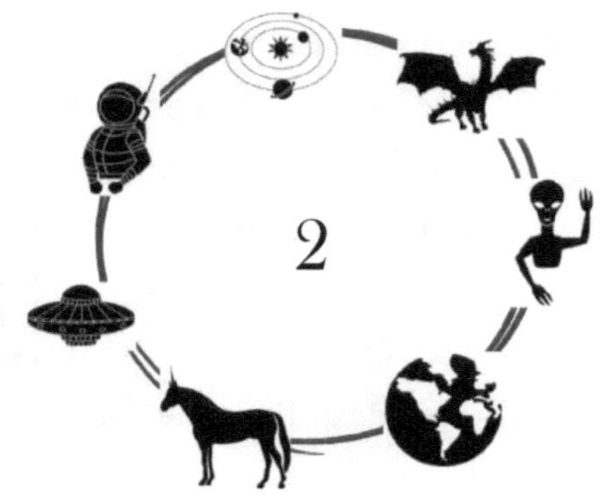

Life Back To Normal ... Mostly

Viera

The sun slanted through the window and warmed Viera's face. It had only been a week in space but being back on Earth and waking up to the sun seemed sinfully wonderful. She stretched and yawned, reveling in the feel of her own bed, her own sheets, and her own pajamas.

After Betsy got out every bit of Viera's story, they drove to pick up her car, take-out pizza, and then sat to enjoy margaritas and a silly movie. Viera was tired from her travels but figured during their next visit she'd give Betsy the third degree about being a pillar and everything that meant.

Today, she had to go shopping. There wasn't any food in the house, not even leftovers from the night before.

She pushed back the covers, weaving around the bag packed with the clothes Thorn had given her. Though the clothes would be strange to wear around town, Viera felt she may be able to wear them on a theme day at school. Touching the fabric, she felt a yearning to see the other woman. She smelled one of the tunics to see if it held a bit of Thorn's scent. She wasn't sure if they did, but she imagined she could smell the other woman.

Then she went to search her dresser and closet for more familiar clothes for the day. She selected jeans, a turtleneck, and a sweatshirt. There was still snow on the ground, though the air was warming up.

In the bathroom—her bathroom, with *her* things—she took a shower, washing away the remnants of outer space, and bringing her completely back to Earth. Clean and dressed, she made her way down to the kitchen. 'The one thing I really miss from the last week was the quick and easy access to delicious coffee. What I wouldn't give to be able to just say, 'computer, coffee.' and have—"

A sound to her left interrupted her. A panel, shiny and black, that hadn't been there when she'd left for school the previous week, and she was pretty sure hadn't been there the night before, sparkled on the wall between the kitchen and the living room. It made a small sound and a mug of steaming coffee materialized ... like magic. Or like alien technology.

So many questions! Viera didn't want to think about it. She wanted to relax and drink the magical ambrosia. With a lustful sigh, she took the coffee and sat at the small, round kitchen table to sip the perfectly made brew.

After a few sips, she got up and searched a junk drawer for a pencil and a small pad of paper. She made a list of the groceries she needed for the week. She hated shopping on a Saturday, but Sunday wasn't any better. Monday would be here soon. and doing anything on a workday was even worse.

Once she'd finished her coffee, Viera gazed at the black mug that had appeared from the panel. *I wonder if I'll end up with a ton of these? I'll have to ask Thorn what I should do with them. Can I somehow get the machine to reuse the cups, or will the damn thing just keep creating them?* Her eyes got wide. *Or is the stupid thing pulling the mugs from some store or house somewhere? Someone will reach into a cupboard for a mug, and they'll all be gone.* Viera snorted at the thought.

She gathered her keys, wallet, and phone, and headed to her car. "Never shop hungry; breakfast first." She turned the car towards a diner. The place was usually busy, but she arrived at a lull. The server seated her in no time. She ordered more coffee, a croque madame, and a sticky bun.

As good as the food had been on her trip, there was something about being handed a menu she could read and eating food she recognized that gave a sense of peace. As she sat, she realized she could pick up the emotions of the people around her. Sometimes her magic seemed to amplify their speech.

"Isn't this place great? It's so busy, I don't know why that woman took a booth all to herself. She could've sat at the bar." Exasperation and annoyance flowed to her from some woman waiting for a seat.

"It's not for us to judge, dear. The server sat her there. Worry about you, not her." Despite his words, the husband's annoyance hit her in the gut like a punch. She could feel their hunger.

"Well, hopefully she won't just sit there all day like so many college students do, unaware of those of us who have actual things we need to get done," the woman snapped.

Viera trembled at their ire. There were others whose feelings and emotions she felt, but that couple was the worst, and it just didn't end.

"Ma'am ... ma'am. When will we be seated? Do you have a table for us yet?"

Viera wanted to shut her ears, but she felt the words as much as heard them. Her belly twisted and she decided she was done. The size of the sandwich was beyond big, so she asked for half of it to be wrapped up for lunch. Once she paid, she was off to the grocery store to fill her fridge.

Back in her car, she took a moment to decompress from the diner. *Everything is so ... normal, if it weren't for hearing and sensing everything and everyone around me. It's almost like I never left home.*

She made it to the grocery store and decided it was better if she was distracted from what she could sense. She knew she had to call her mom, so she slipped her hands-free headset over her ear, and made the call.

"Viera! It's been a week. And you're just now calling me back?"

"I'm sorry, Mom. I decided to take a vacation, instead of a staycation. I ended up in a place without Wi-Fi or internet connection." Viera selected a cart and started down an aisle, searching for the items on her grocery list.

"Why didn't you call before you left and let me know? Or cancel your date? You could have found a payphone, or a landline. It's not like you to just disappear like that, Viera." Her mom sounded accusatory.

For a moment, Viera debated if she'd seen a payphone in the last dozen years. *Are there any payphones ... anywhere?*

She shook her head, focusing back on her conversation. "I know, it just came up. I made a last-minute decision. The traffic was bad. By the time I realized I couldn't call you, it was too late. My phone was dead."

"Goodness, girl, you are such a mess. You can't get anything together, can you?"

Viera sighed. Her whole life, Mom had been managing from afar, never seeing her for the competent adult she was. It was one of the reasons Mom kept trying to set her up with all these men ... even though she didn't date men. "Mom, I'm doing fine. Actually, I think I need to go. I'm at the grocery store and I don't want to forget anything."

"Oh, Viera, you shouldn't multitask, you know that. I'll speak with you later. I'll see if I can rearrange that date from last week."

"No, Mom. I need you to stop. I can find my own dates."

"But Viera, dear—"

"No, Mom. I mean it. I love you, but just ... stop." Viera wanted to snarl at her, but that wouldn't help. "I'll talk with you later."

She got off the phone and finished her shopping. It was good the shopping took some time; she needed every minute to calm down.

When she got home, she brought in the food as well as her mail. Amongst the letters was a large blue envelope. Handwritten on the outside in bold letters was her name. There wasn't a return address.

Curious, she opened the letter.

> *Dear Viera,*
>
> *I was hoping to take you out to dinner tonight. I know you haven't been back long, but I enjoyed spending time with you, my special fire cloud. I hoped we could continue to spend time together while I'm in town.*
>
> *Let me know,*
>
> *Thorn*

Viera leaned against the counter in her kitchen and gazed at the letter, her heart pounding fast in her chest.

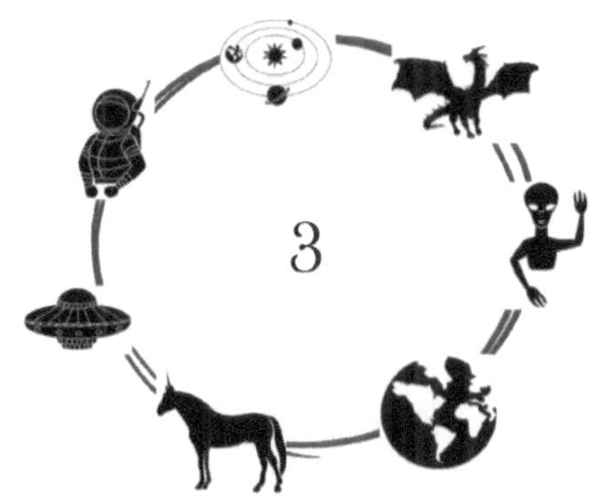

So Many Options ... So Little Time

Viera

After putting away the groceries, Viera searched her cupboards for tea. "Damn it, why didn't I check before I went shopping. All I want is a mug of mint and chamomile tea, is that so much to ask?"

The panel on the wall whirled, and another black mug appeared, steam billowing from the top. The aromatic scent of the tea Viera wanted filled the room, and she blissfully went to collect what the panel offered. "Well, this isn't so bad, now is it. I'll have to ask Thorn about the mugs." She bit her lip. "Thorn."

Viera took her tea back to the table and sat, checking over the note she'd received in the mail. There wasn't any return address, email, or phone number. "I wonder how she expected me to respond?"

She sipped her tea and thought about her week with the alien woman. A warmth filled her as she smiled. Viera texted Betsy. *Do you have Thorn's phone number? I need to send her a quick text.*

Taking her tea and phone, Viera headed up to her room to unpack the new clothes from her space adventures. "I wonder what my students would think of me wearing these doublets?" she mumbled to herself as she squished the clothes in her closet and made space for the new outfits. "Maybe we can do some sort of unit on different cultures, and I can wear these for the week."

She let her mind debate different scenarios as she got her room together. When her phone dinged, she checked the display. Betsy had come through, sharing the full contact.

Viera sat on her bed and gazed at what Betsy had sent. An image. She smiled at the very human-looking Thorn. She'd almost forgotten that representation of the woman she'd spent a week with. Her phone number and her address. She could've looked it all up at school, but that felt like crossing a weird professional line. Now it was all on her phone.

She selected messages. *Hi, Thorn. It's Viera. Betsy sent me your number. You didn't leave a way for me to contact you. I'm not sure if that was a test of my cleverness, but I'd love to have dinner with you tonight.*

It only took a moment for Thorn to respond with a laughing emoji. *Pick you up at seven.*

Viera changed from her jeans and sweatshirt to a long-sleeved navy-blue dress. It was fitted down to her waist then flowed loose to her knees. She wore a pair of black tights with a flower pattern and ankle boots. It was warm enough to go without a coat, so a shawl became her last layer.

At exactly seven, her doorbell rang. She opened the door. It took her a moment to adjust to the beauty standing there waiting for her. She'd known Thorn for most of a year, but only in passing as her student's mother. Scout's mom had only visited her classroom a couple of times. However, she'd spent eight days with Thorn, the alien with glorious purple hair and turquoise skin.

The sexy woman who stood in front of her with dark auburn hair, green eyes—and a slinky red dress that hugged her in all the right places—short-circuited her brain for a moment. Betsy always teased her that she had a crush on Thorn. It had been true before the trip to Torville Station Number Six, and seeing her like this, her previous crush came crashing back down.

"Hi," she croaked out, her voice betraying her.

Thorn smiled wide, leaning down for a kiss. With a groan deep in her throat, Viera stepped in, lifting her hands to the other woman's hips. The kiss deepened for a moment before they stepped apart. "Hi, back at'cha."

"You're stunning in any shape." Viera blushed, realizing she'd spoken out loud.

"And you, Viera, don't need multiple shapes to be beautiful. Now, let's find dinner. I have some ideas: sushi, Indian, Italian. Do you have a preference?" Thorn reached out for Viera's hand to lead her to her car.

"I think Italian sounds wonderful."

"Perfect."

The drive didn't take long. Once Thorn parked, they got into the restaurant and were seated. Viera asked for a table in a corner to minimize the bombardment of the other people while they ate. The restaurant wasn't that full, so Viera could focus on Thorn.

They were quickly making their decisions.

Thorn waved the menu at Viera. "Do you need me to translate?" She waggled her eyebrows.

"Ha, ha, very funny. Do *you* need my help? How long have you been on the planet? Do you know what all the different foods are?"

She picked up the menu again and started reading over the multiple pages. "You know, I've never really thought about it. I always just get pasta and meatballs. What *is* cannelloni? Ossobuco? I could use a bit of your professional tutelage."

Viera was pretty sure she was being teased but she rotated her chair until their legs touched—a small thrill zapped through her body at the contact—so they could discuss everything on the menu.

When the server came, they ordered an appetizer and two entrees: chicken parmesan and gnocchi with lamb sauce.

As they ate their meal, Viera smiled. "So, what do you do when not fighting on a space station for your people?"

"Before those evil bugs came to my planet, you mean? I was a baker, believe it or not. Most of the ingredients that we use on Abritos are different from what you use here. I've tried replicating some of my and Scout's favorites here, but they never work." The wave of sadness hit Viera like a heated, weighted blanket you get caught in and can't easily untangle from.

"Would you want to try to learn to bake together? I've done a little baking. Maybe we could try some recipes together."

Thorn smiled. "That would be amazing. That's what I need, someone local who knows their way around the kitchen."

"Then that's what we'll do," Viera said with finality. She took a bite of her chicken parmesan, savoring the extra cheese melted on top. "If not baking, what have you been doing?"

Thorn finished a bite of her gnocchi with lamb and put down her fork. "I've been focusing on keeping my people together. I'm the chanzii leader on this world, but also the top Commander for all the planets. I'm the one who will make sure my people will all come together again back on Abritos."

"I'm glad you'll get your planet back. It's amazing what you did."

The pride between them grew. Viera didn't want to read both their emotions, but she couldn't help it. With these emotions, she didn't mind. "Thank you."

Once they finished, Viera leaned forward. "You know, we've had a few decisions to make today. Where to eat, what to eat. Now we need to decide: what do we want for dessert?"

"Do you mean where? Or who?" Viera felt her face heat. But Thorn wasn't done. "Scout headed out to one of the other locations where our people are living. He and Juniper, one of our people, are spreading the news of our success. So, we can spend the night at your place or mine, dealer's choice."

"Then let's go back to my place and bake cookies," Viera said with a smile. "I have all the ingredients.'

It didn't take long to pay and drive back to Viera's place. Once they were in the kitchen, Viera started gathering flour, sugar, butter, salt, chocolate chips, baking powder, baking soda, and eggs. She turned to Thorn. "Are you comfortable as you are, or would being in your natural skin be better? I think you're sexy as hell either way. I just want you to be you."

Thorn came over and wrapped her in a hug, dipping down for a deep kiss. Releasing her, she smiled. "I'll stay like this tonight, but we can play around."

Light-headed, Viera went to the cupboard and pulled out her stand mixer. When she turned, Thorn came over and rubbed against her. "It would be a shame for this dress to get messed up from the baking. We should probably get it out of harm's way." She put action to the words and pulled Viera's dress off. "Same for my dress."

Viera had tights and a bra under her dress. Thorn had much less. For a moment, she just gazed at Thorn standing in her kitchen in nothing but tiny panties. She licked her lips, then stepped up to Thorn, running her hands up her sides to her chest, reveling in the silky skin and plump breasts.

She leaned down and sucked a taut nipple into her mouth. Thorn gasped as Viera's hand trailed down. Thorn stopped her hand's progress with a sound of disappointment. "As much as I want this, and we'll get to this soon ... cookies first?"

Viera stepped back, breathing fast. She stared up into the bright green eyes almost glowing with lust and laughed. "Right, baking, that's what we're doing. Maybe put on the apron. I don't know if I can focus otherwise."

Thorn gazed at Viera's light blue apron and smiled. She shimmied once it was on. It had two whisks on it and the tips fell right above Thorn's breasts. Viera wasn't sure if it was that much better.

The two stepped up to the counter and focused on their sweets. It didn't take long to sift the dry ingredients, cream the wet ones, and get the batter mixed. They put it in the fridge to cool before baking, and then a few minutes in the oven and they had their dessert.

"This may be the best date I've ever been on." Thorn sighed as she ate a cookie. "These are great. Next time, let's play with the recipe. I have ideas."

"That's fine, but you're going to have to be okay with a girlfriend the size of a house."

Thorn pulled her in for a kiss. "As long as it's you, I'll take you any way I can have you."

Viera reached over and turned off the oven. "Living room. I can't wait for the bedroom; I want you now. I've been good as long as I can. Couch."

The other woman laughed as they kissed and dropped their remaining clothing on the way to the other room.

On the couch, Viera straddled Thorn, leaning down for a deep kiss. Her hand trailed down the perfect body below her. At the same time, Thorn's hands investigated Viera's body, moving up towards her chest.

The feelings of need, want, and lust were overtaking Viera as she moved over Thorn.

Her hand made it to Thorn's sex, and she slowed her movements, rubbing in a slick circle. She let her finger slide deeper, feeling the heat of Thorn's excitement.

Viera's tongue and finger moved in rhythm, simulating Thorn. She felt Thorn matching her, stroke by stroke, and a wave of pleasure consumed her. She growled deep in her throat as desire built in her gut in waves.

Thorn's fingers shifted and a spike of electricity ran through Viera. Her body tensed as her breathing got choppy. Her hands moved faster as an orgasm crashed through her in waves. As her body quivered, Thorn flipped them, demanding more from her. *Do I have more to give?*

Their legs twined together, clits rubbing together. Viera rubbed up against Thorn as the other woman kept their mouths locked together in a searing kiss. Reaching between them, Viera rubbed Thorn's breast, flicking and pinching until she heard the other woman scream out her own release.

Tracing her tongue along Viera's ear, Thorn whispered, "Nice appetizer. Now we can have our real dessert in your room."

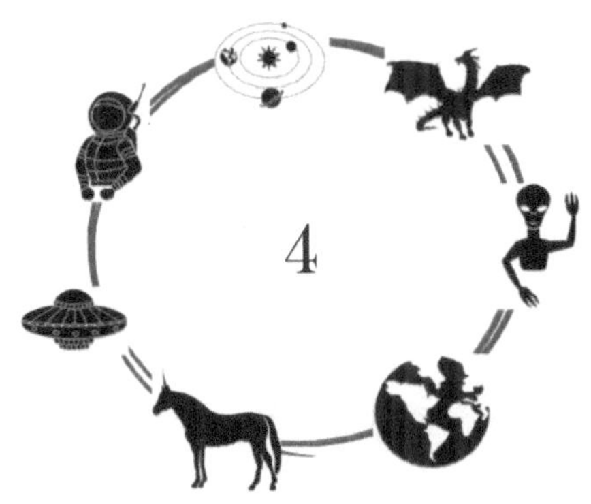

Nobody Likes To Write About Spring Break

Scout

Scout sat on the floor and pet Beaver. He was excited to see her so happy. She loved being planet-side and not on a ship or a silly space station. Being on Earth wasn't the best because she couldn't fly as much as she wanted to, but they had the barn where she could fly without being seen by the Earthlings.

"Okay, Beaver, I have to get ready for school. It's Monday, and I don't want to be late. Not to mention, I miss Ms. Kor. I know we hung out with her all week, but now she's back to being our teacher. Despite that, I have all our new adventures to remember. Do you think she's ever been to Montana or California? Those were fun places to visit."

Beaver hopped around the room, wiggling her body, excited for any attention.

Scout pushed himself up and went to his dresser. No more comfy clothes, just jeans and a T-shirt. He loved his humans-doing-crazy-things shirts, but he couldn't wear those on Earth. They were strictly for off-world wearing. He used to wear them all the time back on Abritos. It was what all his friends wore. Most kids his age ended up on planets that knew about the chanzii. There were a few other chanzii kids on Earth, but for some reason, he was the only one in Wisconsin.

He selected a shirt with three monkeys that looked electrocuted. One covering its eyes, one its ears, and the last its mouth. *See no homework, hear no homework, speak of no homework.* There wasn't a lot of homework in second grade, but the shirt still made him smile.

In the kitchen, he went to the panel and ordered up a plate with eggs, hash browns, and bacon. It tasted better here on Earth where the food actually came from. Mom came down and ordered herself a coffee and a chanzii cereal.

After they ate, Mom drove him to school. He dropped his bag by the door, trying to avoid the snow and puddles, then zoomed off to play with his friends. It had been over a week since he really got to stretch his legs, move around, and play, and he missed it. A couple of kids started throwing snowballs, but Scout just wanted to run and climb.

When the bell rang, he ran with all the other kids to gather his stuff, then he got in line. Ms. Kor smiled when her class got in line the fastest. He had a lot of secrets the other students didn't know, and now he had some with Ms. Kor. She knew he wasn't from Earth, and about the other aliens. Pride bubbled in him and amusement at what his friends didn't know.

"Great job, kiddos! Let's get in out of the cold." Ms. Kor's words pulled him from his thoughts.

She led them to the classroom. "I would like to start with a bit of writing. Tell me about six things you did over spring break. You'll notice you each have a book at your seat. The cover is blank and there are six pages within. Each page is half lines you can write on and half blank. You can add more writing or a picture."

Scout thought about what he could write. Ms. Kor knew everything he did, but he decided to write about the things he did over the weekend. After the grumbles and complaints, everyone got to work and did as they were asked.

The next activity was indoor play. Ms. Kor was excellent about mixing up work with down time. "Ms. Kor!" yelled Sandy, one of the smaller girls in class. "This puzzle is still missing a piece."

Ms. Kor came over to kneel by the crying girl. As soon as she placed her hand on Sandy's back, she perked up, tears gone. "How long has the piece been missing?"

Sandy bit her lip. "Since before break. I dunno. A long time."

Without missing a beat, Ms. Kor nodded, then shut her eyes. A moment later, she stood, walked over to a bookshelf, removed two books, and found the puzzle piece wedged in the seam of the shelf and the wall. She sighed. "I wonder how long that's been there. Here you go, Sandy."

Sandy's eyes were really big. "That was amazing, Ms. Kor. How did you find it?"

Ms. Kor shrugged. "I'm not sure. I think I saw it the last time I put the books away and I've been meaning to track it down ever since. Nothing mysterious."

Scout wasn't sure he believed that. She had new magic ... not that she or he would tell the rest of the class about that. *I wonder if part of her magic found the puzzle piece?*

The day proceeded with lessons and free time. Again, Scout enjoyed getting back into the routine. Despite it being a normal day, Ms. Kor looked tired. Every time the students got loud or angry, she looked like *she* wanted to cry. *I wonder what's wrong with her. Does she miss the Ziner?*

After lunch, she gave the class a wry smile. "How about a movie?"

The class cheered.

During the movie, Scout noticed that Ms. Ko: sat at her desk working. *She's probably getting things prepped for tomorrow.* He also noticed a small glow illuminating her workspace.

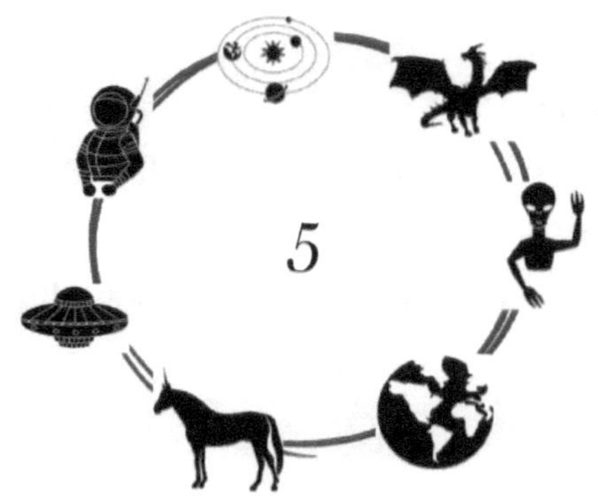

5

Let Me Heal Your Woes

Viera

Viera pulled into her driveway and turned off her car. She sat. The day had been long, and she was so tired. She couldn't believe how many emotions her students felt. There were only twenty-two in the class, but God above, it felt like they spent the day beating her up with their feelings.

She dropped her head back on the seat and let her muscles relax. After taking a few deep breaths, she finally felt she had the energy to open the door. With a sigh, she pushed herself from the car and growled at the mailbox. She trudged over.

As she pulled out the mail, Betsy parked and hopped out of her car, mocking her with all her energy. "Hey, tone down your pep. No one here needs to experience that, not after the day I've had."

Betsy snickered. "Rough day?"

"If you only knew. When I was on Torville Station Number Six it was never this bad. Nor on the ship. But twenty-two students ... I think I'm going to die."

Her friend came over and slipped an arm around her. "Come on, champ, let's go get some wine."

Viera straightened. "Can we?"

"Well, yes, but not until after our first lesson."

She grumbled some very unflattering words about her best friend as Betsy helped her into the house. She dropped the mail onto a kitchen counter. "Food first?"

"Nah, we'll order something to be delivered." Betsy waved her phone. "Let's go outside. We need to make sure tomorrow isn't as ... intense for you."

"Okay, if you can make this ... less, I'll take back half the words I used against you."

Betsy chuckled. "Whoa, half! That's actually not a bad deal. I put in an order for Chinese food." When she got off the phone she sighed. "They're backed up. Apparently, it's a busy time and it'll take them an hour to get here. So, that's how long we have to work."

Viera's backyard wasn't huge, but it did have two separate areas—one with a small table with chairs and a grill and a second with seats and a pit fire. Betsy dragged her to the second area.

"Okay, my friend. First, close your eyes, breathe, and then tell me what you feel."

Snarling, Viera shut her eyes. "I have an overbearing friend who is very amused by me. Though you do have a level of concern for me as well." She breathed in the scent of pine and the cool dry air of winter. It'd soon shift to a wetter air when the April rains took over. "There are squirrels in the trees, four of them. Five rabbits." Viera tensed. "And two coyotes. Holy hell, that's terrifying!"

"No, they are cute critters to have around. They won't mess with you if you don't mess with them. Okay, your sensing ability is good. Weird question, but can you sense the trees?" It sounded like Betsy leaned closer to her. *Or am I sensing that? Grr! Stop it ... there's no extra-credit!*

Viera opened one eye and sought out the trees. *Trees, trees, trees. Right. Trees.* She sighed. Time to throw caution to the wind. She relaxed and opened herself up fully. The onslaught almost knocked her over. She trembled at all the incoming information. Too much to stop. She couldn't control what soaked into her from the world around her. Through it all, she was able to pick out the trees. The story from the trees was low, slow, and long. It felt like a crowd of thousands all clamored to say, 'hello!' She thought her head would explode.

A cracking sound and a sharp pain brought Viera's focus to Betsy as she slapped her. "Close it down! Viera, close it all down. Whatever you're doing, stop it, now!"

Gulping down air, Viera tried. She felt like she was on a superhighway of mental incursion, and nothing would stop it. A cool wave washed through her, and she became aware of Betsy's hand on her forehead. "Viera, come back to me."

Viera shook her head, then rubbed her temples. "Okay, I'm ... okay." Her vision wavered and her head ... wavered, but the extra senses were gone. "Fuck, I don't want to do that again."

"Can you tell me what happened?" The concern from her friend filled the backyard like a rainstorm.

"There are a lot of trees and plants ... they all just wanted to greet me."

Betsy's head swung around, and her jaw dropped. "Good lord. All of them? For Fuck's sake. Let's not do that again."

"No, not even a little." Viera laughed humorlessly. "That was worse than twenty-two students."

Sitting close, Betsy put her hands on Viera's knees. "I need you to learn how to block other people's emotions. You can't spend your days internalizing everything. You'll go crazy. This is a new magic to me, and I didn't realize how intense it'd be."

"Do you know how to make it stop?" Viera could hear the hope in her own voice.

"The short answer is: the opposite of what you did to open yourself up. But I know that isn't enough. You can set up a mental landscape, imagining a wall or a barrier that can help. It will eventually become second nature, but right now, you have to think of something to distract your magic from working overtime before it overwhelms you."

For the remainder of the hour, Viera worked on blocking the concern Betsy felt for her. She imagined herself a princess in a castle, a socialite in a backyard surrounded by a huge wall, a dragon ... or a qynad ... breathing fire at all the extra stimulation she didn't want, and finally herself as a bird flying above it. The last worked the best. When she floated above the quagmire of sticky feelings, she could see them, dip down as she wanted, but avoid when the sensations became too much.

Viera slumped in her chair. "Tell me about your magic. I'm tired of talking all about me."

Betsy waved her hand at a plant that was wilting, and it slowly came back to life. "I have life magic. I can heal. I can do other things with it as well." She leaned back in her chair. "My elemental magic is solid. We can talk about all the magics and what they do, but not tonight. You're tired. I'm tired. And we're both hungry."

As if on cue, Viera heard someone pull into her driveway. Dinner was delivered.

6

Dodgeball

Viera

Tuesday started off better. As the title wave of student emotions tried to drag her under, she imagined flying high, a bird with orange and pink feathers. *I am the all-powerful lesbian fire bird of control.*

At ten, after two rounds of lessons with her students followed by small decompression free-times to allow the kids time to be kids, they were given a twenty-minute recess. Checking the calendar, Viera saw she had recess duty this period. With a groan, she dragged on her boots and winter coat. It wasn't that cold, but while standing around, the chilly air always seeped in.

The number of kids playing—kindergarteners, first graders, second graders, and third graders—was insane. Most of the kids were exuberant to be out playing, and their excitement washed into her, filling her. Like small bee stings, there were a few kids who were upset. She followed the threads of feeling until she found the kids who weren't happy.

"What's wrong?"

A boy sat on the cold asphalt, hugging his knees. "I fell."

"Do you need help?"

His head snapped up. "No!" He popped up, in the elastic way only kids move, and ran off.

As she watched him run, she could see a ball from a game of soccer fly into his path. She ran after him and threw a hand out in the path of the ball, stopping it from tripping him. She just knew if she hadn't stopped the ball, the boy would've fallen and really hurt his arm.

As it was, he hadn't even noticed her intervention.

Shaking her head, she threw the ball back to the kids who'd been playing soccer and walked back towards the school door. In her mind's eye, she could see a small girl slip from a ladder. She reached her hand out to steady her as she walked by. Then a boy started to slip from the monkey bars, and she gave him a boost.

At the door, she shook her head. *Kids slip and tumble all the time. The playground is built for this. Stop fussing and let them be. Moreover, I'm probably just exaggerating things.*

Viera checked her watch; three minutes until the bell. Scout ran up to her. "That was amazing. You've always been the best, Ms. Kor, but you just helped all those kids. And the way you help with emotions. See why you're the best teacher in the galaxy?"

She squatted down. "I don't know, Scout. I think we're both imagining things. I know I'm sensing more, but I think I need to speak with my friend. Now, you have a couple of minutes, go play."

He laughed as he ran off.

Back in the classroom, she started to feel the emotions of the students. Tiffany, a girl who usually sat with a group of other girls, sat alone in the reading corner.

Once everyone in the room had a page of addition and subtraction to work on, Viera sat next to Tiffany. The girl's sadness threatened to take over her ability to 'fly above the emotions of others.'

"What's wrong, Tiffany?"

"My friends don't like me anymore." She sniffed, then tucked her head in her arms which were crossed on her knees.

"Oh, sweetie, I'm sure your friends still like you."

"No! They told me they didn't want me to play with them anymore." She spoke to the floor between her feet.

Heart hurting for the young girl, Viera reached out to pat her back, wanting to take away the sharpest of her pain. As she rubbed the girl's back, she could feel Tiffany settle.

Tiffany sniffed. "Maybe I can talk with them again. They said they were mad at me because I said I didn't like pink. But I could just not love pink, but like it for them. Maybe I was being a bit mean, too." She finally tilted up her head to gaze blankly at the class. "Thanks for listening Ms. Kor. I'm ready to go back to class." She popped up and headed to her desk.

Viera wasn't really sure what had just happened but was happy with whatever she'd done to help Tiffany. She headed back to work with the other students.

In the car on the way home, she dialed Betsy. Her friend's voice came over the car's speaker. "Hey, Viera, how was flying above the crazy today?"

"Well, I think it went ... okay. I still ended up playing a movie. The students are going to know all the kids' movies from the eighties ... and nineties."

Betsy laughed. "You're doing a new kind of education, I see."

"I, uh ... well, Scout noticed this, too. Is seeing things, like premonition, something that people who can sense can also do?"

"What do you mean ... premonition?"

She told her friend about her day. By the time she got done, she was home, in her kitchen, drinking a glass of wine.

"Okay, So, I think we need to talk to a friend of mine. I'll check in with him to make sure he's free, but maybe Friday would work. Pack for the night. We'll be back on Saturday."

"Um ... okay. Are you going to do any more lessons with me, or are you just going to wait?"

"I'm not in town tonight. I may be back Thursday, but let's just wait until after we see my friend."

Going to the plate of cookies she'd made with Thorn, Viera nodded to the empty kitchen. "Okay, I'll see you Friday."

"See you then." Her friend hung up, and a sense of contentedness washed through her as Viera realized it was her first night truly alone since before she'd left for space.

Why Does This Keep Happening To Me?

Viera

Viera walked around her class as the students worked on a science lesson. She was rather proud of her progress. The students had only ended up watching a movie two days this week. The joy and laughter at the cartoon comedies was easier to filter than the disparate emotions of a random assignment. Her battle with her sensing magic continued, but every day it had gotten better.

When the bell rang, she smiled at the wave of exuberance from her students and watched as the kiddos packed up, ready to leave. "Have a great weekend everyone. I look forward to hearing all your stories about the weekend on Monday."

"Bye, Ms. Kor!" echoed throughout the room.

Once the room emptied, she circled the desks, putting away a few items, collecting others, and generally straightening up. She created a pile of papers that needed grading. *I wonder if I can grade in the car wherever Betsy is taking me. If it's far enough to need to spend the night, it can't be close.*

She pulled out her phone and texted her friend the question.

Betsy's response came quickly: *No. Get home soon. We need to be on our way. Grade Sunday.*

Mumbling to herself, she gathered everything she wanted to take home. "What if I don't want to grade Sunday? What do you think of that? Maybe I want to take the weekend off from anything related to teaching." She tilted her head as she put the papers in a folder and the folder in her bag, thinking about Monday. "I may have time to grade on Monday." She carried the papers to her car as a possible weekend grading activity, but if they didn't get done, then she wouldn't stress.

When she pulled into her driveway, Betsy was already standing by her mailbox. "Good, you're home! Let's get inside. I want to maximize our time on this trip. No more dilly-dallying."

"Hi, Betsy. Nice to see you, Betsy. How was your *week*, Betsy?" Viera rolled her eyes. "Do I get five minutes? And why are we going into my house to leave? I mean, my bag is in there, but it's by the door. I can run in and grab it and we can be on our way."

Betsy tugged on her arm. "Hi, my week was swell—save for my smart-ass friend. Come on. And start using your head."

In the house, Betsy looked around. "I spoke with Thorn. She said that one of her people put a panel in your house. Do you know where it's at?"

Viera's jaw dropped. "The fancy coffeemaker? It's in the kitchen."

Her friend snorted. "Yeah, the fancy coffeemaker, that's exactly what it is."

"Well, it makes tea as well," Viera admitted.

"Hmm." Betsy walked into the kitchen. "Bring your bag."

Uncertain, Viera followed her. When she got into the kitchen, Betsy had just finished up at the panel, and stepped back. "You know how to use that thing?" She gazed at the drying rack full of black mugs next to her sink. "Do you know if I can get the silly thing to reuse the mugs? I already have too many mugs and all these black ones are starting to take over my kitchen."

That got Betsy's attention. She gazed at Viera, looking a bit confused, before turning to the sink. She laughed. There was a buzzing sound from the panel. Betsy grabbed her bag then linked her arm with Viera's.

"You just need to program the panel to use the mugs within your kitchen and not create them."

"I need to do what, now?" Viera gaped at her.

Before Betsy could answer, in a replay of what happened two weeks prior, her kitchen started to melt away.

"Oh, shit! I'm not going to space again, am I?"

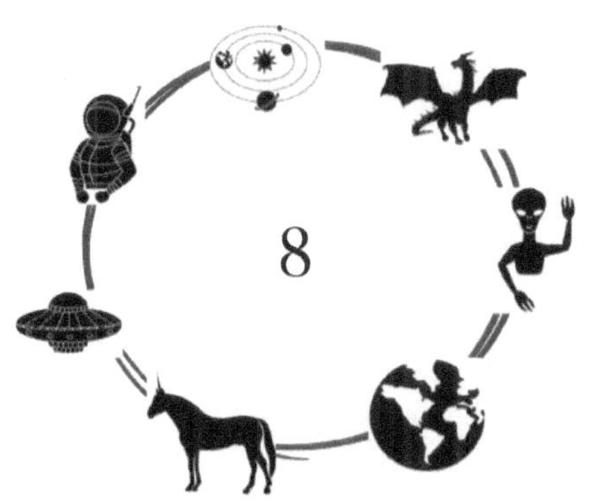

8

Trip Down Memory Lane

Betsy

Viera's eyes were the size of saucers. She gaped at a window and giggled a bit manically. "Okay, not in space. But Wisconsin?"

When Betsy checked the view, she thought she could see the London Eye in the distance, Zuza had a great flat with an amazing view, but she wasn't sure how focused Viera was right now on the views around her. "No, Viera, not Wisconsin."

From behind them, a throat cleared. "Betsy, it's been too long. When was the last time I saw you?"

"In person or does technology count?" She spun and smiled at her friend.

Zuza sat in a chair, crystal blue eyes crinkled at the sides with humor. His light brown hair was swept back in a short style. Like her, Zuza's appearance was deceiving. He looked to be in his mid-forties but was nearly five-hundred years old. "Technology? You know my opinion about the stuff. I was born before it was popular, and I only use it because we don't have much choice." He waved his hand. "This transmittal technology will be picked up by our government soon, and then where will we be?"

Viera shifted. "Transmittal? You mean the beaming?"

Zuza laughed. "Yes, child. The aliens call it transmitting. You get used to the terminology, just like their words for dragons and unicorns." He winked at Betsy's friend. "Don't let an Elder hear you call them a unicorn or an alicorn, they get huffy."

Viera laughed. "Okay, so, you must be one of the pillars. My name is Viera. I'm Betsy's friend. She called you Zuza?"

Zuza stood. "Yes, I'm Zuzalla. I'm originally from ... Poland but have relocated here to London. I like the mellower weather." He held out his hand for Viera to shake. Then he sat back down.

Viera snorted.

Betsy smiled at him. "So, our last time together, face to face, was at the coalition when we figured out how to incorporate all the chanzii into our world. All the pillars were there. I don't think we've been in the same room since then."

"Hm. I think you're right. Crazy times, I tell you. And you ended up with their leader in your back pocket. Dealing with Commander Firoza almost every day. How is that going?"

"It's going. The summit went well; did you hear?"

Zuza nodded. "I did, it went out in our group messenger. Have you checked that?"

Betsy sighed. So much to do, so little time. "No, I've been busy."

Zuza leaned back. "About that ... why were you in such a hurry to get here?"

Betsy guided Viera to a seat and spent a few minutes telling Zuza about the previous week and everything she'd learned from her friend. Viera jumped in with her own details when Betsy faltered. At the end, she let her hands fall. "Her sensing seems to be out of control. I've never heard of a wizard not being able to control their two proficiencies. And I don't know how premonition fits in. That usually is a subset of life, not sensing. Everything about her skills is confusing me. I wanted you to test her and let me know what you can figure out."

Viera shook her head. "Flower Prancer already tested me. That's how we figured out sensing and the proficiency for energy."

Zuza snorted. "That Elder is great, but he doesn't have sensing as a proficiency. He can test for something specific, but I can do a broad test and let you know exactly what you have. Sensing, like you, is *my* proficiency. But unlike you, I've been doing it for several years, and am rather good with it. We'll get you straightened out."

Viera tensed. "Can you teach me?"

A booming laugh blasted out of the man, it was a signature of the other man. Betsy had been waiting for it. "First you question me, then you try to hire me ... how fun. We should be able to set something up once we get you sorted."

Viera nodded. "Okay, I understand." She seemed a bit deflated.

"Hey, I'm your teacher, isn't that enough?"

"Yeah, I guess, it's just ... he's an expert."

"I am. Now, before you get into a silly discussion, sit back, close your eyes, and open up all your magic. But only do it for a moment. I don't want you talking with my plants—we don't have that kind of time."

Viera laughed. "I wish I'd been warned about *that* earlier this week." She took a deep breath before closing her eyes and doing as Zuza requested.

Betsy felt the magic flow from her friend before she shut it off. It was nothing like the deluge from Monday night when Viera lost control.

"Holy shit. This isn't possible. I hate to ask, but Betsy, lock down hard and Viera, one more time." Betsy was locked down, but she felt the blast from her friend again. After the third, Zuza sighed, rubbing the bridge of his nose "Okay, enough."

"Talk. This is not like you."

"Well, this is not like anything I've sensed before. She's hitting my senses as an Elder, not a human."

9

I'm Too Young To Be Old

Viera

"What do you mean I'm an Elder—aren't they the unicorns? I mean, the yonat?" Viera's head spun. What was he talking about, this person Betsy had brought her to? He was a quack! Were all the pillars three steps removed from reality? An Elder, hell, she was barely over thirty.

Zuza sighed, and his expression shifted from being jovial to serious. He'd been light and happy before, but now was time for the serious professor. "Worlds survive with magic."

Viera nodded. If nothing else, she'd learned that. More than that, Earth had a thick blanket of magic spread over it. She wasn't sure what exactly *that* meant. "I've figured that out, yes."

"Good, good. Some creatures are naturally magical, like the chanzii. They can all change shape because they all possess the life proficiency. For the most part, that's all they can do with that magic. Having one proficiency doesn't mean anything among the chanzii or any being, really. Now, having two is the sign of a wizard." He nodded at both Betsy and her in turn. "There are some chanzii with a second ability. A lot of them, actually. Earth is odd that there are only five of us ... well, six, including you. On most planets, wizards are rare, but still make up five to ten percent of the population."

Viera gazed around the room, thinking about the numbers. Half the magic wielders in the world, literally, were sitting in that room. The odds suddenly made her skin crawl. "Why is Earth so different?"

Betsy sighed. "We aren't sure. Evolution hasn't caused more people to awaken their magic. For the current pillars, it's something passed down within the family."

"Does that mean there are more than five pillars when your parents are alive?" Viera just wanted to get this all figured out.

"Yes, but none of our parents are still around. It's been a long time for all of us." Betsy shook her head. "You know what, let's hold off the discussion of family for when we have more time. Let's utilize Zuza while we're here. Back to your question. How can she be an Elder?"

"And what do you mean by an Elder?" Viera cut in.

Betsy rubbed Viera's leg. "Having two proficiencies means wizard. Some wizards study for many years and eventually learn and master a third magic category. Having a third proficiency means you're an Elder." She turned to the other wizard in the room. "She has three proficiencies?"

Zuza grunted. "I don't know how; I just know that she does. From what my test told me, her deepest magics are energy and time. I believe if she'd become a wizard naturally, that would've been her elemental and non-elemental focuses. With what you've told me, it's still very rare. Then, with what the krottel did, if I were to guess, when they bit her, they forced their own sensing into her. It's why she's struggling to control it. We can naturally control what we possess as our own magics. And now she has three ... and is an Elder."

A kick to the gut would feel better. Viera threw her hands up. "Whoa, what you are saying is, not only am I odd as a human, with three proficiencies I'm super odd? Moreover, I can't control my sensing? I'll never be able to control it? And what is time magic?"

An image of stopping time and getting more sleep or having time to prepare for class flitted through her head. Or better yet, pausing everyone in her class when the students were getting wild and just having a moment to breathe.

Zuza narrowed his eyes. "Now, none of that. From what Betsy said, you're already learning to control the sensing. But let's put that aside. The premonition comes from sensing and time. Time has a few aspects. It usually allows the wizard to review the past, but apparently, mixed with your sensing, it's giving you a glimpse into the future. Have there been any other instances where you may have played with time?"

Viera thought about all the times she'd worked with her magic, but nothing came to her. She rolled her mind back through all the instances of training and occasions her body and soul remembered releasing her power. She closed her eyes, and it was like a movie played in front of her eyes. Image after image flashed like a movie on a screen. *But what magic am I using? Sensing? Energy? Time?*

The visions shifted, some became tinted blue, some red, some yellow. When the memory of her preventing the ball from hitting the kid glowed green, a combination of blue and yellow, she understood the colors represented her proficiencies.

Blue was the most common color. Sensing. When the screen flashed all the way to her first lesson with Flower Prancer, she noticed a yellow glow around the pencil. She squinted as the pencil shrank in length. She remembered seeing pencil dust on the table. *Well, I'll be damned. I sharpened the pencil with my magic.*

When she opened her eyes, both Zuza and Betsy were staring at her. She explained what she'd done. Zuza threw his head back and laughed. "I love the adaptations of magic. They never let me down."

Once Betsy stopped snickering, she nodded. "So, there were a few times you've dipped into the time magic. Mostly premonitions. Three different aspects to train. You will be a handful, won't you?"

Viera wanted to growl. "As much of a handful as my sensing. It feels like my power is a group of my students gone wild at recess. Nothing I do really contains it."

Zuza's face softened. "You've had these powers for less than two weeks. You'll figure it out. We'll help. We can set up a regular meeting over the silly technology. You and I will work through the sensing. We'll get you figured out."

A wave a gratitude washed through Viera. "Thank you."

"Now, let's go find a pub and get some grub. There's no learning on an empty stomach. It may be five in the afternoon for you, but it's eleven at night here. So, we need to eat and sleep, then I'll be awake enough to help you tomorrow." Zuza yawned before he led them out to the oddly bustling streets of the city. London, unlike Madison, didn't roll up its sidewalks at nine at night. Apparently bigger cities were awake much later.

Make Me A Gin and Tonic

Viera

"Why aren't there any books? Don't all you wizards have grimoires or magic books or something you hand down from parents to child to help with learning?" Viera slumped after a two-hour session with Zuza. She had to admit she had a better grasp on the Wild West crazy that had taken over her head ... also known as her sensing proficiency.

Zuza chuckled. "Books can end up in the wrong hands. Haven't you ever read any books or seen any movies? It's the heart of half of them. Real magic users' words end up in the hands of the regular people and then all hell breaks out."

Viera narrowed her eyes. "Are you saying if an average Joe on the street read a book on wizardry they could open up their magic and more pillars could evolve on Earth?"

"Maybe." Betsy rubbed the back of her neck. "We're not sure. And that's the crux of the situation. We know our planet is different, but we're not sure why. Do we help the spark of true understanding spread? Or do we keep it hidden?"

"We know what your grandfather thought," Zuza mumbled. "The old swindler. He was always pushing for things the world wasn't ready for."

Excitement at the mention of Gandalf surged through Viera. She knew they didn't like him, but she was still starstruck. "He did bring a lot of ideas of magic and different magical creatures to our attention. Too bad it didn't do more. I wonder what more would be needed."

Zuza smiled at her. "Don't sound too fan-girl in front of Betsy; she's not the biggest fan of her grandfather. Now her dad, he was amazing. It's too bad he didn't live longer. You'd have loved him."

Betsy gave a small smile. "Too true, Dad really was a great man."

"What was he like?" Curiosity filled Viera.

"Everything my grandfather wasn't. He supported me, but also wanted me to be a kid. Grandfather focused on me learning about the aliens and taking over the family job. Magic, diplomacy, languages. Dad knew the importance of all that but also wanted me to be a young, you know, a kid on Earth."

"Sounds wonderful. Did he take you to places like Disney World?"

Betsy laughed. "No, we were a couple hundred years too soon for that."

Viera snorted. *Betsy is such a joker. A couple hundred years.*

Zuza chuckled along with her. "Well, it's only been a couple of hours, but we don't want to overdo it. Why don't we walk around a bit, see the city, take in the sights, then grab food. You can be back home by noon your time. It'll be a long day, but we've gotten a lot accomplished."

A thrill at the impromptu vacation to London had Viera leaping to her feet. "That sounds amazing. Can we see the changing of the guard?"

"We're a bit late for that. There are big crowds and by the time we get there, it'll be over. Next time. But we can see the other big tourist traps," Zuza explained. "And then you can have another meat pie or fish and chips ... done the right way."

Viera smiled like a dork. It all seemed unreal. It had to be unreal. She'd worked all day yesterday and would be home tomorrow. Beamed back and forth? This was insane! "Let's do this unbelievable day."

When they returned to Zuza's flat, it was just after seven local time. He walked over to a panel and started playing with it. Viera sighed. "Everyone knows that stupid language but me."

Betsy patted her back. "I'll get a learning tablet for you. Didn't you say you started?"

"I did, but I didn't realize I needed to continue."

"You'll pick it up. Just give it a bit of time every day."

Viera sighed. "Like all the learning apps on my phone? Remember when we decided to learn Chinese together? That didn't end well."

"For you, my friend. I finished the course."

Glaring at her, Viera grumbled, "Of course you did."

Before they could joke anymore, Zuza gave a curt nod. "Okay, it's time." He came over and gave them each a quick hug. "Off you go, back to America. I'll talk to you soon so we can continue to hone, refine, and contain that wild sensing magic."

She kissed his cheek. "Thank you."

"Of course." He turned to Betsy. "And let's not wait so long next time."

"Agreed."

Viera was ready this time when Zuza's flat shimmered and then was replaced by her living room.

What she hadn't expected was Flower Prancer to be standing in the room, violet eyes narrowed, stamping his hooves impatiently, waiting for them. "Why haven't you answered any of my summons, human? I came to this damn planet to teach you, and instead you plan a day trip to London? What sort of gratitude are they teaching kids these days anyway?"

Viera's jaw dropped as she gaped at the unicorn from every girl's dream. White as a cloud with a rainbow mane and tail. If he wasn't so ... angry at her all the time, he'd be perfect. Then his words penetrated. "Your what? When? I never ..." She shook her head dumbfounded. "I have no idea what you're talking about." Terror washed through her at the thought of offending the yonat. "What are you talking about? What lessons?"

With a huff and a flick of his tail, he turned to Betsy. "Is she simple? Should we put her down instead of wasting my time? What is she babbling about?"

Betsy's face hardened at his words. "You all are idiots, you know that, right? For the record, she's been learning to hone her magic, which you messed up with, by the way. You came to *find* a teacher—well, what do you think *I* am? And we didn't take a day trip, I took her to Zuzalla, because neither you nor I can help her with the sensing magic the krottel forced into her."

As Betsy took a breath, Flower Prancer asked, "What do you mean forced into her?"

Betsy ignored the question. "While you were sending my friend messages on a panel in a language she doesn't speak, I was here helping her. You never sent her a note in the mail. You never sent *me* a message as the local pillar and leader of the human wizards on this planet. I'm shocked you didn't follow *any* of the standard protocol, for all your bandying about doing things properly. All you did was have a panel installed that my friend doesn't know how to use. Brilliant."

"Of course she can use it! She used it on Torville Station Number Six for a week," Flower Prancer said with a snarl.

Viera was tired of listening to them talk about her as if she weren't there, and the battle of their emotions was giving her a headache. If they were going to go on and on without her input, she may as well *not be* there. She headed into the kitchen. She dropped down on one of the chairs, but her escape was short-lived as the two followed her.

"No, the others used the panel because she only speaks English, not Galactic Standard." Betsy swung to Viera. "What can you do on the panel?"

"Um." She shook her head, not really wanting to be pulled into the fight. "I make coffee and tea mostly. I thought I'd ask Thorn why it suddenly appeared the next time I saw her. I mean, fast coffee is nice, but it isn't that hard to make the stuff myself."

Flower Prancer made a pained sound. "It is a glorified coffee maker to you, Earthling?"

Betsy snorted. "Panel: gin and tonic."

Viera groaned. "It can make alcoholic drinks, too? I've totally missed out on the finer points of this panel."

"Make it two."

Two glasses appeared.

The yonat snapped, "It's for communication, humans. It isn't an aid for food and drink!" He was almost yelling.

Viera stood to get her drink. "And how am I supposed to use the panel when I don't speak the language? Say: 'Computer, messages'?"

The panel beeped. "You have twenty-three messages. Thirteen from Flower Prancer, six from Thorn Firoza. Two from Horax. Two from Scout Firoza. Priority?"

Her body went slack and, again, her jaw dropped. She just gaped at the panel. Flower Prancer harrumphed. "Like that. I expect you at the lesson tomorrow, nine a.m." And he walked out of the house.

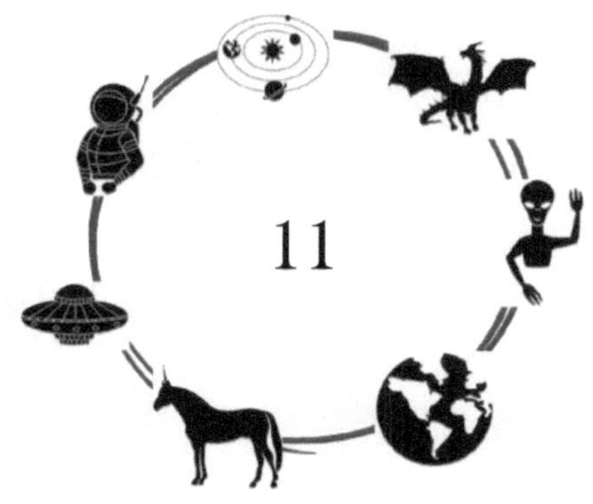

11

Can't We All Just Get Along

Viera

When she woke Sunday morning, Viera felt tired and sore. Her head hurt and her neck was tight. "Goodness, learning magic is a workout! And I have to meet with Flower Prancer today?" She groaned, flopping her arm over her eyes.

After a quick shower, she headed to the kitchen. "Panel, messages."

There was one from Thorn. "Heya, sexy. I hear you'll be training with Flower Prancer this morning. I thought you'd like to stop by for lunch. Scout and I can make you something and we can catch up from the week."

A warmth filled Viera. "Um ... panel, can you send a message to Thorn Firoza?"

There was a beep. Viera waited, then realized the panel was waiting for her. "Hi, Thorn. I hope I'm doing this right. I'd love to have lunch with you. I don't know when I'll be done, or even really where I'll be meeting Flower Prancer, but, um ... lunch. It sounds amazing." She waited a moment, not certain what to do next. "Message complete?"

The panel beeped again. "Message sent to Commander Thorn Firoza."

She just gazed at the strange addition to her computer, uncertain what she thought about it. "Can you make me a coffee, please, with one of my own mugs?" She bit her lip, hoping her collection wouldn't grow. A moment later, one of her favorite mugs, a large blue one with the words, *Today may not be great, but my coffee is.* Appeared in the area the panel used to create ... stuff.

Viera took the steaming cup of coffee with a moan. Not only did this cut back on a set of black mugs, but there was also more coffee in this large vat. She moaned in delight.

After drinking half of her morning salvation, she went about toasting a bagel and slathering it with cream cheese.

Next on her list was finding out where she needed to go for training. While she washed the dishes, a knock came to her front door. She quickly finished the last rinse. "I need a way to monitor who's there without having to check the peephole."

The panel beeped. "At the door, Betsy Doeth. Action: do nothing, call authorities, allow in, or leave for the user to decide."

Viera's jaw dropped. "Um, allow in." She heard the door unlock. "For fuck's sake, how many changes did those damn chanzii make to my house? And what is the difference between 'do nothing' and 'let the user decide'?"

Betsy walked in. "Say 'do nothing,' and the panel stops 'paying attention.'" She used her hands to double quote the last two words. "The panel is always paying attention to some extent in case it's needed. 'Leave for the user to decide' means it's still listening for more directions in case there are more options."

"What options?"

"A shoot out?"

Viera's eyes widened. "You're kidding!"

"Only sort of. If it's someone dangerous, you could be transmitted to somewhere safe. There are more sophisticated actions that aren't instantly in the basic list."

"What the hell have I gotten into? And is there a way to back up to just being a second-grade teacher?"

Betsy chuckled and wrapped an arm around Viera's shoulders. "You're doing great. Now, are you ready for your next lesson?"

"Is that why you're here?"

"Well, Commander Firoza texted that you weren't sure where their area was. She asked that I escort you to training. Since I wanted to make sure Flower Prancer knew all of your magics, I decided I liked the idea just fine."

Viera narrowed her eyes. "You were on your way over here, anyway, weren't you?"

Her friend raised an eyebrow. "Maybe."

With a laugh, Viera gathered her stuff and followed Betsy to her car. "So, where is this ... compound? Do the chanzii live in a compound?"

"They live in a subdivision. It isn't far from here. They live closer to the school than you do, just north." The drive took just under fifteen minutes.

They pulled into *Soaring Arbor Heights.* It made Viera snort. "Wasn't this a corn field, like, ten years ago?"

Betsy smiled back. "Yeah. But *Old Flooded Cornfield* doesn't sell as well."

"Fact. Okay, this doesn't look as cookie-cutter as a lot of the subdivisions. The houses here look nice." Viera gazed at the mid-sized buildings spanning the full rainbow of colors. No regulation gray, white, and a splash of red for flavor here.

"They actually asked for a bunch of architects to come in and create a variety of homes to their specifications." Betsy made a few turns, seeming to head to the center of the former corn field. A huge building stood there. It looked like an athletic training center.

"Is that our destination? There isn't a name on the building."

"Yes. It's the group house and training center." Betsy pulled into the parking lot and parked in a spot by the door.

Before she got out of the car, Viera shook her head. "How did Flower Prancer get from this area to my house without being seen?"

Betsy barked out a laugh. "Your first night home you showed me you could turn invisible, yet *that's* your question? You really are nervous, my friend. Okay, let's get in there."

The door opened to a long hallway that led left and right. Ahead of them was another door, and through that was a large gym-like room. In the center stood the yonat. Viera knew Scout and Beaver, his pet ven, the oversized moth, were also in the room, but after a quick search, she didn't see them. She assumed they hid amongst the pads and equipment on the far side of the room.

"Ms. Kor, I'm glad you finally decided to attend your proficiency lesson. We have a lot to cover, and with your weaker human constitution, we'll only get about one to two hours to work today." He turned to face her, and the tension in the room intensified. "Ms. Doeth, your presence wasn't expected or desired. You can leave."

Betsy laughed. "I don't think so, Elder. I respect you, but there are things you don't know, and can't know, without me."

"I seriously doubt that, human." His tail swished in annoyance.

"You know, if Viera wasn't a good friend, I'd leave, and let you mess up. But she *is* a good friend, so I'm going to tell you what I know. She's too afraid of you to interrupt your grandstanding before you mess up her training and let you know."

"Are you talking because you like to hear your voice, Ms. Doeth, or do you actually have something to say?"

"Maybe a bit of both." She tilted her head with a smirk.

"Enough!" Viera said, using her teacher's voice. "You two are as bad as the eight-year-olds I teach. Should I ask Scout to come and show you the proper way to behave to get along together? I have three proficiencies and at least one language to learn. I feel like I have no time to learn any of this. Can you two just set aside your differences long enough to set up my educational program?"

She heard a giggle from behind her and a ruffling of wings from above. *Ah, the ven isn't on the floor; he took a perch in the high ceiling.*

Flower Prancer snorted, clapping his hoof on the floor. "This is what I'm talking about ... three proficiencies. Again, are we sure she isn't slow? Are all Earthlings becoming less intelligent?"

Viera knew Betsy was about to do something with her magic that she'd regret. She threw a hand out to grab her friend's wrist. "Don't do it. He's an Elder, and you know what they say about the old, the crotchety, and assholes."

Betsy snorted as Flower Prancer's eyes widened. "What just happened?"

Her friend ignored the Elder. "You know, as old as Flower Prancer is ... and he is definitely old, I'm still older than him."

Viera dropped Betsy's arm. "What are you talking about? You're like, what, thirty-seven? Forty?" *She mentioned being old before, but wasn't that a joke?*

With a small curtsy, Betsy winked. "You're close, but no. Let's circle back to my age in a minute." She faced Flower Prancer. "We went to Zuza. She has three proficiencies. She's officially an Elder. Stop talking at her like she's simple; she's not. She's been combining sensing and time to create premonition for over a week. Her sensing is wild, but Zuza is helping her. It's beyond you. But you can help her with time and energy. Her magics are a powerful combination, and without a strong teacher, they'll grow to a place no one wants them to go."

For the first time, Flower Prancer wasn't snarky or condescending. "Three aspects to her magic. What the krottel did to her was beyond unprecedented; they accelerated her entrance to magic and to her third proficiency. This will have to be brought to the council." He faced Viera. "You are correct, she needs me to be her teacher ... but she also needs Zuza, and probably you. It is good she isn't simple."

Betsy sighed. "Okay, we've established she's smart. Now, begin. I'll be over there." She pointed to the wall.

Flower Prancer swished his tail. "We're going to start with practicing your 'energy' magic. It can take on many different forms, from light to sound, even tangible things like fire and chemical manipulation. There are overlaps with gas, such as sound. That's what makes proficiencies tricky. What I'd like you to do first is focus on making a ball of light."

Viera thought about what the yonat said and nodded. She shut her eyes and imagined a softball, floating above her hand, all aglow. She opened one eye. Nothing had happened. *Maybe I need to add more realism.* She thought of the ball flying towards home plate after a pitcher threw it, and the crack of the batter.

A sonic sound resonated through the room. Viera's eyes snapped open to see dust from the windows near the ceiling rain down. Betsy had her hands over her ears. Beaver flew in an agitated circle, and Scout laughed in the corner.

Facing her, Flower Prancer shook his head. "I said light, child, not sound."

"I know!" she wailed. "But I've never done this."

From the floor, Scout looked up at her, eyes wide. "Sure, you have! You do it all the time in class."

Out Of The Mouths Of Babes

Scout

Everyone in the room turned to look at him. Flying around the ceiling, Beaver ignored the adults. Scout kind of wished he'd done the same.

Ms. Kor walked over to him and knelt on the ground so she could look him in the eyes. "What do you mean I do it all the time, sweetie?"

It's like she knows I'm uncomfortable. Well, maybe she does. She seems to know a lot more now.

She placed her hands on Scout's upper arms, and a sense of peace washed into him. He smiled up at her. "Oh! Now I get it."

"Get what?"

He huffed out some air. "In school, you've been doing all sorts of things. During our movies your desk always glows."

Ms. Kor's eyes widened. "What? Did the others in the class notice?"

"No, it looked like you had a small flashlight to brighten your work area. Something tiny to not interrupt the movie. It's only because I knew what had happened to you that I guessed. Oh! And because I saw you helping the others."

Flower Prancer came up. He was a bit scary, but Ms. Kor was there, and she would protect him. He scooted a bit closer to his teacher. He hadn't had many dealings with the Elders. When the other kids in his class talked about unicorns and wanting them to be real, it took all his effort not to laugh in their faces. They didn't understand how mean and scary the Elders could be.

Now, dragons! My friends should all want to befriend a qynad. They're the best!

"Tell us what you mean, young Mr. Firoza." Scout jumped at Flower Prancer's voice. Thinking about Horax had been way more fun than talking to the yonat.

"Um." He leaned on Ms. Kor, who wrapped an arm around his waist. "A few times this last week when a student was really sad, it was like Ms. Kor took away their sadness so they could be happy. Just now, when she touched my arms, it felt like she filled me with happy feelings." He shrugged one shoulder. "It made me less nervous."

Ms. Kor didn't look as happy as he felt. "Did you notice me doing anything else?"

"Well, there were a few times you helped kids on the playground before they got hurt. When you were monitoring recess, it was safer." He scrunched up his nose and looked up to watch Beaver. "Oh! And you kept finding things that had been lost. Like the puzzle piece, the dinosaur figurine, and Jody's mitten. You always knew. I think the other students started noticing that. I heard them making a list of things to ask you to find. They want to make it a game."

Ms. Kor groaned, slumping a bit. She rubbed her forehead with her free hand.

Behind her, Betsy smiled wide. "Anything else, kiddo? You're doing great. I should've asked you to be my eyes on the ground a long time ago. You're excellent at this."

He looked around the room, trying to imagine he was back in class. He saw the dust on the floor and smiled. "Yes, one other thing I can remember. This last week. When the class got really loud, and Ms. Kor was at her desk looking miserable, you know the look, twice I saw her squeeze her eyes shut and then it was like someone turned the volume down on the class. Everything was just a tiny bit quieter."

The arm around him tightened and Ms. Kor's mouth dropped open. It took a moment, but she finally closed her mouth. "I did what?"

"Interesting. Light, sound, sensing, premonition, we are starting to gather a good list." Flower Prancer's head bobbed. "But we need to start at the beginning. A ball of light, Ms. Kor, if you please."

With a small sigh, Scout wasn't sure anyone but him could've heard, she pushed up and walked back to the center of the room. He watched as she closed her eyes and focused on the Elder's directions. He rooted for her, wanting her to be successful. She was such a good teacher, he wanted her to be a good student as well.

"What did you focus on before the loud crack of a sound?" Flower Prancer asked.

Ms. Kor licked her lips. "Well, I imagined a softball sized ball of light. I thought that would be a good size. But when it didn't manifest, I tried to make it more real, so I gave it life. The pitch, the swing of the bat ... the connection of the two."

Scout almost fell on his butt when the Elder laughed. *Do yonat really laugh? I'm going to have to ask Mom about this later. Is he just having a stroke?*

"You added too much realism, Ms. Kor. Try again, but this time, stick with the ball being tossed between two people. Maybe young Mr. Firoza and his ven?"

She nodded. Scout had a tiny thrill at the idea of playing catch with a light ball, though he wasn't exactly sure how that would work.

He raised his hands to hover over his ears ... just in case.

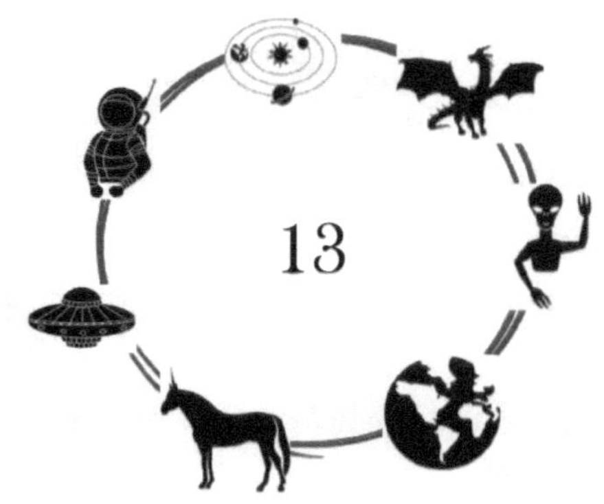

13

Like A Moth To Flame

Viera

Viera dug deep into herself and tried to think magical thoughts. *That's a thing, right. You have to think magic to be magic, and all that jazz?* Instead of projecting a softball being hit by a bat, she tried to envision a game of catch.

She bit her lower lip and tried to think about a blue ball.

Next to her, Betsy whispered. "You've got to *want* it, not just think about it."

"Right ... want it." She sighed. *I really want a blue ball of light to appear.* She waved her hands in front of her, shimmying them back and forth, as if really excited for the ball.

Nothing happened.

Flower Prancer started to say something. She put up a hand to stop him. "Wait, you're all talking to me. Give me a few seconds to think. Believe it or not, despite your words, I'm not simple. Beyond that, I'm a teacher, and I can usually puzzle these things out if given a bit of time to think. You all talking every second doesn't help."

Betsy snorted. "Atta girl."

"You too, Betsy." She pointed to her friend, who mimed zipping up her mouth.

Okay, according to Scout I've done this several times. What did all those situations have in common? The room was dark, and I needed light. Viera closed her eyes and imagined sitting in her classroom with a stack of papers to grade. A movie playing on the TV and all the students transfixed with singing animated insanity. *If only I could see the writing a bit more clearly, the grading would be easier.* She remembered the frustration of the poor handwriting and the low light. She'd rubbed her eyes, and when she'd opened them, everything had been easier.

Viera relaxed, trying to recreate the feelings from her classroom, and breathed out. Holding her hand out in front of herself, she imagined her need manifesting into something tangible.

A few gasps around her told her she'd done ... something. Once again, she peeked out of one eye. Floating a foot from her was a translucent sky-blue ball. It looked to be roughly the size of a softball. Reaching out, her hand passed through it, but it didn't immediately wink out. She took an unsteady breath and looked at the smiling faces around, then shrugged. "I guess I did it."

Scout whooped. "That's great, Ms. Kor!"

"Now, Ms. Kor, can you get the ball to move?" Flower Prancer's voice was calm and pleasant, but it hit her like a thunderstorm. Viera froze and the light blinked out.

Around her, the others grumbled.

"Fu...dge." She smiled weakly at Scout. Blowing out a big huff of air, she tried to recreate the feeling to bring the light ball back.

It felt like it took forever, but it probably only took a few seconds. When it reappeared, elation spiked within her, also mirrored in the others around her.

With a final sense of grounding herself, Viera lifted her hands and imagined the ball flying over to Scout. Her heart skipped a beat as the blue softball sized orb flew to the shocked looking boy. He threw his hands up to protect his face.

Behind her, Betsy gasped just before the blue light ball came to a stop just in front of Scout's hands. Viera giggled. *Do I sound manic?* "It's light, everyone. Even if I couldn't stop it, it won't hurt him."

Flower Prancer's tail swished. "This one is light, Ms. Kor, that doesn't mean they'll all be light. Being wary of a wizard's power is a smart instinct."

Fear surged through her, and the ball disappeared. "What? I can harm someone with my light ball?"

"Of course, Ms. Kor. We're wizards, not simpleton clowns. That's the word for them on this planet, correct? Entertainers? You are not one of them. You are a defender."

She shook her head. "Right, a defender. Then why am I throwing a light ball at a kid?"

He huffed, sounding annoyed. "To learn control."

14

Dinner And A Show

Thorn

Thorn sat in the living room gazing up at the sunny sky. She'd prepared a casserole for lunch, and while it baked, she relaxed. She didn't have much downtime between work and Scout, but today he was watching the magic lesson, so she took advantage of her freedom.

When her people had come to Earth, they'd debated finding areas with pre-made homes. After a bit of searching, they'd realized there were new developments in which they could design and construct their own neighborhoods. Though the outside of the house looked foreign, with Earth specifications, the inside felt more like Abritos, with the glass ceiling allowing her to watch the sky and weather throughout the day.

They'd had to work with a company to manufacture the glass that blocked the harmful rays from the sun. The man from her crew who'd worked with the company ended up starting a car company that used the same technology for his vehicles. It was doing well, though he was becoming controversial and not blending in the best.

The door crashed open, and Scout ran in, followed by a slower-moving Beaver. She'd been moving oddly for a few days. She'd flown when she could, but when on the ground, she'd moved like slogging through muddy water. *I'll need to look her over tonight after Scout's in bed. Maybe I can get a medic over to check her out.*

The ven trotted over to her food and water bowls and loudly made a mess ... as always.

Behind them, Viera walked in, smiling at the two. She looked tired. Thorn still couldn't believe the engineers hadn't left any sort of directions on how to use the panel. The idea that she'd just instinctively *know* how to use it boggled her mind. She'd assumed Viera had been busy and that was why she hadn't gotten back to her.

I should've sent a note with Scout ... such a simple solution.

Viera gaped as she looked up. "That's amazing. You can sit and watch the sky, the weather, whatever you want, from the comfort of your home."

Scout bounced. "It's what all our buildings are like back on Abritos."

The other woman squinted as if in thought as she dropped her gaze down to the boy. "Does that mean all your buildings are single story? Or are only the top floor open to the skies?"

"It's like a cup!" Scout said excitedly. "The middle is always open so you can see you're not locked away from the world. If there are more than one floor, the outside walls are these windows, so no one feels closed in. It's important to have a connection to nature."

Viera squatted down, placing her hands on Scout's arms. "It must've been a big change coming here. We have windows in the classroom, but nothing like what you've described."

Scout's face scrunched up, and Thorn's heart yearned to pull him into a hug. He was trying to be so brave for his teacher.

Before he could say anything, the timer in the kitchen went off. Thorn stood. "Lunch will be ready in five minutes. Scout, please set the table."

Viera stood. "Is there anything I can do to help?"

"Not this time; you're our guest. Maybe next time, though. For now, Scout will show you where to sit. We'll eat in just a few minutes."

They had a greenhouse built in the center of each block of homes. They'd filled the potted plants with dirt from their home planet and kept the temperature a bit cooler than Earth, as was standard. The casserole had chanzii meats, stored frozen, and vegetables from her world. She'd had them tested by the pillars and knew humans could eat them.

She scooped four plates.

Viera gazed at the plate, then lifted it to sniff. 'It smells amazing, but it looks ... are the vegetables pink? And blue?" She gingerly picked up one of the blue ziggers, a vegetable similar to a squash, and tasted it. A smile spread on her face. "Oh! This tastes amazing. What is it?"

"It's a favorite of mine from my planet. We grow our own veggies. I'll show you around later if you want."

Her jaw dropped. "I'm going to have to stop being surprised by everything and start acting chill." She laughed. "But yes. I very much do want. I'd love to see where and how you have vegetables from your own planet on Earth. That's ... amazing."

Scout started to bounce in his seat. "Oh! We can give her the full—"

In the living room, Beaver started to make scratching sounds at the door. Thorn leapt up. "I'm not sure what's gotten into her. She seems insistent on going out. Usually, she wants to be wherever Scout is."

Viera's eyes widened. "She's nervous, and happy ... and really feels a need to get out. She doesn't know how to tell you." She rubbed her head. "Gah, this sensing is insane."

"Mom! You have to let her out. Can't you tell she has some sort of emergency? I'll go with her and keep her safe." Scout's whole body shook with his need.

With a sigh, Thorn opened the door. "We'll all follow, sweetie. I'm not sending you off alone with a pet who's this agitated."

The ven shot off and they all ran to keep up. She flew around to the backyard towards the greenhouse. Behind the greenhouse was a shed with a small open pen behind it. The idea had been a 'doghouse' but none of the chanzii had a dog, so they left it alone for the ven to play in.

Beaver ran to the small structure and ducked in. A high-pitched sound came from inside, and then she tottered out followed by five miniature ven babies. They looked like her, though some were darker in color.

Viera squealed. "Oh, my goodness, she's a mama! She's had babies. And look at them, they're so cute!"

Scout jumped up and down in glee.

Thorn just sighed. *Exactly what I needed. Five more of the creatures to care for. Well, at least they're cute.*

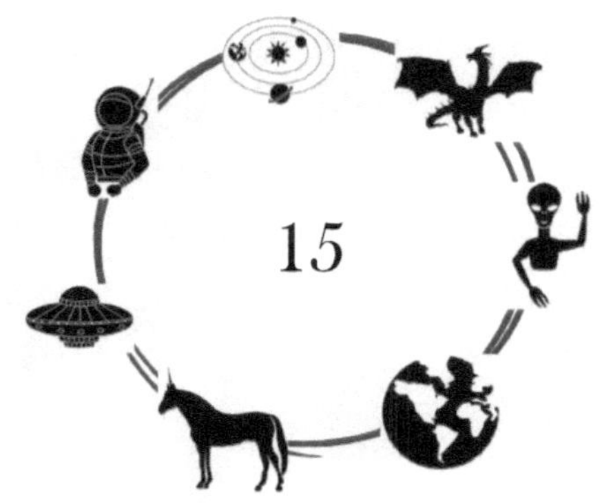

Their Junk Become My Treasure

Viera

Tuesday after school, Viera sat at her desk grading and sorting the last of the papers she hadn't finished over the weekend. After lunch on Sunday, she, Thorn, and Scout spent time playing with the new ven babies. Though she could feel Thorn's annoyance at having more pets, Viera was in love. The babies were adorable. If she had her way, she'd take them all home and watch them play in her living room all day long.

She let the memory of the babies tumbling in the yard replay in her mind. A giggle bubbled out as she remembered them rolling around, knocking over Beaver and Scout.

"Are your students' answers so funny?" Betsy sauntered into her room, a bag slung over her shoulder.

Viera shook her head to stop the movie playing in her head. She hadn't realized she'd tapped into her magic until her friend's voice woke her up from the memory. *Fuck, I'm going to have to be a lot more aware of what I'm doing.* "Yeah, no. I guess I pulled up a memory, and I may have gotten lost in it. It was pretty cool, like watching a movie, but I didn't realize I was using my powers ... again." Her head fell into her crossed arms. "Betsy, when will I start to get a hold on all of this? I feel like I'm being dragged around by this manifestation inside me."

Betsy huffed a small laugh. "It'll get better, and you'll learn control ... or ... you know, we'll have to put you down like a feral dog."

Viera's head snapped up. "What? Are you kidding me?"

A huge smile spread on her friend's face. "Of course I am. Now, want to go on an adventure with me?"

"I don't know. Do I?" She narrowed her eyes. "Last time, I ended up in London. Where are we going this time?"

"Not so far. There's an estate sale, and I want to go junking." Betsy waggled her eyebrows.

"Wait." Viera leaned back. "You want me to go garage sale-ing with you?"

"No." Betsy elongated the word, as if speaking to a kid. Then she spoke at her normal speed. "I said 'estate sale;' no garage involved. Well, actually, we may go into the garage, so I guess, maybe."

"Okay, I've known you for years. I've never known you to go to gara—estate sales. You don't have a bunch of knickknacks in your house. So, talk to me. Why do you want me to go with you?"

Betsy gazed around the classroom. "Do you not want to go?"

Viera smiled at her friend, packing up her stuff. "Oh, no, I definitely want to go, I'm just curious what your ulterior motive is. I mean, you're like, what, a million years old? We never did establish this. How old is Flower Prancer? And how old are you?"

They headed out of the building towards Betsy's car. "Oh, I totally forgot we didn't get back to that."

"Probably your addled old age, I imagine."

"Watch it, Viera." They both laughed. "Okay, Flower Prancer is three-hundred and forty-eight galactic years old. For the yonat, they can begin studying a third proficiency at two hundred years. It's why they, as a species, are considered Elders. They don't allow their beings to leave the planet at under three-hundred galactic years of age, based on their planet's rotation. A galactic year is four hundred of our days. He is about three-hundred-eighty-one human years old."

Viera pulled out her phone and did some quick calculations. "Okay, I see how you got that. And so, how old are you?"

"In human years or galactic years?"

"Betsy!" Viera huffed in annoyance. "Wait, do you actually keep track of both?"

"Nope, I keep track of human years. If you'd asked for my galactic age, I'd have laughed. I only know the one."

"But you just calculated Flower Prancer's!" Viera said.

"Not really, he tries to lord it over everyone. He knows his age on every planet he visits."

Viera laughed. She could just see the yonat doing that. They drove for a few more minutes, Viera waiting. She finally whipped around to glare. "Betsy!"

"Oh! Yeah, you know, my Elder brain ... it's hard to focus." She winked. "I'm three-hundred and ninety-two."

"But you don't even look forty. How is that possible?" Her head was spinning.

Betsy parked in front of a two-story blue house on a block with big lots. The next house was several car lengths away. She turned off the car and leaned back in her seat. "When a creature becomes a wizard, their age slows to about one-tenth the normal speed. For most of us, that doesn't really start until our twenties, thank goodness. But there is a basic rule of ten once we hit our two hundreds."

"Wait, will this happen to me?" Viera's belly did a few backflips. "Will I be a few hundred years old one day?"

Betsy shrugged. "You are an anomaly, my friend, in many, many ways, but that would be my guess."

Viera shook her head. "Okay, so, I should start to care about health since I'm going to be on Earth longer. Good to know." She shook her head. "Yep, don't want to think about it. Why are we here?"

"Why don't we go in and look around. Let me know what you think about the items in the house."

With a grunt, Viera got out of the car. "If you're that old, are you also rich? Are you paying? Because this house looks fancy and I'm a second-grade teacher." She gazed at the manicured lawn and fancy garden. "At a public school, no less, not a fancy academy."

"We'll talk about money, finance, and saving for your very long future. But, right now, let's see what this house has to offer."

Viera sighed. "It's always putting things off until later with you, isn't it?"

"Well, there's a lot for you to learn. I can't teach you everything in a day. Now, inside."

They made their way inside. The living room was light, bright, and full of elegant items. A full mahogany couch, chair, and matching table set. The coffee table, octagonal in shape, was inlaid with light and dark diamond shapes. On the walls were what looked like priceless artworks.

As they circled the room, Viera shrugged. None of it would look good in her house. After a cursory walk through, they headed to a den, which was mostly empty. On an adjacent wall to the one they came in through was an opening to the dining room.

Viera nearly drooled over the ten-foot cherrywood table with inlaid leaf patterns at the corner. There were ten matching chairs. Inset were leaves that would let the table extend even longer. She had no need for the artwork of functionality, but it didn't stop her from wanting it. On the far wall was a matching buffet and dish cabinet.

Along one side, an arched passageway, a butler's pantry, with cabinets and wet bar led to the kitchen and a great room/second living room.

There were a lot of people pawing through all of the knickknacks and displayed jewelry. Others looked at the artwork and furniture. Betsy just gave the room a quick glance. She seemed more interested in Viera's reaction.

When she just shrugged, they headed up the stairs to the bedrooms. The first room was the master bedroom. White, gray, and modern. Again, nothing in the room would work with Viera's decorating style, not that she had one. The only benefit of the room was that it was mostly empty.

"We're zooming through this. Why are we here, Betsy?"

"We can spend more time on the way back down. I just like to do a quick look through first. Let's keep going."

Viera was pretty sure her friend was lying to her, but since nothing called to her, she allowed herself to be led on. In the second bedroom, on the wall of a kid's room, was a colorful boomerang. It sang to Viera. She wasn't sure why; she just knew her senses fired a high alert.

Ignoring everything around her, Viera walked up to the boomerang and traced it with her finger.

Next to her, Betsy watched. "What? Why this item?"

She shook her head. "I don't know. It's hard to explain. It's calling to me. Asking to be brought ... somewhere. What's going on, Betsy?"

Her friend took the item from the wall. They did a quick tour of the other rooms, but nothing else pinged Viera's attention. After paying for the toy, they headed out to the car.

Once the doors were closed, Viera shivered. "Talk to me. What the hell was that?"

"We live on a planet with a huge blanket of magic. A few things happened. The first is those of us who are older lose items that have been imbued with magic. Regular humans find them, not knowing what the items are, and we have to go and find them before something odd happens. The next thing is aliens visit and leave items behind on purpose or by accident. The last, and most common, some items soak up some magic and just become magical. I can scry for magic, but finding the items is a bitch. Using your sensing was amazing."

A shot of annoyance flowed through Viera. "But why didn't you tell me before going In?"

Betsy sighed. "I didn't want you to think too hard. I just wanted it to happen. Magic can be weird, and sometimes when you force it, it messes with you."

Viera slumped. "Okay, I get it. But now what?"

"I'm going to send it to Zuza. You're going to be amazing with your sensing ... one day. But he's very good today. Since it's a boomerang, I'm guessing it works with gas magic, and that is his other proficiency. I'm expecting he'll enjoy the toy."

Viera laughed. "Well, I like that. And he can tell me about it on our weekly call."

Betsy was close to the school, ready to drop her back at her car. "What are your plans for the rest of the week?"

"I have a lesson with Flower Prancer after classes tomorrow, and then dinner with Thorn."

"I could stay hang out Scout if you want Thorn to stay over with you."

Shock and excitement surged through her. "I'll ask her if she'd be okay with that ... because I'd really like it. Thanks."

"Of course. It's about time you started to date."

Viera rolled her eyes at her friend but bubbled inside with anticipation.

16

Mind Games

Viera

During recess, Viera worked hard to get ahead. She knew she had to leave right after class to get to her lesson with Flower Prancer. He'd left a second message this morning to make sure she didn't forget. *As if I'd forget. I only missed the others because I didn't know how to use that stupid panel.*

She rolled her eyes and focused on her work.

When her alarm went off, she hurried to meet her students and walk them in. *If I can get them to focus, I can reward them with a short educational show this afternoon, and get some work done. Win-win.*

As the last of the students filed out of class, Viera spent a moment, eyes closed, decompressing from the day. She didn't care how important the yonat thought her lessons were, she knew time to herself—along with self-care to allow for her own sanity—was just as crucial.

After a few meditative breaths, she packed up her things, and headed to her car. Betsy had drawn a map and written directions to where she needed to go. When Viera checked the directions on her phone they mostly matched up, but Betsy knew a shortcut. The two had gone together last time, and she was good with patterns, so she didn't think she'd get lost.

Ten minutes later, she parked at the training center and took a few extra seconds to ground herself before facing the firing squad ... otherwise known as Flower Prancer.

In the large room, Scout and Beaver played along the far wall. She saw the small ven rolling and playing with their mom. *Now that's an activity I could get behind. I wonder if they've named the cuties yet.*

Flower Prancer stood in the center of the room, his annoyance obvious. "Ms. Kor, for today's lesson, I want you to create the light ball again."

She'd been expecting that. Pulling her focus away from the baby ven, Viera breathed in, then out, then created the ball of light. It popped into existence in front of her about a foot above her. After all the practice she'd done, she was proud at how quickly the blue ball appeared.

"Acceptable. Now make it green."

She clenched her jaw and thought about the request. *It shouldn't be difficult.* After another moment of consideration, the ball shifted to a deep forest green. *Ha! Got it in one!*

Flower Prancer's tail swished. "Purple."

Viera blew out a breath. She tilted her head, gazing at the violet eyes of her instructor, then got her ball of light to match.

He continued to call out colors for twenty minutes, repeating colors as he went. Her head pounded, but eventually she got faster, being able to almost instantly change the ball as soon as he demanded a new color.

Off in his corner of the room, Scout hooted in praise. "That's great, Ms. Kor! I knew you could do it!"

Flower Prancer stomped his hoof in annoyance. "Mr. Firoza, bring your ven over here. It's time for the next step in Ms. Kor's practice."

"Righty-o, Flower Prancer. We're here to help in any way you want." Scout bounced over exuberantly.

The yonat ignored the boy. "Ms. Kor, you'll move the light ball back and forth between the boy and the ven. They'll pretend to play catch."

"Okay, got it."

"Challenge the ven. She needs exercise. Lazy creature," Flower Prancer grumbled as he moved to the wall. Viera followed.

She held her hands out. She didn't really need them to guide the light ball, but their movement helped her mental game. She 'tossed' the ball to Scout who laughed as he 'caught' it and pushed it to Beaver. The ven chased it and batted it with a paw.

Viera had the ball fly back towards Scout in a high arc. Scout swung at the ball and Viera switched directions.

"Ms. Kor, the ball went through the boy's hand. I do not believe a real ball would do that. You're sloppy. Fix your reaction time."

She sighed and continued to try to be the ball. The mental distinction helped her control. When she brought the ball towards Beaver, she had it fly high, so the ven had to use her wings. As the light flew back to Scout, she forced the boy to run for it. *No reason to only tucker out one of them.*

After five minutes of no critique from Flower Prancer, he snapped, "Red."

She shook her head and turned the light ball red.

For the next thirty minutes, Scout and Beaver played, running all over the gym-sized room. Flower Prancer yelled out critiques and random colors. And Viera tried to keep up. When the time was up, she fell to her butt and rubbed her temples. She couldn't believe how tired it all had made her.

"Ms. Kor. Before our next meeting, I would like you to decide on a creature, non-human, that you will create a holographic image of. At first, like the ball, it can just be an image, but eventually I'd like you to include movement. We'll begin that exercise on Monday."

She sighed. "Does that mean we're done?"

"No. We'll work on one other aspect of magic, because of your particular combination. I'd like you to put your hands on Mr. Firoza's shoulders." Flower Prancer turned to Scout. "Mr. Firoza, I'd like you to think of a memory you don't mind sharing."

"Okay, that's easy—"

"Do not tell us, Mr. Firoza, just think about it."

Scout squeezed his mouth shut and opened his eyes wide, as if he were about to explode.

Flower Prancer's tail swished. "Mr. Kor, try to determine the boy's memory."

She wanted to argue but knew that would be useless. She closed her eyes and thought about Scout and what he was feeling, and maybe, just maybe, what he was thinking. She saw him in a kitchen, *his* kitchen, with Thorn, and they were cooking something. He was measuring out what looked like flour and other dry ingredients, making a mess. She was creaming butter and sugar. Viera smiled at the warm fuzzy happiness flowing from the boy. It felt like she was watching a movie.

"Ms. Kor, is anything happening?"

She dropped her hands from Scout's arms and shook her head to clear him and his mom from her thoughts. "Um ... maybe? I saw Scout measuring flour, salt, and other dry ingredients. His mom the wet ones. They were baking together. He was happy."

"I didn't ask for the emotions, just the memory," Flower Prancer snapped.

It was too much. He was an awful teacher and expecting nonsense information. "You can't have one without the other. Memories are more than images. They are the thoughts, emotions, and senses of a time and place. If I'm reading them, I'm reading the whole package. You can't just dictate which part I collect. Not only is it ridiculous, but it's short-sighted of you."

Flower Prancer harrumphed. "Mr. Firoza, is that the memory you'd selected to share?"

His face had paled when Viera had yelled at the Elder, but he nodded quickly. "Yes. That's the one."

"Very good. We'll continue with that on Monday as well. You're both dismissed."

They headed over to the ven babies. Viera picked up the box that contained them, and they left. Scout and Thorn's house was close enough that she didn't feel the need to move her car.

As they walked to Scout's house, she asked, "Have you named these five cuties yet?"

Scout's eyes widened. "Oh! I forgot to tell you. We did. I thought of that movie you showed me, and I named them after the characters."

She'd watched a few movies with him on Terville Station Number Six. "So, tell me, what are their names?"

As he named them, he touched each of their heads. "We have Buttercup, Westley, Fezzik, Inigo Montoya, and Miracle Max."

Throwing her arm around the boy, Viera laughed. "Those names are fantastic."

Scout beamed, letting her into his house.

Why Be Surprised?

Viera

Betsy and Scout planned to take the ven babies out to play. Betsy figured she could tire the lot of them out to the point that she could read while they all slept. It wasn't a realistic plan ... but it was a plan.

After magic practice, Viera stopped to talk with Thorn at her place. As tired as she was, the idea of coming home to Thorn made something in her quake with want. *But, no, this is a short-term thing. Thorn is heading back to her planet soon. Don't get too invested!*

She shook her head to get back to the here and now. Viera wanted to change after a long day at school and magic training. "How about I meet you at my house? I'll quickly shower and change, then maybe I can cook you something there. We can stay in."

Thorn tipped her chin up. "I do plan on spending part of the evening at your place, thanks to Betsy's generous offer, but why not go to a restaurant? Then we don't have to worry about cooking or clean up. My treat. There's a steakhouse I've been wanting to try."

With a soft moan, Viera melted into her for a second kiss. "You know, you're absolutely spoiling me."

"Good."

She drove home quickly and jumped in the shower. Once clean, she wrapped a towel around herself and headed to the bedroom. Thorn waited for her, sitting on her bed in a black, contour dress, and a smirk on her face. "You're overdressed for the room."

"You're one to talk." Viera waved her hand. "Fully dressed. Though with that dress, you may as well be naked." She flushed, her body heating with desire.

"We have a reservation in thirty minutes. I guess I get a reverse striptease. Drop the towel, then slowly slip on your clothes."

Viera smiled at Thorn before doing as requested. She put on a wine-colored A-line mini-dress that ended at mid-thigh.

Once ready, Thorn pulled her in for another kiss before leading her to the car. "I should've requested no panties. It would've made the night more interesting."

Viera chuckled. "Maybe on a night I'm sure I won't run into any of my students' parents."

"I very much hope you *will* run into one of your students' parents tonight. Maybe more than just bump into me. I have plans, Ms. Kor."

Her face heated again. "You know what I mean. And good. I have plans as well."

"Oh? I'd like to hear these plans ... in detail."

The heat intensified. "You would?" Her voice had gone up.

Thorn's deepened. "Oh, yes."

"Well, after dinner, I'd like to take you back to my place." She licked her lips, then slid her eyes to the long legs on display. "After unwrapping the delicious expanse of your body, I'll lay you out on my bed, then slowly run my tongue up your very long legs." Viera's eyes closed, and she squeezed her own legs together, imagining the actions.

Thorn's warm hand rubbed up her thigh, gently making room for her fingers. "Go on. Then what?"

"My, ah ... um tongue will swirl and slick up your thigh." Thorn's finger acted out the words she said. Viera worked at keeping her legs apart. "When I get under these panties, I, um ..." She faltered as Thorn slid her clothes to the side. Viera checked out the car window to make sure no one could see in and spy what they were doing, then her eyes rolled back. She decided she didn't care.

She took a steadying breath. "I'll slowly lick up your center, stroking into you with a finger or two, and tasting you with my flicking tongue, sucking, and playing."

Viera's body trembled with heat and need as she tried to say more.

She hadn't noticed when Thorn had parked "Scream for me, Viera, loud enough that everyone knows how hot I make you." Her fingers continued to move in ways Viera couldn't replicate. "Yell out your pleasure for the world to hear."

Thorn bent, nibbling on Viera neck, licking and tasting up to her ear. Her hand continued to thrust and rub. Then her other hand dove under Viera's neckline to flick her nipples.

Her head fell back as the world around her fractured in sparkles of light and sound. She wasn't sure what she yelled out as all the muscles in her body came to life. Then Thorn's mouth devoured hers and she was lost.

As her breathing quieted, Thorn moved back. She slid her hand out from under Viera's skirt and licked a finger. "Nice appetizer. I think we're early for the reservation. Ready to go eat?"

Viera groaned. "I think so. If I can get my muscles to agree to move."

Thorn snickered. They walked into the restaurant and were seated right away. The walls were covered in old ranch-type equipment. As Viera looked over her menu, a small nagging behind her kept distracting her.

When the server came with glasses of water, they each were ready to place their orders. "I'll have a ribeye, medium rare, a baked potato, and a salad with ranch dressing." Thorn handed her menu to the server.

Viera closed her menu. "I'll take the prime rib, medium rare, a baked potato, and broccoli."

After putting in their orders for cocktails, the server left.

Finally, deciding it was too much, Viera turned around. One of the items on the wall called to her. She thought back to her estate sale with Betsy and knew there was a magical item in the restaurant. She'd been searching long enough that Thorn tapped her arm. "What's going on?"

With a sigh, Viera waved her hands in defeat. "I think there's a magical item in the restaurant, but there are so many things, I just don't know what I'm looking for.

"Why not go to the restroom and see if that helps?"

Viera thought for a second. "That's a great idea, thanks!"

She got up and walked around the room until she saw an arrow pointing to the restroom. As she walked, the feeling got more intense. She finally found the item. It looked fake, but she took out her phone and snapped a quick photo.

Back at the table, she showed Thorn. "Holy hell, that's a minotaur's horn!"

"Wait, minotaurs are real?"

"They sure are."

"And *that's* what you call them. That's a name we have correct?"

"I've stopped trying to guess what you lot get correct or get wrong, it's too hard to try." Thorn smiled and Viera tried not to laugh at her own species' expense.

Once they'd figured out what was magical, Thorn smiled at Viera. "So, what are you doing this weekend? Training with Flower Prancer or Betsy?"

Viera shrugged. "So far, no. Neither of them have put any demands on my time ... yet."

"Oh! Excellent. I'm visiting a friend in Montana, and I thought you'd like to join me."

"A friend? Who?"

"A man ... creature, really. Friendly, but you lot have been trying to chase him down for years. You may know him as Bigfoot.

Viera's jaw dropped. What? Were all the myths to come to life?

18

Imagine That!

Thorn

Saturday morning, Thorn woke up alone in her bed. She yawned and stretched, looking up at the clear ceiling to check out the weather. The scent of coffee wafted up from the kitchen, and it occurred to her she hadn't gone to bed alone. *Is Viera making breakfast?*

Unraveling herself from the blankets, Thorn slogged to the closet to get an outfit. She wanted to take a quick shower before heading to the kitchen for food.

Though it was warming up in Wisconsin, they were heading up to Montana, and there was still snow on the ground at Toby's place. She'd been in contact with the fing a few times since her return to Earth and wanted to check in with the reclusive creature.

She stepped into the shower unit, reveling in the warm water. Though she loved the units on the ship, there was something about the Earth standard way as well.

When Flower Prancer had told her about his living on planet, Thorn had worried about Toby. From what she could tell, Toby had lived in the Montana mountains for years, long enough that even his people forgot he'd come to study the Earthlings. Most exploration parties weren't a solitary assignment. And when they were, they had a strict time limit so that the creature didn't go stir-crazy. Fing, unlike the chanzii, couldn't shape shift.

By the time other species started traveling to Earth, Toby was so established in a pattern of living as a hermit, he continued to avoid contact with anyone he may have been able to socialize with from outer space, including Thorn and her group.

As to why he hasn't made any effort to communicate with the wizards, I'll never know. I'm convinced he came to Earth to disappear.

Thorn quickly dried off from the shower. *I wonder how much of an intergalactic incident it would cause to install chanzii washing systems in our homes.* She shook her head at the familiar thought. *I guess if we get our world back and there's an end date to our time on this planet, then it's not worth pursuing.*

Once dressed, she headed down to the kitchen. Viera moved around the room like she owned it. There was a large mixing bowl, a skillet with ... pancakes? It smelled like bacon was cooking somewhere and, of course, coffee. *If she wasn't a short-lived human, I'd wrap her up and steal her away to Abritos. Scout loves her. She's smart, sexy, doesn't care that I'm from a different world, and she can cook.*

Viera turned, saw Thorn, and screamed, jumping up a foot and tossing the spoon she'd been using to stir and pour the pancake mixture into the skillet up into the air. Her jaw dropped, watching the mess it made as it tumbled through the air. Her hand slapped onto her chest. "Fuck! You scared me."

Thorn laughed. "I hadn't noticed. Don't you have the ability to sense? Shouldn't you have known I was approaching?"

Bending to pick up the plastic spoon and toss it into the sink, Viera breathed heavily, as if she'd just run a race.

"You'd think so, wouldn't you? But maybe I was focusing too much on my next stupid challenge."

Before Viera could get much cleaned, Thorn found a towel and started wiping up the splashes of pancake batter. "The ones on the stove will burn. I've got this."

"Shit!" Viera spun and quickly flipped what had been cooking. She checked in the oven and grumbled, before flipping the pan around. She took a slow breath and shook her head. "Sorry. This was supposed to be a nice surprise, not me being all weird in the kitchen."

"So, challenge. You were cooking and thinking about your next magic lesson? The thing with light that Flower Prancer set for you?" Thorn put the dirty towel down a laundry shoot.

"Yeah. I've decided to try to create a dragon ... no, a qynad with my hologram. Gah! I'll get the names right eventually." Viera removed the cooked pancakes, put butter in the skillet, and poured a new batch. "Anyway, I figure Horax has been really nice. If I mess up one of his kind, they won't be as ... scary as a yonat."

Thorn scrunched up her face, thinking about it. "I wouldn't say all of that in front of the qynad, but I don't disagree with you. I think if you do a recreation of a maimed Horax, he'd laugh."

That got Viera to smile. She finished making the pancakes, and Scout ran into the room. "Are we going to visit Toby today? And pancakes? Ms. Kor, did you cook us breakfast? You know the panel will cook for us, right?"

"Scout! This is a homemade meal! Be nice."

Viera smiled, squatting down. She shot a glance up at Thorn. "It's okay." Then she rubbed Scout's arms. "I like cooking. I know you can get anything you want created for you, and it may be better, but this is a way I can show my appreciation for all you two have done for me, just like when your mom made the casserole."

Scout rolled his eyes. "That's because the r'nik panel can't make anything as interesting as the casserole."

"Scout! Language." Thorn narrowed her eyes at her son. "Where did you even learn that word?" She shook her head. "Now, set the table. Don't forget to pour yourself a glass of water."

Viera stood up and gathered the food she'd made. She brought it to the table.

Thorn took charge of the butter, syrup, and mugs of coffee. In the end they had everything they needed.

The food was good. Better than the panel made. Scout's eyes widened. "I'm sorry, Ms. Kor. You can cook for us any time you want. This is really good." He gazed off to the corner of the room and then his brows knit. 'Horax?"

Thorn turned, not expecting to see their friend, and was confused. He wasn't there. Her head felt fuzzy. Then she saw a qynad in the living room, large and ruby red. "Who are you? What are you doing in my house? Do you need me for something?"

Next to her, Viera looked around the room. "Who are you talking to?"

"What do you mean? I'm speaking to the qynad in the living room. How can you not see it?" Thorn turned to Viera to give her a dumbfounded look. Then she pointed. When Thorn turned back to the living room, it was empty. "What the fuck?"

"Language, Mom," Scout said, in a monotone voice.

She shot out of her seat and stormed into the other room. Head swinging around, she didn't see the beast. When she spun on her heel to question Scout, a large navy blue qynad stood in her way. "What? Where did you come from?" She slowly reached a hand out when the beast neither answered nor moved.

She felt nothing in front of her but air.

19

Did I Do That?

Viera

To Viera's left, Scout thought he was speaking to Horax. In the living room, Thorn waved her hand in the doorway. She mumbled to herself. "There's nothing there ... but I can see it. What's going on?'

She felt so drained. *What is wrong with me? I felt fine while I was baking. I've made pancakes so many times. Though, I was really focused right up until the moment Thorn got here and scared me out of my thoughts*

Viera shook herself from her musings. It wasn't important. She had to figure out what was wrong with Thorn and Scout. "Scout, Horax isn't here. You know that, right?" "What? Sure he is. He's right—" Scout shook his head. "Where did he go? And why wouldn't he talk to me?" He looked around. "He's never not talked to me before. Mom! Where did Horax go?" Scout's eyes widened. "Who is that?"

Frustrated, Viera pulled out her phone and called Betsy. Her friend picked up right away. "Viera. I thought you were going to Montana with Thorn today. Why are you calling? Is everything okay?"

"I don't know. Both Thorn and Scout are acting weird." Viera could hear the frantic note in her voice.

"Weird how?" Betsy had slowed down, as if her pacing out her words would calm Viera down.

"We were eating pancakes, and then they both said they could see dragons." Viera felt her eyes misting up and her voice began to sound frantic. "What's going on? Why are they seeing things? What did I do? Is it permanent?"

"First of all, are you seeing anything? Is it something with the food?"

Viera searched the room. Thorn was cautiously walking through the room and Scout had a frustrated look on his face. "No. I don't see anything but what's really here."

Betsy made a small sound as if making a mental list. "Where did the food come from?"

"I made it."

"Um-hm. And what did you make? Cereal? Donuts?"

"No!" Viera was getting annoyed. "Pancakes and bacon."

"Oh! You make good pancakes. That sounds good." Betsy's momentary distraction amused Viera. Her friend always thought with her stomach. "Okay, tell me about you, my friend. It's morning. How are you feeling?"

"Me? Um, frantic. Confused. Annoyed that you're worried about me when something is obviously wrong with them."

Betsy scoffed. "Did you wake up tired? You're normally an obnoxious morning person."

Viera opened her mouth to answer then shut it. "Actually, no. I woke up early, with a ton of energy, that's why I decided to cook. I made coffee right away in case Thorn woke up, and then started cooking."

"Okay, tell me more."

"There's so much to learn, Betsy. You've had a million years to learn everything, but I'm so behind. I feel like I have no time and three proficiencies to master. I'll never get my feeble brain around it all."

"We already discussed this. You have plenty of time. Don't try to rush anything."

"Okay. Well, I was trying to think about what hologram I wanted to create."

"Wait." Betsy stopped her. "You were focusing on a magic lesson while baking?"

"Yes."

"And when you finished you felt drained?" Now her friend sounded amused.

"Betsy!"

"This may not work, but try closing your eyes, reaching down into your very low stock of magic, and releasing what's left with a command of 'undo.' Don't hang up—I want to know if it works."

Once she'd done as directed, both Thorn and Scout jerked, as if splashed with cold water. Thorn narrowed her eyes. "Where did they go? The qynad?"

Scout walked around the kitchen and living room, searching. "They just disappeared. They're gone. Did they beam away?" He started looking under the pillows.

"It worked." Viera sighed into the phone. "Now, what the hell happened?"

"We'll talk more, but, essentially, you performed your first potion. It's why you're so tired."

Viera needed to sit. "I did what now?"

"I have an appointment. I'll talk to you about it when you get back. No more cooking." Betsy laughed as she spoke.

"Fine!" She got off the phone and turned to Thorn. "I'm sorry. I think whatever happened to you was my fault. Something with my magic. We should get different food. Maybe out."

Thorn chuckled. "Oh! You're a trip. You magicked the food ... by accident. Yes, let's get food in Montana. Maybe Toby will want to eat with us. Are you ready to leave?"

Viera turned to see the mess she'd made. "But ..."

Thorn bent down to kiss her. "Don't worry about the mess. I'll call in someone to clean. Let's just get on our way."

They gathered Scout and their bags and used the panel to contact Toby. He said he was ready.

Within minutes, Thorn's kitchen dissolved, and they were standing in a room that made Viera feel very small. The seats of the chairs all came up to her waist. The tables ... even higher.

A very tall and very hairy man boomed, "Welcome! Are you my breakfast?"

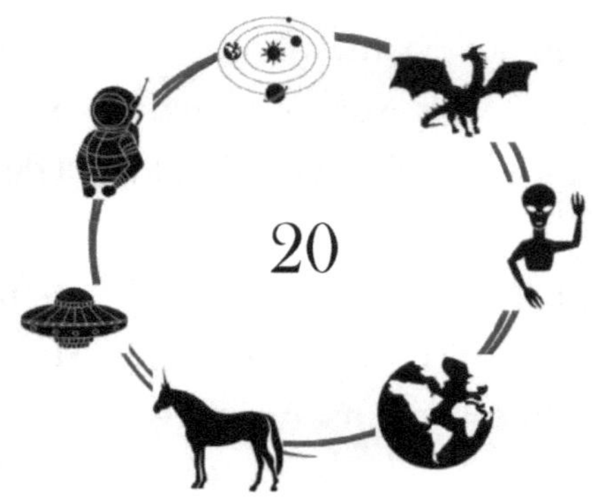

20

Berry Good – A Battle Won

Viera

The big hairy fing stood in front of Viera and gazed down at her. He stood at least ten feet tall with glowing red eyes and long fangs. Viera clasped Scout's arm and pulled the boy behind her. With a shallow breath, she dug deep in her body for whatever magic she had left after her rocky morning and tried to hide.

"Where did they go?" The monster bellowed.

To Viera's right, Thorn's head snapped around. "For fuck's sake," she mumbled. "Viera? Scout? Where did you two go?"

Viera scooted back towards the very large couch. *Can we fit behind it?*

"We're right here!" Scout said, his voice chipper from behind Viera. His voice stopped her motion. "What do you mean, 'Where did we go?'"

Thorn's focus homed in on her son. Viera watched Thorn, forgetting to pay attention to the scary creature, until a low chuckle came from her left.

"Are we playing hide and seek before breakfast? Is this to build up my appetite?" His voice echoed over the large living room.

In front of her, Thorn rolled her eyes. "Toby, did you have something you were going to cook for breakfast?"

"Yes!" His voice sounded boyish in his cheer. "Pancakes and eggs. I have a syrup you'll absolutely die for."

Viera gulped, a tremor traveling down her body. *I don't want to die ... not here, not for him. Why are we here if it's not safe?*

"Why don't you go to the kitchen and get things started. We'll be just behind you." Thorn sounded calm and reasonable.

The ground shook with the rumble of his footsteps as he walked towards an opening on the other side of the room. Without his stare boring into them, Viera realized he wasn't as tall as she'd originally thought—maybe only eight to nine feet. Not the full height of a basketball hoop.

When he disappeared, Viera huffed out the tension and released her magic.

Thorn sighed. "What happened?"

"He called us 'his breakfast.' Are we safe here?"

Behind her, Scout laughed. Thorn rubbed her forehead. "Scout, why don't you go see if Toby needs help." Scout ran off, much to Viera's trepidation. Then Thorn slipped her hands into Viera's. "He meant his guests for breakfast. We are safe, I promise you."

Viera's face warmed. "Sorry. I just ... it's been a long morning. I guess I let my mind spiral."

Thorn wrapped her in a hug, then tipped her head up for a kiss. "It's better to be wary than run into things blindly." She kissed Viera's nose. "I like you just the way you are, though. I like being able to see you." Gazing over her shoulder, she looked at where Scout had been. "I didn't know you could shield a second person. That's fantastic."

Viera rested her head on Thorn's chest, letting go of her anxiety in the comfort of Thorn's arms. "I didn't either.

I just worried, and then did what I felt I could to protect Scout."

Thorn squeezed her tighter. "I love that your first instinct was to protect my son. You know that, right?"

"Hmm," Viera hummed, snuggling in. From the kitchen, the smell of pancakes and sizzling meat filled the air. Her stomach growled. The aroma of something warm and fruity wafted out, wrapping itself around her. She quivered with hunger, and she felt light-headed.

Shit, I've used too much magic. Flower Prancer warned me I'd need to eat more when I was practicing, and I've done a lot.

"Are you still nervous?" Thorn sounded worried.

"No ... yes ... maybe. Mostly hungry. It smells really good. That isn't from any panel, is it? Can I get that at home?"

Laughing, Thorn led her into the kitchen. Viera wasn't surprised that it was just as large as the other room. She felt like a kid walking into the kitchen. A table that came up to her shoulders, with chairs of equal height sat in the center of the room. There were plates, forks, and mugs on the table. Steam billowed from the mugs ... it smelled like ... "Is that coffee?"

Toby turned and gave them a huge smile. She realized he wasn't as scary as she first thought. No fangs, and his eyes weren't red, but rather a dark green. She shook her head, wondering about her own imagination. "It is, tiny human. Climb up. I'll bring the food over."

It took Viera some effort to climb up into one of the chairs. The mug of coffee was proportionately big, and she needed every drop of the delicious brew. *I wonder if I can get some mugs this size at home. This is about perfect for my daily needs.*

Once the food was set out in platters around the table, everyone served up pancakes, sausages, and the fruity syrup. Viera took a bite and nearly swooned.

"This is amazing. What is it?" She couldn't believe how the flavor of the food exploded in her mouth.

Across the table, the large fing smiled and winked. "At the end of July, through August, I spend my time working as a wild huckleberry forager. I collect the berries and ship them all over the state. With the popularity of the internet, my shipments have gone national. I spend the rest of my time baking with the berries and selling sweet treats."

Viera's mouth hung open, shocked. "You're an online huckleberry baker? For real?"

His eyes twinkled. "My people are known for our prowess in the kitchen. Living out here, I was fighting with the berries. They seem to take over my life. I either avoid them or give in and face the inevitability of them. So, here we are."

She took another bite. "This is fantastic. I can't believe how good they are."

He beamed. "I'll send you home with some muffins."

After they ate, they sat in the living room. Viera sat on the floor, playing cribbage with Scout. They were fairly evenly matched.

Thorn sipped her coffee. "You've been on planet for years. Why don't you interact with any of the other non-humans? You don't even talk to the pillars!"

"I came here to learn about the humans, not socialize with other creatures. If I wanted to do that, I'd leave this excellent planet." He snorted at her as if his answer were obvious.

She sighed. "But have you learned anything? Do you have reports?"

"Of course I do! I just haven't sent them in If I do, they'll pull me off planet, and I like it here. It's quiet and the people are nice, and they think I'm a myth. It's hilarious. If I left, what would they do? And now that they have all their cameras, the game's become fun and more challenging! Have you seen all the memes they've made about me?" His eyes almost glowed with his glee.

Viera grinned. *He really is like a kid.*

Across the skinny board, Scout smiled. "Yeah, Mom, he's just having fun. Why leave?"

Thorn's eyes narrowed at her son. "I didn't think you wanted to stay on Earth."

Scout slumped. "I don't, but I don't want to put my wants on Toby. He's allowed his own beliefs, right?" He turned to Viera. "Isn't that what you're always telling us in class? Everyone has their own likes and dislikes and that's what makes things so great?"

A warmth blossomed within her. "That's right, kiddo. Exactly so."

Toby scratched the back of his head. "I just like living here. I don't want to leave."

"Aren't you lonely?" Thorn leaned forward. "You've been here so long. Don't you want any companionship?"

"Nah." Toby said. "I like my solitude and my huckleberries."

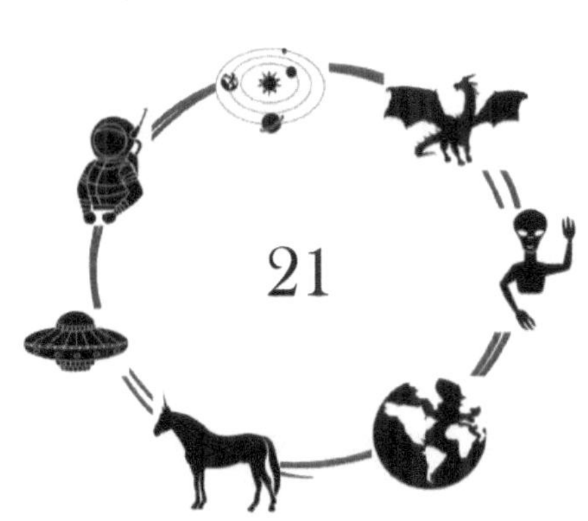

21

Never Yell "Fire" In A Crowded Lesson

Scout

"Blue, red, black, purple ..." Flower Prancer snapped at Viera.

Scout ran after the light ball as Ms. Kor made it fly across the room. He liked the game; it was a lot of fun. The changing colors were funny, though sweat dripped down his teacher's forehead. He wasn't sure why changing the ball's color was important, but he figured his understanding didn't matter.

Beaver leapt in the air to touch the yellow ball before it flew towards Scout. She stayed floating in the air, waiting to see the direction of the next ball. Her babies tried to fly after her.

"Green, orange—"

"Ouch!" Scout flopped onto his butt on the floor, holding his hand. He'd been playing catch with the light ball with Beaver for a while, but this one was the first to hurt him. "The orange ball hurt my hand."

"Stop!" Flower Prancer demanded. "Float that ball to me."

Out of the corner of his eyes, Scout watched as the ball flashed out and Ms. Kor ran to him. "Scout, are you okay? Let me see your hand." She knelt by him, wrapping an arm around his waist and holding his burnt hand in hers. "It looks like it will be tender for a few days, but the burn isn't too bad. Do you want to go home?"

"No, Ms. Kor, don't send me away. I'll be fine." The idea of being sent away made Scout tremble a bit. "I want to watch your lesson."

With a small smile, she nodded. "Okay champ. I'll be more careful." She stood and faced Flower Prancer.

He scowled at her. "Ms. Kor, make a ball, I never told you to dissipate it. I should see it still floating."

Ms. Kor shut her eyes and the ball reappeared, then it bounced through the air towards the yonat.

Scout rubbed the wrist of his hurt hand, trying to stop the pain throbbing down his arm. The palm of his right hand was red from the heat from the orange ball.

He groaned, trying not to be loud enough for his teacher to hear. Trying to ignore the pain, he looked over at his teacher. Ms. Kor's shoulders were hunched as she stood in front of *her* teacher. "I don't know what happened. I thought I had figured out the color change with the ball as it flew around the room. This magic stuff is so hard. And why didn't anyone tell me I could run out?"

She sounds as pitiful as the kids in class when they're in trouble. She must feel bad about hurting me.

"What do you mean, run out of power?" Flower Prancer sounded frustrated.

Ms. Kor sighed. "This weekend ..." She went on to describe what happened when she made pancakes.

Flower Prancer's tail swished. *Oh, no! He's annoyed with her. She should back up, maybe bow her head, or maybe hide.* Scout smiled at his silly thoughts.

The yonat made a low sound before speaking. 'As much as your friend's arrogance annoys me, you need to schedule time to work with her. You're starting to access magic beyond your understanding. You need to learn control, child, before you do harm."

Ms. Kor's shoulders stiffened before she nodded. "I understand your worry. I really am doing the best I can."

"No. If you were doing the best you could, you would stop with that silly human job that's taking up your time," he said. He sounded like one of the school bullies.

Scout took in a sharp breath at Flower Prancer's words, shaking his head. *She's not going to leave the school, isn't she? I like Ms. Kor as a teacher. She really is one of the best.*

Ms. Kor growled low. "I'm not leaving my job. Not only have I made a commitment, my students need me. Educating the next generation is a great honor. If you hadn't noticed, it's exactly what you're doing with me. Now, if you're ready to move on to my lesson, it's getting late, and I need to get back to my 'silly human job' early tomorrow morning."

The tail swished again. "You said your pancakes caused the Firozas to see qynads. Well, let me see what you can do."

Excitement bubbled in Scout. *Will she recreate Horax? What Ms. Kor did with the pancakes was cool. I liked seeing the holograms.*

Ms. Kor stepped back from Flower Prancer. She bit her lower lip and closed her eyes. After a few seconds, she nodded then opened her eyes and lifted her hands.

Scout held his breath, wanting to see Ms. Kor's hologram. Would it move? Would it be as big as Horax? Would it breathe fire?

He almost rubbed his hands together but remembered the burn at the last minute.

As he waited, he realized the hologram wasn't appearing.

"Ms. Kor, we're waiting," Flower Prancer snarled.

She huffed out a breath. "I know. I'm waiting as well. I just ... I know what you want, but a dragon is so much bigger than a ball, and I just burned Scout." She sounded sad.

"A qynad, Ms. Kor, not a dragon, and we all make mistakes on our journey to master a skill. You will always fail on the first attempt, but you can't get to mastery without your first failure. Please, Ms. Kor, fail, so we can eventually get to your successes."

Scout was shocked at how inspirational Flower Prancer's words sounded.

Face hard, Ms. Kor looked ready. Her hands, which had dropped to her sides, lifted again. She grunted, and the image of a red qynad appeared in the gym. Flower Prancer's tail swished, but before he could say anything, the beast began to move. It went from a static statue, to a moving creature. It lumbered forward, seeming to walk and breathe.

Scout looked back and forth between the hologram and Ms. Kor. She shook with the effort she expended.

"Acceptable, Ms. Kor. Qynads can breathe fire. Can your hologram?"

She swallowed and blew out an audible breath. Then the red beast opened its large maw and fire shot out towards a wall, away from Scout, Beaver, or her babies. A holographic image of fire splashed on the opposite wall.

When the fire ended, the wall was black and the curtains burned, smoke billowing to the ceiling. Suddenly the hologram winked out.

Breathing hard, Ms. Kor made a pitiful sound before looking at Flower Prancer. "Fuck! What now?"

22

Magic Run Amuk

Viera

Wednesday morning, Viera's alarm cut through her brain like a chef's knife through butter. She groaned and pushed herself up to sitting. "I don't want to exist today."

On shaky legs, she made her way to the shower. It took a few minutes to get her pajamas off. She waited for the water to warm up and then she climbed in. As the heat seeped into her, she thought about Tuesday.

'Light is the precursor to heat, Ms. Kor. You've started the fire, put it out.'

She'd stood there gob-smacked while Flower Prancer continued to lecture her. 'I don't know how. Tell me how.'

The yonat made a disapproving sound ... as always. 'With your magic, Ms. Kor.'

She reached into herself and thought: I need to take the heat away.

With pure desperation, she imagined herself reaching out and pulling the fire back into herself. The fire went out, but she felt drained. Her head pounded and her body shook with the effort.

'Adequate. We'll continue on Thursday.' And she was dismissed.

Taking a deep breath, Viera scrubbed her hair, and then her face and body. She needed coffee—a Bigfoot sized amount of coffee—and she wasn't getting it in the shower.

Viera sipped her third mug of coffee as she parked in the school's lot. This one in a travel mug. *The school has more coffee. I may make it through the day yet.* Her phone buzzed.

She shut off the car and checked her phone. A text came in from Betsy: *Are you free tonight? I have an activity I'd like to do, and I think you'd be interested in joining me.*

Rubbing her eyes, Viera slumped back. Her life used to be so simple. She texted back: *Will you tell me details when I see you this time?*

The reply came back quickly. *Of course. See you at three-thirty.*

She slipped her phone back in her pocket and slumped in her seat. *How hard can a day of school be?*

With the thought she knew could lead to no good, she pushed the door open and slowly walked through the parking lot towards the building. The screams and laughter from the kids in the playground surrounded her. They were happy sounds, but she knew she needed to take medication for her headache, or she wouldn't make it through the day. She also needed to stop in the staff lounge for more coffee, regardless of how bad it was.

Viera finished the coffee she'd brought from home as she entered the room meant for adults only. There were three other people present, all teachers. One brushed past her as she entered.

"I hate finding a gift for my husband. He's impossible. The ass just gets himself anything he wants. What's the point of working this hard? But the kids want to get him something special ... want me to think of something special ... a surprise. For fuck's sake, this sucks," the woman, Carol Moss, a fourth grade teacher said.

Head pounding, Viera turned to her. "Are you talking to me?"

Carol, whom she'd never spoken to before, gave her a weird look. "No. I didn't say anything. I was just leaving." And then she put action to word and left.

Using her thumb to point at the door, Viera asked the other two teachers, "Was it just me? Did you two hear that?"

Ryan, a third-grade teacher who also taught karate, lifted an eyebrow at her. "I don't know what you're talking about. She didn't say anything. Are you feeling okay?"

Viera moved to the coffee pot to fill her mug. "Yeah, no, headache, but ... yeah. I just thought ..."

Ryan came over to rub her back. He and Viera had been good friends for years. One of her best friends on the staff. "My wife writes the best books. I hope one day the world realizes it."

"What? What did you just say?" *Why would he tell me something I know? I've read all her books, and they are great.*

His brow furrowed. "Nothing. But I'm starting to worry about you."

He patted her arm. An image of a karate class flashed through her mind. *Okay, everyone, kata today, two groups.*

Viera realized he hadn't spoken ... she was reading his memories. Forcing a smile, she backed away from him. "Thanks ... well, have a good day."

Hands shaking, she walked to the door to pick up her students, then led them to her classroom. One of the girls grabbed her free hand. "Ms. Kor, I have to go to the bathroom."

The new puppy is so cute, but why did he eat my favorite stuffed unicorn? A sadness washed through Viera. She pulled her hand from the girl's. "Okay, Cindy, go ahead, but get back to class as quickly as you can."

A boy bumped into her as they entered the room. A pain shot through her leg. *'Oh, sweetie, I know you want to ride your bike, but you broke your leg when you fell out of that tree. You'll be back to your old self soon.'*

But, Mom, I don't want to be inside for six weeks. That's forever! This sucks.

Viera ran to her desk. She felt like every student was a bomb, ready to explode in her mind. Her body shook.

Tiffany came up to her. Before Viera could stop her, she gave her a hug. "Good morning, Ms. Kor!"

'Now, Tiffany, dear, me and Dad will be back soon. You'll only be alone for a little while, maybe a week or two.

There is food and you know how to take care of yourself. Remember, don't tell anyone; it's the only way to be safe.'

But, Mom, it's scary to be alone.

'You're my big girl. You'll be fine. You don't need a babysitter anymore. You're no baby.'

When will you be back?

'Like I said, a week or two.'

Viera clamped down on any emotion from showing on her face. "Good morning, Tiffany. How are you?"

"I'm good." The girl smiled up at her, her brown eyes wide. "Are we going to watch a movie today?"

Head pounding, Viera nodded. "Probably."

"Can I choose the movie today?"

With a small shrug, Viera sighed. "We'll see."

The first part of the day was math. As Viera moved around the room, she avoided touching any of the students. Despite her attempts, she inadvertently learned about a trip to Wisconsin Dells the previous summer, a huge water park near the city. Another kid went to Six Flags Great America and rode on roller coaster rides for the first time. There were birthday parties and Christmas memories. Halloween and Thanksgiving. Kids remembered their first encounters with pets and friends. To say it was hard to focus would be an understatement.

At afternoon recess, she looked up Tiffany's parents' number. Her mother answered. "Hello?"

"Hi, this is Viera Kor, your daughter's teacher."

"Oh! Is everything okay? Did something happen today at school? I can't come in ... I'm still at work, you understand. Business hours. I know that you teachers leave at three, and us real workers work until much later. You're probably home relaxing right now. Such a wonderful job." The woman chuckled.

Did that woman really just say that out loud? What a piece of work. She shook her head, refusing to engage on that level. "Is your husband also at work?"

"Of course." There was a muffled sound as if the woman covered the mouthpiece of the phone. "If you called him, he'd be in a meeting ... very busy."

"Right. So, you two are at work, and where is Tiffany?"

There was a long sigh. "She's at home with a sitter right now."

The words hit Viera like a truck. She'd wanted the memory she's gotten from the girl to be wrong. *How can parents leave a young girl home alone?*

"Oh, okay. Excellent. Thank you." Viera got off the phone, her heart heavy for the little girl playing outside with her friends.

23

Tea And A Muffin

Viera

When Viera pulled into her driveway, she saw Betsy's car parked in the street. Despite the gallons of coffee she'd drunk all day, her head still pounded, and she was exhausted.

Viera pushed open the door and heard, "In the kitchen."

She dropped her bag and headed to the back of the house. Betsy sat at the table drinking a mug of tea. There was a bakery box in the center of the table. "Ready for today?"

"I don't know. Maybe I should just stay home. I'm not good company." Her eyebrows rose. "Are those for me?"

"Now, they're for Kafi, who we're visiting today. But since it's eight thirty at night in Ghana, we have a bit of time. Kafi's a night owl. He won't mind us being a bit later."

"Ghana? That's where you want me to go?" Viera massaged her temples and groaned.

Betsy narrowed her eyes. "Talk to me."

Viera blew out a breath and sat down. "I don't know. First I did that stupid spell. Then my hologram shot out real fire and set the training center on fire." She dropped her head in her hands. "And I don't even know how to create fire," she whined. "And today, God, Betsy, it was horrible!"

She heard Betsy stand and move around the kitchen. There were some taps and a whirring sound. "Drink some tea and grab something from the box. Let's start at the top. There was a lot behind what you said, and we're not leaving until we figure some of this out."

Viera peaked up from her hands, a feeling of hope building within her. "You'll help me with all my drama?"

A laugh helped her relax more. "Of course. Besides being friends, I'm one of your trainers, no matter what Flower Prancer says. Now, drink the chamomile."

She took a sip and selected a chocolate muffin from the box. She let the warm drink relax her. "Will I ever be able to cook again? Watching Thorn and Scout hallucinate in front of me because of something I did was awful."

Betsy reached out and rubbed her hand. The warmth and connection soothed something deep within her. Right until ...

'I'll get everything organized, you don't have to worry. I've been doing this for-"

Viera snatched her arm back. She realized Betsy was speaking to her, but she wasn't sure what it was about.

"Of course. Your magic is strong. I should've guessed with your having three proficiencies. On Saturday, why don't you come over to my place and we can find you a book?"

"Wait!" Viera snapped to full attention. "There are books? I've been asking for books."

"Yes ... well, no. My grandfather had a few books he wrote. They aren't official, but they may help. You can look through them this weekend and see if any of them could help with the potions, and maybe your proficiency for time. He had that as well, as rare as it is. He was always good with his proficiencies."

Viera vibrated in her seat. "You're offering Gandalf's library to me?"

"Not if you make a big deal, I'm not."

Viera slapped her hands over her mouth and shook her head, already starting to feel better.

Betsy narrowed her eyes. "Okay, one issue put on the back burner. Next issue to unwrap and put off, for a little bit at least. You created a hologram?" Her friend's eyebrows danced up and down.

She nodded. "Flower Prancer asked me to make a creature. I chose a dragon. Fuck! When am I going to get this right? It's like when my teacher in third grade got married and I kept messing up her last name. How long did it take you?"

"I learned the word qynad first. But I know what you mean either way. If you use the words you first learned around me, I'm used to them."

Viera nodded. "Okay, well, apparently light and fire are two sides of the same coin."

"That's true. Light wizards evolve to fire." Her head tilted. "Wait, can you create fire?"

Viera had been about to take another sip of her tea, but stopped, with the mug halfway to her mouth. "I don't know how to do it on command. I haven't gotten to that part of my training."

"Have you practiced on your own, played with your abilities, or do you only stretch your magical wings with the Elder?"

Dread slammed into Viera. "Please tell me I won't grow wings."

Betsy laughed. "Don't take everything I say so literally."

"Fine." She shook her head. "No wings. I haven't been doing any practicing because I really don't have time. Sometimes the magic seems to practice without me, though."

"So, I assume, that brings us to that third stressor for today. What happened that was so horrible?"

It was time for more tea, but Viera's mug was empty. She sighed. "More tea, panel. Chamomile mint mix this time." It made the sound, and she got up to get her brew. "My head's been pounding after yesterday's lesson. I don't know if that's caused me to be more magical, less magical, or more chaotic, but whatever it is, it's awful. Every person who's touched me, including you, I'll have you know, I've read a memory." Viera sipped her tea with shaking hands. "Being in an elementary school ... well, it's been a long day."

Betsy's eyes were wide as saucers. "You haven't been taught how to shield? That kin of a donkey's ass hasn't taught you the basics to survive in a populated area?"

"Well, I didn't tell him it was getting bad. It wasn't hard until today. And isn't it dangerous to insult the Elders?" Viera gaped at her friend.

"But you have sense magic. It should've been where he started. Are you going to tell him?" Betsy smirked. She held out her hands and Viera placed hers on top of her friend's. "Remember with the trees, when you opened yourself up? Well, we have to come up with a series of mental exercises you can use to block out the extra stimulation so that it doesn't overwhelm you, so you don't enter memories uninvited."

"What if the memories help others?"

Betsy tilted her head, narrowed her eyes, and leaned forward. "What do you mean?"

"There is a student in my class. Her parents ... I'm pretty sure they went on vacation and left her home alone. I got that from her memory. If it wasn't for this newfound ... whatever, I wouldn't know."

"But do you know the memory is true? Do you have proof?" Betsy sounded so calm and rational.

"No!" Viera snapped. "But you could find out. You're a private investigator."

Betsy sighed. "One thing at a time. Let's fix your shields. Then we're off to Ghana. I'll look into your student tomorrow when I'm in my office."

Viera felt a sense of relief having Betsy in her corner. What would've happened if she didn't? What if one of the pillars hadn't lived so close? She would've been on her own with only the yonat to help her. She shivered.

"Okay, what do I do?" She realized she'd been holding her friend's hands without picking up on anything. "And how come I'm not getting any more memories?"

"I'm blocking. I'm going to drop my shields, but first we have to figure out what works for you. What relaxes you?"

Viera shut her eyes and thought. "A bath? Being outside, like the mountains or the woods? Reading a book? Swimming?"

Betsy laughed. "Are you asking me or telling me?"

"I don't know what I'm doing or what you're looking for. I thought you were going to tell me to imagine myself in a castle, so I'm already off."

With a sigh, Betsy continued. "I'm going to focus on a single memory that will hopefully not overwhelm you. Then you can go through your potential magic blockers. It's all a mental game. To me, the more flexible the better, but everyone has a different opinion. Let's start with the bath. If you're in the bath and touch me, what happens?"

Viera imagined herself in a luxurious bathroom, one from a home improvement show where they redid the room top to bottom. Blue, gray, and white tile, a jacuzzi tub, the works. She got in the bathtub and nodded.

Running through a field. I can't wait to tell Dad. I finally did it! I created my own playhouse from my magic.

With a shake of her head and a quirk of her mouth, Viera gazed at her friend. "How old were you when you made that playhouse?"

"Eleven. It wasn't huge, but I was over the moon." Betsy looked off for a moment before shaking her head. "Okay, that didn't work. Next, think about walking out of a forest into an open field. You can go back into the woods at any time, and the magic is always there, accessible. Like, you can access it, but it can't access you. As for the scenery, you can add some details, the mountains in the background, or other things that make you feel grounded. I'm a bit more hopeful this time."

"Right, woods, mountains, got it." Viera got it all set and then slid her hands back into her friend's.

'Dad! Dad! You have to come see what I created! I know you're busy, but you'll be so very proud of me.'

Viera pulled her hands away with a small shake of her head. Another failure. Part of her wanted to continue to watch the memory to see the structure herself.

Betsy sighed. "Okay, onto the next one. Imagine you have a library added to your house. Not like a library you need a card to visit, but a room with a bunch of books. When you exit the room, you're in the living room, nice and relaxed. Same deal as the outdoor example. You control the magic. It doesn't control you."

Closing her eyes, Viera set up the idea in her mind. She liked the idea of the magic living in books. She walked around the library, a room with floor-to-ceiling bookshelves stuffed with tomes. There was a recliner with a lamp as well as a table with a chair in the room. Easy reading or research, just her type of room. The ceiling was the Abritos glass ceiling, letting in natural light—since there were no windows with all the bookcases. The only opening was the doorway to the living room.

Viera walked through it, cutting herself off from the information in that room. Her hands shook as she placed them on Betsy's. She waited.

Nothing.

She waited a few more moments. Still, there were no memories. In her mind, she walked back into the library.

'Of course Betsy, I have time.'

Viera stepped from the library. "What would happen if I boarded up the library and never returned?"

Betsy tilted her head. "If you boarded it up, you'd degrade your magic. You'd be cutting away part of what you are."

Finishing off the muffin, Viera sighed. "I guess that's not what I want, though things were so much easier before all this happened to me."

"That's true, but things are so much better now. Think of the years you can have with Thorn. Have you discussed it with her? You're long-lived now."

Viera felt like a bucket of ice water had been splashed over her head. *Why didn't I put the pieces of that together?*

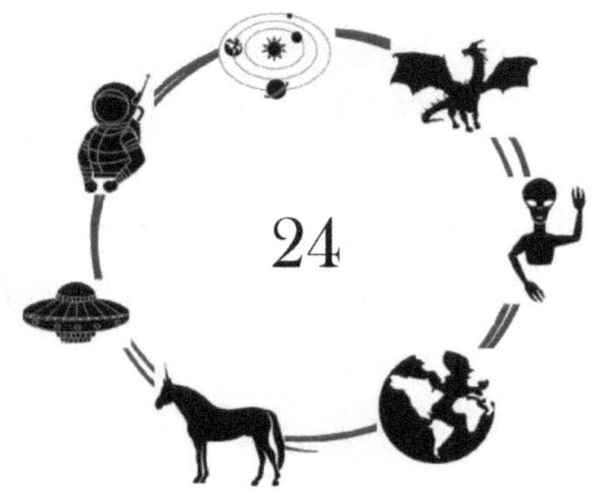

24

Hot Topics

Betsy

Amusement bubbled in Betsy as she watched Viera come to terms with her long life. It wasn't the first time she'd explained it to her friend, but maybe this time it'd get through. As for Betsy, she'd grown up knowing she'd live much longer than the people around her. She'd befriended the other pillars because they were amazing people, but also because they understood what it was like living hundreds of years. Though Betsy and Viera had been friends before, now they'd probably become closer.

Betsy had befriended the teacher when she wanted to figure out if this area would be a good one for Thorn and her people. She'd liked the plucky woman and was happy she had someone to connect with in this cold and dreary state. Viera seemed to love Wisconsin, but Betsy missed the warmer climate she'd grown up in. *One day I'll relocate again, and then I'll choose a place with sun and oceans.*

She shook her head, wondering if Viera's magic was inspiring all her memories to intrude on her time. "Okay, we have places to be. Are you ready? Do you think you're up to it?"

Viera looked miserable. "I've been dragging all day. My head is pounding."

Her amusement turned to frustration. "What has Flower Prancer been doing in your lessons? Hasn't he spent any time on the basics?" Betsy threw up a hand and shook her head. "Forget it, I retract the question. There are ways to block the pain, but we don't have time for a full lesson today. We'll do that on Saturday. We need to start keeping notes. For now ..." She got up and went to the panel. Though the controls were in Galactic Standard, it was a language she knew well. A few taps, and medicine appeared on the pad. "Take two pills and call me in the morning."

Viera had followed her over and had watched her motions. "Isn't speaking to the wall easier?" She took the medicine and swallowed it down with the last of her tea. "And I do have notes on what I've been learning, but nothing about blocking pain."

"Good, we'll review them Saturday. As for the panel, yes and no. I know the controls pretty well, so sometimes I like to just type it out."

Her friend slumped with a sigh. "One more thing to add to my list of things to learn."

Betsy slid an arm around Viera. "On the bright side, you have plenty of time. Do you still have the learning pad from Thorn?"

After a larger sigh, Viera nodded. "I think so. I'll add Galactic Standard to my list. I had been learning chanzii, but I should probably switch. I can learn specific alien languages after I can speak the general one."

"Now that you have that figured out, think you're ready to go?"

Viera gazed around her kitchen. "Nine o'clock at night. Ghana. Sure, instant travel around the world. You've been wanting me to see more than just the greater Madison area." She poked Betsy's side. "More than three hours away, right?"

"Exactly." Betsy smiled at her friend and then typed into the panel. She sent a quick message to Kafi and a second to contact the ship that orbited the planet that could transport them from Viera's house to Kafi's.

The kitchen shimmered around them, and then they were in Kafi's receiving room. Kafi looked the same. His boyish face broke into a smile, his dark eyes bright as he stood and circled his desk to give Betsy a hug. "Betsy!" She loved his deep voice and Ghanan accent. "You made it. I started to fear you were standing me up."

She stepped back. "Of course not, my friend. Would I do that? I have a treat. I'd like you to meet Viera."

His eyes widened as he took her in. "My, my. The woman of the hour. Haven't you caused all the uproar!"

Viera blushed, covering her face with her hands. "God above, I hope not. I'm just a simple second grade teacher from Wisconsin."

Kafi threw his head back and laughed. "There's nothing simple about a human who's caught the attention of an Elder. I hear Flower Prancer himself is teaching you, bless your soul."

"If what he's doing can be called teaching," Betsy mumbled.

Kafi shot her a look. "That bad?"

It was nice that there was someone else who understood that Elders weren't the be all end all of knowledge and respect. "She has three proficiencies, and he hasn't taught her to shield, or to block pain, or how to control even one of her magics." She started pacing as she ranted. "Not only is she randomly picking up memories of everyone around her, but she's also setting things on fire. The other day, poor Viera accidentally brewed a potion. You tell me, how are his lessons going?"

Kafi was biting his lips to stop from laughing. When Betsy turned to Viera, she realized she'd made a mistake. "Oh, dear, I'm sorry, Viera. I shouldn't have–"

"No, you're right. I'm messing everything up." She sniffed.

"But that's just it, you aren't. You're doing some amazing things. A fire-breathing hologram of a qynad is ... well, it's fantastic."

Kafi's hands shot up. "A what now?"

Viera slumped on a couch and told him the full story. As she spoke, he made tea and brought biscuits—cookies—for them to eat.

"Well, now, you came so I could show you what I'd discovered about the boomerang and minotaur horn, but this is much more interesting."

Her friend sat up. "The boomerang? You know what it does?"

Kafi winked. "I sure do. Why don't we head outside? It's dark, but we can get some light going and play."

They headed out of the house and to a field. It was huge and empty. She remembered the field from when she'd done some of Kafi's training years ago. He wasn't even two hundred years old yet, a baby really. It was why he looked so young. For wizards on Earth, the slow aging was strange. When a pillar reached the age of about two hundred and fifty, the first two digits of his or her age would generally look like their perceived age. It was why Betsy appeared to be in her late thirties.

"So, Viera, show me this fire-breathing qynad of yours." Kafi's voice was smooth and soothing.

She trembled a bit but nodded. After a few moments, a large red qynad shimmered into being in the center of the field. It only took a few seconds for it to start moving like one of the real creatures.

Next to her, Kafi whistled. "That's fantastic. Okay, how are you organizing your magic in your mind?"

"My what? How am I ... huh?"

Betsy wanted to strangle Flower Prancer. "Use the analogy of a home library with books, a study area, and a reading nook." She hadn't discussed what the library looked like with Viera, but if she knew the overworked teacher, she'd have to have both areas. "Also, an easy exit to block out overuse. Maybe a secondary spot to hold the books outside of the room."

As she'd described how she imagined Viera's headspace, both her friends nodded. Viera's face broke into a smile. "Oh! That sounds lovely. I don't quite follow what you're talking about, but I think that sounds good. A place to think about magic within the maelstrom of chaos, and a spot in the relative peace outside it all."

Kafi beamed. "Perfect. Imagine the qynad as a book you've pieced together that you can place on the table."

Viera shut her eyes and nodded. "So, this is like a program. I'm setting up a loop to keep the dragon in place. But in this case the dragon's code is kept in a book?"

"I can work with that. Add a parameter for color. Can you change the color of your qynad?"

With a smile, Viera nodded. "This has been what most of Flower Prancer's lessons have centered on. What color would you like?"

Kafi narrowed his eyes. "How about striped."

Viera snorted. "You sound like one of my students. You don't look much older than them. You look barely over twenty! How do you know so much?"

As she spoke, the qynad turned black and white striped. Betsy chuckled. "It looks like a zebra qynad mix."

"Can you make those stripes more colorful?" Kafi asked. "And I'll have you know, I'm one hundred and sixty-three. I'll just have this baby face for another hundred years or so. Now, you? Who knows, coming into magic so late. You may look like that for three hundred years." He laughed.

Viera gaped, but the qynad shifted to rainbow stripes. They all giggled at how goofy the creature looked.

Kafi scratched his chin. "Okay, next. Imagine a second book on fire, but holographic fire. Set that book next to the first and let it burn ... but not really."

As the qynad shot out fire, Kafi balled up some paper from a bag he carried and floated it up on the wind into the stream. It immediately burned. "Nope, that's the real deal. Relax, make it fake."

"Right, fake. It should be easier." Viera's face tensed, but it appeared she tried to relax her body.

The scent of the fire changed. Kafi sent up another ball of paper. Nothing happened. They all cheered.

"Good. Drop the hologram. Follow me." He led them to a small fire pit. "Now start a fire here." He tossed three balls of paper into the dirt.

It took Viera a few tries, but she finally figured it out. "Oh, my God, that was so much easier than I was making it out. The book analogy helped. I think I can keep this all separated in my head. Thank you!" She threw herself at Kafi. He hugged her back.

"Excellent, that means we can have s'mores when we're done with all our work." He winked at her.

"Enough play. The boomerang: what does it do?" Betsy asked.

Kafi nodded. "Right you are. No more lollygagging, we have real work to do. All this play will rot our brains." He winked at Viera. "If you would, Betsy, I need a target. Doesn't matter where. Just somewhere out in the field."

With a wave of her hand, she created a small mound out of the soil on the other side of the field. "Will that do?"

"Perfect." He pulled the boomerang from his bag but faced away from what Betsy had created. "Okay, that's the target." He pointed to his left towards the mound. Then he tossed the weapon straight ahead. It turned in the air, but instead of coming back to him, it turned and thwacked into the dirt. "It took me a bit to figure it out because I didn't have a target right away."

Viera's eyes were wide. "So, it always hits the target? Did you have to add any of your magic, or would it have worked for the family that owned the thing?"

Kafi tilted his head and looked at her. "All good questions. Since I started testing it, yes, it's always hit the mark. I don't have to add more magic to it, but I did have to prime it once. I don't think it'd work for you, unless you primed it ... you know, made it your own. So, no, it wouldn't have worked for that family."

She bit her lip. "So, that's the boomerang. Now the other object I found. And then you'll explain why you have the objects? I mean, you're so young! Right?"

Kafi laughed. "Oh, I really like this one."

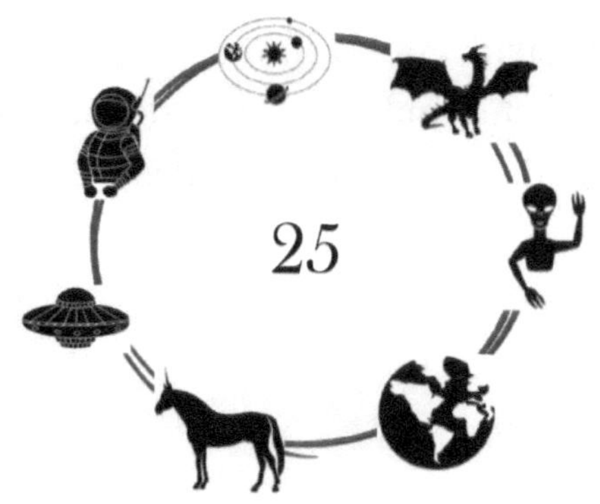

25

School Of Hard Knocks

Viera

Kafi led them to a building on the other side of the field.

"This used to be a school for new wizards," he explained. "When I was your age, maybe a bit younger, I came here to learn to master my magic. Betsy was my favorite teacher. She helped me with life magic. Zuza, you met him, right?" He looked over his shoulder to see Viera's nod. "He taught me to hone my gas magic, though at the time we had a few of the older generation around to help."

Viera swung her gaze back and forth between Betsy and Kafi. "So, five isn't some magical number for the pillars of Earth?"

Betsy chuckled. "No, it's just the most common number. Often, once the kids get strong in their proficiencies, the parents go off-world to explore what they've spent a lifetime studying. They may return, or they may not."

They navigated the hallways. Betsy waved her hand and light balls shimmered to life in front of them. Viera's eyes widened. "But how? I didn't think you had that proficiency."

"I don't, not as something I can do naturally, but we can all study and learn. Making a simple light ball is on all of our 'to learn' lists. When you're born before electricity, light spells are a necessity."

Ahead of them, Kafi snorted. "When you poke around in caves and other places you're not supposed to, you mean."

She flipped him off.

They finally got to an internal room and Kafi mumbled some words and did something with his hands. There was a click, and the door opened. Viera began to tremble when the seal on the door released. "Oh, my God, what is that?"

"It's our room of artifact wonders," Kafi said, waving his arm. The magic swirled around her, through her, like a rainbow of colors and ... *was that smells?*

Viera's body began to tremble as it felt like it filled with the weight of variety and history of powers. Trying to wade through the maelstrom of magic, she realized she didn't know what Kafi had said to her.

Behind her, Betsy rubbed her arms. "Step further away from the library in your mind, Viera, add a curtain, put up a block."

"Why not a door?" There was so much power coming from the room.

"You don't want to accidentally cut yourself off from your magic permanently. Just ... be careful with how you think about it, okay?"

Viera closed her eyes, took a deep breath, and imagined herself standing outside of her magical mental library. It was a maelstrom of chaos. She put up a curtain with a peaceful underwater scene and octopi to protect her from the overflow.

After a few moments she began to feel calmer. She nodded and opened her eyes. "Okay, I'm better."

They entered the room. She could still feel the pulse from the objects on the tables and shelves, but it no longer overwhelmed her. The air felt thick, but she could breathe.

Kafi led them to the minotaur horn. "I figured out what this did when I was bringing this to the room, and it all but dragged me here. It's a power magnet. It senses when something nearby is magical or has any level of power."

Betsy approached it with a small smile. "That's fantastic. We could use it for all our searches. It would save so much time. I took Viera last time, but we don't all have a Viera in our corner."

Kafi replied, but Viera stopped listening to the two of them. Something in the room reached out to her. She felt the pull. As if in a dream, she wandered the shelves. A heartbeat dragged her further into the large room. Her breathing became ragged, and her arms began to tremble. It was close.

As she turned a corner, a song surrounded her. Step by step, the volume grew. Slowly her hand reached out, quivering, about to touch—

"Viera, what are you doing?" A hand landed hard on her shoulder.

She shook her head and turned to see Betsy. "I ... I don't know. There's something here. I don't know what it is, but something is calling to me."

Betsy looked over the objects. "Which item? I'd hate for you to touch something that ends up harming you."

Viera shook her head and looked at the items on the shelf that drew her in. There was a small figurine of a cat, a journal, a pocket watch, a Christmas ornament in the shape of a crown, Shirley Temple cups in the shape of Geisha girls, candlestick holders, and a decorative egg a foot tall. "It's, um, it's the pocket watch." Just calling the trinket released a bit of the intense draw. "Yeah, the watch."

She watched, her hand twitching to grab the pocket watch, as Betsy selected the silver gadget, almost two inches wide, engraved on the top with initials. "I don't feel anything malicious." Betsy handed it over.

As Viera reached out to take it, she saw Kafi watching from the end of the aisle. When her hand connected with the heirloom, a sense of peace settled on her like a blanket on a cool day. She smiled. "That feels good." She looked between the two pillars. "Can I keep it? It feels like coming home, if that makes sense."

The two gazed at each other. It looked like they had a full conversation through their eyes. Finally Kafi's head jerked in a small nod. Betsy turned to her and said, "Keep it. If you start to act different, though, I'm taking it back."

It took Viera a moment to process his words, lost in the feeling that part of her magic was settling. "Different how?"

Betsy patted her shoulder. "Just different. We'll both monitor."

"That ... makes sense. I understand. Now, didn't you mention s'mores before we headed back?"

26

Time For Play

Viera

Thursday morning, Viera debated discussing Tiffany's situation with the principal. But what could she say? Tiffany hadn't actually told her anything. She had no proof of abuse or neglect. She hoped she could get something from Betsy soon that she could bring to the school. As a teacher, she wanted to protect her students.

What she'd learned from Betsy and Kafi helped with her control with her sensing magic, and the day flew by. It almost felt like the days before spring break. When the school day ended, she got in her car and considered going home and continuing the pretense of a day before the insanity of magic and aliens, but it was Thursday, and Flower Prancer expected her.

She made it to the training center in just over ten minutes. With time to spare, she checked her phone and saw she had a text from Thorn. *Dinner tonight after your lessons? Scout is off with Horax for the evening.*

Excitement infused Viera, and she immediately replied. *Sounds delightful. Eating in or out?*

The response was quick. *In. I thought we could bake together again. Horax took Scout to the island. He said he'd return him tomorrow morning after breakfast.*

Viera gazed at the words for a few moments, but they didn't suddenly rearrange themselves to make more sense. *The island?*

The bubbles indicating Thorn's typing took a bit longer. *I forget sometimes how much you're still learning. It's a safe place for the ship's crew to get some downtime from always being in space. It's in the same time zone as us, so everything works easy-peasy.*

She read and reread the message. *I'd love dinner, but I didn't bring clothes for more than that.*

Thorn responded with a wink emoji. *I'll make sure you get to work tomorrow in something decent. See you soon.*

Warmth filled Viera as she stepped from her car. It dampened a bit as Flower Prancer exited the building. "Ah, you *are* here. You're late."

Viera bit back any reply and was happy he couldn't read her mind. He wouldn't appreciate the image of her swatting him right on his equine rump. "I was just coming in. Are we working in there?"

"No, we're heading to a local park. You mentioned having feelings, or premonitions, about kids on the playground." The way he said the word "premonition" made Viera believe he thought she imagined it all. "We need to test it."

Her eyebrow rose. "We do? How?"

He walked away from the training center, and she followed him. "We'll sit at the park and watch the kids play. You're going to tell me what you can ... sense."

"Don't you think a yonat appearing at a park will cause a bit of a stir?" She tried to keep her voice even and steady, but just the idea of the situation made her want to bust a gut. *All those young kids seeing a white unicorn with rainbow hair ... they'd die on the spot!*

"I'll be invisible, as will you. We're there to observe, not to be seen, Ms. Kor. You're smarter than this ... or so I was led to believe." His voice came out dripping with disdain.

Fuck! I'll win him over one day, I swear it! And if not, I'll at least show him I'm a capable pillar.

When they neared the park, he turned to her. "I'll put the invisibility bubble over both of us so that we can see each other. If it were done separately, we'd only be able to hear each other. Overall, that's fine, but we'd lose one other in the crowd."

She nodded. After he performed his spell, the world looked like it was under water. They continued the last few blocks out of the alien creature neighborhood.

Once they arrived in the park, they stood to the side in the shade between two trees. It was a warm, dry April day, and the park was full of adults and kids ready to finally be outside playing. Part of Viera was happy to see such glee, another part wanted to run from what she saw as a continuation of her school day and monitoring recess.

"Ms. Kor, before we do any predicting—premonition— I want to explain that the skill is very rare. The time proficiency itself is rare. Most creatures with the ability over time use it to review the past. Your skill at reading memories, a useful parlor trick, can be honed into something useful. But your theory of seeing into the future is a bit more fantastical." His tail swished. "We shall see." With a small snort, he turned to the park. "Tell me what you see as far out as you can see it."

Wanting to get into the right headspace, Viera shut her eyes to center herself. When she opened them, it was almost like all the kids had a ghost of themselves overlaid moving at double speed. The one moving the fastest was on the balance beam.

She pointed. "The girl over there, she's going to fall, cry out that her knee hurts, then shake it off." They watched, but it didn't happen.

Flower Prancer snorted.

Viera knew what she saw but shook her head. "Okay, on the swings, the boy is going to jump off when the swing is at its highest." Once the boy did just as she said, she pointed to two girls in a field. "The blond will push the brunette and stick out her tongue before running off."

Once the two girls started their fight, Flower Prancer made a sound of disgust. "You teach kids this age. Are you just going to use what you know about the young of your species? I want premonition, not prediction."

She wanted to scream. What she'd told him hadn't been a simple guess about what would happen next. As she gazed around the playground, the image of the girl on the balance beam grew more vivid, but that wouldn't prove her point. Then she found it. "The boy, swinging across the bars, he's going to fall, twist his ankle, and cry out in pain." He fell, but she hadn't finished. "His mom will run over with her phone out, finishing up whatever she'd been working on, and then she'll trip, fall, and hurt her arm." A second yell came from the people in the park, the mother calling for help. "Then she'll realize she's holding a phone and call for an ambulance."

The yonat's tail swished harder. "Fine, but why didn't your sight work on the girl and the walkway she runs on?"

They both turned to the balance beam. As they watched, the girl tumbled off, grabbed her knee and yowled. Then her face transformed into a scowl when a woman approached. "I'm fine, Mom." She leapt up and returned to the apparatus to try again.

With a shrug, Viera said, "I guess I was a bit early. The image of her fall had been a bit light at first, unlike the others."

Flower Prancer's head snapped to her. "Ms. Kor, how is this possible? Time wizards can see maybe five or six seconds into the future, not minutes. It is inconceivable you saw that girl so far forward. Not unless you have an artifact that boosts your abilities."

Her brow knit. "An artifact?"

"A magical item." He growled. "Something with magic that would enhance your range and ability."

She froze, gaping at him. Then she slipped her hand in her pocket and pulled out the pocket watch. "Something like this?"

He huffed. "Yes, Ms. Kor. Something like that." He turned and started walking back towards the neighborhood where the aliens lived. "There is much more to teach you, but I believe we are done for today." She felt the magic snap around her, and he disappeared from sight.

Sighing with relief, she returned to the training center to get her car and head to meet Thorn. She decided she deserved the night with her ... what was Thorn to her? Girlfriend? Friend? Friend with benefits? Well, whatever it was, she deserved time with the other woman.

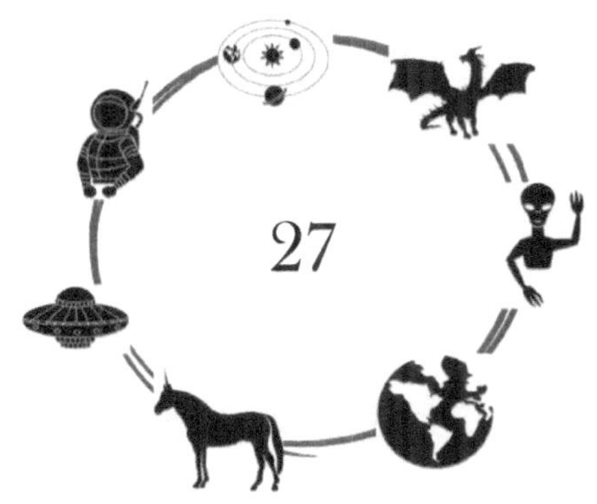

27

Dinner And A Plan

Thorn

Thorn sat at her computer, searching for something fun to cook. She'd tried to cook on Earth, but her flare always kicked in and she ended up messing up the recipes. Between the temperature and gravity, this planet wreaked havoc on her cooking experiments.

Roast with garlic mashed potatoes, Brussel sprouts, and fruit tarts for dessert. I wonder if Viera would be up to doing all that. Her stomach growled as she imagined the meal.

She wrote down the idea and continued to look. Pasta, chicken, stir-fry, there were so many options.

A knock on the door pulled her from her concentration. Wesley and Buttercup, two of the ven babies left behind—the others were with Scout—woke up and ran in circles as Thorn got up. The two furry beasts weaved their way through and around her legs, their antennae swishing back and forth.

Thorn headed out of her office and checked the peep hole. Viera stood on her stoop looking happy but tired. Thorn opened the door and pulled the human into a hug. "Hi! You're early."

The two baby ven leapt up for a pet, which Viera happily gave them. She squatted, giving each baby their due love, then she stood and met Thorn's stare. "I guess Flower Prancer just wanted some basic information about my skills so he could set up my next training session." She sounded more annoyed than hopeful.

The yonat wasn't playing nice during his stay. *I'll need to speak with him. I don't know why he's so insistent on being gruff with his student. Members of his species are usually straight forward, but according to Scout, he's being particularly harsh.*

Pulling back, Thorn wrapped an arm around Viera. She fit so nicely tucked into her side. "Well, his loss, my gain.

I've been hard at work trying to figure out a menu for tonight's dinner. Something we could cook together. Do you have any thoughts?"

Viera signed contently. "I make a mean chicken pot pie. Or if you like mashed potatoes, we could make shepherd's pie."

"Only if the potatoes have a lot of garlic in them."

"Always. What's cooking if there's no garlic?" Viera almost sounded offended. "Want to start now?"

Thorn tilted Viera's chin up and gave her a quick kiss. "Yes. But do we want to make dessert too, or go out for that?"

Viera wrapped her arms around Thorn's hips. "Can't the silly panel whip us up something reasonably delicious for dessert? Then we can get to our second dessert more quickly."

"I like how you think. Now, kitchen, or we'll never eat." Thorn hummed the last word low and seductively.

Dinner was messy and delicious. The potatoes were good and the shepherd's pie better. They ordered blueberry cheesecake doughnuts from the panel and enjoyed them with vanilla ice cream Thorn kept stocked for Scout.

While they savored the sweet treat, Viera bit her lip and averted her gaze. She wiped her hands on her pant legs then shook them out. After a few seconds of playing with her napkin, she finally looked back at Thorn. "I really like you, Thorn."

"And I like you. I think we've established this." Dread intruded on her thoughts. She'd seen enough human shows to know this beginning to a conversation rarely ended well. Her people tended to be more direct.

Viera smiled tightly. "Did you know that the pillars aren't bound by the eighty or so years of life of the average human?"

"Sure. Isn't Betsy older than Flower Prancer? I'm younger than both of them, but I've heard them argue a time or two. I don't know anyone willing to go head to ... well, snout? with that old yonat beside Betsy. She is made of steel." Although Betsy was an admirable human, Thorn still thought she was nuts. The woman may be older than the yonat, but she wasn't more powerful.

"Right, okay. Well, apparently it isn't because of some weird bit of human genetics, it's the magic. Once the krottel opened up the magic in me ... Well, I'm going to age slower. Since it's all backwards for me, no one's really sure how slow or how long my new life expectancy is, but it isn't what it used to be. In essence, I'll be around a lot longer." Her face scrunched up as if Thorn would be upset at the information.

In reality, she wasn't sure what she thought. When they'd started dating, Thorn knew there was an end point to their time together. The rationale was two-fold. First off, their age difference. Second, she'd be heading home to Abritos soon. Neither of these facts pointed to a strong and lasting relationship. Viera just took away one of the two obstacles.

Do I want more from this relationship than something light? Does she? Is that what this is about?

She'd been silent a bit too long. "Are you saying you want what's between us to be more than it is now?"

"I don't know. We're only at the start of all of this. I just wanted you to know. I figure you should have all the facts." Her smile widened and she shrugged.

Thorn nodded. "Okay, good. I really like you and what we have, but I do plan to return to my planet. I assume you want to stay here."

Viera slumped in her seat. "I hadn't even thought much beyond surviving my magic lessons, to be honest."

"Well, why don't we go and see if there's a way to get you to forget everything except us and the present."

Viera's eyes twinkled as her grin grew wicked. Thorn led her to the bedroom and a night she wouldn't forget.

28

Weekend Warrior

Viera

Viera slept in Saturday morning. It felt like a gift. As the sunlight streamed in, it cut across her bed, warming her face. She stretched.

"Good morning, day. How about we celebrate no alarms with some coffee?" She snorted to herself as she got up, dressed, and headed to the kitchen.

"Panel, coffee, please, in my largest mug.' In the freezer, she pulled out two Bigfoot sized huckleberry muffins and put them in her toaster oven. The coffee materialized and she took it to the table. It was steaming hot, and its aroma surrounded her like a morning hug.

She sipped the coffee with a contented sigh. After a few minutes, the sweet scent of toasted pastry reached her, and she got up to get the muffins. As she put the muffins on a plate, a knock came to her door.

She peeked through the living room window and saw Betsy's car. She let her friend in. "Morning."

"What's that wonderful smell?"

"It's called coffee, my friend. It's a new invention, and it keeps people like me from killing other people."

Betsy barked out a laugh. "Coffee is not a new invention, I'll have you know. It's been saving lives, marriages, and friendships for many years. But I meant the sweet smell. Do you have some of Toby's treats here?"

Viera smiled at Betsy. "I do. Let's go enjoy breakfast." At the table, Viera took a few bites of the sweet treat. "Are you really going to let me go through your ancient books?"

"I'm starting to change my mind." Betsy sipped her coffee. "It's been awhile since anyone's pawed through Gramps's stuff. It'll be good for the room to get some positive attention. As you probably have gathered, magical items can pick up on the mojo around them, and my animosity for Grandpa G probably doesn't help."

Viera leaned back. "Do people really ask you about the staff all that often?"

"You wouldn't believe it. Not as much here on Earth, but it bolstered his magic, and off-world, other wizards took notice. Books and movies love to show artifacts imbued with magic. The thing is, when you made the pancakes, a minor spell that would've worn off in less than an hour if you hadn't ended it, your power had been drained for most of the day."

"That's true." Viera recalled how weak and tired she'd felt. The pounding headache and her shaking arms. "So, I didn't need to end the spell?"

"No. There are some wizards with a proficiency for imbuing items. It's probably the rarest of all the non-elemental magic types. The only place it's common is with the dwarfs and even for them it's unusual."

"They're the ones that made the GPS portals, right?" Viera finished her muffin and put the plate in the sink.

"Correct. The items at the school in Ghana have magic, but for the most part they absorbed power from the massive amount of magic on our world. It's why we have to determine, item by item, what each artifact does." Betsy put her dishes in the sink. "Ready to go?"

"Yeah, I'm good."

She spoke quickly and Betsy's eyebrow rose. "That excited to get to my place, huh?"

Viera locked up the house. In the car, excitement bubbled in her like seltzer water. "I've never been to your place; it's super exciting. Now, back to the staff. You were in the middle of telling me about it."

"Was I?"

"Betsy!"

"Okay, fine. The thing is, no one's sure how he got this powerful imbued staff. More than that, have you seen any other wizard use a tool to help in their magic? And then Gramps showed up, hundreds of years old, with his staff, and the damn thing aided his proficiencies." She sounded annoyed.

Viera rubbed her forehead. "I thought in the book that shall not be mentioned in front of you, all the wizards had staffs."

Betsy growled low. "Don't think of the book as being anything but make-believe. I don't know what he was thinking except trying to find more real wizards. Maybe if he'd added more reality into the books ... but he didn't." She spent a few moments focusing on driving. "Anyway, I tried playing around with the staff, as did Kafi, Zuza, and Ania. None of us felt anything but a beautiful stick of wood."

"Wait, what about the fifth pillar? Why didn't he, she, they try it out?"

"Marco? It never really came up. He never knew Gramps. He's also pretty young, still figuring it all out. He's not much older than you, really," Betsy said, as she turned down a two-lane highway. "I know I've made it seem like we've all been doing this a long time, but Marco is in his eighties."

Viera scoffed. "Wow, a baby." She rolled her eyes. "You know, I'm nowhere near eighty, right?"

"Well, he looks like he's twenty." Betsy turned into a driveway.

"I hope you don't think I look twenty."

"Of course not. I just mean, for a wizard, he's young. And now you are a wizard, and young. I should probably get you two matched up. With Kafi, you three can take lessons together."

"Don't those two have their lessons pretty much mastered?"

"They are very good, but a wizard is always learning. Moreover, they'd love to work with you and start to learn more proficiencies." Betsy said this as if it were obvious.

About a quarter of the way to the house, a tight pressure wrapped around Viera, and she grunted. "God, what was that? I felt like we went through a wall."

Betsy swung around to the front of a huge house and parked. "I have wards on my house. If you weren't a wizard, you would've seen a small house and would've wanted to turn around. The mail delivery people just leave everything by the box. If you saw, I have a small area covering my mailbox by the road."

They got out of the car and walked up a set of elegant, half-circle steps, lined with the spring buds of flowers. There were two wine-colored doors with large, cloudy, oval windows with black wrought iron flowers in each. Silver wrought iron trees encircled the doors and decorated about half the front of the house. Sprinkled over the sky-blue side were outlines of simple clouds and a few birds.

Viera took a moment to gaze at the home. "It's amazing."

She could feel Betsy's pride in the appearance of her house. "Thanks. Having a skill in solids, especially metals, should come with benefits. It makes me smile whenever I come home."

Betsy walked up and opened the door without fussing with a key. When she saw Viera's shock, she laughed. "What? Who's going to come here and break in? That won't happen." Viera followed her in. "Okay, do you want to start with a tour or get right to the library?"

She followed her friend into the mansion-sized home. "I guess a tour. I'd love to see what the inside of the huge place looks like. Is it all home, or is it school, museum, and small town as well?”

The snort echoed in the foyer. “It isn’t that big! But, okay, follow me to the right. That’s where I spend most of my time.”

As Viera walked past a winding set of stairs, something urged her to go up. Through the arched doorway ahead of her, Betsy walked into a huge living room explaining ... something. The call from above washed over Viera and her feet turned, taking the steps two at a time.

A wide hallway stretched left and right, closed doors dotting the walls. More of the metal-work surrounded large paintings, some of people, some of scenery, but Viera could only focus on a door near the end of the hall to the left.

She walked robotically. Part of her mind wanted to gape at all the beauty around her, but whatever called her wouldn’t let her stop. She had to get to the room, to what pulled her, to whatever was behind that door.

“Viera!” The words penetrated her fog, just as Betsy’s hands fell on her shoulders. “What are you doing?”

“I need to get in here ... through this door.”

Betsy shook her head. “There isn’t anything behind this door. It isn’t even a room.”

"But there's something there, I can feel it." Viera could feel Betsy's worry and concern, though her face stayed neutral.

"It's a closet. I keep my old coats and boots in there, Viera. I don't know what you think you'll find." Her words sounded reasonable, but Viera knew she was hiding something.

"So, we can look?"

Betsy's blank face broke. Her eyes widened a pinch and her mouth tightened. "Yes." Viera heard the lie but didn't care. She reached out and turned the handle. As the door swung open, a scraping sound preceded the falling of a wooden stick into her hand.

A light flared over the staff, and she heard in her mind. *Home.*

29

Family Heirlooms

Viera

"Betsy." Viera heard the tremor of uncertainty in voice. "What am I holding?" She knew what she held, there was no doubt in her mind, but the idea that Gandalf's staff, *the staff*, had called to her and now spoke in her mind, almost overwhelmed her.

Next to her, Betsy sputtered. "It's been dormant for years. Just a stick, like any twig in my yard. I only kept it because I couldn't *not* keep it. I knew it had magic, although no one could sense it or activate it, but it called you. Like the watch."

Viera nodded. She felt her connection with Gandalf's creation growing. After taking a halting breath, her hand and arm tingling with the feel of the wood under it, she said, "It's more intense than the watch. It feels like the connection is growing. When it fell into my hand, it felt like coming home."

"Like you were coming home?" Betsy sounded confused.

"Yes ... wait, no, like *it* was coming home." Viera rubbed her face. "I'm trying to separate my thoughts from the sensations of the staff."

"That doesn't sound good, Viera. That staff is communicating with you? It's a piece of wood." Betsy reached out, wrapping her hand around Viera's. "Should you put it down?"

"No!" Viera sucked in some air. The images of the bond between her and the staff flitted through her mind. She trembled. "No," she said again more calmly. "It isn't harming me, it's trying to shift its alliance from your grandpa to me. It knows he died and has been waiting for another wizard who ..." She paused, brows coming together in concentration. "Who could do time magic. That's what the staff was made to aid in. It isn't for any other proficiency, just the very rare one." A deluge of information slammed into her, and the world blacked out.

Viera woke up in an opulent living room. Sun streamed in from large windows. She lay on a soft, light brown couch. When she pushed up to sit, she saw overstuffed matching seats on either side of the couch. A table sat across from her with a steaming mug on it.

There were arched openings along the walls. On the left stretched the foyer and the bottom of the stairs she'd climbed earlier in the day. *How long have I been here and how did I get on the couch?* When she looked behind her, there was a lot more living room with artwork, plants, and what looked like a reading nook.

She shut her eyes, but the connection to the staff was weak. It wasn't in the room.

"Hello?" The word echoed in the large room. "Betsy?"

From the opening to the right, her friend's voice came to her. "I left you some coffee. When you feel stable, come join me in the kitchen."

Viera picked up the mug and sighed as she sipped the amazing brew. It tasted like heaven. Halfway done with the mug, she got up and headed into the kitchen. The room looked like it belonged in a restaurant. It was state-of-the-art, huge, and had beautiful marble countertops. The tiled walls had a Mexican flair with blues, whites, and yellows in bright joyous patterns.

Betsy stood at a six-burner stove cooking something that made Viera's belly grumble. She went over to the long and wide island and sat on one of the tall stools. "Smells divine. What are you making?"

"Hashbrown boats with eggs and bacon bits. You collapsed. I thought you may be hungry when you came to." She stayed focused on her cooking as she spoke.

"How long was I out and how did I get down to the living room?" *And where is the staff?* She didn't ask the last out loud, though she wanted to. Betsy had tried to hide it from her, she knew it, but Viera could still feel it ... somewhere.

"I carried you down—you don't weigh that much—and about an hour." Her voice was tight. "And as for what you aren't asking about, I put the staff somewhere safe. I don't think it's a good idea for you to be near it."

Viera didn't agree but didn't want to argue. "Okay, you're the expert in these things, not me. I'm just glad you were there to help. Will we still visit the library after we eat?" She watched as Betsy served up the food.

"Sure, if you're up to it. Since you aren't running to that room in a daze, I don't see any reason to avoid it." Betsy slid a plate to Viera and then came around the wide island to sit next to her.

Once they ate, they finally had a tour of the large mansion of a home ... well, the first floor. They ended up in the library. It was huge. Grander than a school library. "Are all the books related to magic?" Viera traced her finger over a few spines, trying to read the titles.

"No. The majority of the books are somehow related to things wizards need to know, but there are books in here for pleasure reading. I have a whole section on paranormal romances ... you know, for fun."

Viera barked out a laugh. "You're kidding!"

"Nope! Life can't all be about study."

They spent a couple of hours looking through the books. Viera found two of Gandalf's journals discussing the combination of time and sensing magic, the benefits and what to be wary of. There were a few journals from other wizards on light to fire, like, *A Journey Of Painful Exploration* ... and the like.

When Betsy drove Viera home with the books she let her borrow, she had a very serious expression. "Look, Viera, those books are my family's legacy. You can read them, but I will need them back. Moreover, we'll be adding the content of the books to our Monday and Wednesday lessons."

"Of course!" Viera agreed, shutting the car door, and heading into her house.

It wasn't until she sat down in her own living room that she wondered if Betsy's last comment had been a warning or a threat.

Life Back To Normal

Viera

The students sat in groups debating topics from a list Viera had given them to choose from. The assignment was to discuss with the other students, then present a five-minute argument to the class explaining their thoughts.

This had been the easiest week since she'd returned from Torville Station Number Six. She'd figured out how to block other people from her senses. Her mastery of understanding her magic was coming along. Since she borrowed the books from Betsy on Saturday she'd had four nights to read through the journals. There was so much to learn.

Despite what Betsy had said, they hadn't discussed the books during Monday's lessons, but Viera thought they may come up tonight.

Viera shook her head. *Get your head out of magic and back into teaching!* Circling the class, she listened in on the discussions. The first group chose: *Should students be allowed to bring pets to class?*

"When I'm sad, having my pet cat would help me be happier."

"Cats don't behave well enough to bring them to school. Your cat would hide or run off. We'd have to limit the animals to ones in cages or dogs."

"But dogs scare me ... I mean, I'm allergic to them."

It sounded like the group was doing well. She moved to the next set of students. *Are aliens real?*

"If aliens were real, our technology would work better. Dad always complains about how slow his computer is."

"Maybe we have fancy phones because of aliens."

"Or fancy cars. My mom said that car person with the electric cars was an alien."

"That's a joke. There aren't really aliens."

"But how do you know, Tiffany?"

"I just do."

Viera watched the young girl. She'd text Betsy over lunch to see if there was more information about the girl. She felt really bad about her situation. With a sigh, she moved to Scout's group. *Should students go on field trips?*

"When I don't like the field trip, it's a boring day. I have to sit on a bus, walk around somewhere boring, and ride the bus back. It's awful."

"But even when you don't like it, you're still learning it. And if we don't have field trips, we wouldn't go to water parks. We have to take the bad to get the good."

Viera bit back a laugh. This group was getting into their arguments. Before she got to the last set of students, her timer went off. "Okay everyone, it's time for recess. Line up!" She led her students to the playground. It was her day to monitor them, so she stayed outside with them

Should I open up my sensing to know if they're about to get hurt? Should I just be a teacher like all the other teachers? She found a spot to stand away from the other adults. She liked the teachers at the school, she just didn't feel like answering any tough questions, like, 'do you have any plans for after school' or 'how was your weekend?'

Scout ran up to her. "Hi, Ms. Kor!"

She smiled down at him. "Hi, kiddo! How are you?"

"I'm great. This weekend, Mom and I are going out to the island, and Mom said I could invite you."

See, all the hard questions. Though Thorn had mentioned an island before, Viera had never learned what she meant by it. "You're going to have to slow down for me, Scout, you know that." She ruffled his hair. "What island?"

"Oh! Silly me." He bounced a bit. "There's an island in the coast." He snapped his fingers a few times. "Um, the Gulf Coast. No, wait, the Gulf of Mexico, that's it. Out in the water. Pretty far out. Anyway, it didn't have any people on it, so we get to go out there for relaxation. The people on the ship love it. It lets them stretch and stuff. You know. Anyway, Horax is doing a training session on Saturday. Wanna come?" The words all tumbled out of him.

Viera split her attention between the kids running around the play structure and Scout as she debated another trip away from home. She loved being a homebody, and it hadn't happened in weeks. *If I could spend a day just not doing anything, it would be so lovely. Wake up late, drink coffee, read a book, maybe after lunch switch to wine.* She sighed. The offer of a tropical island with her girlfriend sat at her feet—well, bounced excitedly in the form of a young boy—and all she could do was imagine being at home alone.

Am I broken?

"Let me think about it? Okay?"

"Sure!" Scout said, the word full of excitement, and then he ran off.

After that, recess was uneventful. Between recess and lunch, Viera only had to entertain her students for an hour. She had the students think about a story they wanted to write. They brainstormed ideas. If they couldn't think of anything, she had bags with random words and pictures they could use for inspiration. Then they paired up with a partner to help flesh out their ideas. They spent about fifteen minutes in a free write before cleaning up.

Viera had lunch period and recess off, so after she dropped the students off, she got her sandwich and yogurt out, then called Betsy.

"Heya, Viera, any big emergency I should be worried about?" Betsy's voice was light, but Viera knew there was a hint of truth behind her words.

"Not this time. I just wanted to see if you'd found out anything about that student, Tiffany."

She heard papers being shuffled around. "Actually, yes. I was going to call you a bit later. I had to wait for some basic information on the parents, and then I did some snooping, but you were right. The parents are in Greece right now. They've been there for a week and aren't returning for another few days. From what I can tell, there isn't anyone watching the girl."

Viera gasped. She knew it was a possibility, but hearing the truth still hurt. Her heart ached for the poor girl. "I'm going to have to call CPS, um, child protective services."

"I already did, on your behalf. There's a meeting this afternoon at four at the school. They have some questions for you and Tiffany. I was going to call you when your day was over. The principal already knows and plans on collecting the girl at three-fifteen when classes end."

A shiver of dread went down Viera's back. The thought of a girl being torn from her parents always disturbed her, but Tiffany's situation was untenable. "Thank you, Betsy." She paused, her mind finally catching up. "But why are you going to be there?"

"The girl was adopted at a young age, but the paperwork is odd. I just want to meet her, make sure everything is as it should be."

Viera massaged the back of her neck. "I'm confused. How wouldn't it be as expected? She's a scared girl. I would be too in her situation."

Betsy sighed. "I know, I'll explain later. Right now I have to go. See you later."

For some reason Viera's gut clenched. Something was going on, and she didn't like it.

The Creature, The Witch, and The Wardrobe

Betsy

No matter how much I do, the piles on my desk never seem to get any smaller. Betsy grumbled as she glared at all the work she had to do. Between her real job working as one of the interplanetary ambassadors from Earth and her cover-up job as a private investigator, there was rarely free time to do her own things. On top of that, she now added training Viera as a high priority. If Viera turned out to be as good with aliens as Betsy guessed, she could take over some of the ambassadorial responsibilities.

Her phone rang. Thorn's number appeared on the display. "Hi, Commander Firoza. To what do I owe the pleasure of your call this morning?"

The other woman laughed. "I thought we were past formalities, Wizard Doeth. I am calling to inform you that several from the ship are taking shore leave on the island this weekend. They'll be heading down on Friday. Scout, Flower Prancer, and I will head over Saturday, and return Sunday. I'm hoping Scout has extended our invitation to Ms. Kor, Wizard in training extraordinaire, but I don't know about her attendance yet."

Betsy closed her eyes and thought about the tropical island. It was full of white sandy beaches around the edge and lush trees and cool shade inland. The full square footage wasn't huge, but it was a nice escape to creatures stuck in space. "I'm training with Viera tonight, Ms. Kor herself. I'll find out if she's going and put her on my list ... or not." Why anyone would refuse a weekend in paradise, Betsy couldn't imagine.

"Thank you. One of these days we'll get you to the island for some rest and relaxation."

You need to invite me first, she thought sourly. "You know me, busy, busy, busy. Have fun out in the sun and on the water. Keep me informed of anything I should know about.”

“Will do.” And she rang off. She sounded happier than Betsy had heard her since coming to this planet.

It had been fairly simple integrating all the chanzii onto the world. As new developments were built, their people ‘bought’ and moved into the homes. No one was the wiser. The challenge would be when their world was ready for them to return. They’d have to start putting their homes on the market in waves to not shock buyers. The fact that a good chunk of the houses had windowed ceilings was going to cause a stir.

Well, that will go on the list of topics for the next meeting with the leaders. Some of their people will have to start living on their ships to make this transition easier.

She sent a quick message to Kafi who was heading their next meeting to add these items to the agenda, then moved on to her next task for the day.

Before she could pick up a file, her phone rang again. It was Viera. She called for a follow up on her student. Tiffany Anderson. The girl had been found by her parents sixteen years ago in a park in California. The records had been sealed and hard to dig up. After the natural parents couldn’t be found, the Andersons, who’d never had a child of their own, finally adopted the girl.

The first few years had gone well, but then she didn't seem to develop correctly. She was smart but didn't appear to age. As the years progressed, Tiffany seemed to stop aging at about six ... then seven years old. Her adopted parents wanted her to fit in with the other students. They had this crazy idea to create a new birth certificate and records of adoption. They convinced Tiffany to go along. *I wonder if it was her idea?*

The then thirteen-year-old was suddenly being trotted around as a six-year-old, ready for kindergarten in Wisconsin. She was the right size and none of her teachers ever commented that the girl acted any differently than the other kids.

Despite the fact that Tiffany was fifteen, she looked and acted eight. She shouldn't be left alone. Betsy had done what Viera wanted and called child services. The meeting was set, and they'd get to the bottom of whatever was going on!

Betsy drove up to the school. It didn't take her long to find the main office. She had to sit on a plastic bench for ten minutes until someone came to lead her to a conference room. Viera was there, as were several adults, and a very scared-looking girl. She sat next to Viera, holding her hand.

Viera smiled at her. An older woman gazed at Betsy, then at Viera. "Ms. Kor, is this the private investigator you hired?"

"Yes. I had some suspicions, and I decided to get answers before disrupting Tiffany's life." Her voice was calm, but Betsy knew there was more going on than she knew.

"We'll discuss later the proper protocol in a situation like this." That must be the principal. She needed someone to yell at since the parents weren't there.

The men in suits watched mutely. The only difference was one had sandy hair, the other a generic brown. They could almost be twins. The one with brown hair said, "We're here to look into the allegations against Mr. and Mrs. Anderson. We called them, but they both said they couldn't make the meeting. If they left work, they'd be fired. When we called their places of employment, we were told they'd taken a two-week vacation, due back Monday. Checking their credit card records, they are currently in Greece."

Tears dripped down Tiffany's face, but beyond that, she didn't react. She sat quietly. The other man turned to her. "When was the last time you spoke with your parents?"

"I speak with them every night and every morning. They are my parents." Her voice was calm and controlled.

Betsy gazed into the eyes of the other adults, ending on Viera. "How long have they been your parents?" She hoped her friend would read more than the girl would tell the group, but she wasn't sure of Viera's abilities.

She watched Viera as Tiffany spoke. Her friend struggled to keep a blank face, but her eyes widened.

Tiffany's dark brown eyes met Betsy's. "They've always been my parents. They're Mom and Dad."

"And how long have you been going to different schools?" Most kids considered pre-school a school, so this question wouldn't be too odd she hoped.

The girl's eyes narrowed. "Three years. This is my third year of school."

Viera was almost trembling as she tried to keep all the extra information in. "Tiffany, you know before-school-care is often considered a school. Did you go anywhere before this school?"

Tiffany shook her head. "This is the first school I've ever gone to."

Viera's mouth opened then snapped shut. Across from her, one of the men in suits shook his head. "We're getting off topic. Her previous schooling doesn't matter. Tiffany, we need to take you away. You living on your own without your parents isn't safe. We can put you into a foster home until this is all sorted out. But you can't return to your house alone."

Eyes the size of saucers, the girl finally realized what was going on. Her head shook fast. "I have to go home. That's where my parents will find me. I'll be fine. Don't worry about me. I'm not a baby anymore."

"No," the principal said. "But you're not all grown up either. You need someone there to help care for you. You shouldn't be all by yourself."

Tiffany's head swung back and forth. "Can I stay with Ms. Kor? She'll ... I'll be ... I can ... is it possible?"

The men in suits both had sour faces. "I don't think she's on the foster care list, and living with your teacher is a bad idea."

Betsy squeezed her eyes shut. She'd made a lot of bad decisions over the years, good decisions, and strategic ones. One was about to pay off. "I'm on the foster care list. I currently don't have any wards."

The man with the lighter hair pulled out his phone. "Name and foster care ID." She pulled out her own phone and looked up the number. After she rattled it off, he spent a few minutes searching. He had a few extra safety questions, but then he nodded. "Elizabeth Doeth, you've never had any kids. You've been on our list for several years. Why sign up and not take any kids, and why now?"

"I'm usually pretty busy. As for why now, I have the time, and she needs someone. I think I'm the right person." In reality, she knew she was the right person. Maybe Tiffany didn't know what she was, but it was time to learn.

Werewolves Are Not A Thing ...

Viera

Viera read the text one more time. *Temporary care until permanent placement can be arranged. We'll be there in thirty minutes for dinner and your lesson. Want to know what you read off her during the meeting.*

She decided pasta with meatballs and garlic bread would be good. Most kids would eat it. If not, she had chicken nuggets she could quickly make. Cooking for kids was a different skill set than that of cooking for adults.

Almost to the second, a half-hour later, they arrived. As the scared looking eight-year-old entered, she said, "Welcome to my home, Tiffany. I'm sorry this has been such a hard day for you."

She had to remind herself of all the images she saw during the meeting at the school. She wasn't sure how old Tiffany was, but like Scout, she wasn't really eight. So much for a normal day!

The girl curled into herself. "I just want to go home. My parents are going to be so mad at me."

Betsy growled out, "They left you home alone. I'm mad at them."

Moving around the kitchen, Viera stirred the sauce, then placed three plates on the table. She wanted Tiffany to speak freely, and thought if she used a casual voice, like she did in class, maybe the girl would accidentally tell them the truth. She also kept her magic fully open to read all nuances of the room. "Tiffany, why did you lie about schools? And your age? From your memories, you're what? Fourteen? Fifteen?"

At the far side of the table, Tiffany sucked in air, then froze. She stared at Viera and looked scared. After a few moments in which Viera continued to cook and periodically place dishes on the table—she wanted the girl to relax—Tiffany finally spoke. "How did you know that?"

"Well, your memories were pretty loud. You may have more than you think." There were images that felt fuzzy, half memories. Viera had thought maybe she saw deeper things that were buried. "You remember California pretty distinctly." Beaches, sand, and the water. "Especially the ocean." Viera said the last softly, as if she were trying to be careful with her words.

Tiffany blanched. "Is there a bathroom? I need to use the bathroom."

Betsy mumbled something under her breath as Viera pointed to a door.

Once Tiffany was gone, Viera asked. "Why the mumbling?"

"I don't want her to try to slip out. The room is sealed. The only way in or out is through the door or plumbing."

Dread spiked through Viera. "Do you think that was necessary?"

"Yeah, I do. You saw her. We're freaking her out."

Viera sighed. "It's true. I could and can feel her fear. It's getting worse right now. She's probably just now realizing her escape route is blocked."

Betsy gazed at the door. "Quick, tell me what you saw. We need to figure this out."

"Are there such things as werewolves?" Viera sounded bewildered.

"Werewolves? She turns into a canine?"

"Well, no." Viera sighed. "Nothing like that, I was just curious. There's just so many things I don't know."

Betsy breathed out a sigh of relief as she sat back. "Good, because no, there aren't werewolves, or vampires, or other crazy paranormal creatures in the world. We live in the real world, my friend."

"With aliens."

"Yes, with aliens."

"And wizards, and magic, and people that can turn into octopi?" Viera's voice pitched up high at the end of the sentence.

"With ... oh. Oh! She's a cambpulpo. I should've guessed. They are super secretive. If they came to visit, they wouldn't have checked in, like they are supposed to. If they had, then I'd have known they lost a child. For fuck's sake. We have our systems in place for a reason. I'm going to have to speak with Flower Prancer about this one. You said about fourteen years ago?"

"Sixteen." A small voice pulled them both from their conversation. Tiffany stared at them with her large eyes. "I'm sixteen. Yes, I can turn into an octopus. I like that form, but it's awkward around my family. They don't really know

I can do it. I've hidden it. They just think I'm weird in other ways. When my medical records started coming in ... wrong, they stopped taking me to the doctor."

Betsy squatted in front of the girl. "Well, dear. There is nothing wrong with you, except you're in a form that probably hurts. This isn't your natural shape." She darted a look at Viera. "We're going to have to do some quick maneuvering to get this solved. I have some ideas, but we'll need a group. For now, dinner, and your lesson."

Tiffany trembled a bit. "So, what should I do?"

Betsy kissed her forehead. "You'll eat dinner, sleep here, go to school with Ms. Kor, and in the end, we'll make sure your situation is figured out."

"What about Mom and Dad?" Her voice trembled.

Viera served up the food and sat next to her. "Do you want to go back to them?"

"Well, not really. They weren't ever that nice to me. I just don't want to be in trouble. I take long baths, and their favorite punishment is to take away bath time."

Anger welled up in Viera. She could only imagine the need for water for an octopus. Betsy shook her head. "Change of plans. After our lesson, you'll come home with me. I have a pool. It's even salt-water. You can sleep in the pool in your natural form tonight, and I'll bring you back tomorrow."

Viera gaped. "Your pool is salt water?"

"It is now." She snapped her fingers.

Thorn brought Scout over to play with Tiffany in the backyard while Viera had her lesson. Viera had been reading the books she'd borrowed from Betsy and had some questions. "In this book, it talks about stopping time. Do you know anything about that?"

"Besides it being a very advanced spell?"

"I guess that's the first question. So, I am a super novice." Viera knew that, but she'd also done some weird things with her magic. She also wanted to be prepared. "But, if and when I can do something like this, is it me stopping time, or am I just moving really really fast? Also, what is the radius of influence? Do I stop things within a foot or two, or a mile?"

"You'll never *stop* things. Beings that are alive will always be in some sort of motion. In a time spell you'll slow the area around you down while potentially speeding yourself up. As for the specifics, I don't know. I haven't studied the spell. I would imagine an artifact like the watch or my grandfather's staff would help."

It was the first time the staff had been mentioned since her blackout. Viera perked up. Betsy glared. "No. The thing is a menace, like Gramps. I think you're better off without it. Maybe in fifty years we can try again."

"Fine." She deflated. Betsy was probably right. They spent the rest of their time discussing sensing magic and watching the kids play. She used her sense to figure out how many bugs were in her house and then moved them safely out of the kitchen.

"I don't know if I like this skill," she admitted.

"Oh, come on. That was slick! You saved all those critters!" Betsy laughed. "One more thing. Saturday, are you going to the amazing tropical island of wonders?"

Viera sighed. "I haven't had a weekend off since before spring break. I can't believe I'm debating this." Her head fell back. "A tropical island with my girlfriend—"

"Is that what you two are calling each other now?"

"I guess." Viera blushed. "I don't know what to say. We're having fun, but in the next couple of years, she's leaving Earth."

That sobered her friend, if the sympathetic face was any indication. "Yeah, true. Okay. So, you don't have much time with her, and a couple of days on a sandy beach. A definite yay?"

"Yeah, a definite yay." She sounded glum, even to herself.

Betsy's eyebrow rose.

Viera snorted out a laugh. "I have fantasies of reading a book, drinking wine, and doing nothing. It's been so long."

"How about doing that next Monday? We'll take the night off. Talk to Flower Prancer about having Tuesday off as well."

"Oh! That sounds good. If that's the case, then yes. Island life it is!"

Viera smiled happily. "Okay, I'm going to think about this time magic more. I really like it, and this book has a lot of spells. Can you imagine if I could stop time, circle my class quickly to check on cheating, and start it again? Or I don't know ..." She stood to walk Betsy out. They both headed to the back first. "Tiffany, it's time to go."

Betsy gaped at her. "Where the hell did the staff come from?"

Viera stared. In her hand, throbbing with pride, was Gandalf's staff. She could almost feel its pleasure at being needed for time spells. It came because she wanted to do more, and it was here for her. It had bonded, and whenever she needed it, it would come. "It came for me," she said to Betsy. "Apparently, it'll always come for me."

33

Island Life

Viera

Saturday morning, Viera drove out to Thorn's house. She had a bag with shorts, a tank top, clothes for Sunday, pajamas, and a bikini. There were other items in her bag, but she'd checked the weather over the water; it was much warmer than Wisconsin.

When she got to the Firoza home, she saw Betsy's car as well. It pleased her that her friend had been invited to go to the island. No one had told her.

She grabbed her bag from the trunk and knocked on the door. Scout answered with a huge smile on his face. "You made it! Tiffany's coming, too! Did you know? I'm going to see her as an octopus, and I'm going to show her my real form. You know, she'll show me hers and I'll show her mine." He giggled and ran off.

"Scout!" Thorn yelled from the kitchen. "I've told you, that isn't funny!"

Viera smiled as she made her way into the kitchen. Thorn pointed towards the table. "Breakfast?" There was toast, eggs, warm cereal, and a plate of fruit. "We're leaving in about fifteen minutes."

She sat and filled a plate and bowl. Across from her sat Betsy and Tiffany. "I didn't know you were joining us."

Betsy shrugged. "I thought it would be good for Tiffany to meet some other aliens. Also, Scout invited her. I'm busy this weekend, but I feel the girl will be comfortable if you're there."

Tiffany watched them talk. She finally nodded. "I didn't want to go. I don't know anyone. But if you'll be there, Ms. Kor, I guess it'll be okay. Scout said I'll like it. He said there'll be a dragon."

Viera smiled at her. "A friendly dragon. And a bit of a gruff unicorn. But they have different names. Did he tell you that, too?"

"Oh, yeah. He said the dragon was a ... um ... qynad?"

Betsy wrapped an arm around her and gave her a squeeze. "Right in one, kiddo!"

Tiffany smiled up at her. "And the unicorn is called—"

"A yonat, young one. And though I'm okay with a child making a mistake with my species type." Flower Prancer walked in from the living room and eyed Viera. *When did he get here? And is he coming too?* "But you, Ms. Kor, have had enough time to know better."

Tiffany sat up tall, eyes wide, squeaking in excitement.

Apprehension tore at Viera. She'd made another mistake in front of the Elder. "Sorry, Flower Prancer. I was trying to use words the child would understand, not disrespect you."

His violet eyes bored into her. "Very well. I am ready to leave this dreary location. Can we be off to the island?"

After eating the last few bites on her plate, Viera helped clean up the breakfast mess. Then Betsy hugged Tiffany. "I'll see you on Sunday, Tiffany. Stick with Ms. Kor, she cares for you."

"I know." The small girl wrapped her arms around Betsy's neck.

Thorn turned to the group. "Okay, go change into shorts and warm-weather tops. No reason to wear what you're wearing to the island. Two minutes."

Viera headed up to Thorn's room and switched her outfit. As soon as everyone had returned to the kitchen, Thorn went to the panel, typed in some commands, and the room melted.

Suddenly, Viera stood on a sandy beach under a warm sun and a cool breeze tickled her skin. Everyone seemed like they relaxed, even the cantankerous yonat, who turned and walked into the woods.

Gazing out over the clear blue ocean, she smiled. "Wow! I'm on an island."

Next to her, Scout hooted. "Let's swim." He ran out into the water.

Tiffany sighed. "Ms. Kor, may I swim?"

"Of course, dear. Do you need a swimsuit, or are you shifting to an octopus?"

The girl bit her bottom lip. "I don't want to get in trouble." Her voice wavered.

"You won't get in trouble. If you want to be in your natural shape that's fine, just please come back."

She nodded. "I will. I have a good sense of time."

Thorn came up behind Viera, wrapping her arms around her. "We'll be here, either on land, or swimming close to the beach. Enjoy your swim, Tiffany."

Tiffany's expression softened into a smile. Then she shimmered, and a light purple octopus stood on the beach, roughly half the size she'd been as a human. She quickly made her way into the water, slithering across the beach, then disappearing into the waves.

Viera leaned her head back. "I hope she comes back. I don't want her getting lost or running away."

"Did it sound or feel to you like she was lying? Did your senses ping at all?" Thorn's care wrapped around her.

Closing her eyes, Viera considered the questions. "No, it all rang true."

"Can you still sense her? Are you following her?"

With a sigh, Viera shut her eyes. "Yes. I can follow her as she plays."

"Okay, can you continue to follow her? Like, if we swam, can you keep your magical senses attached to where our baby purple octo is?"

Taking a centering breath, Viera thought about attaching a mental bug to Tiffany. When she opened her eyes, she realized it worked. Even without thinking about it, she could follow the crazy antics of the girl. "It worked. Wow! I wouldn't have thought about doing that."

"Well, I'm not only pretty, but I'm also smart. Now, my sexy human, let's change into suits and swim. The water here is amazing."

They took their bags to some buildings camouflaged in the trees. Horax lounged in the shade. "Hi, Horax!" Viera waved happily. Her excitement at coming grew minute by minute.

"Hi, Viera. Nice to see you. I'll be practicing when it cools a bit. I'd love to get your professional wizard opinion."

A snort and swish told Viera Flower Prancer approached. "She is by no means a professional. She is learning."

"Excellent!" Horax bellowed. "I'm proud of you, my friend."

Viera smiled at the qynad. *Why can't he be a wizard? He'd be an excellent teacher!*

Thorn led her into the building. "My room is over here. Or rather, the room I usually use. We can share it. The bed is small, but I think we'll manage it."

They quickly changed and headed back to the water. It was warm and felt like a blanket welcoming them.

They swam and played with Scout. Juniper, another chanzii from the ship, joined them. After a bit, so did Horax. Splashing and diving, they laughed and played.

After swimming and relaxing for about an hour, Viera felt Tiffany approaching, fear pulsing through the connection she'd maintained.

Viera stood. "Thorn, she's coming back. Fear. Terror. Enemy. Chasing her. Help."

Thorn's head snapped between Viera and the water, ready to fight for Tiffany. Horax dove, searching for the small octo-girl.

He flew up out of the water far out in the ocean, roaring. Viera didn't sense panic or anger from the qyrad, only wonder.

Tiffany swam up to Viera, circling behind her, her small purple body quivering in the water. A moment later, two larger octopi emerged, eyes wide and bodies huge. One a dark blue, the other a purple so dark, it almost looked black.

Thorn came to stand next to Viera, tall and proud. She'd shifted to her natural turquoise shade. "Hello. I am Thorn Firoza of the chanzii. I assume I am speaking to representatives of the cambpulpo clan?"

There was a shimmer, and the purple octopus shifted. A tall woman—Viera imagined she was seven feet or more—stood next to the other sea creature. She had black hair and brown eyes. With quick efficiency, she took in each person standing in the water, and those on the shore. "I am Kelpweaver. My husband and I have been searching for our daughter for sixteen of these human years. She was taken from us when she was a baby. Give her back, human."

Viera felt Tiffany's hands on her hips, the tiny fingers digging into her sides. She could feel the girl's terror. "You may be her parents, but right now, all you're doing is scaring her. We aren't your enemy. We didn't take her from you."

"Then who are you, human?"

"I'm her teacher."

Flower Prancer waded out into the water. "She's more than that. She's a wizard of the world, the newest pillar, and she found your daughter amongst her students. It is because of her your kit is here. If you don't calm down, cambpulpo, I will make you calm down."

The creature focused on the yonat and Viera could sense the moment she realized an Elder was in her midst. "Oh, Elder." She knelt, bowing her head. "I am sorry. I didn't realize you were here. Is the council here to return our daughter to us? Will you punish this human for her hubris?"

"Have you heard nothing?" Flower Prancer bellowed.

The other cambpulpo trembled, then shifted. A man, slightly shorter than the woman, bowed. "We are sorry, Elder. We will hear your wisdom."

"You will listen to the human, Ms. Kor. She is the expert here. She is an Elder as well. Respect her."

Viera clenched her jaw to keep it from dropping open. *He does know how to be supportive. Who knew?*

Both cambpulpos' faces paled as they gaped at Viera. Kelpweaver stammered. "I'm sorry, Ms. Kor. I didn't mean to disrespect you, to imply you were less than important in our eyes."

Viera sighed. *Will this never end?* "Look, can we just talk? Tiffany ... who I'm going to assume for now is your daughter, is scared. She didn't know about any of this a few days ago. She was raised by humans. I found her, and we brought her here to allow her to finally have some time in her natural form, something long denied her. She just wants to feel safe."

In front of her, the two adults knelt in the water. Kelpweaver smiled at Tiffany. "Hi ... Tiffany? We were in a park in the big city—" She looked at her husband.

"Los Angeles."

"Right. And we sensed a wizard. We didn't want to check in. Wizards make us nervous. We love how open and uncluttered the oceans are here. We just wanted to be left alone to swim. We ducked behind a fountain in scared ... um, in terror, when Brinediver, that's him," she stubbed her thumb at her husband, "gasped. We forgot Lilyfloater. We dashed back to the park, but she was gone. We searched. We debated finding the wizard, but that human wasn't around either. We finally returned to the water, figuring we'd find our kit when she answered the call of the sea."

Behind her, Viera felt Tiffany trembling. "Mom and Dad rarely let me swim in the ocean, they said it wasn't safe.

When we did go, it was only for short periods of time, and very supervised. This is the first time I've been allowed out in my natural form."

Tiffany's parents growled where they kneeled in the water. Viera wanted to snarl back. Instead, she maneuvered Tiffany so she could wrap an arm around her. "You're safe now. You won't have to go back to them, and you can be in your eight-armed form as much as you like, sweetie."

"You've always been the best. But, Ms. Kor, I don't want to leave school. I want to finish the school year ... with you, and Scout."

"No!" Brinediver snarled. "You're returning to the water with us, and we're getting you off-planet as soon as we can figure out how."

Flower Prancer's tail swished. "If you allow your daughter to finish the school year, we have a ship heading out to Torville Station Number Six in June. You're welcome to join us. If you refuse to let your daughter finish out the year, traumatizing her more and making our lives more difficult, you are on your own. You'd have saved all of us much difficulty had you just checked in—as is policy on this planet."

Face hard and anger rolling off him, Brinediver glared at the Elder. Kelpweaver, equally as upset, gazed at her daughter. "Will you continue to separate us from our child? Keep her from us?"

Viera sighed. "I believe we can figure out a place for you to live with Tiffany. There is no reason to keep you separated."

"Will there be salt water?"

She shrugged. "I don't know, we'll need to speak with Betsy. But you'll have to promise to have the discussion before we can move forward." Her head swam with the logistics that needed to happen. Was this Betsy's everyday life? If so, she couldn't fathom living that way.

Once the two agreed, most of the group left the water. Tiffany wanted to stay, and Scout agreed to swim with her. She stayed in human form, a bit shy around her parents. Horax swam around the deeper areas, monitoring everything.

Thorn started to cook, and Viera said she needed a few minutes. Everything that had happened had been stressful, and she needed time to relax. She walked out into the woods to cool down. She then went into the building and found her phone. A quick call to Betsy would help lift some of her stress. The cool shade of the trees also helped.

Betsy grunted when she got done talking. "So much for a relaxing trip."

"I know! Fun in the sun, mixed with high intensity alien drama. Who knew?" Viera laughed.

"Well, it sounds like you did fine. Do you want me to come out?" Betsy sounded hesitant and hopeful.

"No ... well, yes. It would be fun with you here, but if you're busy ... I just ... I don't know what I'm doing. I wanted to be arm-candy for Thorn, not anything diplomatic. But Tiffany is only really comfortable with the two of us. Though, I probably got past the worst of it."

"Sounds like you did. I think you did fine. I'll see you Sunday."

"Coolio—" Something tickled Viera's senses. She tensed, not wanting to believe what she felt. Her body trembled with the memories crashing down on her. It couldn't be. Not here, not now. Not on Earth.

"Viera! Viera! Talk to me. Where did you go?"

"Krottel." Her voice trembled. "On the island." And she hung up the phone.

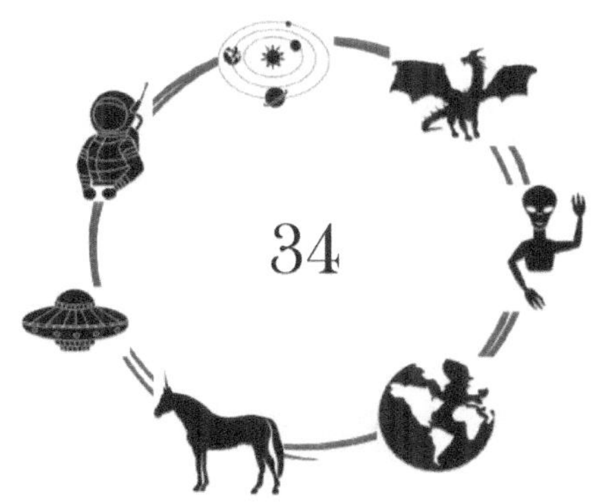

34

You've Been Bugged

Viera

The phone in Viera's hand buzzed. She knew Betsy was calling her back, but she wanted to focus on the bug. According to her mind's magic, there was only one bug on the island. She wanted to make sure that was true.

She closed her eyes and focused. With a push of her will, she spread her sensing magic out, trying to get more pings of the krottel. *I mean, where there's one of the assholes, there'll be more, right? Fucking bugs!*

No matter what she did, only the single bug came to her mind. Her phone stopped buzzing as she searched. She took a few steps deeper into the woods, but her radius reached water in all directions, so she didn't feel the need to move much farther.

Viera took a centering breath, then focused on the bug. It was to her left. She turned in the direction and started walking. After a few moments, she heard something behind her. She checked over her shoulder and saw Flower Prancer and Thorn. Thorn's face was hard; she looked ready for battle. Flower Prancer ... well, he looked like he always did. They didn't say anything, just followed.

It took a bit of walking. Viera had put on shoes, but not more clothes. Traversing woods in a bikini hadn't been her wisest move to date. There was a small clearing about a quarter-hour of walking from the center. Probably closer to ten minutes if she'd had better protection on.

She backed up to Flower Prancer. "There is a krottel, a single bug, about three feet out in front of us."

The Elder shut his eyes. "I can do the magic we need to contain the bug, but it would be easier with Wizard Doeth."

Refusing to take her eyes off the spot the bug was burrowed deep in the dirt, Viera asked, "Is she coming? I thought she couldn't make it."

Footsteps behind her caused her heart to beat faster. Was it Betsy? Again, she didn't want to look away from the spot where she knew the bug was. For some reason, in the back of her mind, Viera was convinced that as soon as she turned, it would disappear.

"There you are," Betsy said softly. "I had to use my paltry sensing spell to follow you. You didn't leave much of a path. Next time, drop breadcrumbs."

Thorn chuckled softly. Flower Prancer's tail swished in annoyance.

Viera smiled, glad her friend was there. "Betsy, the bug is right there." She pointed to the spot. "I don't know how we'll capture it."

"Leave that to me." There was a low rumble, and a chunk of ground lifted. Viera felt the shock from the bug as it tried to escape, but there was a shield around it as if everything was slowed.

Flower Prancer grunted. "The time bubble is in place. Time is slowed for that chunk of dirt. I can hold it for about twenty minutes, then I'll need to stop."

Betsy nodded. "Let's get this back to base and find the bug and get it into a containment unit. The cells there are warded against these creatures' form of communications. It should be safe to drop your spell there, right?"

The yonat nodded, and the group started to move.

Flower Prancer and Betsy jogged, outpacing Viera. She still had little clothing on and worried about the foliage of the woods. When she got back to base, the others had secured the bug in a cell.

They'd waited for her before questioning it. They sat around the caged krottel. Betsy asked, "As a wizard of this planet, and person you are supposed to check in with before landing, I ask, what are you doing on my planet?"

"Why can't I speak with my queen? What have you done to me? She'll come for me if she thinks you hurt me!"

Viera shook her head. "That last was a lie."

Flower Prancer's eyes glowed. "I am an Elder. You will answer me. What are you doing on this planet?"

"We have come to discover if the rumors of the magic are true. We have come seeking the truth. We have come to find the new home for the krottel."

Thank you for reading!

Magic Lessons

Please Leave a review for this book so others know how

much you enjoyed reading it.

Find more information on my books on my website

About the Author

Harlowe Frost has been a teacher at both the high school and college level. Her parents instilled a love of reading from a young age. She grew up in the queer community. Her favorite genre growing up was fantasy and science fiction, that is, until she discovered urban fantasy and paranormal romance. What she never found in those books was the diversity in background, gender identity, and sexuality she saw in the people around her. She decided if she couldn't find that in what she read, then she would write it herself. This started her writing paranormal romance with a LGBTQ+ background.

www.ingramcontent.com/pod-product-compliance
Lightning Source LLC
Chambersburg PA
CBHW032251310726
48973CB00008B/2374

I0705854

PRAISE FOR THE NOVELS OF
KATIE MacALISTER

Memoirs of a Dragon Hunter
"Bursting with the author's trademark zany humor and spicy romance . . . this quick tale will delight paranormal romance fans."—*Publishers Weekly*

Sparks Fly
"Balanced by a well-organized plot and MacAlister's trademark humor."—*Publishers Weekly*

It's All Greek to Me
"A fun and sexy read."—The Season for Romance
"A wonderful lighthearted romantic romp as a kick-butt American Amazon and a hunky Greek find love. Filled with humor, fans will laugh with the zaniness of Harry meets Yacky."—*Midwest Book Review*

Much Ado About Vampires
"A humorous take on the dark and demonic."—*USA Today*
"Once again this author has done a wonderful job. I was sucked into the world of Dark Ones right from the start and was taken on a fantastic ride. This book is full of witty dialogue and great romance, making it one that should not be missed."—Fresh Fiction

The Unbearable Lightness of Dragons
"Had me laughing out loud. . . . This book is full of humor and romance, keeping the reader entertained all the way through . . . a wondrous story full of magic. . . . I cannot wait to see what happens next in the lives of the dragons."—Fresh Fiction

Also By Katie MacAlister

Dark Ones Series
A Girl's Guide to Vampires
Sex and the Single Vampire
Sex, Lies, and Vampires
Even Vampires Get the Blues

Otherworld Dark Ones Series
Bring Out Your Dead (Novella)
The Last of the Red-Hot Vampires
The Undead in My Bed (Novella)
Fistful of Vampires Anthology
Shades of Gray (Novella)

Zorya Dark Ones Series
Zen and the Art of Vampires
Crouching Vampire, Hidden Fang
Much Ado About Vampires
Unleashed (Novella)

Goth Faire Dark Ones Series
In the Company of Vampires
Confessions of a Vampire's Girlfriend
A Tale of Two Vampires

Revelation Dark Ones Series
The Vampire Always Rises
Enthralled
Desperately Seeking Vampire

Ravenfall Dark Ones Series
Axegate Walk

Dragon Septs
Green Dragon Series
You Slay Me
Fire Me Up
Light My Fire
Holy Smokes
Death's Excellent Vacation
(short story)

Silver Dragon Series
Playing With Fire
Up In Smoke
Me and My Shadow

Light Dragon Series
Love in the Time of Dragons
The Unbearable Lightness of Dragons
Something Dragon This Way Comes
(Formerly titled Sparks Fly)

Dragon Fall Series
Dragon Fall
Dragon Storm
Dragon Soul
Dragon Unbound
Dragonblight

Otherworld Adventure Series
Becoming Effrijim
Dragon Revisited
Midnight in the Garden of
Okay and Meh

Dragon Hunter Series
Memoirs of a Dragon Huner
Day of the Dragon
A Confederacy of Dragons
You Seligh Me

Born Prophecy Series
Fireborn
Starborn
Shadowborn

Time Thief Series
Time Thief
Time Crossed (short story)
The Art of Stealing Time

Matchmaker in Wonderland Series
The Importance of Being Alice
A Midsummer Night's Romp
Daring in a Blue Dress
Perils of Paulie

Papaioannou Series
It's All Greek to Me
Ever Fallen in Love
A Tale of Two Cousins
Acropolis Now

Everything is Fine Series
Improper English
Bird of Paradise (Novella)
Men in Kilts
The Corset Diaries
A Hard Day's Knight
Blow Me Down
You Auto-Complete Me
Tell Them Emily Sent You

Noble Historical Series
Noble Intentions
Noble Destiny
The Trouble With Harry
The Truth About Leo

Paranormal Single Titles
Ain't Myth-Behaving

Akashic League Mysteries
Ghost of a Chance
The Stars That We Steal From the Night Sky

Steampunk Romance
Steamed
Company of Thieves

CHERISH

A BILLIONAIRE MARRIAGE CLUB NOVEL

SUPER SECRET PEN NAME

EVIE MARSH

FAT CAT BOOKS

Cherish Copyright © Katie MacAlister 2024
Warrior Copyright © Katie MacAlister 2023
Respect Copyright © Katie MacAlister 2022
All rights reserved

Without limiting the rights under copyright reserved above, no part of this publication may be reproduced, stored in or introduced into a retrieval system, or transmitted, in any form, or by any means (electronic, mechanical, photocopying, recording, or otherwise), without the prior written permission of both the copyright owner and the above publisher of this book.

This is a work of fiction. Names, characters, places, and incidents either are the product of the author's imagination or are used fictitiously, and any resemblance to actual persons, living or dead, business establishments, events, or locales is entirely coincidental.

The scanning, uploading, and distribution of this book via the Internet or via any other means without the permission of the publisher is illegal and punishable by law. Please purchase only authorized electronic editions, and do not participate in or encourage electronic piracy of copyrighted materials. Your support of the author's rights is appreciated.

www.katiemacalister.com

Cover by Racing Pigeon Productions
Formatting by Racing Pigeon Productions

TABLE OF CONTENTS

RESPECT

ONE

"Girl, what you need is a meet cute."

With a near sob of gratitude, I collapsed onto the bench that marked the halfway point around the small lake where Gina and I walked. "What I need is a better pair of lungs, stronger legs, and oh yes, someone to liposuction a good forty pounds off my ass."

"Your ass is fine," Gina said, waving her water bottle at me. "It's curvy. It's sexy. You got to embrace your booty, not wish it away."

"So sayeth the happily married woman." I sipped at my water, my eyes scanning the people who walked, jogged, or biked along Green Lake, hoping to see the man who made my heart race every time I saw him. "If I could find a guy as nice as Herve, I wouldn't worry about my ass."

"I admit he is just about the perfect man—a good father, thoughtful, and smart enough to make a tech company that sold for millions. But that's beside the point. You need to have confidence in yourself."

"That's easy to say, but you don't have to worry about a man who shows up at a date and immediately makes an excuse for why he can't stay."

"Uh oh," she said, tucking away her bottle and getting back to her feet. "Does that mean you didn't like your date last night?"

"I don't know; I didn't have time to find out. I got to the restaurant, said hi, he said hi, and then he pulled out his phone and said he had an emergency gig he had to go to." Reluctantly, I got up after making another scan of the people in our area. Damn. I had really hoped Mr. Handsome would be out jogging this morning. "Tinder sucks balls."

Gina pulled me off the walking path, stopping next to a clump of trees. Ducks floating on the lake drifted our way, quacking hopefully. "You can't tell anyone what I'm about to say," she said, absently using her foot to shoo away one of the more forward ducks that was obviously hoping for a handout.

"Good god, you aren't going to tell me you're in love with me, and want a ménage à trois with Herve, are you?" I joked, expecting her to answer in a similar tone.

"No. I've been holding this back, because...well, I wasn't sure you are ready for it. But you don't seem happy, Sam."

"I'm fine," I protested, confused by her seriousness. "Do I seem depressed or something?"

"No," she admitted. "You seem lonely. And I hate that. So I'm going to give you a phone number. You can't show it to anyone. You can't talk about it to anyone. You can't even admit you know the number exists. OK?"

"OK," I said, slightly worried when Gina pulled out her phone and scribbled a number on a receipt she fished out of her pocket. "What is it, some super secret dating agency?"

"Better than that," she said, making a face when she saw the time on her phone. "Shit, we have to get moving. Gloria has a dentist appointment at noon, and that kid moves slower than a sloth when it comes time to having her braces adjusted."

I said nothing, but it piqued my curiosity. Later, I leaned into my beat up Honda to gather the collection of latte cups, power bar wrappers, and shamefully, a couple of French fries that had evidently been laying on the passenger seat floor for three days.

When I backed out of the car and turned with my hands full of garbage, I took two steps toward the trash bin and stopped in sheer horror.

Next to me, a sleek black sedan had purred to a stop, and while I stared with a mixture of hope and dread, a man emerged. He wore shorts that revealed plenty of muscled thigh and calves, and a sleeveless tee that left nothing to the imagination concerning his biceps and chest.

It was Mr. Handsome, right there next to me, using one of the cement parking lot barriers to stretch.

He glanced over at me, and I realized I had been doing the thing I hate most in the world—I was staring.

Head down, I scurried to the trash, dumped my collection, and was back in my car before I felt my hands shaking. By the time I peeked out of the corner of my eye, Mr. Handsome was off, jogging effortlessly into the crowd of morning runners.

"You're an idiot, Samantha," I told myself. "Men who look like that don't care if people stare at them. It's only you who thinks it's rude."

My phone chirped a warning, reminding me that time was passing and my shift at the store was starting soon.

Sitting in bed that night, I had a particularly horrible conversation on Tinder when a man who said he was a photographer demanded to see a selfie. I sent him one of me looking cute and playful, after which he told me he wasn't into fat chicks, although he knew of people who were, and if I liked, he could give them my name.

I was about to text Gina to complain about him when I remembered the mysterious phone number she'd given me. "What do I have to lose?" I asked myself, then punched the number into my phone.

"Thank you for calling BMC," voicemail told me. "Please leave your name, number, and nearest major city. You will be called within twenty-four hours."

The phone made a beep, obviously expecting me to provide the information it wanted. I hung up.

"I don't even know who you are," I told my phone. "My nearest major city? What the hell?"

A message pinged from the fat-shamer on Tinder, telling me: Hey, my friend wants a picture of your tits before he meets you.

"And that's all she wrote," I said, calling the mystery number again, this time doing as the recording asked. Once done, I blocked the jerk on Tinder, and stared up at my ceiling for a half hour wondering just where my life had gone so wrong.

TWO

The call came when I was at the lowest point, having spent a half hour dealing with a woman who had argued viciously about the return of a half-eaten piece of chicken.

"Samantha Clyde? Jane Washington returning your call. I'm the regional associate of BMC. May I ask who referred you to our service?"

"Um. I'm not sure if I'm supposed to tell you that," I said, remembering Gina's warnings.

"I understand, but we must have a referral or we can't process you for further action."

"All right, but I don't want my friend to get in trouble. Her name is Gina Estevez."

"Ah, Ms. Estevez. Yes, I remember her. She is doing well?"

"Very well," I said, wondering what the hell I was getting into. "Can I ask you a few questions? I don't even know what BMC stands for, or what you do, although I assume it's some sort of dating agency since Gina said I needed a meet cute."

"Why don't you come to my office, and we can talk," Jane said, her voice clipped in what I thought of as a professional manner. "I have time this afternoon if you are free."

"Sure," I said, even though all I really wanted to do was to go back to my apartment. "What time?"

"How about an hour from now?" She gave me the address, and directions on how to get buzzed into the building, then ended the call before I could ask just how much this meet cute service was going to cost me.

An hour and seven minutes later, I ran my damp hands down the material covering my thighs as I perched on a chair in a small reception room. A young man sat at the desk, alternating between answering the phone, typing on a laptop, and reading manga.

I was almost sick with worry. What if the service refused to add me to their roster after seeing me in person? What if they wanted more money than I had in savings? What if it was a scam, and they were going to rip me off, or steal my identity, or worse yet, mock me?

"Ms. Clyde?" A woman in a blue power suit emerged, smiling politely as she shook my hand. "I'm Jane Washington. It's a pleasure to meet you. This way."

I took a seat in what I thought of as a stock photo of an office. It had a desk, a few plants, two chairs in front of the desk, and a low console with generic decorations. "I'm afraid I'm going to be annoyingly persistent with some questions," I told Jane, clutching my bag on my lap. "I still don't know exactly what you do."

"To be blunt, we find you a man."

"OK," I said, feeling she was leaving something out. "That sounds good, but you'll forgive me if I say there has to be a catch."

"It may be hard to believe, but there is none," she said, taking her seat, and examining me for a moment, then pulled a folder out of a desk drawer, and extracted three photos from it, turning them face down. "You asked about our name. BMC stands for Billionaire Marriage Club."

"You're shitting me," I said, slapping a hand over my mouth as I realized how rude that sounded. "Sorry, that slipped out. But come on. Billionaires? Marriage? You have billionaires who need a service to find someone to marry?"

"We do." She clasped her hands. "You have questions?"

"You bet your ass I do! What man in his right mind—no, not man, billionaire—has problems finding a woman? They must have women dripping off them."

"They do, and that's exactly why our service is so attractive to many successful men. Put yourselves in their shoes—"

I gave a harsh bark of laughter that I had to stop immediately. "Sorry again. Didn't mean to laugh, but I live paycheck to paycheck, have to resort to Tinder for dates, and am not the best-looking person in the world. It's kind of hard for me to envision myself as a rich man."

She studied me for a moment. "I see nothing wrong with your appearance. Far from it, you appear to be very earnest."

"Oh, I'm earnest as the day is long, but I am not the sort of woman who hangs out with rich men. They are always handsome as fuck, and smell good, and wear expensive suits, and have skinny women in skimpy dresses clinging to them."

"Exactly," she agreed. "Which is why the BMC was created. There are many successful men who grow tired of the shallow relationships, hangers-on, and those who wish to use them for who they are. Many of them want—for a variety of reasons ranging from convenience to a genuine desire for companionship—a woman who will, so to speak, take them off the market."

"Isn't that the storyline of a Regency romance?" I asked, having no small addiction to them. "Dude wants a fake wife so everyone will stop trying to marry him?"

"That is motivation behind many of our customers, yes," she admitted.

"Except that's fiction, and this is real life. If these billionaires—I feel ridiculous even saying the word—want a beard, then why don't they just...you know...get one."

She cocked an eyebrow at me. "That is, in a nutshell, exactly what they engage BMC to do. We locate women whose personalities are such that we believe they will have success with our client, and the client has a wife who meets their needs and personal preferences."

"There has to be a catch," I repeated, shaking my head.

"There are conditions, naturally," Jane said, giving me a tight little smile. "For one, you must undergo a physical examination at a doctor of your choice. You will need proof that you are not suffering from any sexually transmitted diseases, as well as a general statement of health."

Uncomfortable, I clutched my bag tighter across my belly.

"Likewise, there will be a background check. If you and the client come to terms, then you will be required to sign a prenuptial agreement. There are no exceptions to this, since our client will enter into a legal marriage with you."

"This is crazy," I said, still shaking my head. "Seriously crazy. And while I'm having tests and credit checks and prenup signings, what is this desperate billionaire doing?"

"We require both partners to undergo the preliminary checks," she said, taking me by surprise. "The client will take a physical exam within a week of yours, and provide you with the results. Likewise, we will give you a copy of his background check. The issue regarding the prenuptial agreement is a bit more complicated."

"I thought it might be." I sighed to myself, since for a few seconds, I'd allowed myself to go along with this fantasy.

"You are guaranteed a set amount to be paid into whatever bank account you choose on a monthly or yearly basis for so long as you remain married. If you end the marriage, you will receive that year's allowance, but nothing more. If the client ends the marriage, you will receive a further ten years of the yearly amount unless you marry again, at which time, the client's financial obligation is considered at an end."

"Just for shits and gigs, how much is this set amount?" I asked.

She gave a tiny shrug. "That is to be negotiated between you and the client, although I can tell you that the minimum yearly sum is not to be less than six figures."

For a moment, my mind spun. Six figures for marrying a rich dude? Was she crazy? "How come you don't have hordes of women beating down your door?"

"We are very selective, as I mentioned." She gave me another tight smile and pulled out a second folder. "We rely heavily on recommendations from past clients. Once we have that, we conduct a series of interviews. Since Gina was quite happy to recommend you, I see no hinderance to moving you to the next stage."

"Gina?" My mouth hung open for a few seconds before I realized it. "Holy shit, Gina is...Gina married... you mean Herve?"

"Naturally, I can't breach client confidentiality," Jane answered primly. "Now, I'd like to get a few details before we move on to the three clients who are available in this area."

My mind was still twirling around like it was on a fairground ride, leaving me to automatically answer the series of questions she fired off quickly: everything from a summary of family life and childhood, to personality scenarios.

"I think I have enough background," she said after about an hour, and hit save on the program into which she was entering the info. "As I mentioned earlier, currently there are three clients in the greater Seattle area who have requested our help. I am obligated to remind you that our clients can specify whether they wish to include sexual relations in the marriage. Naturally, we believe consent is of primary importance. If you do not want to consider a physical relationship, then I will show you only clients who do not expect such involvement."

Her fingers tapped gently on the three pictures. I looked at her, trying to determine what I was supposed to answer, but her expression gave nothing away. I thought of my lonely life.

I thought of the assholes on Tinder.

I thought of my drawer full of vibrators.

"Actually, I don't have a problem with sex," I said after clearing my throat, feeling a bit of a blush starting up on my cheeks. "So as long as everything is consentual, then I would be good with a guy who...er...wants that."

"As I said, consent is of primary importance to us," she said, flipping the pictures over. "Our clients agree that violation of that element of the relationship will result in legal charges. Now that the official caveats are over, please consider these photos. All three of these men have expressed an interest in having a sexual relationship, although Mr. B and Mr. C are willing to enter into a chaste marriage if both parties desire that. This is Mr. A. He is a Seattle native. Mr. B. is originally from California, but relocated here when he was a teenager. Mr. C recently moved here from New York. Please take your time looking at them. If one of them appeals to you more than others, we will arrange for a meeting. Obviously, in person contact will be required, but I do like to show their pictures just to get an idea if you are drawn to any of them."

I stared at the middle photo, my palms growing sweaty again, my heart rate picking up.

It was Mr. Handsome, smiling at me with his black hair swept back off his brow, wearing an obviously tailored dark suit.

He looked every inch a rich, successful man, one who should have no problem finding at least half a dozen women. Probably more if they could see him dressed in his shorts and wife-beater tee, with his chest and biceps and muscles and oh dear god, his thighs.

"Ms. Clyde?"

With an effort, I managed to pull my brain back from where it was going into a land of sexy, smutty thoughts. I cleared my throat again. "Sorry. Um. Number two. Er...Mr. B. He's...yeah."

"Very well." She gathered up the photos and replaced them in the folder. "I will arrange for an initial meeting. In the meantime, please set up your medical exam and send in a copy of the results. Do you have questions?"

Only about a half million. "What...uh...what happens if he doesn't like me?" I tried to sound nonchalant, like it didn't matter if this sexy, sexy man found me repugnant, but I didn't pull it off. "What if I like him, but he doesn't reciprocate?"

"The result would be exactly the same should the roles be reversed—both parties must agree. Consent, remember. It covers more than just sexual acts. Are there any other questions?"

There weren't. At least, none that I could get out. I left her office in a bit of a haze, clutching an envelope into which she'd placed a copy of the notes about me she'd taken, as well as the photo of Mr. Handsome.

I waited until I got to my car before I pulled out the photo and studied his face. His smile didn't reach his eyes—hazel, with a black outer ring—and he had lovely black hair that swooped back off a slight widow's peak. His jaw angled sharply, but his gently blunted chin softened the effect. There was also the hint of a dimple on one cheek that melted my insides into a puddle of goo.

"Oh yes, I'll take that," I said before I realized what I was doing.

I was setting myself up to be rejected like I'd never been rejected before. If I thought I'd been at a low when a loser on Tinder turned me down, how would I feel when Mr. Handsome took one look at me and passed?

A little kernel of pride burned in my belly, driving away the insecurities. "Fuck him," I told my car as I started it up. "He doesn't know what he'll be missing."

Famous last words, Sam, my brain thought at me. Famous last words.

THREE

Martin Otieno was a man living a lie.

"—and your two o'clock is running a little late—evidently there's a delay with his flight—but I switched him and your four o'clock." Yasmine, his secretary, tapped on her tablet a few times. "Oh, I see you moved your lunch meeting. Is everything all right?"

"Perfectly. I had an unexpected appointment that I wanted to take today rather than later," he answered, wondering if she could see that he was jittery. Yasmine was unusually shrewd, which was one reason he moved her from the general secretarial pool to that of his personal secretary. Not only was she not interested in him since she was in a long-term relationship with a woman, but she had an uncanny ability to sense what he needed before he knew he needed it.

Except this. He could almost feel the photo residing in his desk drawer, snuggled up against a collection of reports that reassured him that Samantha Clyde was free of any socially contactable diseases, had no criminal history, and was willing to meet with him with an eye toward a marriage arrangement that Martin fervently hoped included lots and lots of sex.

Just thinking about that made him hard, which both annoyed and amused him. It was on the tip of his tongue to ask the efficient Yasmine when was the last time he'd gotten an erection merely thinking about a woman, but decided that was taking her willingness to be all things just a bit too far.

"Have the latest proposals come in on the fiberglass hull replacement?" he asked, glancing at his laptop, his mind not on the yachts that his company built for extremely wealthy customers, but on the woman who he'd first seen the year before.

A woman who clearly didn't have the slightest interest in him because every time he looked her way, she either turned her back so she wouldn't have to see him, or continued walking with her companion without giving him a second look.

He very much wanted her to give him a second look.

He very much wanted her, period.

Yasmine consulted her tablet again and went through details that Martin barely heard. After a few more minutes, she went off to deal with her work while he sat staring out the window at the grey-blue water of the Seattle waterfront.

"Samantha Clyde," he said, and fought the need to pull out her picture in order to trace his fingers down her delicious curves.

Just thinking about those curves had him hot and heavy in his trousers. He wondered what her breasts felt like, whether she was ticklish, and if she liked stubble rubbed on her inner thighs.

He shifted in his chair, his cock growing in hardness until he thought he might have to get either bigger underwear, or a pair of sweatpants to wear at work.

Maybe he should just rub one out. "That would only be polite," he told himself. "No woman wants to be greeted with a rampant erection. It would be the gentlemanly thing to take care of this before Samantha arrives. Besides, I won't be able to think straight with her sitting so close to me if my cock is trying to fight its way out to get her attention."

He lurched to his feet and locked the door, then settled in to deal with his errant desire.

"Let's get this done with so I can concentrate on business," he told his cock once he unzipped his trousers. He thought of propping up the picture of Samantha where he could see it, but decided that objectified her. "It's nicer to do this without staring at a picture of her breasts," he told himself.

He froze for a second, picturing her as she had appeared the week before at Green Lake. She'd evidently already been for a walk, and was cleaning out her car. He had tried to linger around the trash can in hopes she might drop something that he could pick up, or perhaps she'd glance his way and he could make an inane comment about the weather. Something, anything. But no, as per usual, the second his gaze shifted her way, she all but ran off.

His cock deflated a bit at the thought that she might not want him.

"Nonsense," he told it. "I'm not a horrible person. I respect women. I value companionship. I want a wife, not a casual friend with benefits."

What if she was using him? What if the only way she could stand to be around him was the money offered as part of the deal?

His cock softened, flopping dejectedly onto his opened fly.

He glared at it.

"Stop being such a drama queen," he told it, giving it a little shake to let it know he meant business. "If that's the case, then I'll simply convince her to want me the same way I want her."

His cock wasn't convinced at first, but the second he relaxed back in the chair, his hands resting on his thighs as he pictured Samantha's ass waggling when she pulled trash from her car, blood raced to his penis and had it standing at attention.

"Now that's what I'm talking about. Right. Let's get this done so we can both focus. I'll apply a little hand lotion, and now indulge in another mental image of Samantha backing out of her car ass-first, and start a nice easy stroke...shit!"

Desperately, he grabbed at the box of tissue that sat in a lower drawer, just barely in time to keep from having an embarrassing conversation with Yasmine, wherein he had to request some cleaner and several rags.

Ten minutes later, having used the washroom attached to his office, and unlocked his door, he sat down, secure in his ability to meet with the luscious—if elusive—Samantha Clyde with composure, dignity, and possibly a faint air of nonchalance.

"Studied nonchalance," he said a half hour later, straightening his tie in the mirror, and brushing his hand over his hair. Maybe he should have had a haircut this morning. "Just to let her know that although I desire her, I'm not panting after her. There are other women, after all, other women who are just as desirable. Ones that my cock also enjoys."

Said cock, reposing in once-again comfortable underwear, twitched at the thought of Samantha, but Martin ignored it.

"I'll be pleasant, but slightly distant," he told his cock, staring out the window, his hands clasped behind his back. "Now that you are satisfied, I am fully in control. My businesslike demeanor will impress her.'

"Your noon appointment, Ms. Clyde," Yasmine said, opening the door, and moving aside so that a woman could step in.

And just like that, his cock was rock hard again.

"Thank you," he managed to say, his voice coming out a croak. He took a side step so that the chair blocked his crotch. "You can take your lunch now, Yasmine. Sam—er, Ms. Clyde and I will be busy for the next hour. No calls, please."

Yasmine murmured something noncommittal and closed the door behind her. Only then, when she was gone, did Martin allow himself to look at the woman who entered his office.

No, not a woman, a goddess. An earth goddess come to...well, earth. And she was his, all his. Or she would be if she agreed to his terms.

"Um. Hi. I'm Sam. I guess you knew that from my name?" Samantha walked toward him, holding out her hand. The way her hips swayed as she walked toward him damn near had him climaxing on the spot.

"Don't!" he barked, mentally wincing at both the tone and the image he presented as he clutched the back of his leather chair with fingers made white with strain.

She froze, a horrified expression moving over her face. Her gaze dropped along with her hand until she stood awkwardly in front of his desk.

"I'm sorry," she said, and turned toward the door. "This was a mistake—"

"Christ, no, it's not a mistake. It's not you." He swore under his breath at the look of pain that caused her eyes to tear up. "It's...this is difficult...I'm difficult... Christ."

And now he was babbling. Great. She was going to think he was a lunatic, and she wasn't far wrong.

"Is something wrong?" she asked, one hand touching a necklace that glinted on her collarbone. "Did I make a mistake?"

"No." He closed his eyes for a moment, prayed that he wouldn't scare her into running screaming from the room, and took a step to the side, pushing the chair away. "Quite the opposite, as you can see."

She looked confused, adorably so, her nose scrunching up slightly in a manner that pulled up her upper lip. He wanted to kiss her nose. He wanted to kiss her upper lip. He wanted to pound himself into her body and never stop. "Huh?"

He looked down at the bulge resulting from her appearance, now the approximate shape and size of a small lapdog shoved down his trousers.

"Oh," she said, her eyes widening, then to his delight, a little smile curled the corners of her lips even as her cheeks darkened. "Wow, you're really...er...packing. Oh, wait, is that rude? It's sexual harassment, isn't it? I'm so sorry."

"I'm standing here with a cock that wants to do nothing more than pin you up against the wall, and fuck you until we're insensible, and you're worried about sexually harassing me?" he shook his head, then moved around the table—painfully, given that said cock was indeed trying to do everything it could to get her to notice it—and shook her hand. "This is not how I intended on meeting you, Samantha Clyde. Just so you know, I don't normally greet women in an intense state of arousal. Would you like to, by any chance?"

"Let you screw me against the wall?" she asked, immediately grasping the point at hand.

So to speak.

"Yes. I wouldn't ask except that Jane Washington said that you had no aversion to a sexual relationship, and I thought it might be a nice way to get to know each other." He winced even as the words came out.

Samantha laughed, her joy lighting up her dark eyes in a manner that made him feel even hornier, if that was possible, and frankly, he hadn't thought it was. "Yeah, I'd think you plumbing the depths of my vagina qualifies as getting to know each other."

"Is that a no?" he asked, prepared to beg. Her scent, a light floral perfume that immediately went to his head, teased him in a way that had him flexing his fingers to keep from pouncing on her. "Or a yes? I won't ever do anything you don't want me to do, but at this point, there is no blood going to my brain, and I'm not sure what your answer means. I want very much to talk to you, but I can't do that when all I can think of is fucking you silly."

She stared at him as if he was surrounded by dancing penises, her mouth slightly ajar, making him moan mentally at the thought of tasting her sweetness, then suddenly she grinned. "OK," she said.

He took one extremely awkward step toward her, his hands reaching for her, but paused to search her face. "You're certain? You are aware that I am talking about fully penetrative sex, yes?"

"Sure," she said, her eyes dancing at him. "I'd ask you about condoms, but since I saw your medical report, and I assume you saw mine, then I guess we don't need it. Oh, I have an IUD, in case you were wondering."

"I saw that in your medical notes," he said, his hands twitching again as he tried to decide where to start.

"Er...OK. What...uh...what are you doing?" she asked, looking a bit wary.

"Trying to decide where to begin. Do you have a preference? Kissing? Should I touch your breasts? Do you like oral sex? I want badly to taste you, but doing so might actually kill me. Wait, that sounds terrible. It sounds like I don't want to taste you and touch you and make you wild with my fingers and tongue. I do. I want all those things, so if you'd like me to do that first, then I'm happy to do so. But if you could decide how you want me to start in the next few seconds so I don't have a heart attack and die of anticipation, or my cock kills me because I'm talking too much, either of which I honestly think might happen at this point, I'd be grateful."

She laughed again, and then, to his profound pleasure, relief, and gratitude, moved over to stand next to the wall before reaching up under her skirt to pull off a pair of dainty red underwear. "You sure you're up to doing this standing up? I've never—oof!"

He was on her before she finished speaking, his mind, body, and soul intent on one thing—claiming her as his own. "Tell me what gets you off," he all but growled into her neck as his hands were busy unzipping his fly. He swore his cock made a sprong noise when he released it. The feeling of the material of her dress against the sensitive head was almost too much for him. "It's not going to take much for me, so I will do whatever you need to get there with me."

"You're quick, too? Thank god. I really hate guys who insist on poking around forever," she said, moaning and writhing against him in a way that had his eyes crossing. Then she grabbed his head, pulling his mouth to hers even as his hands fought with the material of her dress, trying to move it out of the way. Her lips were sweet, but it was her heat that had him mentally calculating just how long he was going to last.

"Stop that," he said in a mixture of a snarl and a sob as her tongue twined around his. He pulled back to glare at her.

Once again, she looked horror struck, her manner hesitant. "You don't...you don't like that?"

"I like it. Far too much. Dammit, I'm about to come all over you. Stop that wiggling, too. Just stand there perfectly still, and maybe we'll get through this without me having to send Yasmine out for fresh clothes for you."

She giggled, she actually giggled at him, then with a boldness he wanted to applaud, she reached down and touched him.

He twitched, and he had to grit his teeth from finishing in her hand.

"None of that, either," he said hoarsely, bending slightly to grasp her thighs before sliding her upwards on the wall. Clever woman that she was, she wrapped her legs around his hips, which allowed his cock to have full access to all her secrets.

"You're the oddest man—nope, that wasn't—you're too far left. No other left. Sorry, your right, my left. Whoa! That's a no man's zone. Yes, there...dammit, you missed. Did you put lube on, or something? You seem awfully slippery—"

He stopped poking her in a desperate attempt to sink himself into her, leaned his forehead against hers, his hands supporting her hips, and said, "If you have any mercy in your soul, help me!"

"I had no idea you were this funny," she said, and had the audacity to kiss the tip of his nose.

He growled at her until she reached down between them, placing his cock where he badly wanted to be.

"Right," he said, trying with every last ounce of his sanity to regain control. "We are going to do this in an orderly fashion because if we don't, I'm going to—"

She flexed her hips, causing him to sink into her, and that was all it took. He thrust like a madman, one abstracted side of his mind amazed that he had such efficient hip action all the while he plundered her mouth like it was the sweetest of treasures. She kissed him back, her body moving with his in a manner that boded well for their married life, but ill for any chance of lasting more than a minute.

Her back arched just as he was about to warn her he couldn't last much longer, her intimate muscles squeezing him with a strength that he wanted to praise to the skies.

Two minutes later, he staggered to the couch and deposited her there, before collapsing onto it next to her, his cock finally replete.

"That was a hell of a thing," Samantha said, trying to straighten her dress.

"It was," he said, glaring at his penis.

She glanced at his face, then leaned forward to stare with him. "Is everything OK down there?"

"Yes. No. I don't know. It's never behaved this way before."

Her eyes went round. "You were a virgin?"

"Christ, no. I meant that it never saw a woman it wanted and became relentless in pursuit." He prodded at himself, but his cock was in decline. Red, glistening with the results of its exertions, and bearing what Martin could only think was a slightly smug expression, it was definitely happy. "I won't say that it has been comfortable, but at last the madness is over, and now I can talk to you like a normal human being."

She reached out to touch the very tip of him gently.

His cock stirred, exhausted, but clearly willing to put in the effort if Martin was go with the idea.

"They are so funny-looking, really," she said, her eyebrows rising a little as his cock gave a half-hearted twitch. "I can't imagine how you sit with those things in your pants."

"It depends on the cut of the trousers," he said, tucking himself away lest his cock get any further ideas. "I may have to get mine made fuller."

"Are you English?" she asked, giving him an oddly unreadable look.

"No, but my mother was, and I spent some time there."

"That would explain it. I like the way you talk. And speaking of that, I suppose we should have a discussion. Ms. Washington said that we'd decide if we wanted to go ahead with the...the—" She made a vague gesture.

"Marriage," he said, giving her a brisk nod. He approved of her businesslike demeanor. If they both kept the conversation to strictly non-sexual topics, he could get through this without thinking about laying her on the couch, and exploring every inch of her deliciously freckled self. "Yes. We should have a conversation about that. A logical conversation." He shifted a little so he could face her, studying her face, wondering what she thought of him.

He had a horrible feeling that it would not be at all complimentary.

FOUR

"Would you be offended...would you mind...if I said that you weren't at all like I expected, it wouldn't hurt your feelings or make you mad, would it?" I wanted badly to fling myself on Martin, the man who I'd first thought of as unattainable, and now viewed as something of wonder. He had an erection! For me! Of all people, he picked me to pin me against the wall and let the dick fly! It was still a bit staggering to think of, but the fact that my crotch was close to humming with happiness proved that miracles really could happen.

"I can promise not to be angry at you, but as for the rest of your question...that depends," he said, giving me a curious look. I wanted badly to brush back one lock of his hair that had fallen over his forehead, but didn't know if he'd allow the gesture. "What did you expect me to be like?"

"A fitness expert," I said slowly, thinking about how to put into feelings that he was miles away from me. "Maybe a bit snobby? Certainly not someone who would cast a look my way. Whenever I saw you, you seemed so focused—"

"You saw me?" he interrupted. "At Green Lake? You

saw me there?"

"Yes. I walk there with my friend Gina—"

"I cast many a pleading glance at you," he said, now obviously annoyed. "Why the hell did you gag every time you saw me?"

"Huh? Me? When did I do that?" I asked, frantically going through my memories, wondering if I'd vomited at some point.

"Well, it wasn't an outright gag," he allowed, looking delightfully disgruntled. "But every time I tried to approach you, you'd turn away like you couldn't stand to see me."

"Can I touch you?" I asked before thinking about it sounded.

His eyes narrowed slightly. "On my cock? Dammit. Now you woke it up. Go back to sleep; she's not talking about you."

"I actually meant touching your arm or leg," I said, unable to keep from staring at his groin. "I wasn't sure where we were on the whole relationship situation, and if I was allowed to touch you."

"I've been inside you," he pointed out. "Literally inside your body. And while I was having an exceptionally fine time in there, I deposited fluids in a way that made me think that if I had been wearing a condom, I would have blown out the tip with the sheer, unadulterated pleasure of the whole experience. Based on both facts, you can take it as read that you can touch me whenever and wherever you like. Erm...so long as you don't mind if I do the same?"

"Not at all," I said, then put my hand on his thigh.

"Excellent," he said, and placed his hand on my left breast.

Silence fell.

"Well, this is awkward," I said after a minute. "I was going to ask you if you always talk to your dick like it's sentient, but now the silence has gone on too long, and I've forgotten what else I wanted to say."

"I wasn't aware I spoke to any body part, but certainly not my cock," he answered, flexing his fingers on my boob, which immediately woke up and wanted to party again. "But apparently, since meeting you, I do. Does that bother you? Why did you run from me if I did not repel you?"

"OK, one...sorry, I can't think when you do that." I moved his hand from my breast to my leg, hurriedly adding, "It's not that I object to you holding up my breast, but all I can think of when you do that is touching your nipples, and I have a question I want to ask."

He waited, his fingers gently stroking my thigh.

I cleared my throat.

"You've forgotten the question, haven't you?" he asked.

"Yes," I admitted. "I blame your thighs. They're so nice and firm and I like them when you are in shorts—oh! That's what I was going to say. I didn't stare at you because of male gaze."

His fingers stilled in mid-stroke. "You aren't male. I know this. As I just pointed out, probably in too much detail for your ease of mind concerning my general state of sanity, I have plumbed your depths."

"No, I meant male gaze as in I dislike it. A lot. And what's fair for women is fair for men, so even though you're the handsomest man who I've ever seen, and I enjoyed watching you jog, and wished I could brush back your hair when it gets on your forehead, I didn't stare because that would be disrespectful. And I'm very big on respect."

He flicked back the hair hanging over his forehead. "Dammit, I knew I should have gotten a haircut. And thank you. No one has ever been concerned whether I felt disrespected by someone watching my ass. I assume it was my ass you watched?"

"Not really, no," I admitted.

He looked disappointed. "What a waste it was to spend all that time at the gym perfecting the sculpted nature of my ass cheeks."

"Are you joking?" I asked, unsure even though I could swear his baby dimple flashed at me.

"Yes," he said gravely. Then he stood up, and holding out a hand for me, helped me up and escorted me over to his desk. "Take a seat. Let us do this in a properly businesslike manner, because just having you near me is making my cock think it can pull off a miracle and go three for three."

"Three?" I asked, wanting to laugh at his quirky nature. He was a delight, utterly and completely different from what I expected. The thought ran through my mind that I might be in a situation where I was being taken by a couple of brilliant con artists, since wonderful men like Martin didn't happen to women like me, but what on earth could they gain from this setup? A little sex? Hell, I'd all but thrown myself at him. It's not like I lost out on having the most mind-blowingly fantastic sex of my life.

"I had to tug one out earlier." He waved a hand to dismiss the question. "It almost didn't happen it was over so quickly. Think nothing of it. It was a one-time occurrence that luckily, I caught in time." His gaze rested thoughtfully on me for a few seconds. "Although I believe I will ask Yasmine to place some cleaning supplies and extra garments into my bathroom. Just as a precaution for those times when you visit me at work."

I blushed at the heat in his eyes, a warm, happy feeling that stayed with me even as he rapidly went through a series of expectations, monetary renumeration, and living arrangements that would follow our marriage.

I was so bemused, I let it all wash over me, very aware that although he had things worked out on a contract vetted by the BMC, he sought my approval of each point before initialing them.

"Do you have a preference for a wedding?" he asked, pulling my attention from his hands, which I watched for the last few minutes. He had long, mobile fingers that made me shiver.

"Not really," I said slowly. "I was thinking about your hands. I want them to touch me like you mentioned when you were going on about oral sex. Do you really enjoy that? Because most guys don't want to be on the provider side, although I don't know any man alive who doesn't like to have someone playing his skin flute."

He had been leaning back in his chair, his fingers steepled, but at my words, he did an odd sort of jerk that resulted in him falling over backward.

"No, I'm not injured," he said, leaping up almost before I had run around his enormous desk, righting his chair again. "I was merely off balance. It had nothing at all to do with the phrase playing a skin flute, or even the thought of what your mouth would feel like doing that, especially if you gently, very gently, scraped your fingernails along my nuts."

"Can I just...your hair looks annoyed..."

Since he'd told me I could touch him, I gave in to the temptation and brushed his hair back from where his mishap with the chair had forced it down over his forehead again.

He stood froze for a moment like that, then took in a deep, deep breath, and pointed across the room to the couch. "Go."

"Uh..." I watched him for a minute, wondering if I had angered him. "Are you sure you didn't hurt yourself?"

"Quite sure. Go sit over there, where my cock can't see you." He sighed then and gave a little shake of his head. "The things that are coming out of my mouth... what I meant to say but which the image of me going down on you, which, incidentally, I do enjoy...where was I? Oh, what it interrupted was that I can't think when you are this close to me. I keep smelling your perfume. And seeing your breasts move in your dress. And remembering the feeling of your thighs, and then my cock is trying to convince me that I really am a superman, so go over there and keep all your tantalizing bits to yourself."

"All right, but now I'm kind of hot and bothered thinking about your mouth," I warned him before retreating to the couch, where I sat as primly as I could.

He took another deep breath, looking as indignant as only he could.

"Madam," he said in a deep voice that seemed to skitter along my skin. "I will thank you to stop using the word mouth in conversation with me. Also, breasts, fingers, hands, oral sex, and poetry."

"Poetry?" I asked, confused.

"It makes me think of the Kama Sutra, and now I want to work through the whole thing with you. Now, the wedding. What would you like?" he asked as he sat again in his chair.

I felt a giggle rising because he looked so business-like sitting across the length of his huge office, while I sat on the couch trying not to work the word poetry into a sentence. "I kind of hoped...that is, would you mind if we did it without a big ceremony? I realize my role is to keep you safe from all the women who evidently hunt you down as prime husband material, but I see little sense in a formal wedding."

"I don't mind at all," he said, noting something on the document. "I believe, then, we are in accord. I'll sign these and let you take them home with you in case you wish to consult a lawyer. I assure you they are exactly as specified by BMC, but you should always read a document before signing."

I murmured my agreement even as I smiled to myself over the lecturing tone he'd taken. I got to my feet, going to fetch the prenup and financial documents, but he held up a hand. "No! No closer, or I'll end up wanting to bury myself inside you again." He panted for a second. "Fuck. Too late. Fine, three for three it is. I think if you lay on the—"

A knock interrupted him just as he started toward me with a look in his eyes that raised my temperature a good five degrees. He stopped and stared at me for a few seconds.

"Poetry," I said in as sultry a voice as I could manage.

"You are pure evil," he told me before saying loudly, "What is it, Yasmine?"

The door opened and Martin's secretary stuck her head in to say, "You wanted me to tell you when we heard from the engine manufacturer in Panama. Do you want to take the call now? Also, your one o'clock is waiting."

"Yes, yes, I will take it. Ask Damascus to wait five minutes." He avoided looking toward me, waving a hand in my direction. "Yasmine, Ms. Clyde and I are going to be married as soon as we can get a license. Will you set up the pertinent appointments? We wish to marry quickly and quietly."

The woman, who appeared to be in her early sixties, didn't so much as bat an eyelash at us. She just nodded, murmured congratulations, and retreated.

"I guess I'll see you," I said, a little unsure as he backed around the desk. I snatched up the documents, feeling like I should say something, but not knowing what.

"Yes. I'll be in contact."

"'K." I started toward the door, hesitated, and glanced back toward him. "Are you sure you want to do this?"

"Right now I can think of nothing more than getting you into my bed and keeping you happily entertained there for a good year. Possibly nine. Maybe more if I get a supply of erotic creams and unguents automatically delivered each week."

"There's more to marriage than sex," I told him, reaching for the doorknob. "And you'd better add a couple of extra copies of the Kama Sutra to your auto deliveries. All those unguents and massage oils might make the pages sticky. Along with other...fluids. ."

His fingers twitched, and he gave a low moan that filled me with a warm, feminine sense of power as I left his office.

FIVE

Four days later, I stood in the chambers of a judge, having just promised to love and cherish Martin Otieno.

"If you would just sign here," the court clerk indicated on the marriage certificate.

I picked up the waiting pen and stared down at the document, knowing that the marriage wouldn't be legal until we'd both signed it. My name was printed in bold black: Samantha Linn Clyde was married to Martin Austin Otieno.

Next to me, Martin stood. We'd agreed to not dress up for the ceremony, since it was more or less a formality, so I'd worn a dress that I thought covered up all my bad points, and Martin wore a dark navy blue suit that set off his hazel eyes.

"Is something the matter?" the clerk asked, frowning at me. It was after hours, and I knew I was holding everyone up, but suddenly, my mouth went dry.

I set down the pen, and glanced around at the others, the two strangers we'd roped in to act as witnesses, the clerk, and the judge himself who was even now consulting his phone. "I'm sorry, but could I have a few minutes alone with Martin?"

The clerk rolled her eyes. "Sure, but just so you know, you have seven minutes before the cleaner comes in, so kick it into high gear, 'mmkay?"

The judge didn't even glance up as he followed the witnesses and clerk.

"Christ," Martin said, when I turned to him. "You're divorcing me, aren't you? We aren't even fully married, and you're already divorcing me. Is it because I wouldn't let you visit me for the last three days? It is, isn't it? You're mad because I refused to be swayed by your delicious self. Well, I won't have it, do you hear? I will not have it! No woman controls me via my cock! We don't need you. We'll get along just fine without you. I have plenty of hand lotion."

I stared at him, fighting to keep from laughing at the way his mind worked. Dear god, he was wonderful.

He dropped to his knees, taking my hand with its brand new gold band on the ring finger. "Please, please don't leave me to the hand lotion, Samantha. I don't know what I've done to piss you off, but whatever it is, tell me so I can apologize and make things right. I don't want to live my life without you driving me insane with lust, and thinking a hundred things a day that I want to tell you, and hearing about what you're thinking and doing and touching, especially if the last is yourself. Or me. Both is preferable."

"Have I told you how much I like how you talk? It's not so much that you sound like you're English, but when you get on a conversational roll, you just don't stop. It's adorable," I told him when he stopped for a breath, and pulled on his hands until he got to his feet, then dug through my purse until I pulled out a couple of folded sheets of paper. "Here. I want you to have these before I make us legally married."

He opened the papers, scanned them, then looked up. "It's the financial obligations contract. Why are you giving it to me?"

"Because I don't want it." I leaned forward, my lips brushing his as I said, "I want to marry you, Martin, not because of your money, but because I'm head over heels in love with you. I want you making me stand on the other side of the room because you can't think when we're close. I want you going off about my thighs and elbows and hips, and making me melt with pleasure because you don't see my flaws. I want you making my breath hitch in my throat when I see you, because you're so handsome I can't believe you're mine."

"Dammit," he snarled, making me step back, worried that I'd done something wrong.

"I was going to surprise you with this as a wedding gift," he said, looking annoyed as he pulled his own sheet of paper from his suit pocket. "But you just had to be more altruistic than me! Well, I won't have that, either. Here. Take it. I don't want it."

I looked down at the paper in my hand. It was a notarized copy of the prenup. "Why—"

"You idiot," he said, softening the words when he pulled me up against his chest, his mouth hot on my mine as he kissed me until I couldn't think. "I don't give a damn about the agreement, so long as you're mine."

"But why—"

"Because I love you, dammit!" he yelled, giving me a gentle shake, before pulling me in tight again, his body so hard against mine that I couldn't help but melt against him. "I loved you from the moment you first sashayed past me on a walk around Green Lake. I used to pray you would be there, just so I could try to catch your eye. I hate jogging. You know that, right? I loathe it with every iota of my being, but I kept doing it because sometimes, you were there."

I smiled against his lips. "We really are made for each other, aren't we?"

"Yes. Now sign the damned marriage certificate so I can take you to my apartment, and do everything to you that I've been saving up for three days. How limber are you? Never mind, we'll find out together. Also, do you have a preference for heated massage oil flavors? I bought sixteen of them in different flavors because I didn't know what you'd like, as well as a case of the lemon, which is my favorite. I plan on lemoning you up one side and down the other, after which I will lick it all off. Stop laughing, woman, this is a serious discussion we're having."

"Very serious," I said, kissing him. "Get the witnesses back. I have some flavors to pick out!"

Martin's apartment was impressive with its great view of the water, but I didn't get to see much of it since he literally picked me up and damn near raced through it to his bedroom, where he deposited me on the bed, then stood looking down at me.

"Are you trying to decide where to start again?" I asked.

"Yes. Oral sex?"

"Yes, but this time, I get to go down on you—Martin!"

He was on me before I could protest that it was my turn to give him pleasure. I don't even remember him removing my underwear, and I still had on my dress and shoes when he knelt at the end of the bed and pulled my legs onto his shoulders.

"Oh man, your whiskers," I said, clutching the duvet as he rubbed his cheeks on my inner thighs.

"I left them there just for you," he said, sinking one finger in me, curling it slightly in a way that not only had all my vaginal muscles spasming, but made me see stars. "I've been dreaming about this for the last three days. I can't tell you how many bottles of lotion I've gone through thinking about it. Yasmine was beginning to make noises about me seeing a dermatologist for what she referred to as my dry skin condition. Moan for me, my darling. Do you like two fingers?"

"God, yes," I said, squirming beneath the feeling of his fingers moving inside me.

"You can still talk. That's not what I want. You need to be as insensible as you make me feel. Let's try this." His tongue danced along aroused flesh, making my hips rise in time to his rhythm. "You are so sensitive. I like that about you. Now, what if I do this—" He sucked gently.

I almost came off the bed. "I like it a lot, but right now, I just want you to do what you promised."

He frowned. "What—"

"Fuck me silly," I said in a near growl, pulling him over me. We didn't even wait to get undressed; he simply unzipped his fly and sprang out to my waiting hands. "Oooh, so hard. So ready. So silky smooth. What's this? Balls?"

"Oh Christ, no, Sam, don't—you don't know how close I am—" His words faded into a groan as I lightly stroked his balls with my fingernails.

That lasted about five seconds, and then he was spreading my legs, glaring down at me as he hoisted my hips enough to stuff a pillow under my butt.

I fought a giggle at his outraged expression.

"We'll see who drives whom insane with lust, madam. Stop that! You are deliberately tightening on me.

Samantha! I just told you to stop—oh Christ, woman, do you have any idea how good you feel?"

He bucked and heaved and thrust, my body welcoming each intrusion with a thousand pinpoints of pleasure, my orgasm rippling through me with an intensity that left me breathless.

And when Martin's movements got short and choppy, I bit his neck, urging him on to his own climax.

"Some day," he said later, much later, the pair of us lying flat out on his bed side by side. "Some day I'll be able to wait until I get your clothes off."

"Eh," I said, kicking off my sandals before I rolled onto my side, and put a possessive hand on his heaving chest. He was still fully clothed, with just his fly and belt undone. "We have time. I love you, new husband."

He smiled, his pleasure visible in his eyes as I slid off the bed. "My cock wants me to thank you for picking me, new wife, whereas I want you to know that I am so wildly in love with you, I don't know how I'm going to survive the next sixty or so years. What are you doing? You're taking off your clothes? Christ on a crutch, do you know what that's going to do to my cock? It's already exhausted with—holy shit. You are the most beautiful woman—no. No more. Do not show me your hips—grrn. Right. Now you've done it. He's up and demanding serious fucking. You have only yourself to blame for this. Just stand there and let me worship you as is my due..."

WARRIOR

ONE

"Hello. I'm Evan Armstrong. I have an appointment at ten with Jane Washington."

The woman who had been squatting next to a small trash can alongside the BMC office reception desk glanced up, her eyes wide. "That's nice to know."

"Is it?" Evan watched as the woman poked into the trash for a moment, extracting a snack-sized Ziplock bag with an audible sigh of relief. Two red smears inside the bag vaguely resembled squashed raspberries.

"Whew. That'll teach me to clean out my purse when I'm bored." The woman smiled at him and stood up while tucking the plastic bag into her purse.

"Do you work here?" he asked, wondering if, when he'd stepped into the office of the Billionaire Marriage Club, he'd somehow entered a form of Wonderland where attractive women spoke in riddles, and nothing was as it seemed.

"Me? Nope. Oh! You thought because I was—" She gestured toward the trash can. "No, the receptionist stepped out for a minute, and I realized I dumped my emergency berries when I was cleaning out three months' worth of receipts, pens out of ink, tissues that have become furry from smooshing around in my bag, and seriously linty cough drops that got out of their wrappers."

"Ah, my apologies for the mistake." Evan watched as the woman took a seat next to a chair that held not only a large oversized raffia red and white striped bag, but a straw hat, a large metallic water bottle, and a small collection of paperback books.

The woman was certainly not hard to look at. She was a bit shorter than him, clad in black leggings, a tank top, and a gauzy loose top over it. She was a medium shade of tan, with brown hair that was braided and wrapped around her head, emphasizing her heart-shaped face.

She glanced up at him as he took the chair on the other side of her stacked items. "So, you're here to find a wife?"

"That is the idea, yes." He considered her, noting that her eyes weren't just brown, they had flecks of copper and gold in them. She appeared to be of a mixed ethnicity, and was on the plump side, something he appreciated. "I take it you're one of the...er... candidates?"

She heaved a sigh that would have been dramatic on anyone else, but he had a feeling she truly felt each moment of the sigh. "I am. Well, I may not be for much longer. The guy I was matched with is in with Ms. Washington right now, throwing a ruckus. Are you English? You sound English. If that seems like a weird question, it's just that I'm crazy about British mystery shows."

"I was born in California, but much of my family lives in England, so I spent most of my life there. Why would the man they matched you with object to you?"

He wanted to tell her she looked perfectly charming to him, with her copper and brown eyes, delicate features, and body that if he had allowed himself, would likely inspire an erection. Not wanting to be hit with charges of sexual harassment, however, he kept those thoughts to himself.

"He says he's allergic to me," she answered, giving a little shrug, picking up her water bottle. "I mean, I suppose that's possible, but he's been in there for twenty minutes, and I don't see what there is to complain about, other than he sneezes a lot around me."

"Are you wearing perfume?" Evan asked, unable to keep from wanting to know more. He had no idea what sort of woman he expected the Billionaire Marriage Club to find for him, but he wouldn't mind learning more about this one.

She wrinkled her nose. "Nope. Santiago—that's his name, Santiago Dare—says that every time we meet he has an allergic reaction, and complained to Ms. Washington. She didn't believe him, and asked me to come in so she could see for herself."

"Santiago Dare?" Evan frowned, trying to pinpoint where he'd heard the name.

"He's an artist. He owns that animation studio that's been turning out all the hits, you know?"

"Ah, yes, I know the one you mean." He shook his head. "I believe artists are usually somewhat eccentric. Perhaps that's behind his claim."

"Maybe." She shot a suspicious glance toward the door bearing the name of the regional manager of the BMC. Her voice dropped to an intimate level. "It could be that he doesn't like me, personally, because my dad is Indian and my mom is American and Swedish. Some people are...you know..."

"Yes, sadly, they are," he agreed. "However, if that is the real reason he is spurning you, he is not just eccentric, he's an idiot. There's nothing wrong with you that I can see. As a matter of fact, my maternal grandmother was Indian."

Her expression brightened. "Really? Where was she from?"

"Chennai."

"That used to be Madras, yes? Dad was born in Raipur, but met my mom in France, where they were both students. Now they live in a tiny town in the north of Sweden raising goats." She gave a little laugh. "Sorry, that was probably more than you wanted to know."

"On the contrary, I find it interesting how people end up in unexpected places. My grandmother's story was much less romantic—a rich English family took her to England as a servant."

She wrinkled her nose again. Evan always thought it was a silly thing to do, but on this woman, it looked downright adorable. "What is your name?" he asked without thinking.

"Mariah Ray."

"I'm Evan Armstrong. Pleasure to meet you." They shook hands, somewhat awkwardly, since her massive striped bag hindered her ability to reach across to him. Something that had been rattling around in his brain finally came into focus. "Forgive me, but do I know you?"

"Er..." She glanced toward the door leading to the hallway, then gave another sigh. "Not really. That is, we never really met. I used to work in your HR department in the downtown office."

He rummaged around in his memory, but pulled forth nothing other than a vague feeling he'd seen her before. "Used to? Did you leave us for some other company?"

She made a face. "You could say that. The head of HR tried to hit on me, and I called him out on it, and he got all butthurt and made up some bullshit about me acting inappropriately, and as a result, I got canned."

Evan was appalled. He might be focused on the technological side of making better, faster, and bigger RAM chips, but that didn't mean he was completely out of touch with the rest of the company. He didn't remember anything about a sexual harassment charge. "This is unacceptable. Did you report the harassment? The firing?"

Mariah looked uncomfortable, her gaze skittering away from his. "No."

"I'm not trying to victim blame you, but this is a serious issue, and if one of my employees is abusing his position, then I want to know about it. Why did you not report it?"

"Who'd believe me?" she asked.

Evan wanted to reassure her, to eliminate her obvious discomfort, but didn't know how to do that without appearing in the same light as the man who had abused her. "I would believe you."

"Yes, but no one ever got in to see you." Her gaze met his for a few seconds, the lights in them sparkling like they were lit from behind. "So I just left and found a job that I could do at home."

Anger at the fact that she had suffered at the hands of one of his employees mingled with a sense of annoyance at the unspoken accusation he heard in her voice. "I'm not a monster," he protested. "I don't hide from my employees. If there is a problem that needs to be brought to my attention, then I welcome being notified of that fact."

"Oh, I didn't mean that to sound like I was blaming you." She turned to face him, her eyes wide as she reached a hand out toward him before immediately pulling it back. "It's just that there was really no one I could complain to. I mean, he was the head of HR. And I couldn't very well go barging into your office—assuming you were there—and demand that you do something about the ass-grabber."

"He grabbed your...er..." He stopped, his anger heading straight toward a level of fury he hadn't felt since the day he broke up with his fourth wife.

"Oh, that was just the tip of the iceberg, so to speak." Mariah leaned back, her expression much brighter now. "He was a first class grope-copper. Very handsy, you know? And he loved to lean over women's shoulders in an attempt to peer down their shirts. Anyway, that's how I recognized you. But I have to say that I'm more than a bit surprised to see you here. I mean...why?"

"The subject of why I'm here is not of importance," he said, making several mental notes. He'd have his secretary conduct an investigation into harassment within the HR department. He'd pull in the director, a man who came with high recommendations, for an interview. He'd check the security cameras to see if they caught any of the man's actions. "You may think I'm a useless CEO, but I assure you I do not tolerate harassment."

"I didn't mean to imply that you do, just that you weren't around to complain to...oh, hell. Everything I say is coming out like I'm blaming you, which I'm absolutely not." She gave a third sigh. "Let's just drop it, OK? I'm fine. I have another job, and there's no harm done other than the annoyance of dealing with a jerk.”

“My mother was a radical feminist in the 1970s,” Evan told her, hesitating a moment before saying, “May I take your hand?”

“Huh?” She looked down at her hand before her gaze returned to his. “Uh...OK.”

He took her hand and gave it a friendly squeeze, ignoring the fact that he greatly enjoyed the contact. “As I said, my mother was an activist for many causes, and was in and out of jail for most of my childhood. If she thought I allowed someone in my employ to trespass on the personal boundaries of another, she would rise up from her grave and smite me on the spot.”

Mariah giggled, a delightful sound that he felt down to the tips of his toes. “My mom is a bit vocal, too, so I know what you mean. I wanted to cut down a couple of arbor vitae bushes in my yard because they were all growing into one big clump, and she flat out told me no. I’m thirty-seven, for heaven’s sake! I should be able to have my yard landscaped if I want, but man, I don’t dare go against her.”

“That’s not right,” he said, thinking about what actions he’d take against the HR director.

“Yeah, well, you don’t know my mom. She can be very forceful when she wants.”

“No, I meant the situation with you not having a resource available to you for the harassment you suffered. I will make sure there is some sort of recourse henceforth.”

She giggled again, her fingers curling around his in a manner that threatened to make him hard. He didn’t even wonder at that. He simply accepted that this woman was one that appealed to him on many levels. “I don't think I've ever heard anyone actually say the word henceforth."

"Will you be willing to make a statement about the harassment?" he asked. "If the case goes to court, will you testify?"

"I mean...it was eighteen months ago. Does it really matter now?" she asked, her expression fading from amusement to concern.

"Of course it matters." He released her hand and pulled out his phone, making a few rapid notes. "I'll have my secretary contact you, if you don't mind giving me your phone number." She did so, and he entered the information. "Thank you. I'll let you know what I find out after I get back to the office and have a chance to look at security tapes."

"Wow," she said, giving him a hesitant smile. "I guess it's a good thing we're both here at the same time. I never thought I'd get to stick it to that bastard."

"It is an extremely good thing," he agreed, hesitating a moment before adding, "I realize the irony of asking this after discussing making someone who harassed you pay for his actions, but since you have obviously not been matched with the correct person, would you mind if I ask to have you considered in whatever group Jane rounds up for me?"

"I wouldn't mind at all," Mariah answered, and a faint glow on her cheeks indicated she was blushing. Evan was even more delighted. He couldn't remember the last time he'd made a woman blush. "So long as you answer a few questions."

"Ah. Yes. No doubt you wish to know about me." He straightened up. "I'm forty-six, enjoy scuba diving and snorkeling, have no major vices that I know of, and I've been married four times."

"Whoa," she said, blinking a couple of times. "That's a lot of ex-wives. Would you mind if I asked why there are so many when you're only forty-six?"

"Normally, yes, I would mind, but we are in a situation where candor and honesty are of prime importance."

"I really do like the way you talk," she interrupted, her eyes filled with mirth.

"Thank you. I enjoy your conversation as well. To answer your question, I lived with all four wives before we married. I felt that having time together would allow us to determine if we had a future. I was with my first wife a year before we married. We had twin sons almost immediately, and were divorced shortly after that. Wife number two lived with me for three years before we married. She ran off two months after the ceremony. With my then-partner. I divorced both of them at the same time. Wife number three lived with me for five years. I wanted to make sure she would stick, if you will forgive the expression."

"Uh oh," Mariah said, her lips parted just enough to make Evan want to kiss her. "Since there's a wife number four, I assume those five years didn't do the trick?"

"No." He pushed down the pain that accompanied the baring of his soul, feeling that honesty was vital. "She had an epiphany, as she called it, and decided that my lifestyle was too decadent and hedonistic, and if I didn't subscribe to her new homesteading life plan, then we were through."

"I know a couple of people who grow their own veggies and things like that," Mariah said.

Evan nodded. "As do I. However, what my wife wanted was something more in line with a doomsday cult. She insisted that not only do we forego any form of modern medicine and technological devices, but we also would live on a commune and drink water recycled from our urine."

The face Mariah made expressed exactly how Evan felt. "Ew. Wait...your own urine, or someone else's?"

"I believe it was a communal effort," he said, trying hard not to think about it.

"OK, that's just seriously gross. What about wife number four?"

"She kidnapped my sons when they were twelve years old, and held them for ransom."

"Holy shit," Mariah said, her eyes huge.

"She's now in prison."

"I should hope so. I have to admit Mr. Armstrong—"

"Evan."

She made an odd half-grimace. "I'll try, but you were always Mr. Armstrong at work, and I'm not sure I can think of you any other way. I have to admit...Evan... that I'm surprised that all those unfortunate marriages haven't turned you off of the idea of being married."

"I'm not so stupid as to cut off my nose to spite myself," he said, surprised at her comment. "I want to be married. I desire a life partner. My parents were particularly devoted to each other, and I have always wanted to have a similar bond with a woman. Since I've been unable to find one on my own, and I'd heard good things about this organization from a friend who recently married through their services, I decided I would see what they could offer." He paused for a moment, trying to study her without making it apparent he was doing so. "What about you?"

"Why am I here, you mean?" she asked.

He nodded, wondering why a woman so charming, with such a quick mind, would have to resort to a service to find her a man. Then he realized the hypocrisy of such a thought and dismissed it.

"Well, I want money."

His eyebrows rose.

"That is, I want to be married, too. I've tried dating, and all I seem to find are men who are so into themselves, they seem to forget that I'm a living, breathing, autonomous person. I don't want to be an extension of some guy's ego—I want a man who wants me to be his partner. A friend. Someone vital to his life, not just a trophy wife. Not that I'm anywhere near that sort of status," she said with a little laugh as she gestured toward her torso.

"Why not?" he asked.

She gave him a look that was part eye roll, part amusement. "Don't think I didn't see the way you recoiled when I said that I wanted money. I do. Want it, that is. I am licensed for animal rehab, you see, and I want to branch out and make a bona fide animal sanctuary where I can take in sick and old and needy animals of all sorts, and either find them forever homes, or let them live out their days in care and comfort in the sanctuary."

He was intrigued despite himself. Not because he was a fan of animals—he'd never had a pet growing up, and didn't see any reason to change that—but because of the passion that made her eyes sparkle, and her voice throb with excitement. This was clearly something of vital importance to Mariah, and he considered such passion projects as a good sign.

None of his other wives had such lofty goals, not even the last one.

"And you would expect your husband to support the sanctuary?" he asked in what he hoped was a noncommittal tone.

"No, not unless he wanted to. Ms. Washington said that if I match up with a guy and we agree to marry, then I get a yearly stipend, and I'd use that for my sanctuary. I have my eye on a piece of land up north, near the Canadian border that I'd dearly like to buy. But I can't swing it on my salary now."

"That's a very altruistic motive."

"Eh. I'm big on animal rescue. How about you?"

"I'm afraid I have no experience with animal rescue—"

"No, do you like them?" Her eyes narrowed, and he had an uncomfortable feeling his answer was going to make or break her impression of him.

"I don't dislike pets," he said slowly. "But I've never had them. Until recently, I used to travel quite a bit, so it never seemed to be a good time to acquire one. My sons are in college now, but when they were young, they mostly lived with their mother. They had several cats and dogs, and I think some lizards that my ex swore she always found in her bed. But those stayed at her place when the boys were with me."

"Hmm," she said, her expression now guarded.

Evan was about to reiterate that he had nothing against animals, per se, just didn't have experience with them, but at that moment the door opened, and a young red-headed man entered, moving over to the reception desk.

"You the ten am?" the young man asked Evan as he tapped on a keyboard.

"I am. But his lady was here before me." He indicated Mariah.

"Yeah, I know. The shouty dude is in complaining about her being weird." The young man stared at Mariah for a few seconds as if she was something unsavory.

Evan was irritated on her behalf.

He stood up and marched over to the desk, leaning over the youth to drive home his point. "You wil: apologize to Ms. Ray."

"I—what? What did I do?" the young man asked, his Adam's apple bobbing up and down a couple of times. "I didn't do anything!"

"Calling someone weird is insulting. Apologize."

"It's not really a big deal," Mariah started to say, but Evan stopped her with a quelling look.

"It is a big deal. According to my research, this company is well-known for their excellent treatment of the individuals who partake in their services. That does not include referring to their clientele as weird."

Mariah obviously hid a chirrup of laughter with a cough, and Evan could swear he heard her murmur something about the way he spoke, but he had no time for such pleasantries. He turned his irate gaze upon the youth, who melted into a puddle of stammering, redfaced misery.

By the time the door to Jane Washington's office opened and a long-haired man stormed out of the office, the receptionist was begging Mariah for forgiveness.

"—thank you to ensure the next one meets my exacting standards!" the man yelled over his shoulder in a heavy Spanish accent before turning around to see Mariah, who got to her feet, her eyes wide, her body language reading wariness.

Evan moved over to stand next to her even as the man pointed a finger, and said, "I will never again trust a woman to not have an animal stuffed into her tatas!" before he stormed out, slamming the door after him.

"Tatas?" Evan asked, alternating between surprised and startled.

"It means boobs," Mariah told him.

"I know what it means, but his statement took me aback. What a very odd man," Evan said. "I don't know him, but I suspect you just dodged a very large bullet."

"Yeah, that's kind of what I'm thinking, too," she said, glancing over at the woman who entered the room.

"Mr. Armstrong? I'm Jane Washington. I apologize both for the client who just left, and also for the delay regarding our appointment. Shall we commence?"

Reluctantly, he entered her office, taking the chair she indicated, mentally preparing a request to have Mariah included in the group of women the BMC selected.

Before he could say anything, Jane murmured, "If you would excuse me for a moment..." and trotted out of the office, closing the door quietly behind her.

Evan frowned and was about to get up and make sure that Mariah wasn't being picked on when Jane Washington returned. "Thank you for waiting. Now, I have studied your file at great length, since Mr. Otieno was very insistent that we help you out. I have selected three candidates that I believe will suit your particular interests and psychological profile—"

"I'm sure you have," he interrupted, feeling itchy. He wanted badly to know what this woman had said to Mariah. "But before we go any further, I'd like to make a request."

"Oh?" Jane Washington's delicately shaped eyebrows rose.

"The woman who was in the waiting room—Mariah Ray. I'd like her to be one of the official recommendations."

Jane blinked at him for a few seconds. "I'm sorry, Mr. Armstrong, but Ms. Ray has been removed from our list of potential partners because of problems brought up by previous matches."

"I saw nothing wrong with her. I'd like her added to the list."

"I'm afraid that's not possible," Jane said more firmly. "It would be against our policy."

"Then change your policy. She's undergone all the testing and background checks, hasn't she?"

"Well...yes, but—"

"I've paid a sizeable retainer to avail myself of your services. I wish to meet with one of your clients in that capacity. I don't see why this is so difficult for you."

"As I said, we have removed her from our list."

"The solution is simple—add her back in and inform her I'd like to meet her in a location of her choice." He folded his hands, giving her the direct stare that had never failed to intimidate the most obstreperous of clients.

It was clear she objected to what he asked, but she had enough common sense to say, "I'll see what I can do. Now, here are the three women who I suggest you might wish to meet."

Ten minutes later he rose, having rejected all the women Jane Washington had recommended.

"I'm sorry that none of the women interested you enough to meet them," she told him, obviously as frustrated as he was. "I will continue to search for someone who you might find suitable—"

Evan cocked an eyebrow at her.

"—including Ms. Ray," she said with reluctance. She checked herself, then asked, "Do you mind me asking if you know her? You seem quite adamant to have her included for your consideration."

"I met her for the first time about half an hour ago."

"Then why—" She stopped, giving a little shake of her head. "It's really none of my business other than it helps me pinpoint what you are looking for in a woman."

He thought for a moment, then shrugged. "I like her. She's different from my wives and the other women I've dated. Different can be good."

"Ah, but it can also be a disappointment," she said, looking a little self-righteous.

"Time will tell," he told her, and left the office with a much more optimistic outlook than he had going in.

TWO

"So," I said, taking a sip of the tonic and lime a server had set before me. The glass was spotted with droplets of moisture since the afternoon sun beat in on the restaurant's deck overlooking Lake Washington, but it was nowhere as near as damp as my hands.

What in the name of the good, green earth was I doing here? Why was I even considering an arrangement with this man, not to mention hooking up, let alone actual, binding, very legal marriage?

The hooking up part sounds splendid, my mental narrator said with a long, long look at the man who sat next to me. Evan Armstrong sounded as British as a member of the royal family, with a wild mop of chocolate brown curls kept short on the sides and back. I tried to ignore the fact that I'd had a mad crush on him from the minute I'd seen him standing in the building's lobby where his administrative offices were located, but I knew it was a lost cause. Those curls and his pale blue-grey eyes made my stomach flip-flop every time I thought about him.

"So," he agreed, sliding me a look out of those sexy, sexy eyes. "Here we are."

"Yes." I wrestled my mind off the mental image of what his bare chest and arms and thighs and pretty much every other part of him would look like, and onto what it should be thinking about. "Why is this suddenly awkward?" my mouth asked without checking with me for authorization first.

"Because we're considering marriage?" he asked with a little cock of one eyebrow.

My inner narrator threatened to swoon in response. I told her to cool her jets. "Actually, I'm not."

His second eyebrow went up at that. "You're not what? Considering marriage? Am I mistaken in thinking that this meeting, arranged with the blessing of the BMC, and both my attorney and yours, is to discuss our viable future together?"

"Yes. No." I thought for a minute. "Perhaps."

He leaned back against the cloth of the deck chair, one long-fingered hand idly toying with his glass of lager and lime. I gave a little shiver at the thought of those fingers touching me. "I would hate for us to be on different tracks, so to speak. Could you elaborate regarding your intentions?"

"Sure." I took a sip of my tonic water, which I love when half a lime is squeezed into it. "It's just that…well, I'm not sure what it is you're doing, exactly."

A tiny frown wrinkled his brow. "Despite the fact that I've mentioned wanting to find a woman with whom I can share my life?"

"Yeah, I get that," I said, waving away his confusion. "It's just how you're doing it. You said that all your relationships were fine for literally years until you got married, then all hell broke out."

"Yes. Which is why this time, I'm doing the opposite. Instead of finding a woman, getting to know her over a long period, living together so that we can ensure we're compatible, and then marrying, this time I'm going to do the opposite. I like you. You have an interesting mind. The psychological tests we both took for the BMC ensure we are at least somewhat compatible. I would add that I find you physically pleasing, but since that could well be misconstrued as sexual harassment, I won't."

"Ha," I said, making a face at him, wanting to laugh and sing and grab his head to kiss the words right off his tongue. "Nice way to slide that in."

His eyes widened.

I covered my mouth, then spread my fingers and said through them, "Yeah, I didn't think before saying that. Forget you heard that, and I'll forget your comment. Although I appreciate the sentiment. It's...uh... reciprocated." A blush burned my cheeks, but I hoped he wouldn't see it since my upper body was in the shade.

"I'm delighted to hear that. However, I'm still at a loss as to what you are doing here if you aren't interested in going further with the arrangement as described by the BMC."

I hesitated for almost half a minute before answering. "I try to be honest, even when it may not be the easiest thing to do. So I'll be completely frank with you, although I would like to add that I don't intend to be offensive in any way."

He set down his glass, giving me his full attention.

I felt like a bug pinned down by a bloodthirsty entomologist. "I think what you're doing is...well, not terribly smart. That is, more or less jumping for the first woman you see."

He blinked. "What makes you think you're the first?"

My blush kicked up a few more levels. I wanted badly to look away. Hell, I wanted to run away from this insanely gorgeous man, but I'd always made it a policy to clean up any messes I made, and I'd just created a doozy. "I'm sorry, that was conceited of me," I said, trying to calm my wildly beating heart. My hands went even more sweaty than before. "I simply meant that doing the opposite of what makes sense is not the wisest way to find a life partner. Maybe you just had some bad luck with the women you married. Maybe they were in a different place than you, mentally and emotionally, and that's why things ended."

It was his turn to be silent, and I squirmed in my chair, hoping that he wasn't going to put me on blast for speaking my mind.

"What would you do if you were in my shoes?"

I gawked at him, not in the least bit expecting that. "What?"

"You say that I'm going about this all wrong—very well, I accept that by conventional standards, I am an outlier. But I'd like to know what you'd do if our situations were reversed."

"Oh, well..." I thought for a few seconds. "I'd make an effort to find out about the person I was contemplating a life with."

"I did that," he said, taking a sip of his beer.

"Yes, but they moved in with you, right? I mean, that's not really getting to know them, is it?"

"How so?"

"Oh lord, here's where I'm going to put my foot in my mouth again," I said, wiping my hands on my legs again. "You live in a big house, don't you?"

His eyebrows rose again. "I don't think of it as unduly large, but it has eight bedrooms, yes."

"And it's on the lake?" I asked, waving toward the steel-blue water rippling below.

"On the other side, yes."

"Right, and I'm willing to bet you have a staff to do things like clean and cook and mow the lawn, and all that?"

"What point are you making?" he asked, his brows pulled together. "Are you criticizing my lifestyle? Because my third wife already did that—"

"No, my point isn't to make you feel bad about that. I mean, who actually wants to clean the toilet? I'd love to be able to afford someone who could clean my house for me, and it only has one and a half bathrooms. But you had your fiancés move into your world, a situation where they don't have normal, everyday stresses. I think you can't really know someone until you see how they handle the crap that life throws at them."

He was silent again. "You posit that by bringing my wives into my world, I did not see the real them?"

"Yes. Kind of. Oh, hell, what do I know? I only had half a year of doing psychology classes before I got the job in your HR department. I'm sorry, Mr...er...Evan. Feel free to ignore my theories. Clearly, we're not going to agree."

"On the contrary," he said, narrowing his eyes on the glass of lager. His gaze seemed inward until he turned to me, pinning me back with a look that I felt like velvet touching my bare flesh. "I accept your proposal."

"What?" I asked, wondering when I'd proposed. Had I blacked out at some point? I pushed my drink away, wondering if he'd roofied me. But who ever heard of a roofie that only lasted a few seconds? "Look, Evan, I wouldn't mind getting to know you better. A lot better, with everything that means. But I am not going to become your fifth ex-wife. I'm not going to move in with you and live the life of a woman being taken care of by a sugar daddy. That's not me. Not me at all."

He nodded. "I understand now. That is what I am accepting—your terms. Since you don't wish to move into my world, I will move into yours. Shall we say a month's trial period?"

"What?" I didn't understand what he was saying. Did he mean he wanted to move in with me? My brain—and inner narrator—boggled at the idea of what it would be like to have him hanging around my little house, exuding all that masculine sexiness twenty-four hours a day.

Delicious, my narrator purred.

"A month is suitable, I think. Do you prefer longer? I can arrange that, although I will have to leave in six weeks for a tour of facilities in California." He pulled out his phone. "But assuming that doesn't bother you, I can stay with you for as long as it takes for you to be convinced of our rightness."

"Our rightness?" I shook my head, feeling like a deranged parrot repeating everything he said. "Um. It's not that I'm unwilling to put my money where my mouth is, but I don't have a big house. It's a two bedroom, one and a half bath rambler out in the boonies. It was actually my grandmother's house, and I inherited it when she died."

"I don't see a problem with that," he said, giving me a long look. I couldn't read it because my inner narrator was too busy picturing him lying in my bed, every iota of his gorgeousness there for me to frolic upon. "Stefan and Dominic can stay in one room, and I'll stay with you."

It was on the tip of my tongue to repeat "Stefan and

Dominic?" but I managed to stop myself before I really did turn into a parrot. "Who are they?"

"My bodyguards." He turned and nodded toward the bar in the restaurant's interior. "They're at the end of the bar."

"You have bodyguards," I said, my brain giving up all hopes of coping with this unsettling, delicious man.

"Two. Naturally, they will extend their protection to you," he said in a polite tone, just as if I'd been kicking up a fuss.

"Naturally. Dammit." I grimaced.

"Pardon?" His eyebrows were up again.

"I'm repeating everything you say. It's evidently my mind's way of trying to cope with unexpected things. Evan—I'm serious in that I think we should get to know each other in a setting that isn't filled with servants and fancy cars—wait, do you have fancy cars?"

"Several." He looked like he wanted to laugh, but was too well-bred to do anything so uncouth.

"—and I'd be OK with you staying with me for a bit, like maybe a week to see how things go, but my house is tiny."

"Would it bother you if Stefan and Nic helped out around the house, or would that qualify in your mind as having servants?" he asked.

I felt adrift in a sea of...well, adriftness. "No." I said after a few moment's consideration. "I don't consider people pitching in with chores on par with a professional housekeeper. Are you sure about this? My house is like eleven hundred square feet, not counting the garage, which...uh...is not useable space."

"I'm quite sure," he said in a decisive tone that made me wonder if I was mad, or he was. Maybe we both were. "Are we in agreement, then?"

"I guess so," I said, allowing him to pull me to my feet. He held out his hand, which I shook, feeling awkward, overwhelmed, and more than a little turned on.

"Excellent. I'll be by tomorrow. I think we can leave the legalities until after our initial trial period, don't you think?"

"Sure," I said.

"Let us seal our agreement with a kiss," he said, the corners of his eyes crinkling as he pulled me closer, one hand on my hip.

My inner narrator whooped with joy, and after glancing around to make sure we were not the object of anyone's focus, I allowed myself to lean into him. "All right, but I'm not really one for public displays of affection. Although I badly want to touch your chest. And arms. And...hoo."

His lips descended on mine just as I was about to blab how much I wanted him. He pulled my hips closer to his, one hand tangled in my hair as his tongue danced along my lips, wordlessly asking for entrance. I gave it to him, reveling in the taste of the lime on his tongue as it twined around mine, my body wanting to rub itself all over him. I slid my hands under his shirt, my fingers tracing the contours of his chest even as his hand moved from my hip up to areas north.

I moaned into his mouth when he sucked my tongue a little, my nipples hardening as the sensory overload had every bit of me demanding I fling myself on him.

Just as his hand closed on my breast, he froze for a second, then jerked backward, saying, "What the hell?"

"Mouth," I said, staring at him, then realized he was also staring—at my chest. But his expression wasn't one of enjoyment or even lust, but horror. "Huh?"

"Something moved—holy shit! What is that?"

I looked down, straight into bulbous black eyes that peered sleepily at me from a triangular-shaped face. Two pale brown ears tipped forward in obvious question, while the little pink tipped nose wiggled, making a fine fan of whiskers twitch. "Oh, hell, we woke her."

"What—what—"

"This is Bebe. She's a sugar glider."

He looked at Bebe's sweet little head where she blinked at him, up to my face, and back to Bebe. "What is she doing in your—oh."

I nodded. "Yeah, the artist didn't like the fact that I bra-bond my rescues. It's what you do. Sugar gliders are nocturnal marsupials, and sleep during the day, so it's just easier to train them to sleep in your pocket or a sports bra, or even a hoodie with a kangaroo pocket. I put mine in my bra because they just sleep through the day and I don't even notice they're there. Sorry about startling you."

"It's my fault. I should have asked if your breasts were...erm...occupied."

My inner narrator mourned the loss of Evan. It was clear that the surprise of finding Bebe in my cleavage was too much for him. What a damned shame.

"Well. I guess that is that. Thank you for the drink," I said, gathering up my bag. "I'm sorry things couldn't work out."

"What isn't working out?" he asked, watching with his brows pulled together as Bebe, deciding the sunny afternoon was too much, snuggled back down into the valley between my breasts for another nap.

"You're obviously uncomfortable about the fact that I bra-bond my rescues," I said, hesitating before marching off to continue my life alone, unloved, and without a sexy man who made my mouth water.

"I apologize if that is the impression I gave you," he said, finally dragging his gaze from my chest up to my eyes. "It took me by surprise, but I'm not made uncomfortable by the small creature. Although...do you always have them there?"

"Not all the time, no, but Bebe is a new rescue, and I have a home arranged by the rescue organization I work for, so I'm getting her used to being with people. She came from a hoarding situation, and wasn't used to much human contact."

"I did not know people keep those as pets," he said. I could tell he was trying hard not to keep staring at my boobs.

"They shouldn't," I said, slinging my bag over my shoulder. "Don't get me wrong, they're cute as hell, but they can't be house trained, and they mark every surface they consider their territory. And trust me, the smell of that is nothing you want to encounter. I have an exhaust fan running full time in my garage for just that reason."

"Is that why you said the garage is not available?" he asked, one hand on my lower back as we reentered the restaurant. It took me a few seconds for my eyes to get used to the relative darkness, but my entire body was focused solely on the warmth of his hand on my back. It started little fires in hidden depths, causing my narrator to fan herself.

"Yup. I house the rescues there. I had to use tiger pee paint on the walls and floor." He stopped and gave me a look that made me laugh, and add, "It's the type of paint treatment that zoos use for their big cat enclosures. The big cat pee doesn't corrode it, and it's easy to clean off. I had a drain put in the center of the floor, too, so I can hose down the room when the rescues get carried away marking everything in sight."

"Such a little animal," he said, shaking his head, stopping next to two men who stood up when we approached. "Mariah, this is Stefan."

I shook the hand of a black man who was a good foot taller than me. He had a goatee and a wickedly sharp widow's peak. "Hello. Nice to meet you."

"My pleasure," he responded, his voice bearing a distinct Caribbean accent.

"And Dominic," Evan said.

"Hi," I said when the second man, much shorter and wirier, greeted me with a slow, friendly smile and a handshake.

"Hi backatcha." Dominic spoke with the lazy cadence of a surfer bro, making me think of my cousin who lived in California, and who spent every minute he could on with his board. "Dude! Is that, like, an animal?"

"Bebe," I said, looking down to find her inquisitive little nose poking out of the top of my wrap shirt. "Go back to sleep. No nuts for you until we get back home."

"It's a sugar glider," Evan said with a nonchalance that had me giggling. "Mariah breast bonds them."

"Bra-bond." When both men stared at me with obvious disbelief, I quickly explained, finishing with, "Bebe has a passion for nuts, and no doubt she smells the almonds on the counter."

"Can I feed her some?" Dominic asked, picking up the bowl.

"No, those are salted. They aren't good for her. I have some raw ones back home, but I don't feed them when they are in a bra or pocket unless they haven't been fed in a while."

It took another five minutes of questions and answers about my rescues before we left the restaurant, and I headed off on the hour and a half drive home.

"I'll be at your house tomorrow about noon," Evan said as I slid behind the wheel of my car, immediately rolling down my window as he closed the door. "Will that suit?"

I glanced behind him to where Stefan and Dominic were climbing into an expensive sedan type car that probably cost more than my entire house. "Sure, although you might want to mention that I only have one bed in the spare room. And...well, the whole eleven hundred square feet thing."

"It will be no problem. Mariah."

"Hmm?" I was still watching the car, wondering what type it was, and whether it had a driver since both bodyguards got into the back of it. It must have. What man would drive his own bodyguards around?

Evan's head blocked out my view as he moved in for a kiss. His lips were warm, soft, and so steamy I swear my blood pressure rose a few points. "It will be fine. I'll see you tomorrow."

"OK," I said, then as he walked away, called myself all sorts of names.

I was in so much trouble. So, so much trouble.

THREE

To: Mariah

How are the three hoarder rescues doing? The adoptees have requested a date to visit before you are finished acclimatizing them. I've told them I'm leaving that decision up to you, but the family is very excited to see them, so they can start "decorating" what they are referring to as a glider nursery.

Also, just a head's up from the Bellingham office: a group of animal rights extremists have recently begun targeting various exotic rescue and rehab facilities. They broke into a mink rescue last week, and released every last one before setting fire to the barn. Just be careful with anyone who approaches you with a request to see your gliders' living area.

We still on for going to that club in Vancouver on Saturday? We can go early and make a day of seeing the city.

To: Bennet

Dammit! Did they catch the minks? Can they survive on their own? Those extremists really piss me off. And as for the adoptees visiting...can you please ask them to wait a week? The gliders are probably OK to meet them, but I have a...well, situation, I guess you could say, at home that makes it difficult to have people over right now. That also means I won't be able to go with you to the club, so you guys go without me, and have oodles of fun. Hot Canadian guys for the win, right?

To: Mariah

What do you mean you have a situation at home? What sort of situation? Is something wrong with the rescues?

To: Bennet

No, nothing like that. It's just...oh lord. It's so hard to explain. I joined a dating service, for lack of better phrase, and the guy I matched with is staying with me for a week. That's all.

To: Mariah

That's all? THAT'S ALL??? Girl, you have some dude you just met moving in with you? Are you OK? Wait, you're not under duress, are you? Is he holding you prisoner? Shit, why didn't we set up a duress word for situations like this?

Sit tight. I'm coming over just as soon as Elvira comes back from lunch. Don't let the crazy kidnapper see your texts. And don't drink anything he gives you!

To: Bennet

You went from a man staying with me for a week to I'm being held prisoner in, like, ten seconds flat. That has to be a new world record.

There's no reason to come by. I'm not under duress. I invited the man—his name is Evan, by the way—to stay. He's sexy and nice and funny and has a British accent, so stop picturing me in a dire situation. I just don't want to deal with adoptees while I'm coping with my visitors.

To: Mariah

Oooh. Sexy and a Brit? Right, I want to meet him, but I'll let you have a few days to work out all your needs first.

But we really should have a duress word. Just in case. Mine is going to be flibbertigibbet.

To: Bennet

How on earth do you expect to work the word flibbertigibbet into a sentence that would not scream duress word should an actual captor see it?

Also, my word is going to be Sasquatch.

To: Mariah

Example use: My friend Mariah is such a flibbertigibbet that she didn't even tell me she met a man and invited him to stay with her so she can have steamy, hot-guy sexytimes.

To: Bennet

Touché.

I set down my phone and looked at the computer screen, taking a deep breath before putting on my earphones. I had a good three hours more transcription I needed to do before I could stop for the day.

The door to my bedroom opened, and Evan strolled out wearing a tank top and a pair of comfy knee-length shorts that perfectly cupped the lines of his ass cheeks. "—tell them that is not what we agreed to, and if they want to go the legal route, we will. One moment, another call is coming in. Armstrong speaking. Ah, yes, yes, my secretary told me you've been trying to get hold of me. I'm out of the office for the next few weeks—" His voice faded as he wandered into the kitchen, the swinging door closing behind him.

"I am not going to make it a full seven days," I said, looking at the clock. Evan had been here exactly an hour, and already I was extremely aware of him, everything from his physical self as he strolled around the house, to his scent, a heady mix of pine and something citrus.

"Hey, Mariah? I think I broke your toilet. It, like, won't stop running," Dominic said in his surfer drawl as he popped his head around the door of the guest bathroom.

Pounding sounded from the bedroom next to him where Stefan was assembling the frame of a bunk bed that they'd dragged in with the mountain of luggage that evidently made up items necessary to the threesome's wellbeing. Profound swearing followed the pounding.

"—and I told the factory lead that I didn't care how long it took, I want the job done right. Armstrong RAM is better than that." Evan emerged from the kitchen eating an apple as he strolled past me back to my bedroom, where he'd set up a small desk for his laptop, claiming that by working there he wouldn't distract me at all.

Dominic's head disappeared for a second, then returned. "Now something is wrong with the sink. I think the spigot is cracked, because water is spraying up and hitting the ceiling."

"Where's the first aid kit?" The shout came from spare room. "Shit. We got a spurter here. Nic, give me your shirt. And something to wipe up blood from Mariah's wall."

To: Mariah

Told the girls you can't come with us this weekend, and they said pics of the dishy Brit, or he doesn't exist.

I stood up, fixed Dominic, who exited the bathroom pulling his shirt over his head in preparation to give it to Stefan, with a look that warned him I was at the end of my rope. "The water turn off is under the sink and next to the toilet. Please turn both off before you go to the hardware store to buy whatever it is you need to fix what you broke."

He hesitated at the door to the spare room, his expression indescribable. "Do I know how to fix things?"

"You'd better," I told him, then turned on my heel and headed for the garage to check on my charges, and removed Bebe bra to snuggle up with her companions in their soft nest of blankets. I considered putting another glider in for more bonding time, but they were all clustered in a ball, so I left them alone.

"We have to talk," I informed Evan when I marched into my bedroom. He stood at the window staring out of it, while a woman's image shimmered on his laptop screen. "Sorry, I didn't realize you were still on a call."

"Not at all. Claudette, this is Mariah. Claudette is my executive secretary."

"Hi," I said, waving at her image. She was not at all what I expected as a billionaire's secretary—she appeared to be in her late fifties, had salt and pepper short, curly hair, and wore an eyepatch, which bore the image of a Pokémon character.

"Hello, Mariah, it's nice to meet you. You must excuse my appearance. My doctor insists I wear this for two weeks," she said, gesturing toward the eyepatch. "The Pokémon is courtesy of my kid. Evan, are we finished? I told Leigh I'd be out of here at noon to help her wrangle all those kids at the zoo."

"I had hoped you'd be able to deal with issues in the San Diego plant," Evan said, frowning a little.

"And I told you that my marriage would be over if I left Leigh alone with thirty-two twelve-year-olds," she said. "The issues with San Diego are resolved. You're worrying about nothing. If there's nothing more, I'm going to go while I still have a wife who will speak to me."

"That's fine. Be sure to send me any responses you get from the Mexican firm. I told them they have until the end of the day to fix the soldering problem. If they don't, we'll dump their contract," Evan said, turning when someone tapped on the door. "Yes?"

I felt like I was caught up in a whirlpool of activity, a sensation that had stuck with me the entire sixty-three minutes that Evan and gang had moved into my home.

Dominic opened the door, glancing over his shoulder. "Dude! Just get in the car, already. Hey, boss man, I'm taking Stefan to the local walk in. He's, like, bleeding out, and insisting that it's just a minor cut."

"Holy shit—" I pushed past him to find Stefan standing with a stoic expression that would do a Spartan proud, his left arm wrapped in a now-bloody t-shirt. "Oh my god! I thought you were joking about the blood. Let me call the EMS—"

"I'm fine," Stefan said, flexing his jaw a few times. "It's nothing. Nic is overreacting."

"Let's get you to a hospital," Evan said, giving his bodyguard an assessing look. "You probably need a few stitches."

"I'm fine, I tell you," Stefan protested as I opened the door, torn between helping him to the car and calling the paramedics. Knowing that it would take a while for them to get to me, given our rural nature, I decided it was better for the men to go to the nearest hospital.

"'Tis but a flesh wound,' I know," Dominic said.

I stood in the doorway and fretted for a minute while the two men got Stefan loaded into the car, then

Evan and Dominic spent another half minute talking before the latter got in the car and drove off.

"Is he OK?" I asked, worried that Stefan had hurt himself badly. "I feel terrible that he hurt himself the second he got here."

"Nic says he'll be fine, and he's had some experience with first aid. He used to be a lifeguard and did several courses in emergency care. He said I should stay here and apologize to you for the state of the bathroom and the blood on the bedroom wall." Evan's lovely eyes were filled with worry and something that looked like embarrassment.

"That doesn't matter in the least, although I should go make sure that he turned off the water before the bathroom is flooded. I'm just sorry that your friend—bodyguard—got hurt."

Evan shrugged and followed me when I went to check the bathroom. Dominic had evidently found the water shut-off, because other than a bunch of wet towels stacked in the sink, there was no water spewing out of either the toilet or faucets. "They are friends more than bodyguards, although they are both excellent in the latter role. After my sons were kidnapped, Stefan convinced me I needed him to watch out for me."

"That would explain a lot. They didn't seem to be very, 'Yes, Mr. Armstrong,' and 'Instantly, Mr. Armstrong,' when talking to you."

I peeked into my spare room, sighed at a smear of blood on the wall, and went to the kitchen to get some cleaner and a sponge.

Evan gave a short laugh. "The day I hear Stefan say, 'Instantly, Mr. Armstrong,' I will expect hell to freeze over. Now, let me see what he was doing when he hurt himself."

"Are you handy that way?" I asked when I returned to the room with cleaner and a few rags to wipe down the wall. He sat on the floor surrounded by slats of wood, metal frames, and what seemed at least a hundred screws and bolts.

"Not in the least, but someone has to do it, or they'll be sleeping on the floor tonight." He looked up, his gaze catching mine, and leaving me feeling as if someone had just whomped me in the stomach. "Speaking of the sleeping arrangements, I realize I didn't give you much choice about me being with you. I wanted to assure you I will respect any boundaries you set regarding the use of the shared bed."

"Still living in fear of your mom smiting you for getting a bit touchie-feelie?" I asked, my inner narrator scoffing at the idea of him not applying his entire body to mine the second we hit the bed.

He made a face. "Always. She was a force to behold, and I don't for one minute believe she'd let death stop her from setting me straight if she thought I was misbehaving."

I laughed, and left him to the job of sorting out the bed situation, telling myself that he was a delightful man, and if I wasn't careful, I might well fall head over ass in love with him.

Nine hours later, I knew that I'd made a mistake.

I lay flat out on my bed, exhausted even though it was relatively early.

I'd spent the last hour cleaning the rescue room, feeding everyone, and breaking up a minor scuffle when Ward, the dominant male of my family cluster, took umbrage with one of the younger males. But when I found myself just standing there watching the sugar gliders as they zoomed around on faux tree branches, pouches, nests, and arboreal canopy, I realized I was stalling.

"You're not a coward," I told myself as I clicked off the light, flipping on a small nightlight that would mimic the light of the moon, and making sure the windows were locked, returned to the house.

It was empty of everyone...but Evan.

"Oh. Hi," I said, feeling more awkward than I ever have before, and that included a few days before when Jane Washington told me I was not good match fodder for her precious BMC. "Where are the others? Did Stefan's stitches open?"

Evan, who was stretched out on the couch, looking perfectly at home as he did so, glanced up from the laptop that was sitting on his lap. "Hmm? No, they went out, since I promised not to go anywhere."

"They went out? Sorry." I rubbed my forehead. "I'm doing the parrot thing again. It's not any of my business to ask what they're doing."

"It's no secret. They said that after the day you had, they wanted you to have an evening where you could relax and not wipe blood off walls and floors, deal with plumbers, and chop up tree branches while fighting with your insurance agent.

I looked out of the window. The remains of a willow tree could be seen neatly stacked alongside the driveway. "Yeah, that was odd the way that tree came down. It wasn't even like it was windy. Still, the fence needed to be replaced anyway, and assuming my insurance company gets its head out of its ass, then I should be able to afford it."

"I'd be happy to pay—" he said, his fingers dancing over the laptop keyboard.

"No thanks. It's my house, and my weak-ass tree.

I think I'm going to go to bed." The second the words came out, I froze, blushing madly.

"Ah." Evan looked up at that, and I had to fight my body to keep from throwing myself on him. His hair was mussed, his bare arms nicely muscled without going into the zone of bodybuilder, and his bare feet bobbed on the couch to something that only he could hear. "It's that time, is it? Mariah, I want to reassure you—"

"I know, you won't jump my bones unless I give you permission."

"That's right." His eyes, now studying my face, seemed to see far more than I liked. "You're tired. Go to bed. I'll join you later, but you needn't worry I will disturb you with any unwanted attention."

I forced my feet to move me into the bedroom, saying under my breath, "Oh, they are very much wanted."

It took a long, long time for me to fall asleep despite the stress of the day. My body felt itchy all over, like I'd been dipped in salt water and dried under the sun. Not even a steaming shower before I crawled into bed helped. I lay on my back staring up, watching the streetlight dappling the ceiling through the trees, wondering how I was going to survive a week with Evan.

I knew the minute he got into bed with me.

The dip of the mattress when he climbed in woke me from a light sleep, causing me to lift my head and look over my shoulder.

"Did I wake you?" the dark silhouette asked as he froze. "My apologies."

"It's OK. I'm not a particularly heavy sleeper." I put my head down, my back to his side of the bed. He slid the rest of the way in, pulling up the light blanket and sheet.

"Ah. It's a good thing that I don't snore." He moved his legs, one of them brushing mine. "Sorry. That wasn't intentional, in case you think I'm making a move on you. I know you're tired and not...er...interested."

I lay frowning into the darkness for a few minutes. I wasn't interested? Was he insane? Was he playing some mind game with me? I gave a mental head shake. He hadn't given off that vibe at all. I rolled over and stared at where he lay on his back, his hands beneath his head. "What?"

"What what?" he asked, his silhouetted head turning toward me.

I clicked on the bedside light, pulling myself up so I was sitting. "You said I wasn't interested in you."

"You aren't." He lowered his hands as he spoke, a little frown between his brows. "I may not be the savviest of men when it comes to reading women—I believe four failed marriages validates that point—but I'm not an idiot, either. You've barely been able to even look at me today, let alone hold a conversation."

I gawked at him, outright gawked, complete with disbelieving, blinking stare, and slightly opened mouth. "Are you insane? You parade around my house all day with your bare arms, and your calves, and your hair, and then you're on the floor wrestling with that bunk bed deliberately flexing your muscles, not to mention when you had to stand menacingly over the asshat plumber who insisted that I needed to pay for a full toilet replacement when it was just the doohicky inside...you do all that, in addition to being a kind to Stefan when he comes back with his arm wrapped, and even made dinner. You made dinner. You made everyone spaghetti, and you think I'm not interested in you?" I was almost shaking with the desire to throttle the man.

He pursed his lips, his eyes narrowed in thought. "I can't tell if what you're saying is good or bad."

"Argh!" I yelled, and couldn't stand it any longer. I threw myself onto him, kissing his chin, and neck and jaw, the whole time I let my hands go wild over his arms and chest. I had no idea if he was naked under the blankets, but his chest was bare, and for the moment, that was enough.

"Ah. I take it that my actions were good. Erm...Mariah, I would love to reciprocate, but you have my arms pinned."

"I know." I sat up. Somehow, I'd managed to roll on top of him, and now I sat with my knees around his hips, my hands on his biceps. "You're in my power. In my house. In my bed. Muhahahah."

He laughed, the little lines around his eyes crinkling in a way that made warm emotions stir inside. Emotions that weren't pure lust, but which had little tendrils that reached out throughout my being, binding me to him. "I don't believe ever enjoyed being dominated more. Do I take it you have changed your mind about having sex?"

I nipped his chin, stroking my hands up his arms just so I could touch his chest. That glorious chest. "There's no changing of mind. I always wanted to have sex; I just didn't want to walk the same path as your many ex-wives. Now, do you like nipple play? Because there are two little rascals right here demanding that I nibble on them, and I fully intend to do so unless that's not something you like."

"I'd much rather nipple on yours," he said, his breath hitching as I swirled my tongue around one of his tiny nipples, teasing it with my teeth.

I stopped and looked up. "What?"

"You're stopping? You're not doing the other one?" He raised his head and looked down at the unmolested nipple. "Has it offended you in some way? If so, I apologize on its behalf."

"Did you say—never mind, it's not important." I eyed the object in question. "I would hate to be accused of ignoring an innocent nip. Incoming!"

He did an odd little shimmy while I was on my knees, kissing and licking the other nipple. I thought at first that he was simply enjoying the way I was touching and tasting his chest—lord knows I was—but when he suddenly bent to the side, then straightened up, a pair of underwear held triumphantly in his hand, I realized he was simply getting naked.

"Oooh. Is it naked time?" I sat back on his thighs, and ran my hands down my breasts in what I hoped was a suggestive manner. "I suppose I could—"

I didn't even have the chance to finish the sentence. He whipped the tank top and shorts that I sleep in off me, and whammo! I was on my back, his body covering mine. "Underwear off or on?" he asked, one hand warm on my hip.

"Well, it's going to have to be off if we want to do anything more than foreplay," I pointed out.

"Just what I was thinking, but I felt it would be polite to ask first."

"Your mom would be proud of you," I told him, lifting my hips so he could peel off my undies. He knelt between my knees, his eyes glittering like a frosty winter sky as he studied me long enough I was shivering with little zaps of desire and mingled worry. "As fun as this is, if you're going to stare at me much longer while you catalog all the bits that show just how fast I'm heading to forty, I'm going to want my underwear back."

"You have nothing to worry about," he said, lifting one of my legs and propping it up on his shoulder. He kissed first my calf, then trailed fire—or so it seemed—up my leg to my inner thigh. I was doubly glad that not only had I fought with a razor to shave my legs that morning, I had also pruned back the pube forest to something a little less exuberant. "Your body is exquisite, and I wasn't cataloging anything other than all the various parts I want to pay homage to with my mouth. Would it be awkward if I told you I like your pubic area? So many women feel obligated to shave off all signs of hair. If that's more comfortable, then I can't object, but if it's not, then I commend you for going au natural."

"Oh, this isn't wholly natural," I said, dragging my nails gently up his back, making him moan. "But I agree with you. Evan."

"Mariah," he said, his head dipping to nuzzle my bare breasts.

"Why are we discussing body dysmorphia and related subjects when we should, at this moment, be making my bed squeak in a manner that I hope and pray your bodyguards don't hear?"

He laughed again before taking one needy nipple in his mouth, making me arch up and clutch his head. "I'm afraid I'm talkative during sexual times. Does that bother you?"

"Not in the least; I'm a chatty Cathy, too. Do the other!"

He obliged, and by the time he was kissing my belly, I was keyed up, and ready to get down to action. I badly wanted to touch him, but he slid lower, his breath steaming my public mound. "Do you like oral sex?"

"Oh, hell yes!" I said in what sounded like a growl

to me at the same time I dug my fingers into his lovely brown curls, tugging on them in a manner that should inform him I was primed and go for liftoff.

"Good. Now, let me see...do you like it when I touch you just here?" One finger slid into me, curling upwards in a manner that had me close to seeing stars.

"Holy Mary, mother of God!" I said, panting and gasping and unable to breathe, all at the same time.

"Excellent. Let's try this, shall we?"

My pulse pounded in my ears as his mouth moved over me, making me teeter on the edge of an orgasm I hadn't known was there. My body tightened, coiled with the race to finish, my heart beating wildly as the muscles in my thighs trembled and tensed.

And suddenly, he was gone. It took me a few seconds to come down from the frustration of the almost-orgasm to realize that not only had Evan removed his person from my pubic area, he wasn't even on the bed.

I sat up, clutching a corner of a sheet that we'd almost pushed off the bed. Evan stood at the door stark naked. I couldn't see who he was talking to since the door was open only a few inches, but his magnificent ass aside, his body language read tension.

And not the sexual kind.

"Gather everything you can. Tell Stefan to stay with them," I heard him say before he closed the door and spun around, snatching up the clothing that he'd evidently placed on top of a low dresser. "Get dressed."

Fear clutched my heart as I scrambled out of bed, my skin prickling with goose bumps. "What's going on?"

"Your garage is on fire."

"Holy—" Terror filled me as I started to run out of the room, but Evan caught me.

"The animals are out. Nic gathered them up as soon as they smelled smoke. Thank god you have those large dog crates."

"It's what I use to transport—shit. On fire? You're sure all the gliders are out? There are six of them."

He looked as grim as I felt. "Yes, all six. Also, some of their food. Get dressed. Stefan called the fire department. We'll clear out what we can from the house in case the fire spreads. Do you have any valuables in this room? A safe? Jewelry?"

"No, everything like that is at the bank," I said, my fingers stiff as I jerked on whatever garments I could find, tears filling my eyes, making it hard to see.

He disappeared, and I followed on his heels, my mind whirling. I ran to the front door, relieved to see a boxy shape at the end of my driveway with the black silhouette of a man lurking with a flashlight.

Dominic dashed past me with suitcases in hand, while Evan was busy stuffing his laptop and papers into the bag he'd used for them.

"Get out," he yelled at me, shoving his bag at me.

"What are you—"

"Getting the last of the important things. Go check your animals. Dominic was as gentle as he could be, but they were obviously upset."

"God, yes!" I spun around and ran, stumbling down the three stairs, but kept myself from falling. I was up the slight hill of my driveway in what seemed like a split second, kneeling before the large plastic dog crate I used to transport my rescues.

"They seem to be OK," Stefan said, handing me the flashlight. I flicked the light over them. They were squeaking, their normally enormous eyes shining in the light, but thankfully, Dominic had grabbed some of the cloth pouches I used to mimic their nests, and all but the two males were snuggled inside. "Flag down the fire department when they come. I'll go help Evan and Nic."

"Get a blanket if you can," I yelled after him, wanting to fuss over the rescues, but unwilling to open the crate in case one of them dashed out. Instead I told them, "You'll be fine. Just think of this as an adventure."

Memory of the next twenty minutes is somewhat blurred. I remember hovering protectively over the sugar glider crate watching as Evan, Dominic, and Stefan hauled out what items they deemed valuable—their belongings, my laptop, tv, and stereo system, and clothing that I assumed they scooped up from my closet and dresser.

By the time the fire truck arrived, I had moved the crate to the far side of the yard, well away from the house, and covered it with a blanket to not only keep the gliders warm, but to shield them from the worst of the sounds.

At one point, Evan trekked across the yard and stood next to me, watching as the firefighters tried to control the blaze, but it had spread from the garage to the main part of the house. I was numb, my emotions having drained away the minute I realized everyone was safe, so I simply stood there and watched my grandmother's house burn.

"They're wetting the trees so it doesn't spread further," Evan said, his voice sounding strained and tired. "The chief says the house is likely to be a total loss."

I nodded, my throat tight with a lump that didn't seem to want to go away.

He put an arm around me, pulling me up against his side. "I'm sorry, Mariah."

"Do they know—did they say what started it? I had an electrician out when I redid the room for the rescues. Nothing should have gone haywire. Not enough to start a fire."

He was silent for so long that I pulled back enough to look up at him. "The chief said that there would have to be a proper investigation, but he suspects the way the fire started at the back corner, it might be arson."

"Arson? Someone deliberately tried to burn down my house? Why?"

"I have no idea. I'm sure the investigators will have more information." His voice was hoarse and rough with more than mere exhaustion. He had tried to get into the garage armed with the couple of fire extinguishers that sat in my kitchen, but ended up getting a lungful of smoke, instead.

"It's the animal rights people," I said, a fact clicking into place in my head.

"Who?"

I explained about the extremists who had just a few days before had burned down another rescue organization and released the animals to the wild. "It has to be them. The parent rescue organization warned me they were in the area. Thank god they didn't get to the gliders to let them loose. I'd never find them all, and they couldn't last on their own."

"It's lucky Stefan was up getting pain meds, or he might not have smelled the smoke before it ended in tragedy," Evan said. "Did you not have a smoke detector in the garage?"

"Yes, I did. I don't understand why it didn't go off unless...crap. Maybe the batteries were dead?" I felt sick at the thought of how things might have ended, and knelt down next to the crate, lifting the blanket enough to peek inside and reassure myself that the gliders were all safe.

They were, but as I straightened up, I was filled with a strange resolve, clear and focused and as sharp as a razor. Those bastards would pay for what they tried to do.

"I hate to mention this, but we will have to go somewhere for the night," Evan started to say, but I interrupted him.

"Marry me."

His expression went from exhausted to confused. "Pardon?"

I clutched the sleeve of his jacket. "Marry me. Give me the money that the BMC says you will pay me when we're married. I will use it to track down those scumbags who tried to harm my little gliders, and will have them thrown in jail."

"I don't think—"

"No, this won't end up like your other wives. Don't you see?" I shook his arm as I spoke, feeling it vital that he understand the new vision that drove me. "You wanted to do something the opposite of what you did in the past. Well, you have. You moved in with me. And now I'm proposing to you. I hate to ask you for the money that you offered because it seems pretty mercenary, but I'll only take the first year's worth. I'll stay married to you as long as you like, but you won't have to pay me. Do we have a deal?"

"No," he said. "Yes. I don't know. I don't really think this is the time or place to make this decision."

I shook his arm again. "Just do it, Evan. Say yes. I swear I'll leave you alone if that's what you want—"

"I don't."

"Then I swear I won't leave you alone. But I will not let those whoresons get away with this. I won't let them hurt other animals in their deranged vision of what is right and wrong."

"Few people can get away with using the word 'whoresons' while proposing marriage, and yet you've managed it." He pulled me up to his chest, my face pressed against his neck. I relaxed into him, ignoring the whomp that came from my roof collapsing down into the shell of the house. "All right, we'll get married. And I will happily provide you with the allowance that we agreed to, but you will not be using that to track down the extremists. I will fund that particular project. Happily, since not only did they risk your animals' lives, those of Stefan and Nic, and destroyed your house, they also interrupted what was about to be an extremely pleasurable evening."

The tears came then as I breathed in the smokey smell that clung to his jacket. I hiccupped into his shoulder and gave myself up to the comfort that his body provided, praying that I was making the right choice.

FOUR

"And which one is this?"

Mariah paused on her way past Stefan, where the latter was clad in a dark blue hoodie. She pulled open the pouch pocket, and peered in. "You have Bitty and Boo. They're siblings, and like to be together."

"And they won't be bothered if I move around?" The wary expression Stefan bore would have amused Evan if he hadn't a suspicion that he bore one that, if not identical, was at least similar.

"Not in the least, especially not after the last few days. They dislike this motel." Mariah hesitated, looking oddly unsure of herself. Evan admired the quiet sense of competency that seemed to wrap around her , but found her sudden vulnerability reaffirmed his decision. He was right to want her in his life.

She clearly needed him to protect her from self-doubt, he told himself, ignoring the fact that she didn't seem to be overly blighted with such emotions. She needed him, and he would rise to the challenge, not letting this relationship go the way of the others.

"If they are bothering you, I can put them back in their crate," Mariah told Stefan, frowning at his hoodie.

"I just thought they would benefit from a little bonding time, but if you are uncomfortable hauling them around—"

"Not at all," Stefan said, one hand protectively over the pocket. "I can't even feel them there. I just wanted to make sure I wasn't going to give them motion sickness or something by moving around."

"Oh, no, they're fine with you doing whatever is normal, so long as you don't go extra energetic, or press them against anything." Mariah answered.

"I think mine are already asleep," Nic said, one hand caressing the front of his t-shirt. Mariah had slung a soft cloth bag with a long strap over his head, and tucked it beneath his shirt, telling him the sugar gliders liked pouches.

"Possibly, although if you feel them moving around, you should check on them. They have a hard time pushing the top of the bag out of the way if they want out."

"Are they likely to do that?" Nic looked mildly alarmed. "I don't want them to get away."

"No, no, they should be good and sleepy. They were super active last night," she reassured him, glancing around the room.

"As I well know," Evan said, pulling out the top of his shirt in order to look down at the little brown and grey blob that was curled up in the soft fabric pouch that hung between his pectorals. His temporary guest was named Ward, Mariah had told him, and was the dominate male of the group. Evan felt a moment of pride that she chose him to host the leader of the sugar gliders, but that pride soon faded into rampant frustration—sexual, practical, and emotional.

"Sorry," Mariah said, gathering up her purse from the motel bed, and looking around.

He had a feeling she wasn't really seeing him, and felt a moment of petulance over that, then sighed, reminding himself that not only had she had a fright about the welfare of her charges, she had lost her family home.

He just wanted to get the legalities over with, so he could take her home, where he could breathe easy again. "There's no need to apologize. They're nocturnal, so it makes sense they would be active at night. I'm just sorry that they didn't allow us to...er..."

She gave him a quick smile, but he noted the way her eyes glittered at him, and that gave him hope.

He'd had a horrible fear for about five seconds that she was using him solely as a method of revenge for the group that had burned her house, but even though they hadn't been able to engage in lovemaking what with dealing with the investigation, taking care of sudden business matters, and Mariah making sure her charges hadn't suffered from their experience, he knew the truth.

She was a warrior, but even warriors needed help.

She needed him. Warmth blossomed deep in his soul, filling him with a righteous sense of happiness that had been lacking from his life.

This time, he was going to get it right.

Four hours later, he concluded the tour around his house by flinging open one of the double doors that led to his private suite. "And this is my room. Erm...it can be yours, too, if you like. Or if you feel like you need your own rooms—"

"Wow," she said, stopping in the middle of the bedroom and looking around with the same wide-eyed gaze she'd worn ever since they had arrived at his house. "You have a view of the lake. Is that a fainting couch?

I've always wanted a fainting couch. Holy shitsnacks, you have a bedroom deck?"

"It came with the house," he said, a faint worry niggling at the back of his mind, eroding bit-by-bit the sense of pleasure that had followed bringing her home.

"Is this the bathroom?" She opened the door to his dressing room, and stood silent for a moment, taking in the racks of suits, shirts, and trousers.

"The bathroom is through there," he said, pointing to a connecting door.

"Mmhmm."

He held the door open for her, the faint worry growing stronger with each moment.

"This bathroom is bigger than my apartment that I had before Gran died," she said, doing a slow spin to take it all in.

"I feel like I should apologize," he said with hesitation, his happiness leeching away at the lack of expression on her face. That she showed every emotion was one of the things he enjoyed the most about her, and now he felt like she was shutting him out, pushing him away because of who he was. "But at the same time, I am having a fairly defensive reaction. One that wants to say you knew who I was when you signed the agreement."

She turned to him, reaching out, the warmth of her palm on his forearm reminding him just how badly he wanted to get her alone. "Oh, Evan, I'm sorry. I'm acting ungrateful, aren't I? And it's the furthest thing from the truth. I'm just...wow, your house is big. I'm not quite sure how I'm going to fit into your life."

Evan felt for a moment like someone had punched him in the solar plexus.

Mariah sighed, and her shoulders slumped before she carefully positioned herself so that she could hug his side without pressing her breasts into him, or disturbing Ward, who was sound asleep against Evan's chest. "I didn't just say that. Please tell me you didn't hear me. Please tell me you can strike from your memory me being insensitive and ignorant and something else that starts with the letter I, because I like alliteration, but still feel like an idiot complaining about you having a big house. I like your house. I like you more. I want to be here with you. I want us to have the relationship that we both need. It's just…oh, I don't know. I'm not making any sense, not even to me."

"I understand, although I don't blame you for being confused by the last few days. They have been filled with turmoil," he found himself saying, and to his surprise, it was true. He did understand. Her whole life had been upended, and now here she was in his world, in a home that was unfamiliar, and she was worried about not only the welfare of the sugar gliders, but of herself. Her life with him. "I don't want you to be ex-wife number five, either, you know. I wouldn't be pursuing marriage with you if I thought this was going to go the same way as the last one." He stopped and made a face.

She lifted her head from where she'd been resting it on his shoulder, giving a whisper of a giggle. 'Good, because I'm not at all the kidnapping type. And I'm ridiculously grateful that you seem to know what I mean, too, instead of insulting you by treating you like the very same sugar daddy I said I didn't want. Except, of course, for the money we agreed upon."

He laughed at that, mostly because it tickled him to see the light of revenge light up the little flecks in her eyes. He had every intention of helping her bring to justice the people who burned down her house, but he would broach that subject at the appropriate time. Right now, he had to focus on getting his warrior settled. "What can I do to make you feel better about living here?"

She looked up in surprise, her emotions once again visible, which in turn provided him with a sense of relief that she wasn't going to change. "I have to get the furry kids settled, but after that..." She bit her lower lip, drawing his attention to her mouth. He loved her mouth. He loved the curve of her lower lip, loved that she said things he didn't expect, and especially loved the fast smiles she shared with just him. "If I said steamy, sweaty sex, would you think the worst of me?"

"The only reason I am not, at this moment, stripping you naked and flinging you onto the bed so that I can bury myself in you is that we are each hosting small animals that would no doubt protest such actions. So, let us go put them in their temporary home, and then we can get to the steamy lovemaking, all right?"

"Deal," she said.

It took almost an hour before Mariah was comfortable with the large cage setup he'd had rigged up on one side of his garage, pointing out to her that his security system would keep them safe. "The garage is heated, has a separate ventilation system from the house, and cameras that monitor everything inside and out. If anyone goes near Ward and his family, we'll know about it."

"OK, but I'm going to have to find somewhere else to house them, because you do not want them marking their stuff in the presence of your fancy cars." She entered his bedroom and paused again before shaking her head. "Where did you put my things?"

He pointed to the dressing room.

"Thanks. I'll...er...just...you know...get ready for...
uh..." Her shoulders slumped again, and she made a
face. "I am such a boob sometimes. I mean, you had
your face in my crotch. Why is this so hard?"

"I know exactly why it's hard, and that's because
I've spent the last two nights in a hotel room with Stefan and Nic instead of you." He gave her his best leer,
pleased with the way her eye sparks answered him.

"Trust me, you did not want to be in a confined
space with my little hellions. I just hope to god the
hotel people appreciate me duct taping tarps over the
entire room so that the pee smell didn't permanently
permeate their furniture. Right. I'll just go get ready for
sexy times." She tried to stroll nonchalantly out of the
room, but ruined the effect by giggling.

Evan debated helping her disrobe, but decided that
she would feel more in control if he allowed her the
time and space to get used to their new living arrangement.

Instead, he removed his clothing and climbed into
bed, turning off his phone so that nothing would distract them. He thought long and hard about getting
out some massage oil that he favored, but felt that
was something they didn't need. "Things are exciting
enough as they are," he told his toes, where they bobbed
away under the blanket. "It's not like we need enhancements."

The image of Mariah's body spread out before him
like a sensual smorgasbord returned, making his penis—which seemed to remain in a perpetually partially
aroused state whenever he was around her—throw itself wholeheartedly into the game plan of seducing and
pleasuring her to the tips of her toes and back again.

"I like how you think," he told his penis.

Unfortunately, Mariah entered the room at that moment. She hesitated at the door, glancing around. "Am I interrupting?"

She was clad in some sort of blue-green silky negligee, one that skimmed her body like water. Instantly, he realized two things: first, what he'd thought of as an erection couldn't touch the level of hardness that he was now experiencing as he allowed his gaze to follow the delicious curves of her body. The second was that he was a babbling idiot, because he answered her question honestly. "No. I was just chatting to my penis."

"OK," she drawled, then approached the bed much as an antelope would a watering hole known to be in use by particularly hungry lions. "That's...do you always talk to your dick? I mean, I'm not one to cast stones, because I have this inner narrator who is constantly yammering away at me, but I just put that down to the fact that I used to write stories when I was a kid, and she never stopped talking even after I grew out of the story writing phase. Am I babbling? I feel like I'm babbling. You're just lying there looking perfectly gorgeous, like it's a normal, everyday thing for us to be in bed at five in the afternoon, and yet here I am wearing this expensive thing I bought because I wanted to titillate you. Are you titillated?"

"I can honestly say that my tittle has never been so lated," he answered, flipping back the covers on the opposite side of the bed. "Also, you are babbling just a little, but since you caught me praising my penis for its ability to get hard, I am likewise not in a stone-throwing position. Shall we pick up where we left off a few days ago?"

"Nuh-uh," she said. To his delight, she pushed one of his legs aside and knelt between his knees. "Wow.

You are really... hoo. Just so we're clear on everything, I can do all the things to you did to me the other night, right?"

"Short of inserting anything into my lower half orifices, yes," he said.

She grimaced. "Yeah, I'm not into that, either. The back door, that is. Front door is totally fine. Let's see if your dick deserves all the praise you've been heaping upon it."

"I wasn't actually heaping praise—" Words failed him at the moment when her mouth closed on the head of his penis, her hands full of his testicles. He clutched compulsively at the sheet when she found a rhythm that drove everything from his head but the heat of her mouth, the warmth of her body, and the insensible need to drive her as mad as she was driving him.

He was vaguely aware of the fact that he was moaning non-stop, but when she gently scraped her fingernails along his scrotum, it was too much. Far, far too much. He stood panting over her, desperately trying to control his need to lay her back and slate his lust on her.

"Holy cow, Evan," Mariah said, looking up at him. "That was the most amazing move. I've never seen anyone go from lying prone to standing in a nanosecond, and yet you seemed to pull it off. Did I do something wrong?"

"You did something very right." He panted a bit more at her, hoping his heart would calm down at some point. "But I want to give you pleasure, too. It's my right."

"How do you figure that?" she asked, sitting on her heels.

"It's my house. Tell me if I do something you don't like." He whipped the scanty bit of negligee from her nubile body and possessed himself of her breasts. "I love how you smell. It's citrus."

"I used your soap when I was changing. Not everyone appreciates the aroma of a sleepy sugar glider. Lord, I forgot about your stubble." She arched back when he rubbed his cheeks along the sides of her breasts before scattering kisses along them. "You have the best whiskers ever. They're soft, but just there enough to...oh god, not the thighs!"

"You had your turn. Now I shall have mine," he said in his best villain impression, intent on providing the woman splayed across his bed the most exquisite pleasure he could muster. He paused for a moment. "What do you think of moustaches?"

"Like them on men. Not crazy about them on women unless the woman in question really wants to rock one, and then I'm totally 'you go, girl,' with it," she answered, writhing as he nibbled on her inner thighs, allowing his stubble to gently rub on her flesh. "Why?"

"I was thinking of growing one, just so I could twiddle the ends when I menace you with incredibly steamy sex." He sank a finger into her, praying that she was close to being ready to receiving him, because he honestly didn't know if he'd survive any more foreplay. Her muscles tightened around him as she moaned, her hips moving in a restless manner that he took as an invitation.

"Role play? Are you going to tie me to a train track and threaten to foreclose on my house if I don't marry you?" she asked, wrapping her legs around him as he moved up her body, pulling her hips up and deftly shoving a pillow beneath her ass.

"I'll do anything you like," he said, easing himself into her, wanting to make the moment last forever, while at the same time needing to bury himself in her heat. He made himself stop, trying to claw back the control that was so close to slipping. "Do you have a fever? How can you be this hot? No, don't move. If you move, I won't be able to—"

She thrust her hips up, tightening her legs around his ass, forcing him deeper inside the inferno that was evidently her female parts.

"No fever," she said with a gasp of purest pleasure, her hands on his back and ass cheeks, urging him on. "But you are as hot as...as..."

"As a fever?" he managed to say as his libido took over, driving into her again and again, her muscles gripping him with a strength he wholeheartedly commended.

"What? Are you sick?" she stopped moaning and dragging her nails up his spine, her brows pulling together in obvious concern.

"Who's sick?" he asked, not really paying attention to what his mouth was saying. He was too busy being consumed by the ecstasy that his body was experiencing, while at the same time trying to push her to the same state. "Do you like this?" He lifted her hips and dove in at a slightly different angle.

Her legs kicked wildly. "Good god, yes! Do it again!"

"Please image me twirling my moustache in a suitably dramatic fashion," he said in between panting breaths. "Christ, I'm close. Are you—"

"Sweet mother Mary and all the little saints!" she shouted, temporarily deafening his right ear as her inner muscles contracted around him while at the same time her legs went stiff.

He could take everything but the grip her muscles had on him in the midst of her orgasm. There was nothing he could do to stop his own climax—he simply let it have its way, thrusting into her with short, wild thrusts that ended with him doing a little shouting of his own.

"OK, that was truly epic."

The words drifted over to where Evan lay on his back, his eyes open as he desperately fought to get air into his lungs, and his heart rate down to safe levels.

"Award-winning sort of epic." Mariah rolled onto her side, propping her head up on one hand as she put the other hand on his damp chest. "Do they give out awards for sex? Because if they do, we're entering you in the competition. With me. You don't get to do it with anyone else but me."

By dint of a great effort, he turned his head to look at her, his body sated, his mind oddly filled with warmth and pleasure and something that felt very much like love. "I think I'm falling in love with you," is what he wanted his mouth to say, but what it, in fact, said was, "Are you staking a claim on me?"

She looked thoughtful for a few seconds, then nodded. "Yes. I am. You're mine, Evan. I don't want you looking for wife number five. You have me, now. If you want to get married, we can get married. If you want to just live together in this incredibly large house, then we will live here, although I would like to find somewhere nearby for my animal sanctuary."

"I'm falling in love with you," his mouth finally said. Then, because his mind was as it was, he added, "I could have a building put up on this property for your sugar gliders."

She shook her head, and for a horrible moment, he thought she was rejecting his declaration of his feelings. "I want a proper sanctuary. If I take the insurance money for the house being burned, and add it to my yearly stipend from you, then I should be able to buy that piece of land up north and have it built."

"Is that all you have to say?" he asked, trying to keep his expression neutral, and not at all like that of a man who'd bared his soul without reassurance that the feelings expressed were returned.

"Oh, no, I have a lot to say. For one, I think I'll quit my job. Not that I want to mooch off of you, but I assume you won't be wanting me to kick in for electricity and cable and food, so I won't have to spend all day transcribing medical records. Also, I could help you cut if you had something that was within my wheelhouse. I'm good on the computer, although I don't know anything about the components you make."

"Is that it? That's all you want to say to me?"

She pursed her lips. "I'm sure I will think of other things later, but yes, right now, that's the top of the list."

He stared at her, waiting.

She tried to stifle a giggle, failed, then scooted over until she was partially draped over him, planting a kiss to the corner of his mouth. "Evan, I had the biggest crush on you back when I'd see you marching through your building, exuding sexy intensity and curly hair. You can't possibly think I'm anything but madly in love with you now that I know just what a wonderful man you are."

Relief, happiness, and the blossoming sensation of love filled him, allowing him to relax into the softness of the mattress, holding her close, reveling in everything about the woman in his arms. "Good. We're in agreement, then. You think I'm wonderful. I think you're a warrior. We will be happy for the rest of our lives."

"Warrior?" she asked, tipping her head back to kiss a pulse point.

"You're the bravest woman I know. Well, aside from my mother. She would approve of you. She didn't approve of my first two wives, and wasn't alive to meet the other two. But you—yes, she'd like you. She'd see you are a warrior, just like she was."

"Warrior," she repeated, but this time in a softer tone, clearly considering the word. "I think that's just about the nicest compliment anyone has ever given me."

"I have something else to give you, but it will have to wait," he said, sleep pulling at him despite the fact that it was so early.

She laughed, and patted his penis, which was in repose after having given its all. "I can see that."

He didn't correct her, his mind swinging lazily between thoughts of just how she seemed to complete him, and what he'd do to ensure that she was just as happy as he was.

Two months to the day, he smiled at Mariah as the car pulled off a main road, and bumped its way down an unpaved drive.

"This had better be a hell of a restaurant," she said, clutching him as they hit a pothole. Stefan, who was driving, swore and apologized. "Or I'm going to have to give you new shocks for our one month anniversary."

"Ah. About that." He hummed softly to himself as they rounded a bend, and the car stopped. Ahead was a long, low house, a small barn and a scattering of outbuildings, all surrounded by several paddocks and pastureland. "There's not a restaurant here. That was a ruse so I could give you your wedding present."

"My wedding present? We've been married for a month, and besides, you gave me that pretty emerald necklace as a present."

"Ah, but that was just part of the present. This is the true one." He opened the door and held out his hand for her. She looked from his hand to the buildings. He knew the minute she understood what he'd done, because she whooped and leaped out of the car, flinging herself on him.

He lifted her up and twirled her around in the best romantic comedy manner, then set her back on her feet when she peppered him with questions.

"You bought the land? For me? This looks bigger than the one I picked. Is that house included? How much land is there?"

"Yes, yes, it is, yes, and eighty acres." He pulled out the papers and handed them to her. "I bought it, but once you sign these, it will all be in your name."

She glanced at the papers, her eyes widening. "Ray Animal Sanctuary. Oh, Evan, that's the nicest thing that anyone has ever done for me. I just feel bad that it's so far from Seattle. It took three hours to drive here—"

"If you flip the page, you'll see the architect's plan for a new house. One large enough for you and me, and my boys when they visit, Stefan, Dominic, and a housekeeper. We'll build another smaller domicile for any staff who you want to live here. And then there are the animal buildings—"

His arms were full of his fifth—and best—wife; his words stopped by her delicious mouth as she kissed the breath from his lungs.

And for the first time in a very long while, Evan truly felt he was home.

CHERISH

ONE

"You are, hands down, the single worst loss protection employee I've ever had."

"Flattery will get you anywhere," I said flippantly. I knew that doing so would drive my boss, Terri, into a full-fledged rage rather than just the pissy mood she was in now, but she'd had it in for me for the entire two years I'd been working at the store.

"What did you say?" She whirled around from where she'd struck up a dramatic pose next to a potted palm.

"Was there anything in particular you wanted to address?" I asked, tired of the corporate environment, tired of the job, and tired of being Terri's personal punching bag. She called me into her office on average once every week to yell at me for perceived slights, writing me up for the most asinine things, most of which were so trivial that HR simply told me to ignore it and do my best to comply with her wishes. "I should have been on the floor six minutes ago."

"I will not stand for insubordination!" she all but screamed at me, leaning on the desk, fury twisting her face. "You will apologize to me. Now!"

It took me a good seven seconds to make my mouth comply. "I'm sorry if I offended you by asking if there was something you wanted to discuss," was what came out.

It wasn't what she wanted, but I'd be damned if I gave her any more fodder for the perpetual power trip she reveled in. Her eyes narrowed and her jaw worked a few times before she snarled, "Unlike you, I attend to the cameras. There's a group of four teen girls in the couture section. They look like trouble, so get out there and get them in the act of shoplifting."

"Oh, come on. 'Look like trouble'?" I asked, disbelief rife in my voice. "You always say that about teens."

"And I'm always right," she snapped back, stabbing a finger at me. "I can smell trouble, and those girls are it. Now, go do your damned job and catch them!"

I frowned, mentally sighing. There was nothing Terri loved more than catching thieves in the act so she looked good to management, whereas I took the route of stopping crimes before they could happen. "I'll go stop them before they resort to shoplifting."

Terri didn't like that at all. She snarled out an expletive before adding, "You are to watch only until you see them take things. Wait for the video proof of their acts, then nail 'em."

"It's so much easier if I can stop them before they do anything wrong—" I was fully ready to argue as long as it took, but Terri was not one to suffer charity.

"Just get out there and do your job. And don't forget that I'll be watching. You mess this up and it will be my extreme pleasure to have your ass canned."

I said nothing, despite wanting to rant and rave about the vendetta she had against me, and instead reminded myself that my lease was up in a few weeks, and

I had to make a decision about whether I could afford to stay in my apartment or I had to find somewhere cheaper to live.

With that thought in mind, I swallowed my pride, and went out to do my job.

Ten minutes later, a conversation caught my attention as I was lurking around the women's wear. It had taken me a while to track down the group of girls Terri had ordered me to catch, but at last I found them in a small alcove dedicated to cruise apparel and beachwear. I moved into the area that held four girls who looked to be in midteen years, and pretended to eye a rack of beach cover-ups.

"What do you want me to say?"

A girl who was almost as tall as me, and definitely on the curvy side (also like me), asked the question of the other three.

I kept my head down as I shifted to the side and pulled out my phone, making "mm-hmm … no, not in that size" murmurs to no one while flipping through a group of linen tunics. That, plus the fact that I looked innocuous as hell, had the girls dismissing my existence.

The two skinny ones didn't even bother lowering their voices. "Whatever you want to say," Girl A answered with a roll of her eyes, adding in a much put-upon tone, "You need to own your own shit, OK? I can't do it for you."

"We can't do it for you," parroted Girl B. "So just do it."

"This is stupid." The fourth girl, who wasn't as curvy as the first, nor as cheerleader svelte as the other two, glanced worriedly at the three others. Her voice dropped to an almost inaudible level. "What if we get caught?"

The way her shoulders pulled up, and the protective manner she was holding herself in, set off several mental alarm bells.

"What about green?" I asked my phone, praying I wouldn't get a call while pretending to be speaking to someone. I pulled out a hideous sage blouse covered in rhinestones. "They have green."

"You won't if you do what we told you to do. Cat will take care of the camera, and we'll block the aisle. So just do it."

"Pink?" I gave a little shake of my head, shifting so that my back was to the girls. Unfortunately for them, I could see their reflections in a glossy chrome wall panel bearing the logo of the store. "I'll look."

The first girl shot me a curious glance, but was evidently satisfied that I was nothing but a boring adult who wasn't paying the slightest attention to them. "It'll be OK, Rory. No one will see."

"I still think it's stupid," the fourth girl repeated, her body language screaming unhappiness and subjugation.

"No one's making you do anything," Girl A said, admiring her nails. She had a manicure that probably cost as much as my day's wages. "This is all you. You said you wanted to join our mastermind. Everyone in it has to undergo the ritual, or else you don't get in."

"Everyone," Girl B said, nodding. The two of them were side by side, obviously physically intimidating the fourth girl. The chrome panel didn't let me see expressions with much accuracy, but I thought it was interesting that the first girl didn't appear to be either intimidated or nervous.

"Here, I'll send you a picture," I murmured into the phone, and made a show of taking a picture of the blouses.

The fourth girl said something, but I didn't catch what. I did watch in interest as their reflections split up, Girls A and B moving to the entrance of the alcove, while the tall girl moved over to where a camera covered the entire area. With a quick glance around, she peeled off the hoodie tied to her waist and threw it toward the camera. It took her three tries before she managed to get it to hang precariously over the camera; then she turned and made shooing motions at the fourth girl. Just in case the store's other cameras didn't catch everything, I turned on my phone's video recording, and put my hands behind my back as if I was contemplating a rack of extremely ugly palazzo pants in various shades of dirt.

The fourth girl looked around, obviously working up her nerve, and with a quick gesture snatched up a couple of swimsuits and stuffed them into her bag.

"I really wish you hadn't done that," I said with a loud sigh, turning to face the girls as I did so. Two of them bolted before I could do more than take a step forward. Luckily, the other two seemed to be frozen with fear. "It's just going to make all of us miserable. Come on, ladies. I'm afraid I'm going to have to detain you."

Thirty seconds later, I had a firm grip on both girls' shoulders and was marching them toward my office while alerting the security team that the two others had attempted to escape, and to watch for them at the exits.

"What—what's going on?" the fourth girl kept asking me, her voice quavering and thick with tears. "What's wrong?"

"Let's save the discussion until we're in my office, all right?" I kept my tone firm, but I couldn't help but feel empathy as the girl crumpled up on herself and sobbed the entire way to the back area of the store.

It took ten minutes to calm her down enough so she could give me her name, address, and parents' names.

"I didn't mean to do it," she repeated for the twelfth time, taking the fresh box of tissues I slid her way. She'd gone through the one that sat on my desk for just such a situation. "It was a stupid dare. The As said the only way I could join the mastermind was to—to—"

"Shoplift," I said, since she once more dissolved into tears.

She nodded, her body rocking in the chair as she clutched tissues to her face.

"The As?" I asked the first girl. She sat in the chair looking distressed, but I realized with a start it wasn't concern for herself, but for her friend Rory.

"Angel and Astley," she answered, giving me a curious glance. "It's their mastermind."

"Are you in it?" I asked, wondering about her. She seemed relatively calm, but her gaze kept returning to her friend, although she made no move to physically comfort her.

"Yeah." She made a face. "I don't know what a mastermind is supposed to be, but Angel says it's a coming together of consciousnesses. Or some such crap. Rory wanted in, though, and since—" She stopped speaking, biting off the last word.

I didn't need to hear what she left unsaid. Rory Tellison showed every sign of having been bullied.

"You said your name is Cat Tomas," I said, tapping on the keyboard to enter information into the theft report. "Is Cat short for Catherine?"

"Caterina."

I made note of it, then asked, "Parents?"

"One," she answered.

I shot her a quick look to see if she was being a

smart-ass, but her expression was placid. I kept my gaze steady on her, saying nothing. It was an effective tool against those who thought they could bullshit their way out of repercussions.

"My dad," she answered after a good forty seconds of silence. "I don't know where my mom is. She dumped me on Dad when I was a little kid."

"I'm sorry to hear that. And your father's name?"

"Izán Tomas."

"Ethan—" I said, typing.

"No. Yes. It's pronounced like Ethan, but it's spelled differently." She spelled the name for me, making sure I put in the accent mark. "My grandparents are Spanish."

"Are they," I said politely, wondering why the name sounded vaguely familiar.

"Yup. Dad was born here, but only because my grandma was visiting her sister's family. Grandpa was pissed, but Dad says it's all good because now he's a US citizen, so we match. Can we go?"

I typed in a brief summary of the event before looking up at the girls. Rory had stopped sobbing, but looked as miserable as a person could. Her face was red and blotchy, her nose was running, and she had an air of fragility that made me feel like the biggest bully in the world.

And I really, really hated bullies.

"Do you think it's as simple as that?" I asked Cat.

"I was kind of hoping it would be," she said, wrinkling her nose and looking wholesomely winsome.

I hardened my heart. Loss prevention may not be the greatest job in the world, but it allowed me to survive. "I'm afraid it's not that simple. You girls were caught stealing. Unfortunately, your friends got out before security could find them, but that doesn't mean you are off the hook. In this situation, police are called, a loss report is filed, and then your parents are notified to pick you up."

"My parents will kill me," Rory said, and lurched forward to a small plastic trash bin, where she vomited, then collapsed on the floor in a ball, sobbing again.

My shoulders slumped.

"Rory's parents are kind of religious," Cat said, picking up the box of tissues and handing it to her friend, moving over next to the latter while she rocked and cried. "Can you—maybe you could pretend I was the one who stole the swimsuits?"

I started to shake my head, but Rory retched again.

My heart ached for the girl, but I reminded myself that I had a job to do, and Terri would make sure I followed the rules.

One glance at the wet, sweaty, red face of Rory, and I regretted having ever left the teaching job I'd dumped after getting zero support from the school district with regard to bullying. "I'd let you go with a warning if I could, but you guys were caught on camera." I gave Cat a long look. "The one you didn't cover. And with video evidence backing up the store's policy to prosecute all shoplifters, my hands are tied."

"But ..." Cat glanced from Rory to me. "I'm just saying to blame me, not Rory. I can take it, but she can't."

I was shaking my head before she stopped speaking. "Even if I did agree to do that—and honestly, I can't; it's illegal, and I could lose my job—I'd still have to call your parents."

"Yeah, but if you wrote down that I stole the suits, then you'd just have to call my dad, right?" Cat offered, a distinctly wheedling tone to her voice.

"Both parents will be called." I felt like a monster saying the words.

She glanced at her friend, who was now curled in a ball of misery on the floor. "But her parents would think I did the stealing. I could tell them that Rory tried to stop me."

A faint headache started in my forehead, causing me to pinch the bridge of my nose. "You'd still be in trouble," I pointed out, about to continue when she interrupted me.

"That's OK. My dad's always pissed about something—he's Spanish, as I said, and his side of the family are so drama llama—but he won't threaten to not let me go to Cabo, which Rory's parents would do."

"They would. They will," the ball of misery that was Rory said from the floor. "They won't let me go anywhere until I'm thirty."

I fought the smile that wanted out in response to her maudlin tone. I glanced at the report open on my screen. I knew what I should do. I reminded myself that I hadn't forced these girls to steal—they'd made that choice on their own, and they had to learn that their actions had consequences.

Like you never made a stupid choice because you were bullied, the honest part of my mind pointed out.

I hesitated, torn between compassion for Rory and the knowledge that entitled teens turned into entitled adults.

"Did you—ah. Good." Terri threw open the door with so much force it bounced back and almost hit her. "Glad to see you acted like a responsible employee for a change. Wait, why are there only two girls here? There were four! I saw them on the camera!"

"Two got away before I could—"

"That is unacceptable!" she almost screamed, then obviously managed to get a grip on her temper. "I will address your lack of control of the situation later. Have you called the police yet?"

My spirits, already depressed due to the situation, sank even further. "No. I didn't think they were needed. The whole thing was really nothing more than a dare, and I think—"

"You're not paid to think. You're paid to catch thieves," she snarled, shooting a glance filled with smug pleasure at the two girls. "Call the parents, then the cops. I'll expect your report on my desk within the hour."

The silence that followed her departure left me slumping in my chair.

"I don't like her," Cat said, glancing at the door before turning to face me again. "She's just mean."

I would have loved to add my own opinion, but swallowed it down to study the two girls before me. My heart broke for them, but my back was up against the wall. "I'm sorry, but I'm going to have to talk to your parents."

"Please." Cat slid down to her knees next to her friend, her head bobbing above the top of my desk.

"What are you doing?" I asked, startled.

"Begging," she said, and clasped her hands before her in a seriocomic attitude. "You can call my dad, but please blame me for this and not Rory. I swear I won't let her get into trouble again."

"And what about you getting into trouble?" I asked, surprising myself by considering what she was asking, really considering it.

I knew I'd lose my job if Terri found out, but I couldn't see the purpose in ruining these two girls' lives over what amounted to an act of bullying.

"Oh, I never steal," Cat said, her gaze forthright and as innocent as a newborn. I didn't believe it for a minute. "It's part of my code of conduct. My father is very big on personal codes of conduct. I don't steal, I don't take anything for granted, and I own my mistakes. Dad is a bit deranged about owning mistakes, too, which means he's constantly beating himself up for making a bad choice with my mom. At least, that's what Denny says. Denny is my therapist. Denny says that Dad also has trust issues."

"I'm willing to bet he'd also have an issue with you discussing such intimate details with a complete stranger," I pointed out, amused. Despite the situation, there was something open and honest about Cat that appealed to me.

"Yeah, but I'm doing it to show you how real and sincere I am. Denny says that people relate to real and sincere, and I want you to relate so that you do what I'm asking—begging—so that Rory can go with me to Cabo in a month. Is it working?"

"Cabo?" I asked, pretending to be confused.

She cocked a knowing eyebrow at me. "Is my sincerity wringing your heartstrings?"

"Sadly," I said with an exaggerated sigh, "it is, but only because I'm so wholly against calling the cops on underage kids, not to mention your two friends who instigated the whole thing, then ran off leaving you to face the music. Right. I'll do this for you, but if I see either of you in this store in the next six months, I reserve the right to revoke my heartstrings. Deal?"

"Deal," Cat said with a cheeky grin, and nudged her friend. "Stop crying, silly. Ms. … er …"

"Bela Turner," I said, then put my fingers back on the keyboard. "What's your father's number?"

She gave it to me. I filled in the rest of the incident report, changing the culprit from Rory to Cat, then printed out a copy and slid it to her.

"Are you sure you want to do this?" I asked, still torn between compassion and my employment security.

"Yup. You want me to sign a statement saying I give you permission to blame me and not Rory?" she asked.

"God, no. That would get me fired in an instant. I just want your word of honor that you are willing to take whatever repercussions come from this choice."

She nodded, and helped her friend back onto her chair. "I am. We both are. Right, Rory?"

"Oh, yes, absolutely. Cat's dad is so nice, and mine is …" She made an odd gulping noise.

"I'll do this on one last condition," I said, eyeing Rory, well aware that what I was doing was extremely unethical.

"Wha-what?" she stammered, her gaze shifting to Cat.

"I want you to talk to someone about what those two other girls are doing to you. A school counselor, or a friendly teacher, or someone in your church, if you go to one. Just tell someone that you're being bullied, OK? Someone you trust."

She blinked a couple of times; then big, fat tears welled up and spilled down her cheeks. "OK," she said, grabbing for the tissue box again.

"Right. Let's get this done, shall we?" I picked up the store phone and dialed the number Cat had given.

"Yes?"

"Izán Tomas?" I asked.

"That is correct. Who is this speaking?"

I don't know what I was expecting Cat's father to sound like—I had a stereotypical mental image of a hotheaded Spaniard with a sexy accent—but to my surprise, this man sounded like he'd grown up in a posh section of London, all liquid vowels and very upper-class pronunciation.

"Bela Turner. I'm with Shandlers. I'm afraid that your daughter, Caterina, has been detained after an incident involving the theft of two swimsuits."

"What?" The word was barked into my ear. "That's ridiculous. She doesn't steal. It's part of her moral code. You are wrong, Bela Turner."

"Regardless of her code of conduct, I will need you to pick her up from our downtown branch."

Profound swearing in Spanish followed. Being half-Hispanic myself, I understood enough of it to raise my eyebrows at the level of his inventiveness.

"The depth and breadth of that was impressive," I told him when he ran out of colloquial steam. "But nonetheless, I will need you to come to the security office to pick up your daughter. When can I expect you?"

"Are you Spanish?" he asked in that language.

"No," I answered in English. "My mother was from Guatemala, but my father was from Maine. I'm afraid that I must insist you retrieve your daughter. As she is only fourteen, I can't release her into her own custody."

"That's ridiculous. She's an exceptionally smart fourteen," he argued. "And mature."

I pursed my lips as I eyed Cat. She grinned in response. "Uh-huh. What time can we expect you?"

He swore again, then demanded to speak to his daughter. I handed her the phone, watched with amusement as she chatted with her father.

"Yup. No. Well, it was a dare. I know. Well, maybe—OK. No, not at all. Bela's been nice, so you don't have to. Dad! No! Right." She handed me back the phone with a quirk of her lips. "He says he'll be here in half an hour."

I hung up the phone and studied her for a second. "Why do I have the feeling he was trying to urge you into claiming I had acted inappropriately instead of you?"

Her lip quirk turned into another flash of a grin. "He's very protective. Denny says that it's part of his overcompensation, but I think he's just one of those people, you know?"

The next call didn't go nearly as well. Rory's mother made a big scene on the phone about her daughter betraying their trust, switching immediately to how much she distrusted the girls she ran around with. It took me five minutes just to get her to understand she needed to come down to the store to collect her daughter.

The girls moved over to the couch once the calls were made, and to my surprise, Rory's mother showed up within twenty minutes, spilling ire upon Cat's head when she spotted her, alternating with asides to me about how children raised by fathers alone never turned out good, but luckily, she didn't remain longer than a minute before she hustled Rory off, promising her the lecture of a lifetime for her misguided choice of friends.

"I hope she'll be all right," I said when the door closed behind them. Cat stretched out on the couch, her phone in her hands. "I'm afraid her mom may make it hard for her to go with you on vacation."

"Naw," Cat said with an unworried wave of her hand. "Her mom bitches a lot, but she is impressed by my dad, and Rory's dad told her she'd be crazy to stop Rory from hanging with me."

"It doesn't sound like her mom is overly supportive, although I understand being upset by stealing," I said slowly. "I worry that Rory won't understand that she can't always rely on you or your friends to bail her out of regrettable situations."

"They're not really my friends, despite me being a part of their mastermind. And I told Rory she should go see Denny, but her parents think therapy is stupid. They told her she just needs to pray through her issues like they did when they were her age. Maybe I'll take her with me to one of my sessions, and let her have Denny for a half hour instead of me."

"That's a generous thought, but I'm not sure smuggling her in to your therapist is the answer. She needs to find an adult who has her back."

"Yeah. There's a teacher we both like—Ms. Lisa. She does female empowerment. I'll tell Rors to talk to her."

I glanced at the clock. "I hope your father doesn't intend on holding us up much longer. I really need to get back to the floor."

She set down her phone and studied me. "It's kind of a bad job, isn't it?"

"I—you're very forthright," I said, leaning back in my chair.

"Dad says I take after him in that. He says it's always better to say what you mean. You don't like your job a lot, do you?"

I was a bit taken aback by her blunt question, but decided I could give as good as I got. "Not really, but that is often the case with employment. Sometimes we have to take jobs that we'd prefer not to do. This one isn't great, but really, it's better than my last one."

"Were you a prison warden?" she asked, sitting up, her eyes lighting with interest. "Did you work with hard-core prisoners? Like murderers and bank robbers and terrorists? Have you seen someone in the electric chair? Wait, do we have the electric chair in this state? I know some places shoot you up with drugs to kill you. What do we have?"

"You are the oddest person I've met," I told her, both amused and surprised by her stream of consciousness that she clearly considered suitable conversation.

"I get that a lot," she said with obvious modesty. "So, were you?"

"A prison warden? Not quite—I was a high school teacher, so almost the same thing, but minus the actual death penalty, which I don't believe we have in this state."

"Oh." She apparently lost interest in me, returning her attention to the phone.

I was about to ask her why she hung out with friends who expected others to steal just to be a part of their clique when the door was flung open, air swirling around me, stirring up a stack of papers on my desk and sending them flying.

In the doorway stood the handsomest man I'd ever seen. He was tall—taller than me, which said a lot, since I cleared six foot—with thick blue-black hair that waved back from a widow's peak. His eyes were a startling shade of teal with a couple of black splotches in the iris.

But it was the sense of barely contained anger that hit me like a Mack truck, leaving me blinking and speechless as he strode into the room, pinning me back with those beautiful eyes.

"You are the woman who has accused my daughter of stealing?" he asked, his eyes glittering with teal fire that seemed to do something to my insides.

Something dangerous.

"Yes, I am," I answered, my voice sounding alien, as if it belonged to another person.

"Good." He took two long steps forward with the same grace as a stalking panther, then placed his hands on the desk and leaned forward to say in a dark, menacing tone, "You should know that I take it as a personal affront that you would charge Cat with an act she clearly did not do. I am not a pushover. I will not have her accused falsely, and if you think I will take such actions without fighting, you are not only very wrong—you will find yourself in a great deal of trouble."

"Oh, I think I'm already there," I said, my body coming to life under the effect of his nearness, while at the same time part of my mind went into a full-fledged panic attack. How on earth was I going to deal with this magnificent, dangerous panther of a man?

TWO

Izán Emmanuel Hugo Tomas was not a happy camper when he marched into a downtown department store.

"I could do without this, Jacob," he told the man who was both the head of his personal security team and a trusted confidant. "What with Cat driving off Mrs. Simpson, and your sister-in-law swearing she'd rather submit to waterboarding than tutor Cat this summer, and then there are her actual tutors, people I pay to teach her things that she needs to know."

"Failed you, did they?" Jacob asked, his tone, like his expression, filled with mild interest. But that was Jacob to a tee—he never raised his voice, never seemed to be possessed with the emotions that made Izán feel as if he were an emotional powder keg. A volatile emotional powder keg.

"It's my parents' fault," Izán grumbled, pulling out the slip of paper upon which he'd written the name of the woman who called him. "If they hadn't insisted on having me, I wouldn't be in this situation."

Jacob raised his eyebrows at that, but made no comment on how idiotic Izán was being. And that irritated him even more—he knew he was being unreasonable, but he just couldn't help it. Not when Cat drove him nearly to the point of insanity.

"Maybe you'd better look at that place your mad cousin told you about," Jacob offered.

"Which mad cousin? I have a plethora of them," Izán answered moodily.

"The artist one."

"Oh. Him." Izán considered that idea as the two men wove their way through the large department store, taking the escalator upward to where the administrative offices were located. "Billionaire Marriage Club."

"That's the place." Jacob gave a curt nod. "The one that does all the psychological tests to find the perfect mate for you."

"There is no such thing as a perfect mate," Izán answered, moving his shoulders under the suit coat. His skin felt irritated, like burrs were prickling along his arms and back. "And what makes you think I want another wife?"

"The fact that you've mentioned finding a woman who can take Cat's education in hand every day for the past seven months, mostly." Jacob nodded, lifting a hand in greeting when a person descending on another escalator called out. Izán was always amazed by the number of people Jacob knew, but chalked it up to the latter having worked security in the area for more than twenty years. "Desdemona thinks it's time."

"Does she?" Izán replied, saying nothing more. He had nothing but respect for Jacob's wife, who, due to an accident, seldom left her house. She was a charming, erudite woman whom Izán had known since he was a child, and although she put up with him, he had a feeling she disapproved of his present lifestyle. And that made him feel even more itchy. "I'm just not sure that a wife is the answer. What if she turns out like the first one? What if we don't deal well with each other? What if Cat dislikes her?"

"That's why the BMC place is the answer," Jacob answered as they rounded a landing and continued to the next floor. "They'll take care of all of the figuring out who would work well with you, emotionally speaking. All you'll have to do is show up, meet a bunch of the women selected to match your likes and dislikes, and sign the check."

Izán flinched at the last word. "That's another thing I don't like—it's so transactional. It smacks of the arranged marriages of the past, and if I want that, all I have to do is let my mother have her way. Oh lord. It's June now, isn't it? Damn. She messaged that she's coming out with three more prospects. She'll be here at the end of the month with more women filling my home."

His tone adequately expressed the disgust at the memory of his parent's visit eight months earlier, but Jacob laughed nonetheless. "I sure wish I'd been there to see your mother in action, but when treatment at the Mayo Clinic comes up, you go."

"Of course you do, and we're all glad you did, because Desdemona has been much improved since then. But as for the other …" Izán paused next to a map of the department store and located the security offices at the far end. "You most certainly do not wish you'd been here. Not only was my mother here for three long, interminable weeks—she brought with her two adult cousins, a collection of aunts and uncles, and what Cat called the Battalion of Potential Brides. Three weeks, Jake."

Jacob laughed again. "Like having a house full of gorgeous women who would do anything to make you happy is such a hardship? All you have to do is pick the one you like the most, marry her, and let her take over with Cat."

"Three weeks," Izán repeated grimly as he strode through a dazzling array of women's intimate garments. "They hunted me, hunted me like the prey I was. They followed me everywhere, giggling, and flirting, and batting their false eyelashes in an attempt to lure me into their clutches. No, Jacob. I'm not letting my mother railroad me into a marriage like my first one."

Jacob said nothing, but Izán could feel him thinking things.

That fact also irritated him, until he realized just how idiotic he was being. That was followed immediately by a punch of guilt. "You're right, though. I should let BMC handle finding someone for me. A nice, maternal, competent woman to serve as stepmother to Cat, one who won't bring drama to my life. In fact, a direct opposite of my first wife. Someone … solid."

"What about happiness?" Jacob asked softly as they approached a door labeled SECURITY. "You deserve that, as well as Cat."

Izán's left shoulder twitched as he reached for the door handle. "Romance is overrated. I'll settle for getting along tolerably. Right, let's go see what that out-of-control child of mine has done now."

Jacob said nothing, but Izán knew he was thinking more things. He braced himself, and jerked open the door to the sight of his daughter.

At his arrival, Cat, who had been lounging on the sofa, sat upright and looked pleased to see him. "Yay! You're here."

"I wouldn't start celebrating just yet," he said, shooting her a look that warned of dire repercussions, a dark future, and little hope of escaping punishment. She beamed back at him in a way that always melted even the most hardened of his intentions, and completely negated his attempt to drive home the point that he was the father, and she the daughter, and thus, she needed to heed his dictates.

It was best to take a dominant stance right off the bat. For that reason, he took two long steps forward, then placed his hands on the desk and leaned in to say in a dark, menacing tone to the woman who sat there, "Are you the person who claims my daughter has stolen items from your store? Before you answer, you should know that I take it as a personal affront that you would charge Cat with an act she clearly did not do. I am not a pushover. I will not have her accused falsely, and if you think I will take such actions without fighting, you are not only very wrong—you will find yourself in a great deal of trouble."

Jacob gave a half-laughter, half-snorting sound that had a bubble of humor rising up and making Izán want to laugh. Instead, he donned his most impassive expression.

"Yes, I am," the woman answered. Her voice was the first thing that caught his attention. It was lower than most females of his acquaintance had, reminding him of sultry singers in dark Spanish nightclubs. He narrowed his eyes to warn her that he was not going to stand for any trouble. "But I am also not a pushover, and thus, here we are."

Her voice was husky and low and as smooth as dark water flowing over marble.

It was an oddly erotic voice, one that he felt to the tips of his toenails, but he'd sworn after his cheating ex-wife dumped him for her massage therapist that he would never trust his heart to a woman who could so easily throw it away. That way lay madness, as he well knew.

"The charge against my daughter is ridiculous," he said, firmly quelling the libido that was suddenly interested in the woman before him. He donned his most intimidating frown, the one that sent employees scattering before him, and leveled his gaze at her. "She is not a thief. It is against her moral code, as I told you."

"People don't always believe me," Cat said, nodding as she collected her backpack, and stood up, obviously waiting for Izán to spring her.

He sent her another look, this a bit more effective. Cat sat back down, and heaved a drama-laden sigh.

"I'm sorry Mr. Tomas, but as I said, your daughter has admitted to stealing the swimsuits, and it's for that reason she's being held."

Izán stopped glaring at his child, and shifted the glare over to the woman in front of him. The demand for the release of Cat dissolved on his tongue, and for a few seconds, he felt as if he stood wobbling on the edge of a sinkhole.

The woman's eyes were smoky jade: not a true green, but a beautiful mixture of green and gray that pulled him into their depths. He didn't know if it was the thick chocolate-brown lashes that highlighted the color of her eyes, or the way her dark hair seemed to explode in a riot of curls from a bun at the top of her head, or even if it was the scattering of freckles across her nose and upper cheeks, but her appearance hit him in the gut with the impact of a kicking mule.

"Since she is only fourteen, I opted to call you rather than the police," the woman continued, "although I should point out that store policy very much encourages us to report the thefts to the police, and in fact, my supervisor is going to be very unhappy when I release Cat without doing so."

Her voice was even more erotic than he'd first thought, and his libido ratcheted up several notches as he took in her eyes, and face, and the silky hair that he suddenly wanted to feel slithering across his naked belly.

No! No hair. No belly. And certainly, no slithering.

"I hope this can be a learning lesson to Cat in the folly of giving in to peer pressure," the woman said, cocking an eyebrow at Cat as she fed a few pieces of paper into a shredder. "It's for that reason that I'm going to shred the reports that would go to the police."

He glanced at his daughter to see how she reacted, aware that she had inherited not only his blue eyes and black hair but also his tendency to impulsiveness. He half expected her to at least roll her eyes in a dismissal of the woman's statement, but to his surprise, Cat sat with her hands clasped meekly, and what he imagined she believed was a chagrined expression plastered all over her face.

"I'm very sorry for giving in to peer pressure and stealing the swimsuit," Cat said, making him stare at her in surprise. He knew her character as well as his own, and she was not a thief. "I have learned my lesson, and will never do it again, I promise."

His gaze swiveled back to the woman, who was now standing as she watched him, clearly waiting for some sort of a response. And it was at that moment that he realized he'd been so stunned by his physical reaction to her that he'd been standing there as silent as a bump on a log … and about as charming.

"I don't believe it." The words were out before he could contemplate whether they should be spoken.

"You don't believe your daughter stole a swimsuit?" For a moment, the woman looked faintly sick, but she shot a look at Cat, and squared her shoulders. "You heard her admit to it."

"Yes, obviously it was a false admission," he said quickly, dismissing both the ludicrous idea that Cat could steal and his body's demand that he trot out his charm in order to woo the tempting—if misguided—woman. "What I want to know is, what's going on between you two?"

"Between us?" The woman stepped back, her expression stunned.

"And this is one of those times when I give up hope about you ever understanding me," Cat said, and this time did roll her eyes as she got up and moved over to stand next to the security woman, just as if she was offering support.

Against him, her own father!

"It's an idiotic claim," he told her.

"Yeah, it is, but it was the only thing we could do," Cat admitted, and watched the smoky-voiced woman with what he realized was worry. "And I promised Bela that she wouldn't get into trouble."

"Bela," he said, unable to keep from rolling the word around on his tongue. As a name, it suited her—it was just as mysterious and intriguing and unusual as she was.

A smile flashed across her lips. "You say it just like my grandfather Luis. He was from Guatemala."

"My family is from Seville," he answered without thinking, mentally sorting through possible explanations for what was going on. In the end, he decided the easiest way was to simply demand answers. "Did Rory steal the swimsuit?"

"Yes," Cat answered, pursing her lips at her phone when it pinged at her. "But if her parents knew, she'd be grounded for life, and wouldn't be able to go to Mexico with us. So I had to say it was me."

Izán was many things, but a stupid man was not one of them. He quickly accepted what Cat had done, and moved on to the important point.

Getting to know Bela better.

"And you felt comfortable allowing this?" he asked Bela, a full-fledged mental war playing out over his body's demands concerning her. He badly wanted to kiss her, a fact that shocked him, since he'd never before met a woman and immediately wanted to taste her, and yet here was a woman wrapped in intrigue and sensuality and groin-tightening curves, and all he could think about was kissing her over and over again until her eyes went dark with passion. He cleared his throat, willed away the imminent erection, and tried to focus on something other than his libido. "That seems counterintuitive to the precepts of loss prevention."

To his dismay, her cheeks flushed, and her gaze dropped to the desktop. "'Comfortable' isn't quite the word I'd use regarding the situation; however, I did agree to your daughter's plan, and it's largely the reason I opted not to get the police involved. My hope was that parents of both girls would make it clear to them that a path of theft is not going to end well."

"And yet you lied to me," Izán said, more annoyed than angry. He was all too aware of how persuasive Cat could be, and he had no doubt she'd turned the full extent of her charm onto Bela. "You told me my daughter was a thief."

"That was wrong of me, and I know it. Regardless, it is the course of action I chose, and I stand by it," Bela said, taking him by surprise again. He'd expected her to shift the blame to Cat—where most of it belonged—but instead, her gaze was level on his, clearly braced and ready for more of his annoyance with the entire situation. "The girl in question was evidently being bullied, and I have little tolerance for such things. Plus, it's a swimsuit. Yes, shoplifting is wrong, and all the girls should be punished for their role in the event, but at the end of the day, it's just a swimsuit. As for lying to you … I apologize again for that. I realize my decisions don't excuse my actions, but I hope they explain why I agreed to your daughter's plan to save her friend from more grief."

"I told Bela you wouldn't mind," Cat informed him, her eyes flashing in a way that was far too familiar for his peace of mind. "So you can't get mad at her about it. It's not fair. She's helping us."

"Us?" His eyebrow rose as he studied Bela's face. The red cheeks were returning to their normal shade of tan, the freckles standing out a bit in relief.

Lord, he wanted to kiss those freckles.

"Rory and me," Cat said, still standing defiantly next to the object of his sudden fascination, obviously championing her. "Bela saved us so that we could go to Mexico."

"On the contrary," Bela said, shifting slightly to the side. Behind her, a photo of a horse with a young, green-eyed girl with braids sat in a place of pride. "I did it because I've witnessed far too many examples of how bullying can ruin a child's life. What I did was not right, Cat, but I've found that sometimes you have to do what's wrong for the right reasons."

"Yeah," Cat said, crossing her arms as she met his eyes. "We're righteous."

"That's not what I said—" Bela protested, but was interrupted when Cat, who had turned to look at her, caught sight of the photo that had evidently been hidden from her view. "Is that you? You ride? Is that your horse? I have a horse, too, but Dad won't let me ride him, which is just so unfair, because he says I ride horribly, but he won't teach me, and the woman he hired ran off with money from the stable, and now there's no one to help with Dave."

"Dave?" Bela asked, looking a bit stunned about the eyes. Izán knew just how she felt. Conversation with his child frequently left him in a similar state, and more so with each passing year.

"My horse," Cat told her. "He's a German warmblood gelding, trained for eventing, but Dad said I could do dressage with him if I keep my grades up, only the woman from the stable didn't do more than come out to look at him and talk to Dad about what sorts of things she could teach me. Wait—you said you're a teacher. Do you teach riding? Dressage? Or jumping? I'd love to learn how to do real jumps, not just logs lying around in the pasture. Could you teach me? Dad! Bela could teach me instead of the stable lady!"

"Whoa," Bela said (the unintentional pun amusing Izán), holding up a hand to stop Cat. "Yes, I was a teacher, but I taught high school English and math, not riding. And my knowledge about dressage is limited to what I need for the three-day eventing team I ride with … or, rather, I used to ride with." Her gaze dropped to the desk again, and Izán felt a punch of empathy at her response. Clearly, something had happened to keep her from a hobby that had given pleasure.

He reminded himself the enticing woman in front of him was not his problem or responsibility, whereas the same could not be said for Cat. He needed to keep his mind on her, and what was best for her. "Regardless of what Ms. … er … Turner said, I am not so easily swayed with tales of peer pressure," he told his daughter. "The fact that you would be a part of such a plan is disappointing."

"Hey!" Bela moved immediately to Cat's side when the latter, with drooping shoulders, shuffled over to pick up her backpack and phone from where she'd left them on the sofa. "I appreciate that you think badly of me because of my participation in this situation, but that's no reason to blame Cat. I mean, yes, she was the one who suggested it, but I agreed with it."

"Cat should know better," he said with as much sternness as he could muster, which admittedly wasn't a lot, since his body was attempting to break his control so it could woo Bela as she deserved. Once, he had given in to such an overwhelming passion for a woman, and it ended up with a wife who viewed him as an ATM more than a partner in life. He was older and wiser now. "As should you. You have responsibilities."

He took a step back when Bela exploded in a whirlwind of words. "That's sweet coming from a dad who clearly puts the minimal effort into knowing what his teenage daughter is up to. Maybe if you spent more time with her, you'd know what's going on in her life! And before you protest that you are the best dad who ever lived, I know what it's like to have a deadbeat dad, one who promises you the moon and stars and doesn't even bother to show up, let alone care what happens to you. So you can take that attitude and—" She stopped, blinked a couple of times, and evidently realized what she'd been about to say, because her cheeks turned dusky pink again.

"My dad isn't deadbeat," Cat protested. "He's a good dad. He's always telling me I can be whatever I want, and he doesn't mind at all if I change my mind. And he does spend time with me"—she looked at him, her expression tinged with doubt—"when he can. He's busy a lot, but he always calls if he's not going to be home at night."

"I apologize again," Bela said, her hands on her cheeks briefly before she did the shoulder-squaring again, her eyes so beautiful, it almost hurt to have her gaze on his. "What I said was out of line and I regret it."

"You get full marks for that apology," he said, still struggling to hold back the need to reassure her he wasn't offended. Much. "It was given honorably, and did not attempt to blame anyone else. That said, I would suggest that before you make a comment on someone's parenting or lifestyle, you ascertain the truth first. And now, since we seem to be overstaying, we will leave. Cat, get your things."

Bela was obviously miserable when she said, "Again, I apologize for what I said. My temper got away from me, and as you said, it's not right to make judgments without knowing all the facts."

He acknowledged the apology with a curt nod, and before he gave in to his body's demand to pull her to his chest so he could plunder the rose of her lips, he marched to the door, holding it open but saying nothing as Cat slouched her way out.

"Thanks for everything, Bela," she called from the doorway, lifting her hand to wave. "I'm sorry about Dad. I'll explain it better to him so he's not mad at you."

Izán took a deep, deep breath, turned his head to nod again at the enticing Bela, and resolutely marched out of the office, regret trailing his steps.

THREE

"You're lucky that Vihaan is out of the office today, or you'd find yourself on the street right now." Terri threw open the door to my office, slamming the flat of her hand on the door to emphasize her words, warning she was in one of her rages and making me jump. "Where's the paperwork, Turner?"

"What paperwork?" I asked, my gut clenching despite not knowing why she was so furious.

"The parent acknowledgments from yesterday. From two of the four girls you managed to catch." She panted a little, and for a second, I worried she was going to have a rage stroke. "You only turned in one release form. Where's the other one, Turner? Did you even get the parent's signature, or did you let it go just as you let everything else go? And while you're looking for that, you can just upload the copy of the police report to the server so I can add it to the file."

Oh goddess, the parental release for Cat! In the mental haze that had seemed to roll over me when Izán stormed into my office yesterday, I'd forgotten to have him sign the form acknowledging Cat's actions and the store's policy regarding her.

"I'm sorry," I said, hating to say the words, but my mother had raised me to own up when I did something wrong. "That's my mistake—I neglected to have Mr. Tomas sign the form. I'll give him a call and see if he can drop by and do it today."

She slapped the door again. "And the police report?"

I stared at her for a few seconds, my mind whirling like a deranged wolverine. I managed to get my thoughts in order before she completely lost it on me.

"I'll upload you a report just as soon as I get back from lunch," I said, hoping against hope she wouldn't ask me if I'd sent the police the report. I was happy enough to write it up so long as it didn't actually get sent to the authorities. She wasn't known for her attention to detail, so I prayed the fact that the report was never filed escaped her notice.

"You'll do it now." Her gaze raked scorn down my body, her upper lip curling. "You could stand to miss a meal now and again."

"I do not have to take this abuse," I said, getting to my feet despite the fact that I hated confrontation. But there was confrontation, and then there was being a doormat, and I refused to be the latter. "If I've done something you don't agree with, I expect you to discuss it in a professional, respectful man—"

"Get me the signed release and the police report in the next hour, or you'll be out. You got that? Get your shit together!" Terri slammed the door behind her as she stomped her way down the hallway.

Nausea, worry, and a touch of dread filled my belly until I thought I might burst into tears, projectile vomit, or curl into a fetal ball and sob.

I did none of those, of course. Instead, I tried to calm my madly beating heart and shaking hands, and, consulting my laptop, found the phone number I needed.

"Hello, Mr. Tomas? It's Bela Turner. I'm sorry to bother you, but I was remiss yesterday by not having you sign Cat's release form. Would it be possible for you to stop by sometime today and do so?"

The silence that followed left me wanting to squirm with mingled embarrassment and worry, but at last Izán spoke. "Why should I sign something that isn't true? You admitted yourself that Cat didn't do the stealing."

"She was a part of the group that did, however, and I really do need her release signed," I explained, a bit annoyed even though I knew that wasn't fair. It wasn't Izán's fault that I messed up, although he didn't have to be so obstinate about it. "I'm aware this may seem trivial to you, but I assure you it's not to me. If you're busy today, I can stay late so you can come by this evening."

"No," he said with a finality that had my worry spiraling. Just as I was about to protest—or, more likely, beg—he added, "But if you wish to bring the damned thing here to my office, I'll sign it. Under protest, because I don't like signing my name to a lie, but if it's that important to you, then I will do so." He ended with the address of his office, which I absently wrote onto my calendar.

"Oh. Er …" I thought quickly about my day. As usual, Terri had shoved a split shift on me, so I was working for the next four hours before I had a three-hour break. "I could come around one, if you're available then."

"That's fine, although I have a meeting shortly thereafter, so if you are late, you'll have to wait."

I rubbed my arms against the goose bumps that rippled down them at the intimate sound of his voice in my ear. Although he sounded mostly upper-class English, there was a hint of Spanish inflection now and again. It was an oddly erotic voice, leaving my skin feeling both hot and too tight. It wasn't an entirely comfortable feeling, but then I had the mental image of Izán speaking directly into my ear, his breath brushing my face, and my body turned into one giant erogenous zone.

"Ms. Turner? Are you there?"

"Sorry," I said after wrapping my arms around myself in a desperate attempt to get my emotions under control. "I won't be late. I'll see you at one. And thank you."

There was another silence, but this time, he didn't sound annoyed when he spoke. "For signing a false statement about my daughter?"

The words, "For being you," trembled on my lips, but I managed to keep them back, and simply murmured, "One o'clock, then," before hanging up.

I had planned to leave during my three-hour break and head straight to the address, but but remembering how his voice had felt in my ear, I headed home and pawed through the meager contents of my closet to find something a bit more suited to an office space than the casual clothing I used to look like a shopper.

Exactly two minutes before one, I entered an impressive building a few blocks away from my store, and gave my name to the two ladies at the reception desk. "I'm here to see Izán Tomas."

The nearest woman began typing. "Turner, Turner … I'm not seeing you listed."

I glanced to the right as a couple of men and a woman entered the building, laughing and talking as they tapped their ID badges and proceeded through what I figured must be a metal detector.

"Do you … I'm sorry, this is kind of an out-there question, but do you get people bringing guns into the building?" I asked.

The woman who wasn't at the computer froze in the act of flipping through her phone and turned to look at me. Likewise, the one helping me paused, her eyes examining me.

I pointed at the metal detector. "I've never seen one for an office. I just … er … wondered if you guys got shot up a lot."

"What did you say your name was?" the other woman asked, setting down her phone.

"It's Bela," I said slowly, feeling someone approach behind me. I glanced behind to see one of the security guards that sat at a desk near the metal detector now moving up toward me, his eyes narrowed.

"Crap! I'm not … I don't have a gun. I don't even like them—I'm a pacifist. I was curious about why you guys are worried about them, that's all. Look, I'm totally unarmed," I said, lifting my hands in the best western-movie manner.

I won't go into the next four minutes, mostly because it was so embarrassing that I prefer not to dwell on the fact that I managed to get myself thrown out of a building within two minutes of arriving.

I leaned up against the building, aware of the guard who'd more or less frog-marched me out to the sidewalk now standing just inside the doors, watching me with obvious mistrust.

"I'm so sorry," I said when I dialed Izán and he snapped a, "Yes? Who is this?" at me.

"Bela Turner. Again. I'm sorry to bother you—"

"It's now three minutes after one, and you are late, Ms. Turner." His voice slid over me like water over silk, once again sending a little shiver of delight down my spine. "Despite assuring me you would not be so."

"I know, but—"

"You may not consider punctuality important in your dealings with others," he said in a voice rich with satisfaction. "But I do, and I encourage you to embrace the lifestyle of the prompt and on time."

I grimaced at his tone. "Yes, but I was—"

"As it is, I have a meeting I need to be at in now ten minutes, so I'm afraid I will be unable to await your eventual arriv—"

"I was kicked out of the building!" I interrupted, my ire up. "And much though I appreciate the lecture of punctuality, I would prefer if you told the people at reception that I'm not weird just because I asked about the metal detector. You have to admit it's kind of odd, especially since it looks like that building just has offices in it, and nothing that people would bring guns to, like a jewelry store or maybe something with drugs."

"Many of the larger buildings have metal detectors," he answered slowly. "It is a regrettable sign of our times, but not at all unusual, I assure you."

"Oh." I made a vague gesture that he obviously couldn't see, and cleared my throat. "I didn't know that."

"Where are you?" Izán asked after a good ten seconds of silence. His voice sounded odd, strained almost.

"Outside on the Fourth Avenue entrance," I said, alternating between mortification that he thought I was such a loser that I'd never seen a metal detector before, and amusement because, really, when had my life turned into some twisted form of French farce?

"Go inside and tell Sierra—she's the one with pink hair—to send you up to me."

"OK, but you'd better tell someone you're expecting me, because that guard said if I tried to get back in, he'd have to call the cops."

"My secretary has already called her. Be quick, though, because I'm leaving for my meeting in five minutes."

I didn't wait—I murmured my thanks and, after taking a deep breath, marched back into the building, avoiding glancing toward the security desk, and heading straight for the woman named Sierra who had first helped me.

"Hi. It's me again," I said as she hung up the phone. I was aware of movement to the side of me, assumedly the guard coming back to run me off. "I just talked to Mr. Tomas, and he asked me to meet him in his office."

"That's all right, Bernie," Sierra told the guard, who clamped a hand down on my shoulder. "I just got a call from the Tomas Group. She's expected."

I smiled at the man only after reminding myself he was just doing his job, and accepted the visitor's badge that I clipped onto the front of my sunflower sundress. I'd thrown a pale-peach-colored shrug on to cover my arms, hoping I looked professional enough, but it was with no little doubt in my suitability that I stopped at the metal detector and divested myself of all metal, my phone, and my purse.

A few minutes later I arrived at the top floor, which was evidently taken up by Izán's business.

I stopped in front of a glossy oak desk, and smiled at the young man who was clearly the receptionist. "Hi, I'm—"

"Ms. Turner?" The man nodded toward the wall behind me, which bore a couple of soft butter-colored leather sofas and three matching chairs. "Mr. Tomas is busy, but he will be out momentarily. Can I get you a beverage?"

"I'm fine, thank you." I moved toward the couch, smiling politely at two women who were also evidently waiting for people.

"Hi," said one of the women, a blonde who looked almost as tall as me, although she had a willowy figure, whereas I was of more epic proportions (as my cousin liked to call our shared body type). She eyed me in a manner that left me feeling a bit itchy. "I'm Serena Benson."

"Bela Turner," I said, taking a seat in one of the chairs, my palms a bit sweaty. I wasn't normally anxious around people, but just the thought of seeing Izán again—even if for the few seconds it would take for him to sign the form—had my body reacting with sweaty palms, a heart that beat faster, and decidedly jittery nerves.

The second woman studied me for a few minutes before saying, "You're here for Izán Tomas, aren't you?"

"Yes, I am," I answered, wondering what her point was. "I assume he's a busy man—"

"We're here for him, too." Her expression turned sour, which was a shame, because she looked like a supermodel, her face expertly made-up and her hair a glorious mane of glossy black.

She wore what I thought of as club wear: a bodycon short black-and-red dress with spiky red heels that I knew would cripple me if I ever tried to wear them. "And by 'for him,' I mean just that. The BMC didn't say they were sending a third girl."

"I don't know who you're talking about, but I wasn't sent by anyone but myself. That is, I have something that Mr. Tomas needs to sign."

"Oh, you're a courier?" Serena, the much friendlier blonde, leaned back against the couch and smiled. She, also, wouldn't have brought any shame to a fashion house had they put her on the runway. The two svelte women had me shifting a little in my chair so I could unobtrusively suck in my gut and smooth out the dress I'd put on because I was seeing Izán. "I'm so glad you're not competition. It's bad enough with Kim there looking like she stepped off a cover of Vogue."

I didn't quite know what to say to that, but before I could respond, the receptionist called my name, gesturing to follow him. "If you'll come with me, please."

"What about us?" the woman I assumed was Kim asked, getting to her feet. She actually snapped her fingers when she added, "We've been waiting here longer than her. She's not even a viable client! Why is she getting priority over us?"

"I'll remind Mr. Tomas that you are waiting," was all the receptionist said as he hustled me past the wall that separated the entry area from the rest of the offices, and down the right side of the building to the back, where a set of imposing double doors loomed.

Just as we reached it, the doors opened and Izán emerged, a frown wrinkling his brow.

"We're late," he said, and, not pausing to greet me, simply took my arm and tugged me after him. "I have a very small window of time to speak with this vendor, so you'll have to be patient for a few minutes."

"Mr. Tomas!" the receptionist called after us.

Izán stopped and glanced back.

"The two ladies from the BMC are waiting for you."

Izán looked very much like he wanted to roll his eyes. "Tell them I'll see them as soon as I'm done with Ms. Turner."

"Sorry if I've messed up your day," I said as we continued down a hallway. "I wouldn't bother you if this wasn't important."

"It's not you who is bothering me, but the endless hordes of women my mother has sent my way," he said under his breath, but loud enough he clearly intended for me to hear.

"Your what?" I asked, throwing grammar to the wind. "Your mom is matchmaking for you?"

"Yes." The word was gilded with so much disgust, a giggle rose within me and fought to be released. "It's not bad enough she hired a company to send women for consideration; she is also rounding up whatever eligible women she can find in Spain."

I eyed him. He was so handsome, it almost hurt to look at him. And yet, at the same time, he was completely lacking in anything I connected with male models. He wore a nice suit, but he didn't reek of aftershave, or seem to be wearing any sort of cosmetics. Even his hair looked fairly untamed, and he had no jewelry but a signet ring and a small wristwatch.

I looked at all that, and still shook my head. "I can't believe anyone has to find you women."

"It's a subject I will happily discuss another time," he answered, taking my elbow and hurrying me forward again before suddenly pausing. "I've learned not to make assumptions about how people deal with my personal assistants, but I hope you don't have a problem with them. They are cojoined, and although they insist they are happy to answer questions about their circumstances, I would ask that if you are uncomfortable with people bearing physical differences, you remain in my office until I'm done."

I stared at him for a second, then, without thinking,

whacked him on the arm. "I appreciate the heads-up, because I wouldn't want to offend anyone by looking surprised, but I can assure you that I'm not a stranger to differently abled people. My sister is partially deaf, and our cousin is fully so. Oh lord! I just hit you! I'm so sorry! It was sort of an automatic thing. I apologize if I hurt you."

He seemed to study my face for a moment, then a slow smile curled the corners of his mouth, making me feel like I was standing in a shower of sunshine. "You didn't hurt me, no. Let us proceed."

I followed him into what was clearly a small conference room, now filled with a handful of people, two being the twins in question. I gave them a smile before looking a bit nervously at everyone else.

I had no idea why Izán insisted I accompany him, but the last thing my libido wanted was to hurry him along.

Ten minutes later, we all rose when the video call ended.

"Mr. Somsri says he will have the documents sent this afternoon," a young man who translated the callers' part of the discussion told Izán as he headed for the door, taking me with him. "I'll follow up as soon as I get the specifications."

Izán nodded, and started to haul me across the office (again) but hesitated before shooting me a curious glance. "Have you had lunch?"

"No, but—"

"Good. I missed breakfast this morning, because Cat was having a crisis and needed some things, so I'm hungry. We'll have a quick lunch now; then later we can talk about whatever it is the store wants. Do you have any food allergies?"

"Shellfish," I said, a bit bemused as he spun us around and marched us toward the front of the office.

He shot me a disbelieving look. "In Seattle?"

"I know, I know. It's sacrilegious, but unfortunately, if I don't want to have saucer-sized hives covering my body, I have to forgo all shellfish. Er … not that I want to disarrange your schedule, but all I need is a signature; then I can leave. You don't have to take me to lunch."

"Lunch?" The voice of the clearly annoyed Kim whizzed past me like a bullet as she got to her feet when we emerged at the bank of elevators. "You're taking her to lunch? Is she even registered with the BMC? Ms. Washington told me that this woman and me were the only ones who fit your profile."

Izán swore in Spanish under his breath before squaring his shoulders and turning to the two women. "My apologies, Ms. Boyle, is it? I'm afraid you've been misled as to—"

"And now you think it's OK to disrespect Samantha here and me—"

"Serena," the woman in question murmured, although she, too, had gotten to her feet. She looked decidedly uncomfortable, however, and clutched her purse with fingers that were white around the knuckles.

"—to the point of leaving us hanging around like we're nothing to you, while chicks off the street can stroll in and be taken to lunch. Well, I won't have it! I simply will not have it! I am reporting you to Ms. Washington and the heads of BMC!"

"What's BMC?" I asked Izán in a whisper.

His gaze flickered away. "It's a company that helps people find committed partners."

"Again with the matchmaking," I said in what I hoped was a light, carefree tone, and not at all one that spoke volumes about the regret that solidified in my belly like cement.

"You are very disappointing," Kim told him as she skewered him with a pointed look before stomping off to the elevator, continuing to glare until the door closed on her. "I won't forget this for a very long time."

"I feel like I should apologize," Serena said with a hesitant gesture.

"There is no need." Izán took a deep breath. "Naturally, I would be delighted if you would join Ms. Turner and me for lunch."

"Really?" She brightened and offered Izán a timorous smile before sharing it with me. "That would be lovely."

"I appreciate the offer of lunch, but I just need a form signed—" I started to protest, but Izán interrupted.

"You must eat; you might as well do it with me." He watched as Serena gathered up her things, surprising me when he said in a near whisper, "Unless you have a reason not to, I'd appreciate it if you came with us to lunch."

I stopped the protest I was about to make, catching an odd glint in his pretty blue eyes that made me want to laugh.

And that's how, half an hour later, I looked out at the gray-blue water of Puget Sound from my perch at a popular seafood restaurant that sat on a pier, and felt more uncomfortable than I had in many a long year.

"It's so interesting that you manufacture those memory things, but aren't geeky," Serena was telling Izán. Despite the awkward situation—I very much felt like I was a third wheel at their date—I had to admit that Serena chatted just as much with me as she did Izán.

She was, quite simply, a nice person, and with a little pang of pain I pretended not to notice, I thought how well she would likely fit into Izán's life.

That thought sank my spirits almost as much as the feeling of pushing myself into their company. I dwelled on that for a while, wishing I'd just gotten the signature and left.

Anything would be better than watching Izán's attention focused on Serena.

"And how about you?" Izán asked a few minutes later, turning to me.

I pulled myself out of a reverie in which I skulked in a snowstorm outside a brightly lit window that showed a glowing holiday scene with Izán and Serena and Cat, all happy and content in their joyous familyhood, while outside, I huddled against the sleet and snow, near starvation and frostbite, with just a touch of leprosy to make everything that much worse.

It was maudlin at best, and it took me a few seconds to pull myself from my pity party to look at Izán. "Leprosy."

One glossy brown eyebrow rose. "Your hobby is … leprosy?"

"Oh god." I was horrified for a moment that I'd spoken without thinking, but then decided to just embrace my outburst. It wasn't like I could compare with the nice Serena. "No, of course not—I was just thinking about … er … never mind. What was the question? Hobbies?"

Serena, who had frozen in midbite of sushi, looked horrified.

"Yes, that was the question." Izán leaned back in his chair, and I had the feeling that for the first time since we entered the restaurant, I had his full attention. "But what I'd like to know is what you were considering to toss out that word."

I managed to pull out a smile, even though I wanted badly to go somewhere quiet where I could continue my wallow in self pity. "You truly don't want to know. I'm afraid I'm going to have to leave soon, but that salmon was delicious. Thank you for lunch. If you don't mind signing my form?"

He watched me with an unreadable expression, leaving me feeling alternately hot and cold. "Of course."

"I'll be back in a minute. I just need to ...' Serena rose and made a vague gesture. "I'll let you talk business in private."

It was on the tip of my tongue to tell her she didn't have to leave on my account, but she hustled off before I could do so. I looked back at Izán.

His eyes glittered like pale blue topazes flashing in a clear stream.

"She's nice," I said without thinking, then blushed like mad at my inability to keep a thought unspoken. "I like her."

"Do you? I had rather the opposite impression," he said slowly, his expression still unreadable, but his voice sounded a little stiff.

"You didn't like her? You seem to be getting along great," I protested, then immediately damned my tongue again.

"I agree that she seems to be quite pleasant, but I was referring to the fact that you have barely spoken during the lunch. I assumed you didn't care for Serena's company."

"I'm sorry if I acted to the contrary," I told him, my spirits damp and depressed after the last hour. "But I meant what I said. She's a nice person. Friendly, even."

"But?" he asked, gesturing toward a waiter, who bustled up with a check, pausing to clear a few of our lunch plates.

I eyed him. "But what?"

"That's what I'm asking you. You said she's nice, leaving an implied 'but' that would negate in some way your statement."

"There's no 'but' in this instance," I insisted.

He gave me a long, long look from the corners of his eyes, obviously accusing me of being less than truthful.

And that was the point where I broke. I don't know what pushed me over the edge—perhaps it was the effect of sitting next to Izán at a small table for a half hour, or hearing his delicious voice as he chatted with Serena, or even the way he occasionally brushed his hair back off his forehead.

There was something about the gesture that made my stomach seem to wobble, but it was ridiculous to stay here where I was only torturing myself.

"Look," I said, suddenly pugnacious. I fought down the emotion, not wanting to be obnoxious. "I don't like lying, because I'm so bad at it, so I just tend not to do it. I meant what I said. I think Serena is a very nice person."

He steepled his fingers as he continued to watch me. "So, it's your recommendation that I should have a relationship with her?"

"Sure, if you want," I said after a good half minute's struggle against telling him I didn't give a damn what he did with his fine, fine self, that I hoped they would have long, happy lives together, and finally, that I didn't have any more time to waste bolstering his male ego.

I didn't say all of that, because it wasn't true.

"Gotta run or I'll be late getting back to work," I said, flustered under the continued watchful—and silent—gaze that rested on me. I snatched up my purse and murmured another thanks before bolting for the door.

"Idiot." I swore to myself as I faced several blocks of uphill hikes before I made it to the shopping district. "Now he knows you're a bona fide boob. Oh, god. Could life get any worse?"

Fifteen minutes later when I entered my office to find Terri ranting, I realized it could, in fact, get worse.

I'd forgotten to have Izán sign the damned form.

FOUR

"Cat says you are a former teacher, and has suggested that I ask if you'd be available to tutor her this summer."

Izán's voice nestled up next to my ear, as usual, sent a little ripple of excitement down my back. I paused on my way through the store, keeping an eye on a young mother with a suspiciously growing diaper bag. "Hello, Mr. Tomas."

"Izán, please. I've been thinking of you as Bela for the last few days, since all I hear from my child is 'Bela is fabulous,' and 'Bela is so nice,' and 'Bela is intriguing,' so I can't help but think of you as Bela. I hope this doesn't offend you."

I stared sightlessly at a pair of jeans I'd picked up as cover, so startled I didn't know what to think. "Cat thinks I'm intriguing?"

A slight cough emerged from the phone. "That might have been my interjection, although I'm sure if I asked her, she'd agree with me that you are intriguing."

"Oh, good, because otherwise, I was going to have to talk to her. Er … I'm sorry, that's probably your role, but I've never had someone think I was intriguing, especially a teen, so it's a bit startling. I mean, I like Cat. I don't have a problem with her visiting me, although I'm limited in the amount of time I can give her."

"I believe the crush she has on you is entirely horse-based," he said, which was the last thing I expected to hear.

"Horse-based?" I shook my head. "I told her I don't have my horse anymore. I can't go riding with her, if she's looking for a buddy to do that."

"I'm sure she'd love that if you could, but I was referring to her lust for riding instruction. She has you in her sights for that, and has asked me if you could teach her. I pointed out that she had promised to better her grades at the time I gave in and provided her with a horse, but as such, she hadn't fulfilled her part of the agreement."

"If you're looking for riding lessons, I'm afraid I wouldn't be a great instructor," I protested, mildly confused, but at the same time oddly excited to be talking with him.

And just how bad was my life that even a phone call with a man made my day?

My brain brought up the memory of sitting next to Izán for lunch, and decided that I'd take what I could get, even if it was just a sexy, sexy voice in my ear.

"I'm more interested in you tutoring her in math this summer, with riding lessons—whatever you are willing to provide—as a reward for doing the work."

"Ah. Gotcha." I thought madly for about fifteen seconds, then had to admit the truth. "I'm afraid that I wouldn't be able to do either form of teaching. I work split shifts, as I think I mentioned last week, and it just wouldn't be feasible."

"That is a shame."

An awkward silence followed, one that had me glancing around the store in realization that I'd lost the lady with the suspicious diaper bag. I hurried down the main aisle, trying to scan the customers without obviously doing so, but entirely aware that Izán was still on the phone. I could hear the faint tapping of a keyboard in the background.

"Er … this is none of my business, but did you get on with Serena?"

"Serena? Ah, the woman at the lunch. The one you wanted me to date."

"I did no such thing," I scoffed, realizing when someone shot me a curious glance that I was frowning. I smoothed out my forehead and smiled before moving on, still scanning the people shopping. "I just said she was nice. And she was."

"She was," he answered, then said nothing.

Ten more seconds of silence passed.

"So did you?" I couldn't stop my mouth from asking him.

"Start a relationship with her?" he asked, his voice rumbling around my ear in a way that sent another ripple of goose bumps down my back. "No."

I almost sagged with relief, then mentally told myself to get my shit together and act like an adult.

I wanted to do many adult things to Izán.

"Have you had to fend off any more women today?" I asked, trying hard to make it sound like a casual question.

He sighed. "Three in the last week, but I believe we are at an end of the pool of potentials. I would celebrate this fact and relax, but unfortunately, my mother continues her attempts to find me a suitable partner. What about you?"

"What about me?" I asked, more than a little taken aback by the question.

"Are you dating someone?"

"No."

"Ah."

The way he said the word reminded me of my abuela's cat when she curled up in a spot of sunshine on the floor—satisfied.

"Have you thought of finding a girlfriend yourself?" I couldn't stop from asking, leaning against a rack of leggings and pants. "Rather than using a dating service, that is."

"I'm not using a dating service. The BMC is ... it's something different. Well ... somewhat. But that's neither here nor there. Obviously, I have made myself open to having a relationship if a woman came along who was suitable, but ..." He let the sentence trail away.

I toyed with the idea of pressing him, but I really could do without hearing the rest of the sentence, which I was sure would be "but I have yet to find her," and instead I moved on. "Thank you for the offer of tutoring Cat. I wish I had the time to do it, but I just don't."

Izán started to speak, the words coming out in a slow cadence. "I don't suppose you'd—"

"There you are! I could see you on the cameras just lounging around talking on your phone, wasting company time as usual!" Terri stormed down the main aisle, her face red with anger.

"Shit. Sorry, I have to go," I said quickly, then hung up without waiting for a response, hastily tucking my phone away before facing my furious boss.

Three days later, I was still stinging from being raked over the coals (and barely surviving with my job).

"Your shadow is here looking for you."

I looked up from where I was donning what I mentally referred to as my disguise—really, just casual clothes and a couple of shopping bags to sell the idea I was a shopper—and frowned when Gustavo, one of the security trainees, popped his head into my office. He had a pronounced Adam's apple, long, thin limbs, and the general air of gawky uncertainty that I mentally associated with men in their late teens.

"Also, Terri said that if I saw you, I'm supposed to tell you that she wants to see you in her office. Like, right now," he added.

Of course she did. She called me in every day to yell at me over perceived slights to her authority. "OK, thanks. Where did you see Cat?"

"Coffee," he answered before dashing off on whatever errand Terri had sent him on.

I took a look at myself in the mirror, and grimaced at the annoyed expression that seemed to be stuck on my face. "Stop it. Stop thinking about him. He doesn't give a shit about you, because you aren't in the least bit the sort of woman who wears bodycon like Serena and Kim. You are nothing but a tutor to him. It doesn't matter if he has nice thighs and a spectacular chest; he's way out of your league. So just get your act together, go out and be nice to a kid who clearly lacks some feminine input in her life, and get through the day."

The me in the mirror didn't look at all happy about being lectured, which led me to the mental image of my mirror self telling off my real self, so by the time I entered the small coffee shop strategically tucked away next to cosmetics, one part of me was amused, while the other worriedly vaguely about my grip on sanity.

"Bela!" Cat stood up and waved vigorously at me,

oblivious to the attention she drew from the other shoppers.

I fought the urge to turn around and leave, but instead said under my breath, "This is all good cover."

"I hope you don't mind I came today when I said I had swim practice, only I'm on day one, and day one is always a gusher, the kind where not even an industrial-strength tampon can cope, so I told the coach it was shark week, and she said to go home, so here I am. You don't mind me talking about shark week, do you?" she asked, her voice dropping on the last sentence as she glanced around with narrowed eyes.

"I don't mind, no, and I'm sorry your period is here. Do you need some ibuprofen? I'm afraid that's all I have in the line of painkillers, but I can get you some if you are crampy."

"No, I'm good there. I don't normally get bad cramps," she said, hurriedly dumping her cup and plate in the receptacle before following me out of the café. "Dad says I take after my mom in that respect. Not having cramps, that is, not the day-one gushing. I don't know anything about that."

"Is your mother …" I bit off the question, reminding myself that despite Cat visiting me, it was better if I didn't get involved in her life.

My heart sang a sad song at the thought of never seeing the gorgeous Izán again.

"Is she dead? No. She's living in South America. Chile, I think. I can ask Dad, if you really want to know, although he tends to get a bit snippy when he talks about her. I mean, he tries to be nice and not say anything bad about her, but I'm not stupid. She left us when I was a kid, and I've only seen her a couple of times since." She gave a shrug that, on the whole, Bela thought was unconcerned. "It's OK, though, because she was mean to my dad, and I don't like people who are mean to him."

"Mean how?" came out before I realized what I was doing. "Never mind. You don't have to tell me."

She glanced around, and then leaned in and said in a whisper, "I'm not supposed to know, but I heard Jacob talking about it with Des—that's his wife—so now I know. She dumped my dad for some massage dude she met doing yoga. Can you imagine that?"

I thought of Izán's eyes and chin and what I was willing to bet was an equally beautiful chest, and couldn't even remotely imagine walking away from him. "No, I can't," I said honestly. "But it's often hard for people not in a marriage to understand what happens in it."

"Have you been married before? You're not now, right? You said you didn't have a boyfriend, so I figured that meant you weren't married, either."

"I've never been married, no," I said, and fought like the dickens to ask more about Izán.

"OK, good. Anyway, because of what my mom did, Dad is always going on about not letting my heart rule me, and to use my head instead, blah blah blah. Which I do! But yeah, he's lonely."

I stared at her. "How did you get from using your head to make decisions to your father being lonely?"

"It's like ... logical," she answered with a scathing look that told me I had let her down in the comprehension skill. "He is way too logical when he dates. He usually only goes out with women he meets at work, and they're all workaholics, and are ... I dunno, so cold, you know? Like ... glossy and shiny, but not someone who's going to hold your hair when you're spewing in a toilet. Dad needs a hair holder."

"Indeed," was the only noncommittal thing I could think to say.

"Anyhoozlebee, I thought, if you didn't mind, you could meet Smythe, and we could talk to you about this great idea we had."

"Smythe?" I frowned, my gaze automatically scanning the area for any body language that might alert me to potential problems. I didn't normally walk the floors at this time of the day, but figured a little break in the routine would be fine … unless Terri caught me.

I pulled my attention from my own world of woe to focus on what Cat was saying. From what she'd told me, there were no women living in her household, and I suspected she was in need of female input and general friendship. "And lucky me, I'm it," I said under my breath.

"Huh?" Cat asked, pausing to tip her head and look at a midriff-exposing cashmere sweater before shaking her head and proceeding on what I'd come to think of as her standard path wandering throughout all the areas of the store. "Smythe is Jacob's replacement when he's not available, and Jacob is Dad's bestie. Well, he works for Dad, too, but they are more like friends. I told you about him, right? He used to be in the military, in some superspy place that Dad says Jacob can't talk about because of the government."

"How interesting," I murmured, wondering if there was a point to her conversation, or if she was simply indulging in one of her normal streams of consciousness.

"Yeah." She slid a look at me from the corners of her eyes. "He knows how to do a lot of spy stuff, like looking people up, and doing background checks, and things like that."

"That's a good ability to have if you are in security, as I assume Jacob is," I answered blithely. Just the mention of Izán was enough to derail my best intentions to not think about the fascinating, annoying man who'd charged into my office two weeks before.

"Yeah," she repeated, but slower, as if she was thinking hard. "Smythe's on duty today because Jacob is busy with Des, his wife. She broke her back when she was young and can't walk. You don't like your job, do you?"

I paused and frowned at her. "Where on earth did that come from?"

"It doesn't seem like you like being here very much." She gave a one-shouldered shrug. "Wouldn't you rather be doing, you know, something else? Something fun?"

"Like riding?" I asked, shaking my head as we started off on the path through women's wear. "I really wish I had the means to ride to my heart's content, but alas, some of us have to do the plebeian jobs so other folks don't have to."

"Yeah, but there's bad jobs, and then there's boring jobs," she said, gesturing at a stack of leggings.

"Again," I said, trying to hold on to my patience. "Sometimes, we don't have a choice. I have to support myself, and that means I have to do what it takes to eat, and sleep in a place that isn't a dump, and even, sometimes, do fun things like ride. But it doesn't happen without work."

She was silent for a couple of minutes. "So, that's why you keep working here despite that lady you said was toxic?"

I glanced around, and hustled us toward another display. "I really should not have mentioned that. Would you do me a big favor and forget anything I said about my job?"

"I'm not sure I can," she answered, wrinkling her nose. "But I'll try if you like."

"Thank you." I absently straightened a rack of shirts that had been left in disarray while we'd pretended to examine them.

Cat made a face as she studied me, blurting out, "You want me to help you find a better job?"

"Wow. That's not at all what I was expecting you to say," I told her, holding a shirt up to her when a gaggle of what looked to be high school students danced by, obviously recording themselves in a TikTok stunt. "On the whole, I prefer to look for my own jobs, but I'm not stupid. If you know of a great job that doesn't require a whole lot in the qualifications department, and which pays really well, then by all means let me know about it and I'll take a look. Otherwise ..." I heaved a sigh before I realized it. "Otherwise, I'll just hang in here. There's always the chance that management will heed my complaints."

She shot me a look that said a lot, and none of it was an expectation that miracles would happen

Silence returned for the next seven or eight minutes as we made the rounds. Cat was good cover, but I drew a limit to her visiting for just fifteen minutes—the time allotted for one of my breaks.

"Yeah," she said suddenly just as I was glancing at my phone to check the time. "I see what you mean, but I think if someone were to ..."

"If someone were to what?" I asked, glancing at her. During the last fourteen days—in which she'd visited me eight times—I'd discovered that she wasn't the type to let sentences hang.

She frowned before turning and snatching up a pair of jeans, pretending to examine them. "You said—the day we met—you said that sometimes you have to do what's wrong, but for the right reason. You meant that, right?"

"Yes," I said slowly, pausing to watch her. I had a horrible presentiment that she was about to tell me her father had decided to sue me, or otherwise destroy me, for my part in the incident. A wave of nausea hit me, and for a moment, I thought I might have to dash for the bathroom.

"OK, good," Cat said with obvious relief. She shoved the jeans back haphazardly, and without thinking, I straightened the jeans and folded them properly before replacing them on the stand. "Because I wouldn't want you to be mad at me unless there was a good reason. And since you did the whole turn-bad-to-good thing, then it won't matter."

I stopped her as she was about to move into the lingerie area. "Cat, what are you talking about? What did you do that I might be angry about? Is it something to do with your dad? Is he annoyed with me?"

"Not that I know of," she answered, looking thoughtful. "He went to Spain a couple of days ago because my wela wants him to marry some model, and every now and again he has to go see the grandparents and get them to back off with the hot babes, but he came back last night."

"I called my grandma wela, too. Er … hot babes?" I asked, visions dancing in my head of Izán standing on a sandy Spanish beach, his body glistening with water, the tiniest of white Speedos highlighting just how gorgeous he was. "A model? Is he … er … engaged?"

"Nooo," she said on a drawl, looking momentarily horrified before flashing me a big grin. "But that doesn't stop Wela from trying. She's always nagging him to get married again, and Dad says she's combed the entire country of Spain for suitable candidates. She comes out to see us every year and brings women with him that she wants him to marry. Not all of them, of course. Just one."

"Your father must be flattered to have so many women trotted out before him," I said, hoping like hell she didn't hear the distaste all but dripping off my words. I took a moment to mentally yell at myself for being so interested in a man who clearly had to pry the women off him with a shovel, but that lasted only as long as it took for Cat to drop her bombshell.

"Not so much, really. That's why Jacob told Dad to use the marriage place."

"Oh, the dating app?" I asked, for a split second wondering which one, and how hard it would be to set up an account. "Yes, I've seen some of the women who match with him."

"No, it's a bureau. A marriage place, not dating. People like my dad sign up with them to find a woman or man who is a perfect match."

"People like … I'm sorry," I said with a little shake of my head as we strolled through the collection of lingerie. "I hate sounding like a parrot, but I don't understand what you mean, unless it's an app that matches up extremely handsome men with women of a similar quality."

And as Kim and Serena had proved, they were well out of my class. Not, I reminded myself, that I was interested. Not after finding out that Izán evidently had women all but oozing out of the woodwork.

And how sad is it when you lie to yourself?

She stopped, a lacy thong in her hands as she glanced around in another furtive gesture of suspicion before leaning in and whispering, "Like, loaded. Dad owns a company that owns other companies that make computer parts. He told me if I want to run it one day, he'll teach me how, but I have to get a business degree first, because he didn't work his ass off just to have me run his business to earth supporting a stable of expensive horses." She giggled at the end of the statement, her joy downright infectious.

"Which you would absolutely do," I told her, my stomach undecided whether it should continue to feel dicey.

"Yup," she said, her eyes squinting with laughter before she sobered again. "That's why I had to do what I did. So you understand, right? It's to help Dad, because I'll be going to college in four years, so it's good if we take care of everything now."

"What do I understand?" I asked before shaking my head. "Cat, you know I'm happy to have you visit me at work, so long as you don't interfere with me doing my job, but if you have some idea that I'm going to … I don't know, date your father … then I'm afraid you're going to be disappointed. For one, your father has no trouble meeting women who could fill the position, and for another, we've only met a couple of times, and at least one of those meetings, he was extremely irritated at me."

"He wasn't, though," she corrected, setting down the thong to squeal at a pretty tiger-striped sports bra before snatching it up and holding it to her chest. "When you caught Rory and me? He was pissed at me for getting involved with the mean-girl mastermind, but he said you were really nice to us, and that I deserved to be locked up in a medieval tower that sits on the corner of my abuelo's land in Spain until I'm eighteen, but he doesn't really mean that, either, because come on. A tower?" Her eyes sparkled with amusement. "Me? It's like he's never met me!"

"Regardless," I started to protest, but she cut me off by throwing down the sports bra and heading for a sale table.

"I know, you guys just met, but my wela says that he's too close to the problem, and can't see the forest for the trees. Or something weird like that. My wela is ancient," she confided to me, a handful of brightly colored sale undies in her hand. "Like, the sort of old that always forgets how to change her ringtone."

I raised my eyebrows at such a shocking exposé, and glanced at my phone. Two minutes left.

"She's like sixty or something!" Cat finished with a face that said she expected me to join in her disbelief that someone so ancient could possibly exist.

"You do realize I'm forty-one," I told her, tidying the undies that she pruned out of her bouquet.

The expression she turned on me was filled with disbelief. "You are not!"

"I am," I said gently.

"But that's so old! Oh man, that came out wrong. I don't mean that you're old, just that … just that you …" She stopped, flushing with obvious embarrassment.

"It's OK," I told her, giving her shoulder a friendly squeeze. "I'm resigned to my ancient status."

"Oh, good." She relaxed and gave me another bright smile, then suddenly froze, her eyes narrowed on the underwear in her hands. "Wait a min. Let me figure this out. Dad is … he was near thirty when I was born. I remember Wela saying he still had time to have kids even though he started late. He's probably forty-something."

An "and he's a damn fine specimen at forty-something" almost burst from my lips, but I managed to keep some dignity.

"It doesn't matter," Cat declared, first shaking her head before switching over to giving me an approving nod. "Dating Dad isn't going to keep Wela from shipping more potential wives to the house. The next batch is due soon, and even if we escape them, there will just be more. Des says Wela is hell-bent on getting Dad married off. So that's why the best thing is to follow the plan."

"What plan?" I asked, glancing at a text. "And I'm afraid my break time is up."

"You're going to have to sign up with the BMC, and then you'll get matched with Dad, and then Wela will stop finding skinny women for him. Dad hates skinny women. He says he likes women to look like themselves, not what other people think they should look like," she said in a rush of words as I headed for the escalators.

"Bully for him," I said, a bit uncertain as to how to respond. Clearly, she had an image in her head of Izán and me together in an attempt to save him from his matchmaking mother, but just as clearly, she was borderline delusional if she thought it could happen. "I'm sorry, that was rude, but you have to understand that I've never been one for a blind date, so while I appreciate the fact that you want me to help your dad, I'm afraid it's just not going to happen."

"He also doesn't like perfume," Cat added absently, not paying attention to me, although she did make a few delicate sniffs around me before adding, "You don't wear any, so that's good. There's Smythe. I've got to go, because I'm mostly grounded until our trip to Los Cabos in a month, except Dad lets me come here to see you. He says it's good for me to have a strong female role model, and I wanted to come and explain everything, so you wouldn't be mad. I'm so glad you're you, and not anyone else."

A little grunt escaped me when she suddenly lunged forward and enveloped me in a bear hug. "Cat, I—"

"And then you can teach me eventing!" she said, before dashing off to meet a tall man with a tight, tailored suit, and the physique and stance of a man who's had a lot of physical training.

"Definitely security," I murmured to myself, having a cousin who had been in the army in a not-discussed position, and recognizing the way Smythe automatically scanned and rescanned the environment for potential threats.

His gaze paused on me, but I decided enough was enough. I had a job to do, even if it was becoming steadily more unpleasant as Terri worked hard to make my life miserable, so I turned around and resumed my casual stroll through the store.

It wasn't until I was in my office three hours later that I checked my phone.

Your application has been accepted, read the email subject line. I was about to hit the spam button when I noted the sender's name was merely three initials: BMC.

"Right, if you signed me up for a time-share or something, Cat, I will be calling your delicious if annoying father to discuss your actions," I said to my empty office as I opened the email, prepared to save it to use as evidence if Izán demanded it. Instead of a sales pitch, the email contained the oddest message I've ever read.

Per your request, your application for participation in the BMC has been received. Please visit the sites listed be-

low, where personality tests have been arranged for you to take without charge. Upon completion of the personality tests, your application will be moved to the next stage.

"Oh, you did not!" I sputtered, wondering if I should look up Izán's phone number and tell him his daughter was evidently trying to set us up. "I am so not going to let you get away with this, kid or not—"

"You are aware that it's against store policy to be attending to matters of a personal nature when you are not on a break or off the clock entirely," came an acid voice from the door, causing me to whirl around and almost drop the phone that I was about to use.

"Of course I do," I said, biting back my true feelings about my boss targeting me in ways that HR flat-out ignored. "And for the record, I was going to call the father of one of the girls I detained a couple weeks ago."

Terri said, "You may think because you're Hispanic and thus fill a quota, you can't be fired, but that's just not true. You've been pushing boundaries for months now, and I've just about had enough. Naturally, I will do everything I can to make sure you don't step over the line and require action by management." She smiled a grotesque parody of a smile and, with a flip of her bob, marched off to blight others.

"Oh yes, you want to help me, all right," I muttered, turning off my phone. "Your racist self wants to help me right out the door. Fine. I won't call Mr. Sexy, but I am most certainly not filling out a bunch of personality reports."

And that's where I thought it ended.

Two days later, I was out on the floor watching a couple of young men who were giving off nervous-energy vibes when I got a call to return to the office, because there was an issue I needed to deal with.

Imagine my surprise when I entered the office to find it jammed full of people, everyone from the head of HR, a charming Indian man named Vihaan, to Terri, a local police officer … and Cat, who held a store carrier bag and was speaking to Vihaan with lots of hand gestures.

"—and of course I know it's wrong to steal, but Bela said she'd take care of everything, and that she wanted me to enjoy myself. Oh, hi!"

"Cat?" I asked, my stomach suddenly feeling as if it were filled with cement. "What are you doing here? Is something wrong?"

"Something is very right, as a matter of fact," Terri said in a voice that was filled with triumph.

The cement in my gut turned to lead.

"Ms. Turner, perhaps you'd like to address the allegations this young woman has made," Vihaan said in his gentle voice. I was horrified to see that rather than bearing his normal mild expression, his face was somber and stiff.

"What allegations? What's going on here?" I asked, confused, and worried to the point where I thought I might vomit.

"Oh, don't pull that act," Terri said, stomping over to my desk and flicking a piece of paper on top toward me. "We know all about your scheme to rob the store blind. I'm just sad I didn't catch you before this, but regardless of that, justice is nigh! Officer, take her away!" Terri finished with a sweeping gesture toward me.

I looked at Cat. "I don't steal, which you know. Did you tell Terri I was robbing them, or was it one of the friends you were with a few weeks ago?" I asked her, my life suddenly becoming a whirlpool that threatened to suck me down into its depths.

She grinned at me. She actually grinned, her eyes sparkling with joy and happiness, and I've never, ever felt so hurt in my life as at that moment, when I realized she had betrayed me in a way from which I doubted I'd ever recover. "It's OK, Bela. I explained to them that you were just getting me a few things because you know I can't afford them."

"Am I going insane?" I asked Vihaan. "Or is everyone else?"

"I'm sorry," he said with genuine regret evident in his voice. "But I'm afraid that this young woman's allegations, along with the evidence, is well beyond store policy."

"In other words, you're canned," Terri said with a smug smile that made my palms itch. "We don't want thieves like you at the store."

"I didn't steal anything—" I protested, but it fell on deaf ears.

I stood silent while Terri, Vihaan, and ultimately the local cop all discussed the situation. They'd sent Cat out of the room, but I was so stunned with her betrayal of me that my brain seemed to be floating in a vat of molasses, unable to function.

Terri pushed for my immediate arrest on the grounds of theft and child endangerment, but luckily, Vihaan had a cooler mind, and spent a half hour explaining to me that although he didn't believe I had done anything wrong, the evidence presented by Cat, coupled with Terri's push, meant my employment with them had come to an end.

"And you're damned lucky we're not suing you," Terri spat out as Vihaan herded her out of the office. The cop waited while I cleared out the few things in my office that had value to me, then walked me out of the room, saying nothing, but looking infinitely bored with the whole situation.

To my surprise, Cat wasn't waiting outside the office for me.

Instead, she was out on the sidewalk, and pounced the moment my box of belongings, the cop, and I exited the building.

"Don't return," the cop advised. "They'll just trespass you."

I gave him a brief nod, my throat aching with the attempt to hold back tears, while my mind was still whirling with the events of the last half hour.

Why would Cat do that to me? Why would she lie? Was it a prank by her and her friends? What had I done to justify her causing me to lose my job?

And more important, what the hell was I going to do now?

"There you are! I was hoping you'd be out soon. This is Smythe. I told you about him."

I turned my head to look where Cat had hurried forward from a sleek black car that was double-parked, followed by a tall, dark-haired man who eyed me curiously. My throat grew tighter with the lump of unshed tears. I wanted to scream and yell, to demand an explanation about why she'd destroyed my life so quickly and easily.

She blasted me with another of her high-wattage smiles. "I'm glad it didn't take long. Now you can come with us and meet Dave. That's the German warmblood my dad bought. He has a big German name, too, but his stable name is Dave. I'm sure you'll like him. Here, I'll take your things so you don't have to carry them."

"I understand from Caterina that you've agreed to take on the job of tutoring her," Smythe said, his voice somewhat flinty.

I shifted my gaze to him, rage filling me as he spoke so nonchalantly, just like nothing the least bit life-changing had happened.

"I'm sure Mr. Tomas will have some forms for you to fill in," he continued as he reached for the box with my framed photo, my favorite mug, and the few office supplies I'd brought in. "Insurance and the like."

I stepped back so he couldn't take the few things that were left from my job, and turned back to Cat.

"I thought you were my friend," I told her.

"I am," she said, her sunny expression slowly fading as I blinked rapidly to keep from bawling right there in the middle of a busy Seattle street.

"No," I said, and backed up a couple more steps before turning to leave. "I was wrong."

I left before I said anything further, beyond devastated, but not willing to say anything to her that I'd later regret.

It took forever for me to get home on the midday crowded buses, and when I did arrive at the studio apartment that ate up most of my paycheck, I just sat on the floor and stared at nothing for two straight hours.

FIVE

"Houston, we have a problem."

Izán didn't bother to glance up when Jacob entered his office, his fingers flying over the keyboard as he whipped through a proposal, editing it to better reflect his offer. "Deal with it. This consolidation in Uruguay is going to drive me to the brink of insanity, if I'm not already there."

"About that … this is something you're going to want to deal with," Jacob said, filling the doorway. "Cat has … well, I won't say made a gross miscalculation, but the end result is fairly problematic, not to mention her method in accomplishing her goals."

Izán smiled at one of the three monitors that filled his desktop. "She may not have learned much from me, but her negotiation skills are going to be formidable if she continues."

"They're formidable, all right. So formidable, they're going to land you in a lawsuit. Izán."

He glanced up at that. Jacob, although his oldest friend, preferred to maintain a professional relationship when working and usually referred to him simply as boss. "What has Cat done that's upset you?"

"It's the woman from the store. The one Cat has been visiting. You remember?"

How could he forget her? The memory rose of Bela's smoky jade eyes, the riot of chocolate curls, and the curves that made his groin heavy with need. Oh, yes, he remembered her. Far too much for his peace of mind.

"I remember," he said, leaning back to consider Jacob, a little ping of worry snaking through his brain. Cat, on the whole, was very like Natalia in her spontaneity and generous spirit, but she was also impetuous and had a tendency to act without first thinking of the consequences. "Does she object to Cat visiting her? I told her she could do so only if Bela—Ms. Turner—had no issue with those visits. I thought all was going well there. Has Ms. Turner changed her mind?"

Jacob just looked at him for a few seconds before saying, "She lied. No, not Bela Turner—Cat. She lied to me. Flat-out lied. She told Smythe I was on board, and had him do most of her dirty work, but in the end, she lied."

"When?" Izán asked, then added, "And about what? It's not like Cat to lie."

Jacob's expression grew grimmer, if that was possible. "It was a few days ago, when I took Des to consult with the surgeon in LA. Cat twisted Smythe up in her plans, telling him I was OK with it. I didn't find out anything until I took her to school this morning. She says she's doing wrong for the right reasons, and that Ms. Turner would be grateful in the end, but the fact remains that she lied. To me."

There was no denying the pain in his friend's voice, but still, it was a lot to ask to believe Cat could do something underhanded.

"What did she lie about?" Izán asked, aware that Jacob had more to say. He knew his daughter relatively well, or as well as anyone could understand the mind of a fourteen-year-old, and she didn't lie any more than she made a habit of stealing.

"She told me—and Smythe earlier, when I wasn't around to catch it—Ms. Turner agreed to leave her job and become her tutor, swearing she'd talked to you about it. Naturally, he did a background check on the woman, and was about to set up an appointment for her to go in and meet with HR, but then Cat informed him Ms. Turner had applied to the BMC with the end goal of enticing you into marriage."

"She what?" Izán was no stranger to being chased by women who saw him as an ATM, but for one to announce such a thing to his daughter was beyond bearable.

"It's not like that, not really," Jacob said, holding up a hand. "At least, it isn't now. Cat lied about all of that, Izán. She's never lied to me before. Fibbed, yes ... I expect that from a teen. But not outright lying. Not to the point where she set up Ms. Turner with some sort of a prank that ended up with her in trouble. It was only after I got the report this morning from Smythe that I realized what Cat had done, and that she—Bela Turner—was not part of Cat's grand plan, as she insists on calling it."

The threads of worry triggered by Jacob's words turned to shards, ones that stabbed into his brain with swift jabs of pain. "It's not like Cat to lie," was all he could say, his mind being busy with swearing up a mental storm.

"No, it isn't." Jacob's gaze was steady on his.

Izán sighed, and with a resigned slump of his shoulders asked, "Where is she?"

"Cat?" Jacob tipped his head toward the door. "Waiting to see you. She didn't want to, mind."

"I'm sure I'm the last person she wants to see right now," he said, rubbing his forehead where the worry shards continued to dig into his brain. "Not that she's usually afraid to face me."

"It's not that," Jacob said quickly with a brief shake of his head. Despite the concern that gripped him, Izán was warmed by just how immediate Jacob's defense of Cat was. "She said she wanted a chance to fix things before she had to explain it all to you, but I thought it was better you take a hand in the situation."

"Tell her to come in," he said, then added, "Give me half a minute."

"As you like," Jacob said, then quietly exited.

Izán leaped to his feet and took up a position at the window, one where he'd be backlit, leaving him in a position of power, while Cat had to take up the less desired chair facing the window.

"She's not a subservient sort of person," he muttered, the idea of his child groveling before him leaving a foul taste in his mouth. He moved over to sit in an armchair, his legs crossed casually, but that felt like he was undermining his own authority. "She doesn't deserve me being overly sympathetic," he told the chair as he rose, and ended up standing solidly at the end of his desk, his arms crossed, his mind filled with various statements of disappointment that he planned on sharing with his child.

"Before you say anything, I know I fucked up," Cat announced as she flung open the door and stood in the doorway.

"Is that really the language you wish to use?" he asked, managing to keep his voice calm despite the fire of his own emotions. He leaned one hip on the desk and tipped his head to study her, this girl who stood with one foot firmly planted in adulthood, while the other remained in childhood. He remembered her as a wild sprite running through the house in a cacophony that would do a herd of oxen proud, her eyes flashing with humor, joy, and love. The memories warmed him despite the anxiety stabbing through the love.

At least she had the decency to look contrite. "Sorry. Messed up," she corrected. "I messed up, and I know it, and I'm going to fix it. Could you hold off yelling at me until I do that?"

The faintest hint of a throb in her voice, not to mention her unusually shiny eyes, told him she was not as indifferent to the consequences of her act as he feared. Instead of reading her the lecture of her life—following by a grounding until she was thirty or so—he inclined his head toward the sofa and took the chair he'd just rejected. "Why don't you tell me what you've done first, and then we'll discuss what you can do to make things right."

She heaved an obvious sigh of relief but, instead of taking a chair or the sofa, knelt at his feet, just like she used to do when she was little and wanted to wheedle something out of him.

He ignored the fact that she was more often successful than not, and donned his sternest expression, the one he usually kept for his mother when she was in full matchmaking mode.

"Bela was unhappy at her job. Like, seriously unhappy, not the sort of unhappy that you say everyone is."

Izán didn't recall making such broad generalizations, but he let it pass.

She sat cross-legged, and stared at her knees while she obviously gathered her thoughts. "And her boss is mean to her. She has it in for Bela, and keeps giving her split shifts, whatever those are. Bela doesn't like them, and her boss is always riding her for not doing her job well, but she is! She totally caught us, and we were super stealthy."

"I believe the less said about that unfortunate event would be for the best," he replied, continuing to project a calm, sober expression despite the need to protect his little girl.

But she wasn't so little anymore, and judging by the somber cast to her eyes and expression, he suspected what was about to come was going to be a stiff learning moment for her.

"Yeah," she said, giving a short nod before she went back to knee-gazing. "And you said I need a tutor this summer to make up for that stupid trig class—who ever uses trigonometry? It's like ancient technology!—and since Bela used to be a high school teacher, I figured she would be perfect. Except she didn't have time, because of her job. I asked her."

Izán pursed his lips when Cat met his gaze, her eyes filled with an earnestness that almost melted his resolve.

She's fourteen; will be fifteen in eight months, he reminded himself. If she did a wrong, she needs to face the consequences of her actions. "I'm glad to hear you have discussed the subject with Ms. Turner. Did it not occur to you that you might also mention it to me, your father, the one who will pay the salary of anyone engaged as a tutor?"

"That's why I'm here." Her brow furrowed, and with obvious reluctance, she amended the statement. "Well, that and to tell you that it's OK, I knew I fu—screwed up, and I'm going to fix it. I just have to explain the whole thing to Bela."

"There's more to your plan than to have her leave her job in order to tutor you—" As he spoke, a thought struck him. Anxiety intensified as he rubbed his forehead again. "Why do I have a horrible suspicion you did something that ensured Ms. Turner would have the time to tutor you?"

"It's part of the plan," Cat said, a mulish expression stealing over her face.

Unfortunately, he was all too familiar with the mood, since he'd frequently told her mother that she could out-stubborn a mule.

"What, exactly, was the complete plan?" He didn't really want to know, but he couldn't let Cat harm anyone else any more than he could tolerate her being hurt.

She took a deep, deep breath and obviously braced herself for an outburst from him. He was pleased, however, to note that she met his gaze while she admitted to her transgressions. "So, the idea was to make it easy for her to leave the job, and also, to get a little revenge on the bitch boss."

Izán allowed one eyebrow to rise a quarter inch. Although he was known to indulge in the use of profanities when the situation warranted, he had strong ideas about fourteen-year-old girls doing the same. He kept quiet, however, wanting her to finish the soul-baring so he could ascertain just how much trouble she was in. Or, rather, had put him in.

"When I heard Jacob telling Desdemona about saying you should get that wife place to find one for you so Wela doesn't keep bringing those skinny models to wear thongs aggressively at you, it struck me that Bela would be the perfect answer to all the problems."

"How," he couldn't help but ask, the mental picture of her words all but dazzling him, "how do the potential brides wear thongs aggressively?"

"They waggle their butts at you when they walk. And stand. And prance around trying to get your attention." Disgust and scorn mingled in her voice. "I'm sure you like it, but, Dad, it's just impossible to eat your lunch out on the patio while Wela's potentials wander around with their butt cheeks hanging out all over the place."

"While I am not against thongs in general, I don't happen to enjoy your grandmother's selection of women parading around in them," he said in the same calm tone, although inside, he was having a good laugh at her disgust. "Charming as they were, I've never been attracted by women whose sole purpose was to seek my attention."

"See, and that's perfect!" Cat slapped her legs, her expression brightening. "Because Bela isn't at all the sort of person to wear thongs. At least she said she didn't when I asked her about some pretty ones that I was thinking of getting. She said they ride up and it's really awkward if you get an itch, and some other stuff about trimming parts that I'm not going to say, because I would never violate the privacy of our conversations."

Another wave of mental laughter hit Izán, and it took him a moment to get control of it. "I'm sure Ms. Turner is grateful for such consideration," was all he managed to say, and even then, his lips quivered a few times.

Luckily, Cat was frowning at his legs now, obviously too deep in thought to notice his amusement. "My point is that she's a nice person, and that's what made the whole thing gel, really." Her eyes met his again. "Because when I talked to Des later, she said that it was important that you and me both like whatever woman saves you from Wela, and I like Bela, and I think you would if you got to know her like I do. She's awesome, Dad! You're always saying we should walk the walk when it comes to being charitable, and she so does that. Plus, she knows how to ride, and she does wrong things for the right reason, and was nice to Rory and told her to get help to keep the mastermind from bullying her."

It was on the tip of his tongue to ask her what on earth a mastermind was, but he decided he'd wait on that point.

"I take it that you intend for me to marry Ms. Turner?" he asked in what he thought of as his most reasonable tone. "Has she agreed to your plan?"

"No, of course not." The look she leveled him was filled with pure irritation. "I'm not an idiot, Dad. I mentioned the marriage place because I had to find out if she was interested in getting married, and she is. At least I think she is." She was silent for a moment, long enough that Izán was about to speak. "I can see that's part of where I went wrong. I will ask her if she'd like to get married, first, before springing you on her."

"Again, your thoughtfulness is touching," he said dryly, wondering if he should let her continue, or if it would be best for him to step in and fix whatever problem she'd created. He had a horrible feeling he'd be finding employment for the enticing Bela at the very least.

"Smythe did the check on her, as I said, and then I told the marriage club people about Bela, and that she'd be perfect for you." She slid him a glance out of the corners of her eyes. "And I know what you're thinking."

"I very much doubt you do," he told her, fighting to keep the inner laughter down. Dear god, how he loved Cat. She seemed somehow to take the best traits from both her mother and him, and mingled them together to make a perfectly charming, if slightly eccentric, young woman.

It was the eccentricity that threatened to drive him to madness, however.

"You think that the people at the marriage place wouldn't listen to me." Her gaze was filled with defiance. "And you're right. So I sent the emails from your laptop."

Now, that was beyond eccentric. "Did you, indeed?" he asked, a flicker of anger tempering his amusement. "Despite the fact that you know my computers are off-limits?"

"Yes," she said, her hands clasped together, her eyes still on his. "I'm sorry that I went against that rule, but I thought it was for the best, and I'm prepared for you to punish me."

"Good," he said simply. "Because tolerant though I might be, there is a reason that I do not allow others to use my computers."

"I know, and I didn't touch anything except send an email, I swear. Well, I did move the response they sent in return to your folder of my emails, but that's it."

He rose without another word and went to his desk, tapping on the keyboard to check his email client. Sure enough, there were a couple of messages in the folder he kept for communications from her school, the stable where she went riding, and other such sources. He returned to the chair, decided the silent tactic was working well, and stuck with it by giving her a long look.

"The thing that went wrong that I have to fix is

that Bela didn't understand the plan. I mean, I talked to her about it. I thought she'd understand, but ..." Cat blinked rapidly a few times. "But she didn't. She was going to cry when she left, Dad. I could see it in her eyes, and even Smythe said she was upset. She almost dropped her box of stuff, and wouldn't let me carry it for her. She wouldn't even let us drive her, and just left us there. It was horrible, and I know I have to fix it. And I'm going to. I figure if she doesn't want to marry us, she could just be a tutor and teach me how to ride instead. And she could live with us because she said her apartment takes up most of her money, which doesn't leave her any to pay for riding. She had to sell her horse a few years ago. I can't imagine how horrible that feels. If you sold Dave, I'd never get over it!"

He rubbed his forehead a third time. "What did you do to the poor woman?"

Silence filled his office for half a minute before Cat said, "I told the store people she said I could take clothes without paying for them. I knew her boss would fire her for it, and that she'd be mad—Bela, not her boss—but that once I went back later and told the store people that I lied, and Bela was innocent, they'd offer her the job again, but she could turn them down because she was going to marry you and tutor me. Or just tutor me and teach me dressage and eventing if you don't want to go ahead with the marriage thing."

He stared at her, this child of his, and wondered what the hell he'd been thinking a few minutes earlier. He'd thought her eccentric? She was nothing less than a force of chaos bent on ruining his life. "You lied in order for her to be fired for theft?" He took a deep breath, his hot temper riding him, but he kept his voice level as he spoke. "Did they arrest her?"

"No, Smythe said something to the store people, and they just fired her." Cat looked utterly and wholly miserable before a look of determination filled the eyes that so closely matched his. "I see now that I may have been wrong in doing that, so I'm going to make that better, too. I'll confess to the store people, and make sure they understand that Bela had nothing to do with it."

"Christ," he said, giving in and running a hand through his hair. "The lawsuits that are bound to come from this …"

"Not if you marry Bela," Cat said, watching him with an expression he found himself unable to read. He thought it might be a bit of hopeful cunning. "Desdemona says a wife can't be forced to testify against her husband."

He blinked, mildly startled that Des was giving Cat that sort of advice. "Regardless of that point, spouses are very much able to testify against their partner if they so desire."

"Oh." She stiffened her back and lifted her chin. "Well, we'll just have to get her to want to be with us, so she doesn't sue me for lying to the store."

Izán wanted badly to point out the sheer folly of not only her actions but her plan to fix things, but something inside him fractured a little at the thought that she wanted a wife for him so much she'd go to all this work to get to know Bela before lining her up via the BMC.

"That's the extent of your plan to fix things?" he asked instead of reading her the lecture of her life. "You'll admit to the store security that you set Ms. Turner up for dismissal? What are you going to do about her?"

"Convince her to marry you?" Cat asked with obvious hesitation.

He shook his head. "I have not been required to coerce a woman into marrying me before, and I'm not going to start now."

"Then you'll have to, you know, take her out and stuff." A dusky pink rose on her cheeks as she glanced away. One hand waved vaguely in his direction. "Take her on romantic dates and trips and make her laugh. Then she'll fall in love with you, and will agree to marry you, and can teach me without us having to hire a tutor."

It was on the tip of his tongue to point out to her that her leaving him open to a lawsuit would cost far more than the saving on a tutor's wages, but once again, he bit back the comment. He needed to focus on what the best steps forward would be.

"I can see you're pissed at me, but you like Bela, right? And you wouldn't mind marrying her?" Cat asked, her arms wrapped around herself until she looked like a human pretzel. "She's really nice, and funny, and although she doesn't speak a lot of Spanish, her being part Hispanic will make Wela happy, right? So that's good."

"Get up," he said, suiting action to words. He gathered up his phone and keys, and shooed Cat out the door when she asked what he was doing. "We're going to see how bad the situation is. Jacob—ah. I suspected you would be close by."

"I figured you might need me," his friend answered, cocking an eyebrow at him that asked a silent question.

"Jacob's awesome at fixing things," Cat said brightly.

Izán narrowed a glare at her before stalking forward to the stairs that led down to the garage block. "We are going to have many, many conversations about your day's work, one of them being how you involved Jacob in actions that I suspect you did not make perfectly clear."

"She told me a version of the events," Jacob said, obviously torn between wanting to protect Cat from a father's wrath and needing to exonerate his own involvement. "I didn't realize Ms. Turner had not consented to Cat's plan."

"I didn't say she did," Cat protested, but when Izán stopped next to a car and looked her dead in the eye, she blushed again, giving an annoyed toss of her head. "Well, I didn't! I said I talked to her about her job, and how she was a teacher and that I needed a tutor, and how she could teach me to ride, and she said she didn't have time for that because of the way her mean boss was scheduling her. I can't help it if Jacob believed something I didn't say."

"Caterina," Izán said in his best impression of his father at his coldest.

"Fine!" she said with a roll of her eyes and much stomping around the car wildly waving her hands. "I may have not made the whole situation perfectly clear, but I didn't lie! You know I don't do that! I would never lie about Bela! She's nice, and I like her, and she likes me, and you don't lie about people who like you!"

"And yet, Smythe said you did so to the people at the store," Jacob started to say, but Cat cut him off with another dramatic wave of her arms and loud explanations.

"That's different, though! It's part of the plan, and I'm going to tell them the truth so they don't blame her anymore."

"I believe we've had enough histrionics," Izán said, prepared to take the wheel, but Jacob beat him to it by a hare's whisker.

"Don't think I don't know what you're doing," Izán told his friend, glaring to drive home the point.

"She's your kid," Jacob said, and shut his door.

"I can have you fired!" Izán yelled before giving in to the inevitable, and taking a seat next to Cat.

"Yeah, but you won't," both Jacob and Cat said in unison, the latter going so far as to pat him on his arm.

"Dude! You don't fire a bro," she told him, then pulled out her phone and began to rapidly text god only knew whom. Izán didn't, despite Cat telling him every thought she had. He loved that about her, loved that she was so open with everyone, and hoped it was a trait she retained past her teen years.

That said, she was in deep, deep trouble, and he intended on driving home to her just how outrageous her actions had been.

The rest of the trip to an outer suburb consisted of him delivering a lecture that left her alternately bristling in indignation and teary-eyed in regret.

"—and if you ever so much as think of pulling this sort of a stunt again, I will not only ship you off to Spain, but I will also tell your grandfather to put you in the tower and toss the key down the well." He stopped in front of a door, glancing at the number. "Is this it?"

"According to the information Jacob has, yes. Here, you take this." Cat shoved a bouquet of flowers they'd picked up on the way out of the city.

He frowned. "You are the one offering the heartfelt and profound apology, not me."

"Yeah, but she likes you more than me. Especially now." Her expression was glum, her eyes not in the least bit sparkling with her normal joie de vivre. He hated it when she looked sad, and he had to fight with himself to keep from taking over so she would be happy again.

Some lessons learned were not just painful to the child, he reminded himself, and, with a pointed nod at Cat, stepped back so she could knock. "I highly doubt that. Proceed."

"Hi. I know you hate me right now, but my father has some flowers for you," Cat said when the door opened in response to her gentle tapping. "Please don't yell at us. We'd like to explain."

Izán opened his mouth to tell Cat she could do better, but the second his brain registered what his eyes were seeing, he stood and stared like the horniest of teenage boys.

Bela Turner stood before them wearing a pair of black leggings, an oversized shirt that swathed most of her torso, and a disbelieving expression highlighted by red, swollen eyes, and an obviously running nose.

She'd been crying.

His resolution crumbled.

SIX

"I want to apologize and explain what happened. Why I did what I did." Cat, to my complete dismay, stood at my door and glanced hesitantly at her father, who appeared to have turned into a statue.

I knew how he felt. I stiffened at the sight of his gorgeous eyes with their thick black lashes, my breath catching in my throat, which was still a bit achy from crying.

"Er ..." I said, seemingly not able to kick-start my brain.

"Just so," Izán said, his knuckles white on the massive bouquet of flowers that he held frozen in front of him.

"Can we maybe come in so I can tell you everything?" Cat asked, drawing my attention back to her.

I thought for a moment, then shook my head "No," I said, and closed the door on them.

My heart beat wildly while I stood there wondering what I'd done.

Was I mad? I just shut the door on the handsomest man I'd ever seen, one who haunted me at night when I was at my loneliest and most vulnerable.

And his daughter, who had hurt me to a point where I doubted I would recover from the betrayal.

A fourteen-year-old girl, my brain pointed out. One who desperately wanted to be my friend.

"Getting me fired is not the way to do that," I told the door.

"What?" came a muffled voice.

Dammit. They were still there.

I thought of walking away and hiding under the covers on my bed, but my curiosity, and the need to vent my spleen on someone who wasn't a child, convinced me otherwise.

I opened the door just enough to peer out.

Two identical sets of topaz-blue eyes gazed back.

"You didn't leave," I told the eyes, opening the door up a little more.

"No, we didn't," Izán answered, exuding sexiness from every pore. Even his voice was sexy, damn him. "My daughter would like very much to apologize, as would I. May we come in?"

"Anyone can apologize," I said, managing to tear my gaze off his handsome self to consider Cat. She looked hot and uncomfortable, her color high, while her gaze kept meeting mine before flitting off. "That doesn't imply the sentiment is sincerely felt."

Cat bowed her head for a few seconds, and my heart felt as if it had contracted. "I really am sorry, Bela. I didn't think exactly how you'd feel about the plan. I thought because you said that doing bad for good reasons meant you'd understand that I was doing the same thing, but I see now you didn't, and I'm really, really sorry about embarrassing you."

"Got a lecture on the drive over here, did you?" I asked.

Her gaze flickered toward her father, then back to me with a flash of a grin. "For hours! It started at home, and took the whole ride here."

"Good." I eyed her with an odd sense of detachment before looking at Izán. "And what about you? Are you here because you're worried I'm going to sue you because of Cat's actions?"

"Worried?" he answered after a moment's obvious thought. "No, I'm not worried. I believe you would be within your right to take legal action, however."

"And you're here to squash that likelihood," I said with a tired nod. Suddenly, the emotions of the day hit me like I'd run smack-dab into a steel wall.

"No," he repeated, taking me by surprise.

"Why not?" I asked, too tired to keep a filter on what I said.

He took his time examining my face. I was more than a little impressed that he had cast only a fleeting glance at my chest before locking his gaze on mine, and keeping it there. "I wouldn't blame you at all if you were to sue. I'm not saying I'd enjoy it, but I am not here to dissuade you from doing anything."

"You don't mind if I were to sue you?" I asked, not sure my brain was functioning. What man would be so unconcerned about a lawsuit that he would be sure to lose?

"I didn't say that." He gave a half shrug. "I would regret the time and money it cost, but at the same time, I would do whatever it took to keep my daughter safe while recognizing the harm she's done to you. If settling compensation on you for her actions is what you'd prefer, then I will make it happen."

Fury hit me like a red wave. "I may be a lot of things," I told him, blinking rapidly to beat back the tears that burned at the back of my eyes, "but I am not the sort of person who can be bought off by someone who has more money than is probably good for him! Thank you for your offer of bribery, but no thanks."

I slammed the door shut before either of them could speak.

This time I lasted less than thirty seconds before I opened it again.

"I'm sorry," I said, my head held high, my dignity wrapped around me like a tattered cloak. "That was rude of me, and I regret my hasty words. As for you …" I turned to Cat. "I appreciate your apology, but I'm afraid I'm going to be too busy looking for a new job to hang out with you like we have been the past few weeks."

"What? I … but I … oh." She took a step back like I'd kicked her in the gut, and instantly, I felt like the world's biggest ass.

"Oh god, this is what my life has come to," I said, sliding down the door to crumple into a miserable blob on the floor. "Picking on fourteen-year-olds in an epic emotional meltdown. Can it get any worse?"

"Yes," Izán said, and, handing the bouquet to Cat, bent down to me. He hesitated before asking, "I wish to help you up and into your apartment so you may have a meltdown in private. Do I have your permission to touch you?"

I couldn't help myself—I started to laugh through the pity party I'd sunk into. "Yes. You can touch me anytime you want." That last bit surprised me, but my brain was clearly wallowing in its unfiltered state without the slightest hint of restraint.

"I'm delighted to hear that. Naturally, I will offer you the same consideration," he said, his voice deliciously English, all smooth and round with liquid vowels. I took the hand he offered, well aware of his other hand on my back as he guided me into my apartment. His fingers seemed to burn an imprint on my spine.

"Really?" I needed to get a little distance from his too-sexy self, but couldn't stop from facing him, our toes almost touching. "So if I wanted to punch you in the belly, you'd let me?"

"I would," he said immediately.

I stared at him for a few seconds, aware of Cat, but too drawn in by the look of mingled concern and something much, much warmer in his fathomless eyes. "Is it because I'm a woman and you think I can't punch very hard?"

"It's because you're a woman, yes, but my reasoning has nothing to do with your ability at bare-knuckle fighting." I swear his gaze heated up a notch, because I felt like I was a particularly untidy dumpling in a steamer.

"Jeez, Dad," Cat said, waving the flowers as she spoke. Two yellow rose heads and a white carnation hit the floor. "You're supposed to convince her not to hate me anymore, and to teach me how to jump, not tell her she fights like a girl."

Izán didn't so much as glance her way. He just gestured toward the door and told her, "Leave the flowers, and go to the car."

"But I have to apologize!" Cat said, making another hand wave with the bouquet. Another three flower heads separated from their stems. "I have to make her understand!"

I sighed and, with a faint worry that the apparently so-wealthy-he-didn't-mind-a-lawsuit Izán would see my pitiful studio apartment and judge me for my inability to get my life together, took the bouquet, marched over to the small sink, and filled a mason jar that served as my vase before placing the flowers. "I'm not sure that I ever will understand, but I do have something I want to say."

"But I need to—"

"Cat," Izán interrupted quietly, steering her over to my sofa, now pulled out into a bed. "Ms. Turner wishes to speak. You owe her the courtesy of hearing what she has to say without interruption."

"Sorry, Bela," Cat said, sitting on the foot of the bed. She stiffened just as if she were going to take a blow. "Go ahead."

Silence filled my little apartment for an entire minute, broken only by the sound of a siren as a cop car raced past my building.

"I like you, Cat," I told her, surprising everyone there (including myself). "You have a wonderfully imaginative mind, with a strong sense of adventure, and a sunny disposition that warms me—but at the same time, you ruined my life with some half-baked plan to … what? Get me to be your tutor? Teach you how to ride? Marry your father, with whom I've exchanged less than a few hundred words? All those options seem pretty unrealistic to me, but I'm willing to accept that you didn't intend any malice with your actions. Unfortunately, I'm still waiting to hear from the police about whether or not the store is going to pursue charges against me for your grand scheme, so I won't be available to fulfill any of the plans you had for me."

I bit back a lot more about thinking before acting, but felt that was up to her father to discuss. Judging by the narrow-eyed look he was giving her, I had a feeling that lecture was forthcoming in the near future.

"They aren't going to," Cat said, beaming at me.

"What?" I marveled at her mercurial nature before asking, "How do you know?"

"My dad and I told them you weren't to blame, and that I was trying to help, but it went wrong. Dad got pissed when the police said they could charge me, but it all worked out in the end. Except for me, because Dad moved the girl that was responsible for cleaning the stable to work with the gardener, and now I have to muck out the stalls, and pick the fields, and haul the water, and feed Dave, every single day for the next three months with no days off except our trip to Cabo, but I'm not allowed to ride him the whole time."

"And why is that?" Izán asked in a voice so velvet, it sent a quicksilver shiver down my spine.

Cat heaved a massive sigh. "It's the consequences of my actions."

"And what did you learn?" he asked.

Her shoulders slumped. "That I can't toy with other people's lives just because I think I can make them better. That I am never, ever to make Jacob and Smythe believe Dad said things he didn't really say."

"And?" he prompted.

Her slump was truly a magnificent thing to behold. It was almost as if her spine turned to rubber. "That I have to own my mistakes and make a genuine apology. Which I have! Really, Bela, I am very, very, very sorry. I couldn't be more sorry. But Dad fixed everything with the store, so it's going to be all right in the end. Except for me not being able to ride all summer, but I'm hoping that after you guys get married, you can talk to him about how unfair it is for you to have all that riding knowledge in your head but not be able to teach any of it to me."

I glanced at Izán. His expression was one of profound martyrdom. I almost giggled at the sight of it.

"The situation with the store wasn't quite so cut-and-dried as Cat makes out," he said, meeting my gaze with the same straightforward manner of his daughter. I realized that she got that from him, and for some reason, it pleased me. "But I wanted to make sure your former employer knew that you were in no way at fault. They now understand that. Unfortunately, I could not secure on your behalf your job."

"I'm not surprised," I said, wanting to curl up and pretend the world didn't exist. "They were more or less looking for a reason to can me. That's why I was trying so hard to keep off their radar."

"I'm so, so sorry it didn't turn out the way I thought it would," Cat said, back to looking miserable. "But other than your work stuff, the rest can work out. You just have to be willing."

"To do what? Tutor you? Even if I wanted to, I'm afraid that's not going to be enough to support me, and given the current state of education, there are oodles of tutors offering their services. I'm not sure I'm up to that competition."

"That's part of it, but if you and Dad got together, you could live with us and wouldn't have to worry about paying for your apartment," Cat said, looking at her father for support. He just stood quiet with his arms crossed, his gaze on her, his expression now unreadable, but I thought I saw the faintest hint of amusement in his eyes. "I know you aren't in love with my dad, or anything like that, but he needs someone to save him from my wela's—"

"No," Izán interrupted, giving her a stern shake of his head. "You will not attempt to guilt Ms. Turner just because your grandmother is misguided to the point of derangement when it comes to my romantic life. Say what you must without attempting manipulation."

Cat curled into a ball, pulling with her a soft blanket from where it was folded on a chair, holding it to her chest as she said, "This is so unfair! I can't say anything right, and now Bela hates me, and Wela said she's got some leads on women she thinks would be perfect for you, and that means the house will be filled with a bunch of skinny women in thongs who pretend to be nice to me so they can get into your pants, but really are awful people who don't know anything about horses, or even precalculus, and Bela knows about both. Plus, if you married her, then Wela would back off with the rampaging Thong Women, which would be the best thing of all time."

"Ahem," Izán said, one eyebrow arching in a manner that evidently Cat knew well.

"God!" she said, tossing the blanket in order to stand up and face her father, slapping her thighs in obvious irritation. "I'm trying, OK? I'm trying really hard, but you keep interrupting when you said you would let me handle it."

"I told you I would let you offer an apology and explanation. You have done the former, but not the latter. Get on with it so that Ms. Turner can decide whether she wishes to accept our offer." Izán looked so annoyed I had to stifle a short bubble of laughter.

"If you think I'm going to take you up on an offer to save you from hordes of thong-wearing women, you can think again," I told him.

"Really?" He did the cutest head tip that I'd ever seen on a man. It went a long way to melting the icy fury that remained in a knot inside my belly. "Is it me, personally, you dislike, or are you opposed to marriage on the whole?"

"Wow," I said, taken aback to the point where I busied myself refolding the blanket that Cat had dumped. "You really went there."

"I don't play mind games with people," he told me, his eyes on mine. I wasn't any great shakes at reading people's expressions, but his was wholly without guile. "I believe in saying what I think, and admire that trait in others. It occurred to me that you share the same philosophy."

"I do," I admitted, then shook my head. "No, the whole thing is ridiculous. We don't know each other. I'm not saying I'd be opposed to going out on a date with you, but even that would be very much a learning process and not a slippery slide straight to a marriage of convenience."

"And yet, such marriages can be incredibly successful given the right people," he answered, his eyes glittering with an emotion I had a hard time pinpointing.

"The whole thing about meeting someone who you mesh with is why the marriage peeps do tests," Cat said, bouncing up and down a couple of times on my couch mattress until I glared at her. She stifled a giggle at the look. "They look at your personality and will tell Dad if they think you guys will, you know, mesh." She accompanied the last word with a gesture of her hands that involved entangled fingers.

"The personality tests are a function of the marriage bureau," Izán said with a fast frown at her. "I prefer to assess the suitability myself, and don't require their tests to determine a potential partner."

"Oh really?" I wanted to mimic his head tip but knew I couldn't pull off the gesture as he did, so instead,

I plopped down in a wooden chair, and waved him to the only armchair. "I get that you know what you like, but it seems to me like the personality tests would allow you to determine quickly if someone shares the same traits and values as you do."

"I can't imagine anything worse than living with someone who bears my nature," he answered, his eyes studying my face again. "I did that once, and with the exception of a daughter who sometimes makes me want to pull out my hair, no good came of it."

"Mom is very much the female version of Dad," Cat told me. "Or so Wela says. She also says it's her biggest failure, and it's why now she goes around looking for women who are completely opposite him."

I watched Izán as he finally took the seat I offered. "May I ask you a question?"

"Yes," he said, crossing his legs with an elegance that sent a shiver of heat up my back. "Whether I will answer it is something I won't guarantee."

"Fair enough." I gathered my thoughts for a moment, then with a glance toward Cat asked, "Why do you need help finding a woman? Forgive me if I'm being overly familiar, but you're drop-dead gorgeous, and evidently you are solvent enough to not be bothered with the idea of being sued."

I liked the fact that he took his time in answering. "I didn't say I wasn't bothered about a potential lawsuit. … I'm simply not worried about it. As for your question, I am a busy man. Not only do I take a direct role in running my company, I make sure I'm present for Cat."

"That doesn't mean you can't go out now and again to meet people. I'm sorry, but I just can't imagine looking like you do and having to rely on some psychological dating company for romantic partners."

"I haven't yet had to go to that length, although I'm told by my cousin—who is a part owner of the organization—that it has a very high success rate thus far." Izán didn't look at all bothered that we were having this odd conversation. "I've been divorced for the last twelve years, and in that time, I've not had a relationship that lasted longer than half a year before the truth came out."

"Cousin Santiago says they're gold diggers," Cat said, draping herself with the blanket. "And only after Dad for his money."

"That is not quite fair," Izán protested with a little frown at her.

Cat peered over the edge of the blanket at her father. "The last one wouldn't even go out to a movie unless you paid for everything. That's not fair. You told me it's important to be responsible for yourself when I go out with my friends."

"And so it is, but there is a difference between being used and treating someone," he pointed out.

I couldn't help but wonder what sort of woman wouldn't want to go away with Izán. Someone quite insane, no doubt.

"Yeah, but that's all they wanted from you," Cat argued, clutching the blanket. "That's not right."

I was silent, continuing to have a problem that someone as successful as Izán couldn't find a woman on his own. There had to be another reason he was here, and that reason wasn't at all one I relished.

Still, he was obviously baring his dating history for my benefit. I eyed him, trying to ignore the way just looking at him made my stomach feel like it was turning somersaults, so I could determine if he was doing what I suspected.

"No," he said when I looked away from him, wrapped in my dark thoughts. "It's not because I believe I can seduce you into forgetting what happened today. I'm simply willing to compensate you for the significant harm my daughter has done."

I shot him a startled look, amazed he could so effectively read my mind.

"I didn't mean it," Cat said, swaddling herself with the blanket.

"Your emotional flip-flops exhaust me," I couldn't help but say, not wanting to address the fact that Izán knew about my dark suspicions.

"Tell me about it!" she said, falling onto her side, her arms pillowing her head as she watched us. "It's a million times worse living it."

"I don't really expect monetary compensation for what happened," I said, watching as Izán noticed the taxidermied armadillo in a lion-rampant pose that stood on the small half-moon table in the corner. His expression almost had me laughing out loud again. "I appreciate the offer, but other than clearing up my innocence with the police and store, I don't need anything, so you can put away your metaphorical checkbook."

"Is it ... why is it on its back legs?" he asked, still looking at the armadillo.

I smiled fondly at the admittedly odd decoration. "He used to sit astride a ceramic horse, but that broke when I was seven, so now he just stands up. He's supposed to be Don Quixote."

"Bela's mom was a famous taxidermist in Guatemala before she was born," Cat piped up. "Bela, not her mom. She said people brought her mom all sorts of weird animals, and she stuffed them. She even did an ocelot once."

"I come from a somewhat eccentric family," I told Izán when he managed to drag his eyes away from the armadillo.

"Something I'm very familiar with," he murmured, casting one last dark look at Don Quixote. "As for the compensation, although I would not disagree that you are due a monetary amount for the loss of your income as a result of Cat's thoughtlessness—"

"Dad! I said I was sorry!" Cat pulled the folded blanket over her head. "Just embarrass me to death!"

"—I am in agreement with Cat that should you desire to work as her tutor, I would be happy to employ you as such."

"Without even checking out my credentials?" I asked, wanting to laugh at the ridiculousness of the situation. Just the fact that I was able to swing from utmost misery to amusement spoke a lot of how comforting I found Izán's presence. "I can't imagine how you are as successful as Cat says you are without at least checking to make sure the people you hire have the qualifications they say they have."

An uncomfortable silence fell. Cat peeked out at me from under the blanket.

I looked from her to Izán. "You did not!"

"Me, personally?" Izán shook his head. "No. My head of security conducted the background check on you. He did so the day Cat stated her intention to visit you."

"Dad makes me check when I want to go see new places or people," Cat explained before retreating back under the blanket. Her voice came out somewhat muffled. "He says someone tried to steal me when I was four, and ever since then, Jacob checks out people and places for potential kidnappers."

The steadiness of Izán's gaze told me a lot. I wanted to protest being the subject of an investigation, but I had to admit that even if my teenage daughter wasn't targeted by nefarious people, I'd want to know whom she was with, and if they were suitable company for her. "OK, I'm going to let that go, because I suppose that if I were in your shoes, I'd do the same. Also, I'm horrified that you've had to grow up fearing kidnappers."

"Eh," she said, the blanket moving as if she was shrugging. "That's why we have Jacob, and Smythe, and Maria, who drives when Jacob's busy with Desdemona, and Dad's cousin Santiago, who's a famous artist. He taught me self-defense for six months when a guy in school got grabby-ass. He's got like three different black belts, and said that someday, if I focused, I could get a belt, too. I told him I'd rather learn how to do three-day eventing." Her head popped out of the blanket again. "You said you competed in that, right?"

"Yes," I told her, then stood up, and opened my front door. "I appreciate the offer of monetary reimbursement and/or employment as Cat's math tutor, but the answer to both is no. I hate to seem ungrateful, but I'm about at the limit of my mental and emotional strength, and I really want my blanket back so I can curl up and hide under it like Cat."

Reluctantly, she peeled off the blanket, and made a half-assed attempt to fold it. "OK, but what about if you just marry Dad?"

"I don't have many rules in life, but one of them is that I get to propose for myself," Izán told her. "Go out to the car."

"Fine, but you have to make sure Bela understands that we need her," Cat said, pausing at the door to give me a bear hug with a fervently whispered, "I swear I didn't mean to hurt you, and I'm really, really sorry," before she left.

Izán handed me a small slip of paper that turned out to be a business card. On the back he'd written a phone number. "I won't press you now, because I can see you're upset. But I would appreciate a call when you are able to discuss the future."

"I'm not marrying you," I told him. "Not that you've asked me."

His lips twisted in a wry half smile. "I believe my daughter has done that for me, but I understand your feelings." He was silent for a moment, his eyes pulling me in like no other man's eyes could. "Were you being polite when you said you'd like to go out with me?"

A blush rolled up from my chest. "I seldom say things I don't mean," I answered, my heart suddenly beating loudly in my ears at the same time my palms went straight to sweaty nervousness.

"I'm beginning to see my way through to a solution that might help us both, but I need some time to fully flesh out the details. Would you be available tonight? For dinner? We can go out, or I'd be happy to cook for you."

"You cook?" The words were out of my mouth before I could think about how rude it sounded.

"I do. Not terribly well, but early on, I made a habit of cooking with Cat once or twice a week, and we've continued to the present. We make a mean lasagna, although the last few years, Cat's insisted that we use ground turkey instead of beef and lamb."

"I'm glad to hear that. I try not to eat much beef, although I do love lasagna," I said, torn. Part of me badly wanted to continue to see him, to watch his expressions, and to lose myself in his eyes, but the other part warned that his daughter had already changed my life for the worse, and I didn't have the strength to cope with the heartache that would follow should I fall for him. "I think, however, that it's probably better if we keep things as they are."

"Hard?" he asked, blinking his impossibly long lashes at me.

I have zero excuse for the fact that I glanced at the front of his pants, and of course, he caught me doing so.

"I wasn't hitting on you, if that's what you imagine," he said quickly, a little frown pulling down the corners of his brows.

"And of course you caught me staring at your groin," I said, covering my face as I let myself sink onto the foot of my bed. "Seriously, this day could not get worse than me not realizing you were talking about the awkwardness of the situation, and not a physical manifestation of your ... er ... self. Please go away and let me die of mortification and regret."

He was silent long enough that I slid apart my fingers so I could peek up at him. He looked puzzled rather than offended. "If you are feeling that desperate, I am happy to call someone—"

"I'm not suicidal, no. Just emotionally drained, and missing my normal mental filter that keeps me from blabbing the first thing I think. I apologize for misunderstanding your comment."

"What makes you think you misunderstood it?" he asked, causing me to lower my hands and stare at him. He stood with his hands on his hips, and his short hair—black as a sinner's heart, and with enough of a wave that it seemed to ripple back from a very slight widow's peak—stood on end as if he'd been running his hands through it.

I had a mental image of doing the same, my mind filled with the thought of how silky that hair would feel on my fingers … and belly … and breasts … which just meant those inner parts that were excited to see him returned to an anticipatory state despite me telling them to cool their jets.

"Ms. Turner?"

My breasts grew heavy with need and want and many, many desires that were all wrapped up in Izán.

"Bela?"

"Hmm?" I had a mental image of myself lying naked in a seductive pose on a green velvet chaise, and him bending over me with those eyes, and his hands, and pretty much all the rest of him.

"Are you in medical distress?" He squatted down so he was level with where I sat, his eyes now filled with concern. He pulled out his phone. "Would you like me to call emergency services?"

"Huh?" All of a sudden my brain snapped back from the Land of Izán and realized that I was making an even bigger fool of myself than I'd done a few minutes before. "No! I was just … that is, I saw your hair, and … oh lord. There's no way I can finish that sentence without straying into potentially offensive territory."

He touched the swoopy wave that rolled back from the little widow's peak. "You think my hair is offensive?"

"Are you insane?" I asked him. "You must have a mirror at home."

He stared at me for a second, then hoisted himself onto the bed next to me. "I have a feeling we are talking at cross-purposes, so let's roll back the conversation to the point before everything went wrong. I asked you if you'd like to have dinner with me, and you said no. At least I think you did. Then you apologized for something that I'm unsure about, following which you seemed to be lost in your thoughts about how much you dislike my hair. I'm afraid there's not much I can do with it other than keep it reasonably short."

"Your hair, like the rest of you, is utterly gorgeous, a fact that I'm sure you very well know, given that your house is filled with thong-clad women who desperately want you in all meanings of the word," I said alternately annoyed at myself and worried he would think I was mentally unstable. "I like your hair, Izán. Er, Mr. Tomas."

"Izán is fine," he said, doing the head tip again. "So long as you don't mind me calling you Bela, and I hope you don't, because I already think of you that way, and I'm sure to mess up and offend you if you do mind. Why don't you want to have dinner with me? I don't think you're so angry with Cat that you refuse to see her, although you certainly have every right to be so. I was hoping that we could discuss a solution to your employment problem during dinner. If you are busy tonight, we can do it tomorrow."

"Why?" I asked him, suddenly struck with a profound thought.

"Why tomorrow? I have an appointment on Thursday that unfortunately will take me to California for most of the day—"

"No," I interrupted, putting my hand on his arm without thinking. "Why aren't you passing me along to your lawyer to deal with? Not that I'm going to sue you, because Cat's intentions weren't cruel, but still, if you're worried that I'm going to sue the hell out of you, you can relax, because I won't."

"As I said, I'm not concerned about a lawsuit, although I would appreciate not having to deal with it, especially since I'm sure Cat's reputation would be impacted, and she's working hard to go to a prestigious college with strict admission standards." His gaze fell to where my hand still rested on his arm; then to my utter joy, he put his hand over mine. "As for why I want you to come to dinner, I simply wish to talk to you in a more pleasant circumstance, one where Cat and I can ply you with, if not excellent food, then at least comfort food, wine, and possibly chocolate if you like it. I hope you do, because both Cat and I have a secret love of dark chocolate that we normally keep just between us, but we would be willing to let you into our secret club."

"You have a secret dark chocolate club?" I asked, unable to keep from laughing despite the fact that my body seemed to be on fire with just the light stroking of his fingers on mine. "An actual club?"

"Well … " he admitted with a little bob of his head. "It's actually my ex's former office, but ever since Cat was little, we'd get together on Saturday nights and have chocolate tastings while watching Bollywood movies."

"Sounds like heaven to me, although I'm afraid I'm more of a milk chocolate girl than dark chocolate. I do love Bollywood movies, though. The more singing and dancing, the better."

He beamed at me, and I could instantly see where Cat got her smile. "Then you'll join us tonight? We will do dinner at home with chocolate tasting afterward, despite it not being our regular night. Then we can talk about your future, and a way to ensure we are both protected."

"Both protected from what?" I asked, but he simply gave my hand a squeeze, then rose.

"We'll talk about it tonight. Is seven too late for you? We tend to keep later hours now that Cat's older."

I shook my head. "That's fine, but—"

"Excellent." He went to the door and opened it, turning to face me. "We'll pick you up then. Do you have a preference for salad dressings? I wouldn't ask except we'll have to get some things in for the meal, and I want to make sure your tastes are accommodated."

"Blue cheese?" I asked, wanting to laugh.

"Works for me. Cat doesn't like cream-based salad dressings, but she's a heathen. We'll see you at seven, then." He exited and was about to pull the door closed but stuck his head in to add, "And in case you were wondering, no, you did not misconstrue my earlier statement. I was being inappropriate, for which I apologize."

The door closed softly before I could gather up my startled wits.

I stared at it for a few minutes before saying, "He was flirting. With me. The handsomest man in the world flirted with me." I looked down at my slumped self, and immediately straightened my back. "Holy shit, girl. He flirted!"

I flitted around my tiny apartment for a good hour after that, examining my limited wardrobe for a dress that wouldn't shame me, trying to resuscitate long-unused cosmetics, and finally pulling out a flat iron that never seemed to cope with my hair, but which didn't stop me from hoping one day it would actually give me hair that wasn't bent on living its own life without consideration of my desires.

It wasn't until it struck me that he might be lying, not to get me to drop a potential lawsuit, but simply because he was the sort of handsome that had women dripping off him, and that form of attention did a number on your brain.

Men that handsome simply had no need for forty-something women of bulk.

That thought remained with me the rest of the afternoon, leaving me feeling as if I were sucking on a rotten lemon.

SEVEN

I don't know what I was expecting when Izán and Cat came to pick me up, but it wasn't Cat banging on my door and loudly demanding I get my crap in gear because her dad was double-parked, and if we didn't get to the airport in time, we'd lose out on the good helicopter.

"What on earth are you talking about?" I asked when I opened the door, at the last minute snatching up my grandmother's shawl that had been left to me when my mother died. "What helicopter?"

"The one we have to take to get home, and we don't want the crappy one. It always smells like barf. Come on! Dad was already swearing in Basque, and he only does that when he's seriously pissed." She spun on her heel and ran down the hallway of my apartment with approximately the same amount of noise as a small herd of cattle.

"Helicopter," I said to the air before grabbing my purse and turning to close the door. "Who takes a helicopter to go home?"

Izán, evidently, although that thought faded away when I noticed an envelope taped to the front of the door. Inside was a notice that per the imminent arrival of my lease term date, the rent was going up by 25 percent, effective next month.

"Not now," I said through my teeth, crumpling the note and stuffing it into my purse before I straightened my shoulders, lifted my chin, and told my libido that just because life was crapping on us lately, it didn't mean we had to let down our morals. I didn't have to give in to the lure of Izán and his magical eyes. I could behave with dignity for the dinner and not be a slave to my inner urges.

Especially the ones that wanted me to touch his thighs. Or run my hands over his arms and chest. And most of all, I didn't want to gaze deep into those eyes just before he kissed the breath straight out of me.

By the time I made it outside, I was fanning myself with the crumpled letter.

"Hurry, or we'll get the barf copter!" Cat urged me. She stood next to a muddy black SUV's open front passenger door. "Jacob said you can ride shotgun."

"How considerate of him—oh, hello. It's nice to meet you." I shook hands with the man who was evidently Izán's bestie, and head of security. He was tall, African American, and had lovely warm brown eyes. Although he appeared friendly, I noticed signs of hypervigilance.

He murmured something about it being a pleasure, but given that several cars were loudly protesting the fact the SUV was more or less blocking the flow of traffic in both directions, I hurried into the car, a little startled to find Izán driving.

"Sorry if I'm late," I offered, glancing at him with a bit of worry. He didn't say much when I got in other than muttering what I assumed were rude things in

Euskara, the language of the Basque region. "People in this area take their parking very seriously and tend to get a bit shouty when they get held up."

"So I see," was all he said, his attention focused on getting us out of my busy neighborhood.

Cat chatted endlessly during the ride, so I didn't have to come up with any witty repartee, which was a big relief because I couldn't stop glancing toward Izán's thighs. There was something about the interplay of muscle as he drove that had my hands itching to touch him.

A sudden realization that Cat had stopped talking had me aware of the air of expectation that filled the car. "Er … sorry?" I said when it was clear she'd asked me a question.

"I asked if you wanted to see Dave. Dad said I'm not supposed to pressure you, but since you have a horse and obviously love them, I thought you might like to see him."

"Had a horse. As I mentioned, I had to sell her. And yes, I would be happy to meet your horse." I looked out the window, fighting the urge to cry again. "I'm sure he's lovely."

"Sorry, I forgot about … sorry," she said, giving my shoulder an awkward pat. "You're welcome to ride Dave. At least, I don't mind if you do, and since I'm not allowed to ride for the entire summer, you might as well. Because if you don't, Dad will have to exercise him, and no one has any fun when he does that."

"Your attempts at guilting me are feeble at best," Izán told her, cocking an eyebrow at her in the rearview mirror.

She giggled, and proceeded to tell me everything about her beloved horse.

At one point while we were at a red light, Izán mouthed what was clearly an apology while Cat was waxing poetic over the many fabulous points of Dave.

I looked away, but immediately felt guilty, and turned back with a wry smile. "She's just excited," I said in a whisper to him.

He nodded just as Cat demanded, "What? I didn't hear what Bela said."

"My ears are ringing from the recitation of your horse's lineage, so I can understand your lack of hearing. Ah, I see we will fulfill at least one fantasy tonight," Izán said blithely, not even glancing in the mirror when Cat sputtered a protest before asking, "What fantasy?"

"The clean helicopter," he answered, pulling into a parking spot at a small airport in the suburb where I lived.

"Why do you have to take a helicopter to go home?" I asked, getting out when everyone else did, although I was a bit wary. I'd sent a message to my sister with my plans for the night, just in case Izán et al. turned out to be psychopathic murderers who preyed on statuesque, if beaten-down-by-life, women.

"'Cause we live on the other side of the lake, and traffic this time of night takes forever, so Dad had a helipad put in. He was going to buy his own helicopter, but said he'd wait until I'm through college." Cat ran off toward one of the small buildings dotting the tiny airport, throwing over her shoulder, "I'm expensive!"

"You're something, all right," I said under my breath, immediately regretting it when Jacob, who was behind me and evidently designated to suffer the traffic as he drove the car home, snorted, but managed to turn it into a cough.

We exchanged glances for a few seconds before he got behind the wheel, and I turned to follow Izán, who had stridden ahead to the biggest building and paused to hold the door open for me.

Twenty minutes later, I was holding on to the seat belt that strapped me into one of the four seats in the helicopter, Cat sitting up front and chatting with the pilot.

I dragged my gaze off the dizzying sight of water speeding by under us as we zipped across the lake, and turned to look at Izán. To my surprise, he was watching me.

"I'm surprised," I told him.

His beautiful eyes narrowed a little as he clearly chased down my odd statement. "By the existence of helicopters, the lung capacity of my only child, or the fact that I'm not flying the copter?"

"The last," I answered, pleased for some reason that he understood what I was saying without actually saying it. "Although the second one—"

"I heard that!" Cat said, twisting around in her seat to pin me back with what I'm sure she thought was a scathing look, but which reminded me of an annoyed puppy who was only too happy to forgive and forget. "If I wasn't going to be a professional rider, I'd be a singer. My mother used to sing with an opera company, but she stopped when I was born, because she said I ruined her vocal cords. That's why I'm never going to have kids. Also because you can't ride if you're pregnant, and who wants to give up that for nine months?"

I looked at Izán. "Your ex was an opera singer?"

"Amongst other things." The martyred look was on his face again, although it flitted away pretty quickly. "She was also eccentric."

"You seem to have a lot of odd people in your life," I said without thinking, then immediately apologized. "I'm sorry, that came out rude, and I didn't intend it to be. My filters are just gone today. I even took a nap so I'd be able to watch what I say, but I guess it wasn't long enough."

"I like your unfiltered state," he told me with a gravity that made me want to laugh.

I won't deny it was nice to not have to sit in traffic while going to Izán's home, but as I took his hand to exit the copter, I was more than a little nervous.

"I'm going to say something that you may very well find offensive," I yelled to him as we ran off the helipad, the wind whipping around us as the copter geared up to take off. "But I really don't mean it that way, so I'd appreciate it if you weren't offended … oh. That's better."

The pilot took off, allowing me to speak in a normal tone as Izán gestured toward a rambling three-story house that probably technically fit the definition of mansion.

"I can't imagine what you'd say that I could find offensive, unless it was to accuse me of luring you to my home so I can do wicked things to you."

I stopped, watching his back as he strode on for a few feet before he realized I wasn't beside him.

"Ah," he said, no doubt accurately reading my expression. "I take it you were going to suggest that I have nefarious plans for you. Would it reassure you if I swore that my motives, if not exactly pure, would be considered beneficial in nature?"

"Beneficial to whom?" I asked, then shook my head before he could answer. "Never mind, it doesn't matter. I wasn't going to accuse you of bringing me here just so you can abuse me, but I do want you to know that

I told my sister I was meeting you for dinner at your home."

He thought for a moment, gave a little shudder, then nodded before turning to resume the walk over lush green grass toward the house.

"You shuddered," I said, quickly catching up. My interest in Izán kept flip-flopping between pure sexual yearnings and an amused enjoyment of him, personally. Particularly his mind. "I saw it, so you can't deny it. I'm sorry that I made you shudder in horror at the idea of me protecting myself—"

"You misconstrued a simple gesture of horror and denial," he interrupted, surprising me by offering his hand when it came to a set of stone steps that led up to a verandah. The warmth of his fingers around mine made every single erogenous zone in my body sit up and take notice. "It was in no way aimed at you, and was, in fact, a reflection that in just a few years I will be sitting up worrying like hell about Cat's dates. I approve of your policy to tell family where you are, and just hope I can convince my headstrong child the wisdom of doing the same."

"A few years?" I asked, glancing toward the house, where Cat had loped off without a word to us. "She's not dating yet?"

"No, and for the love of all that's holy, don't put the idea in her head. I'm far happier with her being obsessed with her horse than roaming around hunting for boys to seduce." He gave another shudder and, to my regret, released my hand. "Here we are. To the left is the kitchen. I'll change and meet you there."

Cat was in the kitchen, perched on a wooden stool, chopping up red and green peppers while talking nonstop. It wasn't until I entered the kitchen proper that I noticed she had her phone propped up and was clearly video chatting with a friend.

"I just hope you're wrong. If she doesn't go with the flow, the house will be filled with—oh, hi! Rory, it's Bela. You remember her?"

I said nothing about the sudden stiff manner that had turned Cat's happy, chirpy voice to one filled with discomfort, and instead waved to the slightly blurry figure on the phone screen. "I hope things are going better for you, Rory."

Her face was flushed, but she looked pleased. "Oh yes! My mom was pissed for a week, but my dad told her it would be stupid to ruin my vacation with Cat, so we can hang again."

I was a bit confused by the conversation, but Cat quickly filled me in after ending the call. "We're going to Mexico next month. Maybe you can come with us?"

"I don't think my finances are going to be up to vacations for a little bit," was all I said, and moved over to the opposite side of a massive marble-topped center island. The kitchen itself was larger than my entire apartment, but I tried to ignore the opulence surrounding me.

"Dad says I'm not supposed to ask you to help chop things, and that because my knife skills are atrocious, I have to prep all the veggies. You like peppers, don't you?" She paused in the act of chopping, a piece of green pepper halfway to her mouth while she waited for me to answer.

"Yes, I like peppers. Would you like me to chop up that onion?" I nodded to a couple of large yellow onions perched next to her.

Her smile was almost blinding. "That would be great, but Dad said—"

"You may have to respect your father's wishes, but I do not," I said with what I hoped sounded like a light laugh as I washed my hands quickly.

"That's a pity, considering I have a good deal of wishes that I believe you might enjoy. Ah. I see you managed to off-load the onions to Bela." Izán entered the room, suddenly filling the space with an intoxicating mix of a pleasant electric awareness of him as a man, and downright sexual attraction that had all my inner bits revved up and ready to party. He wore a simple black T-shirt and jeans, but the way the material caressed his chest, arms, and legs had me averting my gaze to the onion I was about to chop. "You are shameless, child of my loins."

"Ew!" Cat said, chomping loudly on another piece of green pepper. "You're not supposed to mention your loins in front of me. It'll traumatize me or something, and I'll have to go to more therapy than you already make me go to."

"For one, I do not make you go to therapy." Izán picked up a couple of tomatoes, hefted them, then returned one and picked up a replacement. "You asked to speak with a therapist, and I made it happen. And as for the mention of loins, considering the conversation you were loudly having with your friend last night about some K-Pop boy band, I believe you'll survive without any undue trauma from the restatement of your parentage. How are you on garlic?"

He asked the last question of me, glancing over as he put the tomatoes in a pan of boiling water, no doubt to blanch their skins.

"Oh … uh … good? That is, I like it."

"Excellent. We are garlic lovers here, but I was prepared to forgo it entirely if you had an aversion to it."

"He means because of kissing," Cat said with the same sort of blithe indifference her father used when tossing off something equally unexpected. "Not that you're going to kiss him tonight, but he said that some women don't like to eat garlic because of that. I don't think I'll ever want to go without garlic just to kiss someone. I mean, garlic is garlic, right? You need it in food! You don't need to kiss."

Cat dumped her chopped peppers into a sauté pan, and waited for me to finish with the onions before adding them.

I glanced at Izán. He held a knife poised over a few cloves of garlic, watching me with avidity.

I blushed.

His lips twitched, and for a moment, I felt like a web of static electricity had wrapped around the two of us, isolating us from the rest of the kitchen, but leaving us tingling with awareness.

"Unless it's a horse," Cat said, dumping the tomatoes into a bowl of ice before carefully picking off their skins, in the process severing the spell that Izán seemed to wrap around me. "I mean, I always kiss Dave on his nose. He likes it. Especially if I bring him a molasses Popsicle. He loves molasses! And peppermints. Did your horse like molasses, too? The one you used to have? Is that the horse in the picture that was behind your desk? Dad, did you see it? It was an event-win pic. I don't know what for, but I'm sure Bela will tell us when she feels more comfortable with us. That's what Ms. Banner says, anyway, and she's got some sort of a diploma for family psychology, so she should know. If you don't want to talk about your horse, you don't have to, because I know how hard it must be to give one up when you don't want to."

I looked down at where I'd been rinsing off both the knife and the cutting board I'd used, blinking rapidly to alleviate the burn of tears that threatened to escape. "Yes, my horse liked molasses. And no, Bo—the horse I competed on—is not the one in the picture, but she is still around. Just not with me. I had to sell her earlier. Luckily, the woman who owns the stable I used wanted her for her daughter, so Bo got to stay in a familiar home with the other horses she liked."

"That's good, because it's important for horses to have companions, since they're herd animals. We have a mule named Tara for Dave. He loves her, but she is pretty cranky and doesn't like people. Just a warning. We can't get rid of her because animals are for life, and also, it would be mean to Dave. Jane said that. She's my trainer. Well, former trainer." She paused stirring the vegetables as they sautéed, in order to fling a glare at her father. "She was thirsty for Dad, so she left, and he refuses to get another one, because he wants me to run his businesses instead of being a world-class equestrian."

"I want no such thing, and I will thank you to not make misleading statements based on your erroneous beliefs. Thoughts on sun-dried tomatoes?"

"In lasagna?" I asked, since he held out a jar toward me. "Is that something you guys normally do?"

"No, but we like to expand our palate when possible. Cat?"

She shrugged, busily tapping with one hand on her phone while she stirred veggies with the other. "They're a bit oily, but I don't really care either way. You can throw them in here with these guys if you want."

The discussion turned to food for a good twenty minutes while Cat and Izán assembled the lasagna, popped it in the oven, then turned their attention to a garlic bread with a touch of honey and chili flakes that ended up being so delicious, I happily gobbled down several slices, and a massive salad with a vinaigrette that Izán mixed for Cat.

I tried to help, but was firmly told to sit down and enjoy being waited on. Instead of that, I spent the time watching the interplay between father and daughter, at first amused by their sometimes rambunctious teasing banter, but I quickly moved to admiration for a man who clearly valued his daughter, encouraged her participation and contribution to choices, and gave gentle guidance to which I suspected Cat was completely oblivious.

"And now, I hope you will accompany me for a stroll to work off at least one of those slices of garlic bread I consumed with somewhat disgusting gusto," Izán said as I helped them clear the table and load the dishwasher. "Cat has stable chores, so we won't have to put up with her pestering you for more details on every event you competed at."

"You think that's going to stop me from asking?" Cat tossed her head and dashed out of the room, her words trailing her. "I'm so going to love having Bela here!"

I looked from the now-empty doorway to Izán.

"Ouch," he said, wincing before gesturing me through the kitchen door, and pointing to the left where a large living area sprawled with floor-to-ceiling windows. "I was hoping I could approach that subject later, after we've filled you with chocolate, but I suppose now will do just as well as when we're in a chocolate haze."

"I'm not going to marry you," I said more abruptly than I liked as I stepped out onto the stone verandah, pausing to take in the glorious sunset. Peach, pink, and golden light seemed to tip the deep-green lawn that rolled out before us. To the left were a few smaller buildings, one clearly a stable block, with attached pastures. "And yes, as I said earlier, I realize you haven't asked me, but since Cat keeps assuming I'm here for mercenary reasons, I thought I'd get it out there immediately."

"Why are you here?" he asked, then stopped, his face somewhat stiff. "This may seem suspicious given our discussion, but would you object if I was to hold your hand?"

"Hell, no!" I answered without my brain giving the OK.

He laughed, then made a show of bowing and taking my hand in his, his fingers rubbing briefly over mine, making me mentally squeal with a girlish reaction that was downright embarrassing. "Thank you, assuming that was a compliment. Did I just put you on the spot? I did, didn't I? Don't feel like you have to answer if you don't want to. I will admit to being curious, however, since you seem adamant about not accepting payment for the situation Cat caused, and yet, I can't imagine that you so enjoy Cat's company that you're willing to put up with her boring father just to spend time with her."

"Boring? Dude, really?" I asked him, wanting to laugh for some absurd reason. Maybe it was the fact that he was holding my hand, or the sense of irony that I was there at the home of the girl who had ruined my life, and her entirely too handsome father.

He slid me a look. "You think I'm indulging in false modesty?"

"No," I said after a moment's thought. We had stopped next to the wooden rails of a paddock containing a fat mule and a leggy brown horse that was following Cat around as she stalked the pasture with a pitchfork and wheelbarrow. "I don't think that, but I also don't think you are unaware of the effect you have on women."

He propped an elbow on the top rail and leaned his head on his hand. It was almost as cute a gesture as the head tip.

To my surprise, he winked. "All right, I will allow you that point. However, that has nothing to do with the situation at hand."

"Which is what, exactly?" I asked, leaning against the fence, as well. "You feel bad because Cat destroyed my job. OK, I get that. You are her parent, and you feel responsible for her actions, especially when they harm another person. But I've already told Cat that I don't blame her for what happened. I accept that she was doing something she genuinely thought would help me. I'm not going to sue you. Hell, I'm not even going to rant and rave, because what good would it do? I'd still be out of a job, with an apartment that's about to get five hundred bucks a month more expensive. No amount of crying is going to fix that."

"You shouldn't have to fix anything," he said, the light of humor fading from his eyes. They were filled with earnestness now, an emotion that was strangely compelling. "You were the one harmed, and yes, I am responsible—to some extent—for Cat's actions, especially when it involves something as catastrophic as losing your employment. Which is why I'm more than happy to help you recover from the results of Cat's grandiose plan to save us from the very real threat of my mother showing up with another dozen women she considers suitable brides."

"Uh-uh," I said, shaking a finger at him. "You told Cat she can't guilt me with the threat of the Invasion of the Thong Women, and that means you can't, as well."

"Nonsense," he said, dismissing my objection with a wave of his hand. "She is young and has no experience with the hellish nightmare of a matchmaking parent. Do you have one, by the way?"

"A matchmaking parent?" I asked. He nodded. "No. Both my parents are gone. My mom died of cancer when I was about Cat's age, and my dad a few years ago. He drank himself to death."

"I'm sorry to hear that you've lost both your parents so tragically." He patted my hand, then withdrew to look out over the paddock, watching as Cat swatted away the mule when it started nipping at her T-shirt before she jerked the wheelbarrow forward to the next pile of manure. "The fact remains that we—Cat and I— have done you a wrong, and I want to fix it."

"I'm not marrying you," I repeated. "Again, not that you asked, but I'm disgustingly traditional when it comes to the idea that I be in love with the man I marry."

He shrugged. "That is for you to decide; however, I would ask that you listen to my alternative suggestion."

"You want me to teach Cat to ride?" I gave an abbreviated shake of my head. "I wouldn't mind doing that in the least, although I can only take her so far, and that is not to competition level. But I couldn't live on the wages that come from only one student, and before you say you'll pay me enough to live on, don't. One of the few things I learned from my parents was the importance of making your own way in life. I'm not disparaging people like you who were born to generational wealth; my mother's family is quite wealthy, as a matter of fact, but once she met my father, they cut monetary ties in order to make it on their own. They didn't want to be supported by their families any more than I want to be supported by you."

"If I told you that I did not come from generational wealth, would that matter?" he asked, still watching Cat, who was now—with a pair of chunky headphones slapped to her head—dancing around the paddock as she finished cleaning up the horse poop.

"Yes," I said after a minute's thought. "That is, somewhat. I thought your parents were loaded? You said your dad has a tower on his property. That sounds like generational wealth to me."

"As a matter of fact, both my parents did come from what could be called the landed gentry, but their respective families lost everything in the civil war."

"That was before World War II, yes?" I asked, my knowledge of Spanish history less solid than the culture.

"They overlapped, yes." Izán's lips thinned. "My father was a lawyer who managed to attach himself to a land-development company, and ended up making a fortune on a lucky purchase of land that was unexpectedly rich in oil. My mother worked as a nurse until I was in my teens, by which time my father realized the value of his oil rights. Our life changed after that, but I assure you that I grew up in a home that was very modest by all standards."

"My mom was an artist who never really hit it big. My dad was an accountant," I said in the spirit of sharing. "Unfortunately, neither of my parents struck it lucky like your family."

He slid me an odd look from the corner of his eye. "You don't ... er ... have your mother's artistic tendencies, do you?"

"Still shook by Don Quixote, huh?" I asked, leaning against a fence post in order to better consider the man next to me. I had to admit, the more time I spent with him, the more I realized he had the winning combination of good looks, wealth, and a hefty amount of charm. He seemed wholly real and not at all artificial ... but then, the jaded part of my mind pointed out, if he was as successful as I thought he was, he had probably perfected his persona, and I was being taken in by his pretense of normalcy.

What man successful enough to take a helicopter home really cooked dinner for his daughter? I ignored the mental whisper that Cat and Izán worked very well together in the kitchen, just as if they'd done it for years, and instead tried to rally a protective wrap of general distrust.

A few expressions flitted across Izán's face, ending with something that looked a whole lot like embarrassment. "I am fully cognizant that beauty is in the eye of the beholder, and that art takes many different forms, but your mother's vision for the ... er ... departed armadillo escapes me."

"They are weird, so don't worry that you're insulting my mother's memory by not liking them."

"Them?" he asked, reeling back a step. "There's more than just the one?"

"Yup. My cousin is a manager at a storage facility and lets me share a unit with her for no charge. My half is filled with my mom's creatures." I couldn't help but smile as he fought to keep disbelief from his face. Despite my attempt to remain on guard against the lure that was Izán, the fact that he tried so hard to keep from insulting my mom's oddball art warmed my heart from the depths of its icy cage. "Don Quixote got left in my car when I was moving everything after Dad died, so I ended up keeping him. It was kind of a way to maintain my mother's presence."

"I would happily discuss your parents, and particularly your mother's vision for her art, but since Cat will be finished in five minutes or less, and will no doubt want you to then go admire her horse, I will drop all polite conversational conventions and get straight to the point."

"OK," I said, straightening up to face him. To my surprise, he had resumed his spot at the fence, his arms resting on the top bar as he stared into the gathering shadows. "I will warn you that I'm not going to take money from you, but since you seem determined to do something beneficial, I am happy to listen."

"Good. I value the listening skill highly, since so few people seem to have it these days." He turned his head to examine me, his eyes never leaving my face. "Would you enjoy teaching Cat? Not just equestrian skills—she needs help with math, which is a subject I am notoriously weak in, despite trying to take some classes in it. My mother claims I take after her, since she is horrible at any sort of mathematics, but the fact remains that Cat needs a bit of remedial help this summer with various math endeavors if she is to thrive in school."

"Yes," I said after thinking about it a minute. Cat, as Izán had predicted, was finished picking the paddock, and hauled the wheelbarrow out of sight to no doubt some sort of compost area, still dancing, the mule and the horse following right on her heels. "I believe I would enjoy teaching her. She is very bright—something I'm sure I don't need to tell you—but isn't rigid in her thinking. If you would agree to standard tutoring charges, I would agree to work with her. Although

I would have to seek other pupils, as well, since I'm not going to let you pay me a full-time salary when I wouldn't be earning it."

"Actually," Izán said, his eyes still on me. "I was thinking of not paying you a salary."

Unexpectedly, a faint hint of fear gripped my stomach, squeezing it painfully. "Oh?" I managed to ask before clearing my throat. "I mean, I get that you want to make Cat happy, but I have to support myself—"

"I want you to marry me. No." He held up his hand to stop the protest I was in the middle of making. "Don't refuse until I've had time to explain. If the situation with my family was different, I would happily hire you to tutor Cat, and would assist in finding you other pupils. And while that would make Cat happy—and by extension me—it would do nothing to solve my problem. And as my child has pointed out with prescience unusual for her, you coming into our lives offers the opportunity to improve both significantly."

"I'm not—"

"The marriage, of course, would be strictly a business deal, one that will mutually benefit all three of us. It can be as temporary as you like, but I think a year would be good compensation for the injury you have suffered at Cat's hands, and at the same time would be good for her, educationally. After the period of the year, you would have the option of ending the marriage without any fuss or bother."

"You sound like someone out of a historical novel," I told him, wanting to laugh at the absurdity of the idea that anyone so handsome and charismatic would wish to marry me. "Or like you've been watching one too many reality TV shows. I assume the transitory nature of the marriage would not be made known to your parents?"

He shuddered. "I may not live in fear of my mother's matchmaking attempts, as I have managed to stave them off for the last ten or so years, but I will admit that I would dearly love to have her focus her attention anywhere other than on me. For one, she insists I provide a son to carry on the family name, but I am content with Cat, and don't want more children. Er … I assume you don't have children, yourself?"

"No, I never had time for kids, either," I answered. What sort of a man didn't care if he had a son to carry on?

One who valued his daughter, and felt she was enough.

Another piece of ice broke off my frozen heart.

"Just so. Are you opposed to divorce?" he asked.

"Not in itself, no," I said slowly, wondering how much of myself to reveal. He made it so easy to believe I could trust him, but … Cat came back into view, still bopping to her music as she started to refill water buckets. I didn't want to put into words how much Cat had hurt me when she destroyed my trust, but I fully believed Izán genuinely felt guilt for her actions, and I couldn't twist that particular knife in its wound. "But … look, even if I said yes, which I'm not going to, but let's pretend I will."

"Let's pretend," he agreed, looking interested. That was one of the things that was so irresistible about him.

It took me a couple of minutes to figure out what I wanted to say, and thankfully, he waited for me to speak without pressuring me. "Even if I agreed, it wouldn't work. For one, I'm not going to indulge in connubial activities just for a roof over my head."

Izán nodded, which took me by surprise yet again. "I agree to your terms. Not that I would refuse if you wish to indulge in the physical side of the marriage, since I am a mere man and you are an extremely tantalizing woman, but I would respect whatever level of intimacy you decided was appropriate between us. If you wish for us to have a chaste marriage, then that is what we will do. If you think there might be a future for us together … physically … then I will be happy to give you whatever time you need to get to that point I prefer the latter, but would be content with the former."

"And if we do hook up and then decide after a few months that things aren't working?" I asked, part of my brain marveling at the proposition he was offering me, and the other part up to its armpits in doubt.

"Then we will deal with the situation like adults," he said firmly, his gaze never wavering. "I dislike mind games, as I said, and if you find that you are unhappy with us, then I will honor whatever choice you make regarding our future."

"And then there's money," I said somewhat desperately, my heart warming up even further with his willingness to bend over backward for me. The skeptic in me wanted to dispute the veracity of what he was promising, but I ignored the warning and continued. "I'm not saying I want to be supported when I've done no work to earn it, but if I am tutoring Cat, then I would expect to be paid for that time."

"That is a bit trickier," he said slowly, his gaze having shifted to Cat. "Because my idea is to present our marriage as a very real relationship, except to those who know the truth—namely, you, Cat, Jacob, and his wife—all of whom will respect our privacy. If I pay you for teaching Cat, questions might arise in people's minds as to the marriage. It would be best, I think, if I gave you a monthly allowance in lieu of wages."

I'd be lying if I said the idea of not having to fight and claw for every dollar didn't make his proposal that much more tantalizing. I did have to push down the guilty thought that I was putting materialism over common sense, but what could it hurt if, just once, I came out ahead in life? "And your parents? You'd tell them … what?"

His gaze flickered off to the paddock. "My mother won't stop throwing women of childbearing years at me if she doesn't think we are well and truly wedded. I would hope you would go along with that pretense … at least for the time she is visiting."

Several words rose to my lips, but my brain managed to stop them all from coming out in a tumble of sounds.

"Look," I finally said, feeling a bit like I'd just stepped into a whirlpool, and was being tossed around with increasing velocity. "I'm not going to say that it's not a tempting offer—it is, and I fully appreciate your generosity in offering it—but it's just not going to work."

"Why?" Izán asked, his brows pulling together just enough to make a line between them. I wanted badly to smooth it out. "Is it the marriage you object to, even though I will happily sign whatever legal documents you desire to protect you? Or is it the idea of living with us for a year?"

I wanted to ignore the pain that resulted with his matter-of-fact method of proposing—if you could even call it a proposal—but reminded myself that I wasn't under any romantic delusions concerning Izán. Or any man for that matter.

"Or perhaps you have another reason for not wishing to stay with us," he said after an uncomfortable moment's silence. "Are you—is there a romantic partner in your life?"

"No," I said without thinking, then blushed at how bald that sounded, and decided my ego deserved a little salve. "I haven't had a lot of free time in the last eight months since I've had to work split shifts."

"Ah, good," he said, relaxing. "I was worried for a moment, but if it's just your pride that is causing difficulties—"

"Have you even watched Pride and Prejudice?" I asked, outraged by the idea that his offer pricked my pride. "The good version with Colin Firth, not the remakes."

"Of course I have," he said, amusement dancing in his eyes. "Cat insists on a yearly rewatch right before Christmas. If I have offended you or injured your pride with my suggestion, then I apologize. I simply wish to make it clear to you the benefits of marrying me, even if it's just for the short term. If you don't like a year, name a time period with which you'd be comfortable, and I'll make it happen."

I was shaking my head even before he finished, one eye on Cat as she finished with the water and disappeared into a small barn, no doubt to feed the horses their evening meal. "And what happens when it's over? If I marry you and stay with you for a year, what will you tell everyone when I walk away at the end of that time?"

"I will tell them whatever you'd like, and if you wish to leave it to me, then I will simply say we decided we were better friends than married partners." His gaze was as unflinching as ever, but I couldn't maintain eye contact. Not knowing it would break my heart to leave even a pretend marriage if it concerned him.

"And what about Cat?" I asked, playing my last card.

He was silent for several minutes. "I see what you mean," he said at last, casting a glance toward the barn. "She has a very loving heart, and I would ask you not trample on that, not that I think you would."

"I wouldn't," I said quickly. "But even if she knows from the start that the marriage isn't ... for lack of a better word, traditional, would she be all right when it broke up?"

"That is a valid concern, and one for which I don't have an answer," he admitted, his gaze flickering away to the barn when Cat appeared and hallooed at us, waving her arms wildly. "But if I reassure you that I will work with both her and her therapist to ease the transition—should it come to that, and I'm hoping you will like us enough to stay for at least the year—would that be enough to ease your worries?"

"I don't know," I said, lifting my hand in response when Cat repeatedly screamed my name and gestured at me. "It's not something that I think can be decided with a moment's thought."

"Silence!" Izán bellowed to Cat. "It's rude to yell! If you have something to say, come over here and say it like a normal human being."

I cocked an eyebrow at him.

One corner of his mouth curled up, and I swear to god, my knees damn near buckled at the expression. I thought nothing could be cuter than his head dip, but the half smile just about did me in. I grasped the railing with both hands, stiffened my legs, and said, "Much as I appreciate the offer—"

"Think about it," he interrupted, taking both of my hands in his, giving my fingers a squeeze that seemed to light up all my innards with happiness. "Don't make a decision tonight. I wish I could tell you that you have as long as you need, but my mother called shortly before we left to pick you up, and she will be here in less than two weeks. If you have any mercy in your soul, marry me now. You can divorce me at any time if that's what you want, but marry me now so I can avoid filling the house with fertile women determined to get into my bed."

So many thoughts were whirling around in my head like a hamster ball filled with deranged hamsters. I decided that I was going to have to ask the biggest of my questions, and trust my judgment for the minor concerns. "Why do you want a wife so badly? Not because of your mother—you could hire someone to pretend to be your wife—" I ignored the fact that what I was doing was coming perilously close to that definition. "But why a wife?"

He was silent for a lot longer than I expected, his gaze watching Cat for most of the time before he turned his beautiful eyes on me. "Loneliness, mostly. I miss having a partner. I miss having someone randomly hug me, or kiss me, or initiate lovemaking. I miss talking in the middle of the night. I miss sleepy coffee mornings. I miss traveling with someone who wants to see more than whatever local horse-related activities are available. I want a woman who fits well with me."

"And you haven't found one in all the time you've been divorced?" I couldn't help but ask, my heart melting at what I knew must have been an uncomfortable confession.

"No." His eyes seemed to burn a path to my soul. "I've always told myself that I'm not a romantic man, that I can get by with casual sexual partners, and for a while, that worked. But with each passing year, those types of relationships become less desirable. It struck me about a year ago that what I really wanted was a wife, someone with whom I wanted to share my life." He gave me another long look. "I hope that person could be you."

"How can you say that when you don't know me? Not really, anyway," I asked.

"I know enough about you to be confident we would mesh well together, and no, that was not a sexual innuendo, although if you enjoyed it being so, I will happily consider it as such." He looked like he was about to do the head tip again. "And learning more about you is something to which I look forward."

It took me a full minute before I could respond. "What happens if you find someone you want to marry? For real. What if we got married, and then one of those Thong Women turned out to be the one for you?"

"Then we will discuss the matter and work out a solution that is satisfactory to both of us," he said with more than a hint of stubbornness. "I warn you that I'm difficult when it comes to romantic partners. Most of the women I find interesting want something from me, usually money, but sometimes business deals or other such financial considerations. You, on the other hand, don't want money."

I grimaced. "On the contrary, I very much do want it. I have none, and I need it, but I'm not willing to become what amounts to a sugar baby for it."

"And that right there is the difference between you and every other woman who sought to gain something from a relationship with me," he said with a seriousness that wrung my heart.

I wanted to point out to him that life wasn't so easily tidied up as what he was suggesting, but kept my tongue behind my teeth when Cat loped up, excitedly chattering about how she wanted to know what I thought of her eventing horse.

"Think about it," Izán mouthed to me when Cat grabbed my arm and more or less hustled me to the barn.

I nodded, but my spirits sank.

My heart knew what it wanted, no matter how unreasonable it was to be infatuated with a man who not only was out of my social reach but could have any woman he chose. To spend my life in a pretend marriage with him only to have him leave me for a woman he loved, or to run through the established period of marriage and be sent on my way with a friendly wave and murmured thanks … I'd rather die than go through that particular hell.

Izán drove me home a few hours later, just the two of us in one of his shiny black cars.

He kept the conversation on neutral topics, discussing Cat's love of horses, his family in Spain, and even a few tidbits about his ex-wife. I suspected he tossed in the last one in an attempt to show me how honest he was being, but I already knew he was an honest man.

"I'll let you know," was all I said when he saw me to my door.

"Would I be pushing my luck to ask for a goodnight kiss?" He leaned against my open door, his eyes once again sparkling with a topaz-blue light of what I realized was mingled desire and mischievousness.

Both of which were almost irresistible to me.

"Yes," I said, then pushed the door closed, leaning against it for a minute, listening intently. I smiled to myself, then opened the door again, fully intending on letting my libido have its way. I might not be willing to marry the man, but by god, I'd enjoy kissing him the way I wanted since I first laid eyes on him.

The hall outside my apartment was empty.

EIGHT

The call came before Izán was awake.

"Hrn?" he mumbled into his phone when it persisted in singing the latest Taylor Swift tune Cat had set as his ringtone.

"Good morning. Did I wake you up? It's almost eight." The voice caressing his ear was low and husky, with a smoky quality that seemed to stroke his skin in a way that left his nuts tight, and his cock at the edge of an erection.

"No. Yes. What was the question?" He pulled himself up into a sitting position, rubbing his head as he squinted at the light coming in through the blinds. "It's eight?"

Bela gave a little chuckle that he felt down to his toenails. He frowned at that sensation, not entirely pleased with his body's reaction to her. While he very much wanted her to fall in with his plans for a marriage to help them both—and Cat—he didn't intend on giving any woman the sort of power to destroy his heart like his ex had done. Bela as a companion, yes, that was good. Bela as a sexual partner was even better. But he'd be damned if he went through the hell of falling in love with a woman only to have her betray him. Again. "I'm sorry, Izán. I thought you said you had a morning meeting, so I figured you'd be up and about. I can call back later—"

"Absolutely not," he said, pulling himself together. "I am delighted to hear from you. Wait—am I delighted? Or are you calling to dash my hopes, and tell me I have to face the horde of women my mother will unleash upon me without you serving as protection?"

Silence filled his ear for about a quarter minute. "Actually, I have a counterproposal."

He pulled a couple of pillows behind his back and got comfortable. "Excellent. Please proceed."

She giggled. "So businesslike! Very well, we'll do this formally. Would you like a bulleted list, or do you need a PowerPoint presentation?"

"The list is fine. I have a secret love of bulleted lists."

"So do I!" Her voice sounded excited for a moment, before she evidently reined in her emotions. "OK. Point one: I have calculated the money I would earn from teaching riding three times a week, along with math tutoring five days a week—that's assuming she has a bit of catching up to do before school starts in September."

"Yes, she's failed the last two math classes, and it will impact her college future if she doesn't rectify it in the next semester. Five days a week is perfect, although I suspect she will ask for more riding lessons."

"I have a second amount covering that possibility," she said, and he heard the rustle of paper. It both amused him and warmed his heart that she had done so much work on the proposal. "I will text both bids to you for approval."

"Consider them approved," he said, scratching a spot on his chest, then, distracted, looked down at himself and wondered what she'd think of his body. Did she like men who didn't wax their chests? Would she be offended by the fact that he had chest hair? Some women liked it, while others seemed to have an aversion to anything beyond a scattering of hair. Hmm.

"You don't even know how much they are," she protested with laughter behind the words.

"It doesn't matter. I'll pay whatever amount you like. I assume you will agree to the marriage?"

"Yes," she said slowly. "That's actually bullet point four, but we'll skip ahead to it if you like."

"I wouldn't dream of disordering your list. Proceed to point two."

"Since my landlord made an illegal visit to my apartment an hour ago to inform me that I have to move because he wants to sell the apartments. I have decided that I would happily accept your offer to live with you for a year, with a proviso that we can mutually agree on a different time period should it be needed."

"Agreed," he said, wondering what she'd objected to in his proposal. He suspected it had something to do with intimacy.

"Point three is that I want my own bedroom." She gave a slight cough, and added in a rush, "I'm not saying that a physical relationship is out of the question, but to begin with, I want my own space where I can be alone if I choose."

"I am happy to provide you with a suite of rooms including a bedroom, dressing room, and a bathroom that is large enough to house a small pony. I know this because Cat did just that when she was six, and thought she could hide a pony she 'borrowed' from a friend." He swung his legs out of bed and moved to the window to stare out the open blinds at the dewy green lawn.

"Oh lord, I bet that was a nightmare to clean up. Um. OK, point four." She took a deep breath, and Izán marched into the bathroom, putting his phone on mute so he could piss without offending her. "I will agree to marry you—with suitable prenup to protect your assets, of course—but only on one term."

He turned off the tap, absently drying his hands. "And that is?"

She took another deep breath, and he braced himself. "We don't tell anyone."

"The whole purpose of marrying—"

"I know," she interrupted. "It's to save you from all the women who want to give you babies. I'm aware of that, but I'm not comfortable lying to people by saying we're married."

"But we would be married. Legally," he argued, staring sightlessly into the mirror.

"It's still a lie by omission," she said somewhat cryptically. "I'm sorry, Izán, I just can't tell everyone we're married, because of what it implies. And that isn't true for us."

His shoulders slumped. "Very well. Naturally, I wouldn't consider forcing you to do anything that displeases you."

"However!" she interrupted again, this time her voice sounding warm and filled with pleasure. "I am willing to tell everyone that we are in a blossoming relationship. It's the truth, after all, even if we don't expect the relationship to last longer than a year. Hopefully, if you tell your mom that you have a girlfriend, she'll back off with the Thong Brigade."

He would be insane to point out that claiming to be in a romantic relationship was no different from allowing people to believe they married for love. "I'm not sure that my mother would view a girlfriend as a permanent solution to what she believes is a problem in my life, but if that is the line you have drawn, then I will agree to it." Reluctantly, but he realized this was the best he was going to get, and since with every passing hour it became more important that Bela fall in with his plans, he would do whatever it took to make that happen.

"Thank you. I know that disappoints you, but it is important to me," she said, her voice now positively golden with warmth.

"And point five?" he asked, making a face at himself in the mirror.

"There is no point five. What about you? Do you have any points you want to discuss?" she asked, and he was once again warmed by the obvious empathy she felt for others.

"No. I have presented my case to you already. Let's see … I have an hour free at one today. Can you be ready to go to the courthouse with me to deal with the marriage license? We will stop by my lawyer's office first to sign the prenup, as well."

"That's fine with me. I'll be ready for a break from packing and cleaning by then."

"May I offer you Cat and Jacob as helpers?" he asked, studying his belly, and wondering when he'd lost the six-pack that was once the object of female admiration. Now he just had a belly. He sucked it in, and studied the result in the mirror.

He looked ridiculous.

"Sure, if you think they wouldn't mind."

He hung up five minutes later, several points pinging around in his head, but as he stepped into the shower, he made himself two promises: he'd do everything in his power to make Bela happy while she was with him, and he'd start doing sit-ups. He wondered how long it would take to make a difference to his belly, and despite his penis being willing to seduce Bela, he admitted it might be better if they waited a month just so he could take care of the belly issue.

Once he had that under control, he was sure Bela would be more receptive to romance.

He didn't bother to wonder when he'd gone from being physically attracted to Bela to the point where it became of primary importance to have her in his life. It simply was.

His lawyer had everything arranged despite the short notice, and they duly signed forms, including wills, a stringent prenuptial agreement, legal agreements as to Bela's allowance, a few other protections for them both, and finally a slew of paperwork that the BMC insisted was the bare minimum allowed.

"It's intended to protect both parties," Izán explained when Bela read over the documents. "I would have declined to use their services, but they became involved with the security and psychological checks, so we are bound to sign their documents, as well. Your lawyer didn't have any objections, I assume."

"Not so much ..." Bela finished reading the short statement that outlined payments to her account for work with Cat. Izán had insisted on increasing the amount she requested, claiming it was a cost of living adjustment that the BMC required. "That is, I had a friend look them over earlier. She's a paralegal, and knows a lot about contracts, and she didn't see anything wrong. In fact, she said the terms were pretty balanced, and didn't favor one person over the other. Is this the last of it?"

It was, and it was with real regret that he dropped her off at her apartment.

"There's no need to walk me to my door," she said when he got out of the car, about to do exactly that.

"Ah?" he said as noncommittally as possible, hopefully hiding the spike of pain that she didn't want him in her space.

"My place is a disaster zone right now," she admitted with a small smile. "Packing and cleaning, that is. My friend Carla—she's the paralegal—said she'll help when she's done with work."

"Cat said she'd be more than willing to help, although Jacob is attending his wife today. She has medical needs that sometimes require his attention. I can send her over in an hour, if you like." He saw Bela hesitate, then added in a completely neutral tone, "I will understand if you would prefer not to have her overly enthusiastic self underfoot."

"It's not that," she said, shaking her head, and for a brief moment pressed his forearm. He was oddly touched by the gesture. "I really do like her, you know, including her exuberance for life. But I'll be going in and out all day getting everything to the storage unit, and I'm sure Cat would be bored to death."

"I'll tell her you're too busy to entertain," he reassured her. "And now we have three days to wait before we can proceed with the marriage. I would invite you to dinner, but unfortunately, I have to fly to Denver tonight, and I won't be back until the day after tomorrow. Would you mind if Cat visited you during that time? I know she will want to make herself useful, and I hesitate to quell her do-good spirit."

Bela laughed. "I would be delighted to have her tomorrow. The worst of the packing should be done by then. She can help me sort things to be given to the local charity shop."

It was agreed, and Izán left with an odd sense of reluctance, which he chalked up to relief that he would finally have a way to divert his mother's attention.

Three days and several hours later, Izán offered his hand to Bela as they approached the bank of elevators in the courthouse building. "Do you mind?" he asked when she glanced at the hand.

She hesitated a few seconds, then took his hand. "I don't have an aversion to being touched, if that's what you were implying."

"Good. Cat, you will remember what we spoke about earlier."

To his amusement, Cat, standing on the opposite side of Bela, linked arms with her, flashing a brilliant smile at Bela's surprise. "Yup. I am to be supportive, but mindful of the moment, as is right in a best woman. Did you want me to be your bridesmaid, too? I think I can do both."

"Oh. Uh … sure," Bela said, her lips twitching in a way that warmed Izán's heart. "I'd be happy to have you be a bridesmaid, although I understand that your first duty is as your dad's best woman."

"That's OK. Dad said if I made myself useful to you, and didn't talk the whole time about my plans for the summer, then he'd let you give me riding lessons now, although I'm still not allowed to just hack around on my own until the summer's over, because I'm learning about consequences and other shit like that."

"Caterina," Izán said in his most quelling tone.

"Sorry. Crap like that," she said with the merest hint of an eye roll, then leaned in to Bela and said in what she no doubt thought was a whisper, "Dad swears a lot, but most of it is in Spanish, because he says the English version is too unpoetic, so he doesn't like me dropping 'shits' and f-bombs everywhere."

"Especially not in public," Izán said, pausing outside a set of doors. "This is the office. Is everyone ready?"

"Yup," Cat said, and released Bela's arm to open the door with a low bow and a grand, sweeping gesture.

"Ready and willing to act as witnesses," Jacob said, pushing Desdemona's wheelchair.

"I'm still admiring Bela's lovely poppy sundress," the latter said, smiling the gentle smile that never failed to bring joy to Izán. He had known Desdemona since childhood, and although he regretted the accident that robbed her of an active physical life, he rejoiced that his two best friends had found happiness together. "I am definitely going to have to visit that consignment shop you mentioned, Bela, although I doubt I'll find anything even half so gorgeous."

"You are beyond kind," Bela murmured, but Izán, as he released her hand and waved her into the office, couldn't help but notice that she brushed a hand down the dress and looked pleased.

His lawyer had everything arranged despite the short notice, including a nondenominational officiant who had been given a bare-bones wedding ceremony.

The whole thing took all of three minutes before they had exchanged rings. Bela opted to wear hers on her middle finger, and Izán—after a moment's thought—had her place his on the ring finger of his right hand. He wondered for a moment if she'd be offended, but her smile both reassured and irritated him.

He wanted to argue the point of not hiding the marriage, but he'd agreed to her terms, and wouldn't break them without her consent.

"OK, I get it why some people don't want a big wedding, because honestly, it's so wasteful what with all the stuff people do and make and eat, but this seems a bit … I don't know. Kind of boring, maybe?" Cat said, glancing around as they left the lawyer's office. "Dad said you would probably want to go out to dinner afterward, but that's bound to be boring, also, because he won't let us go somewhere fun, like a club. I thought we could go home and have cake, instead. Des made a huge cake for you, and we could put on some music and have our own club. What do you think? Dad said it's up to you what we do."

"The phrase 'Dad said' has become my new pet peeve," he murmured into Bela's ear as he put a hand on her back, escorting her toward the bank of elevators. Behind him, he heard Desdemona stifle a laugh. "Do not allow her to sway your choice in how you wish to spend the evening. There's a very nice sushi place we like near the waterfront, or if you prefer Italian, there's a restaurant closer to home."

Des and Jacob discussed various restaurant options as they rode down, and found the car waiting for them. Although Izán owned a limo, he didn't often use it, since it had horrible mileage, but more important, he found it too ostentatious for his life. There were times when it was handy to have, though, and this was one of them.

"If you want my honest opinion," Bela said once she settled in next to him, close enough that he could feel the slight pressure of her hip against his, "I'd just as soon go to your house, since I haven't had the chance to unpack and arrange things in my room. Would it be too anticlimactic to just have dinner there? I'm happy to make my mom's killer chicken tostadas verdes if you like those."

"Verdes? That's green, right? Green sauce is the best. We can do that if you want. I'll help," Cat offered.

"I'm happy to lend a hand," Desdemona added from where Jacob had pulled her to his side, the wheelchair folded next to her. "Although I don't think I've ever made tostadas with a green sauce, it sounds delicious."

Izán watched Bela from the corners of his eyes, not wanting to make her uncomfortable by being the focus of everyone's attention. If she looked at all unhappy with the idea of simply returning home, he'd gently persuade her to go to a restaurant.

"The more help the better," Bela said with what Izán deemed a genuine smile.

He relaxed, and considered how he needed to keep his libido in check until he determined if Bela was at all interested in a physical relationship. He suspected she was—not being a stranger to the signs a woman wanted to engage in sexual acts—but he'd allow her to set the pace for any intimacy she desired.

"We're going to need a few things," Bela continued, glancing at him. "I'm not sure what you have in stock, but if we can pick up a couple of rotisserie chickens, that would be great."

"We will stop and get what you need," he answered, feeling suprisingly content. He didn't know if it was because he was surrounded by Cat and his friends, or if he was just relieved to have the matter of Bela's immediate welfare settled.

Half an hour later they entered the house, everyone carrying bags of groceries for what Cat excitedly declared would be a killer wedding dinner.

"I think we should have the cake Des made first, though," she said, charging ahead when Izán, his arms laden with groceries, held the door for Bela.

She hesitated for a few seconds on the threshold, and Izán knew the reality of the last few days was hitting her.

"We're not monsters," he said softly, wanting to reassure her. "But if you aren't comfortable here, you can leave at any time."

She said nothing, but nodded and proceeded into the house.

He took a deep, deep breath, and sent up a prayer that she would find the haven he suspected she needed.

He was certainly starting to see that what he thought of as a solution to several problems might well become his saving grace.

NINE

"It's fine. I'm fine. Everything is fine."

"The lady doth protest way too much," Carmen, my sister, misquoted somewhat tinnily, since I had her on speakerphone while I unpacked. "Are you sure that rich dude didn't hide something weird in the contracts and prenup you signed? I mean … you know I love you, but it doesn't make sense that he picked you to marry."

"Gee, thanks," I said, glaring at my phone.

"You know what I mean. You're a wonderful person, Bel. You're sweet and caring and love animals, and that's awesome, but it's not billionaire sort of awesome, you know? I mean, even if you consider his über-pushy mom, it's still pretty much a telenovela level of weird."

"Oh, I am well aware that I am now living in make-believe land. And thank you for your vote of confidence," I said as I finished decanting my clothes into a lovely oak dresser and a massive walk-in closet. "Because there's nothing like knowing your sister isn't supportive of your life choices."

She made a snorting sound. "You know I have your back. I just worry about you. I don't want you hurt by Mr. Big Bank Account. You haven't had a lot of luck in the romance department, and this guy sounds like a whole new level of cray. I'm afraid you're not up to the sort of games he might play with your affections. Rich guys never care about who they hurt."

"There's more to Izán than just his money," I said somewhat snappishly, her words prickling along my skin. "He's a very nice man. He loves his daughter even if she is a bit extra—but in a good way, not like cousin Teo—"

"That's good, because I heard he's run off to some hermit's cave up in the mountains so he can marry a tree," Carmen interrupted.

"Teo?" I asked, momentarily distracted.

"Yup. He says it's his soulmate."

"So weird," I said, then shook my highly eccentric cousin from my mind, and finished my sentence. "—and most of all, Izán isn't looking for a baby mama."

"Pfft," Carmen said. "You've known him for what, a week?"

"Three weeks, actually," I corrected, glancing around the room. The bedroom itself wasn't huge, but it had an entire wall filled with windows that looked over the pastures, and a second room that Izán mentioned I could use as an office if I liked. On the other side, a glorious bathroom sat with gleaming brilliance. "And you're just going to have to trust me, Carmen. I know what I'm doing."

"Do you?" she asked, stirring up all the doubts that had been rolling around inside me for the last few days. "OK, I'll trust that you're savvy enough to see the red flags if your dude is flying them, but call me if things start to go sideways, like if he won't listen when you tell him there will be no sexy times, or he wants you to do things you don't get into."

I blinked at my image in the mirror. "I don't get to have sex?"

"Of course you can have sex. Just not with Mr. Man."

"Why not Izán? He smells nice, he's so handsome it hurts to look at him, and he gets my motor running."

"Bela! You just met him!"

"Three weeks ago, as I just mentioned," I said with an obvious scoff in my tone. "And I am in my forties! If I want to have a sexual relationship, then I will do so. As long as Izán is agreeable, and he said he'd honor whatever decision I made in that regard."

"That's just a clever man manipulating you," she warned. "Look, kid, I have to run. Just protect yourself, all right? You may be my annoying little sister, but I don't want you hurt by any man, let alone one you married for a year because his daughter is a bit extra."

"Thank you for big-sister concern showing itself as your usual bossiness. Love you," I told her, smiling despite myself.

"Love you, too," she said. "Be happy. And use protection if you're going to give in to your baser nature!"

The next two hours were spent cooking, eating, meeting the two men and one woman whom Izán employed for security purposes that Jacob couldn't cover, and allowing myself to be dragged back out to the stables so I could undergo a second—and, to Cat's mind, more thorough—introduction to her horse and mule.

The whole time, I was wondering if I really wanted to have a sexual relationship with Izán.

"Oh, who am I kidding?" I murmured to myself, trailing behind Cat as she raced back to the house. It was almost dark, but much of the grounds was lit up with solar lights, making delightful twinkles everywhere. "I just want to touch and taste and stroke, and, dear god, have him do all those things to me."

"Huh?" Cat asked, waiting for me to catch up. "Did you say something? If you don't hurry, we're going to be late for chocolate tasting."

"We just had that delicious cake Desdemona made," I pointed out.

She rolled her eyes and giggled at the same time. "Yeah, but that was hours ago. When are we going to start lessons? Tomorrow? Dad said he wants to take you away on a trip for your honeymoon, but he can't do it this week because my wela's coming."

Ice filled my veins, or at least that's what it felt like. I stopped and grabbed at Cat's arm, halting her. "Your grandmother is coming? Here? Izán said she was due soon, but not this week! I thought I'd have a little more time to get settled before I had to meet her."

"She's not mean or anything like that," Cat reassured me, slipping out of my hold and trotting to the house, leaving me marooned on a bit of tiled walkway. "Dad says she's really smart, but her wanting him to get married gets in the way of that. But now he has you to protect him. Come on or you'll miss first choice at the chocolate selection! Tonight we have an orange chocolate from Switzerland that is my fave, but I'm willing to share. Unless you don't like it, in which case it's all mine, because Dad knows how much I love it."

"Chocolate orange is also my favorite," I yelled after her, alternating between an urge to laugh at the absurdity of the situation, and a desire to curl up into a ball in my new bedroom in order to hide from the world.

I'm not sure how I thought the evening would go, but I knew it would be all shades of awkward, and I was right.

"You're uncomfortable, aren't you?"

We were sitting in the small room with a large TV (currently playing a recent superhero movie) and several comfy chairs. Cat was stretched out on a sofa with her phone propped up before her, a tray with a selection of chocolate within arm's reach.

The words had been whispered to me.

"No, of course not," I said in a similar whisper.

Izán cocked an eyebrow at me.

"OK, yes, it is a bit awkward, but it's just because this is a new situation."

He nodded, glancing at his phone when it burbled at him. He swore under his breath, then, to my surprise, stood up and held out a hand for me. "Let's take a walk. There's a call coming that I will need to take."

"A walk?" Cat asked, wrinkling her nose. "And leave the chocolate?"

"You may remain here. Bela and I would like some time to ourselves," he said, giving her a look that I suspected he thought was filled with sternness and command, but really overflowed with affection.

Inexplicably, that made me feel a morsel better about the situation. I took his hand, reveling in the warmth and strength of his fingers on mine.

"OK, but if Bela wants to see Dave again—"

"I've seen quite enough of him for the day, thank you," I told Cat, managing to keep from laughing at the look of disbelief that Izán sent her. "I'm sure we'll visit him tomorrow."

"Yeah, when the lessons start." She almost fell off the couch leaning out to yell after us as we left the room, "I'll get up early so we can start as soon as you've had breffy. Does seven sound good? I can do earlier if you like."

"Oh, lord," I swore under my breath as, my hand now firmly clasped by Izán, we headed out to the garden at the rear of the house.

"Ignore her. She was raised by badgers," Izán told me. "My mother just texted me that she will be calling in a few minutes, and I want to introduce you to her. Are you OK with that?"

"Sure," I said slowly, suddenly nervous.

Izán must have felt that, because his fingers gave mine a quick squeeze of support. "She will love you, trust me."

"Mm-hmm," I said, thinking of all the books, movies, and TV shows that featured very different outcomes. Denial of the worry that gripped me had me asking a question that was hovering in the back of my mind. "Does your mother always warn you she's going to call?"

"Ever since the day I made the mistake of answering a call while I was in the bathroom shaving, yes. She insists on warning me so that she doesn't have to talk to me while I'm on the toilet. Not that I have ever answered a call there, but she is a bit of an odd character, so we humor her. Ah. This will be her. Ready?"

"Yeees," I drawled, shooting him a look from the corners of my eyes. Dear god, even in darkness broken by a few solar ground lights, the man was sexiness personified. If anything, now that he was out of a business suit and wearing a pair of faded jeans and a T-shirt that did marvelous things to his chest and arms, he was even more attractive. My libido got one glance at his profile as we strode through a small formal garden, and I immediately discounted my sister's words of advice.

Izán gave me an odd look, ignoring the noise of his phone when it blared out what was obviously another of Cat's choices in ringtones. "Are you all right? You look like you might want to vomit onto that very nice rosebush. I don't know the name of it, but Des does, and she loves it. Please vomit on the other bush, if that's what you're going to do. Also, I'm going to angle the phone away, since I'd prefer not to let my mother see you doing so. She's always had a gag reflex that doesn't tolerate such things."

"I'm not sick to my stomach," I said, laughing at the turn of his mind. It struck me even harder than before just how nice he was, how his consideration for others was truly ingrained in his soul. "To be honest, I was thinking how handsome you were, and it made me feel a little giddy. Oh lord, that must be the champagne talking." I put my hands on my cheeks, blushing like crazy over the fact that I'd said exactly what I was thinking.

"I am flattered, and will respond with my thoughts on just how lovely you are, and what my body wants to do to yours—assuming you are willing to allow that—but this is the second time my mother's called, and if I don't answer, she'll text Cat to tell me to pick up. Ready, again?"

"Yes," I said, and, warmed when he stuck out his elbow for me, took it, feeling a delightful cocktail of silliness, excitement, and arousal. I couldn't think of the last time I felt any single one of those emotions, let alone all three together.

"Mother, what a delight it is to see you," Izán said as he tapped into the video call. "You look beautiful as ever."

She responded in a flurry of Spanish so fast that I could only pick out a word or two. I made a mental note that if I stayed with Izán, I'd have to arrange for a tutor so I could really learn the language, but stopped when I realized I was even considering remaining with him.

It wouldn't be hard at all to fall for him, I told myself as I watched him nod and periodically try to get a word into the sheer wave of verbiage that poured out of the phone and over us both.

That was just the problem, though. I'd fallen hard before for a man who was not even half as gorgeous as Izán, and look how that had ended: with me in a dating slump that had lasted more than eight years.

Life, I thought as Izán—with several quick apologetic glances at me—continued to try to stem the flow of his mother's conversation, would be much easier if I kept to the terms of our agreement. I'd stay with Izán and Cat for a year, then go on my way with enough money to restart my life.

Leaving behind my heart, a thought whispered in my mind, but at that moment, Izán's mother ran out of steam, and he was able to say, "That's all very interesting about the Tomas cousins, but since they are on Dad's side and not yours, it's probably best to let them do what they want. You know how crazy his side of the family is."

"Yes, but still, it will affect us, and you know your dear papá does not like to be so bothered. But why are we speaking in English? And is there someone with you?"

I had moved aside while he was talking to his mom, but now took a step toward Izán. Yet another frozen piece of ice over my heart crumpled into nothing when he wrapped an arm around my waist and gently pulled me against his side. "There is indeed, and that's the reason I asked you to call me. Mother, this is Bela Turner, who, against all odds, has agreed to be what Cat decrees the best girlfriend ever. Bela, my mother, better known as Amalia Mata Garcia."

"A girlfriend?" His mother—who looked to be in her late sixties, with dark hair streaked with gray, and the same eyes that graced her son and granddaughter—studied me as I smiled awkwardly.

"It's a pleasure to meet you, although I'm sure there was a better way we could have told you about our relationship."

"A better way?" she asked, her face still frozen in the expression of surprise that had greeted Izán's declaration. "A better way to meet you? Is such a thing possible?"

I didn't know how to answer that, let alone interpret her expression, which had shifted to something I couldn't define. I glanced at Izán, worry gripping my belly with biting fingers. "Er ..."

Amalia went off into another long, so-fast-I-couldn't-understand statement in Spanish, and I felt lower than a slug's belt buckle. Obviously, Izán's reassurance that his mom would welcome me in his life was completely wrong.

"Wait for it," Izán told me softly, and winked.

It was the wink that did it. One second, I wanted to be swallowed up by the earth, and the next, Izán winked at me, including me in the way he dealt with his mother.

I took a deep breath, feeling as if I could fill my lungs for the first time in years, and a sense of being shackled and bound seemed to drop off me.

Izán had winked at me.

It was such a simple act, and yet, it rocked my world.

"What?" he mouthed at me, a slight frown pulling his brows together.

"You rocked my world," I whispered back.

He looked first surprised, then smug as he leaned in to brush a kiss across my lips. "Not yet, but assuming you give the green light, I'll do my damnedest tonight."

I stared into his endlessly blue eyes, and knew there was nothing that was going to stop me from falling toes over ears in love with him.

"This, this is what I like," Amalia said, pulling our attention back to the phone Izán still held. "You look at each other with such emotion. Your eyes, they sparkle, my Izán. You are part Hispanic, yes, Bela? It is not important in the least, of course, but when my Caterina texted me that she has a new tutor whose mamá was born in Guatemala, I knew that fact would please my husband. He is very traditional, you understand. I, myself, am not so, and am far more pleased that my Caterina raves about you, and says that you are the nicest person she has met aside from her horse, which makes no sense because a horse is not a person, but still, that is high praise."

Izán smiled at me, which came damned close to melting my knees. "It is the ultimate praise, the heights of which I have not scaled since she was six and I bought her first pony. But in Bela's case, it is well-deserved praise. We are, in fact, quite happy, which means you will have to break it to all the women you have rounded up to fly out here to look me over."

"Bah," she said, waving a hand as she continued to study me, but I had relaxed from my first concern that she was going to go psycho mother-in-law on me. "Two of them have run off with each other, and the third one decided she didn't want to live in the US no matter how handsome you were, so it is good that Bela has taken you in hand."

I looked at Izán. His lips twitched, telling me he was having the same inappropriate reaction to her statement, which just warmed my heart even more.

Izán chatted with his mother for a few more minutes before he ended with, "We were just going to take a stroll through the gardens so we can make out without Cat pestering Bela to go tuck Dave in for the night."

"'Make out,' Izán?" Amalia scoffed at her son. "Sometimes, I worry that you are so out of touch with young people. How will you converse with my Caterina if you do not understand what it is people of her generation are saying?"

"What term would you prefer? I refuse to say 'get jiggy with' Bela, Mother," he answered with a sternness that didn't deceive anyone present. "I have some standards."

"Oh, my dude," I said, shaking my head in faux regret. I knew from getting our marriage licenses that Izán was only a little older than me, but that didn't mean I couldn't tease him a bit. "That phrase ages you so much more than making out."

"What would you say?" he asked, thinning his lips at me. For a reason I didn't fully understand, instead of being worried that he might think I was criticizing him, I was comfortable enough to answer as I wished.

"Smash and dash," I suggested, fighting to keep from laughing aloud.

He rolled his eyes. "Ignore Bela, Mother. She's clearly far too overcome with all my manliness to be sensible."

"Hit it and quit it," I said, unable this time to squash the laughter that followed the words.

"Booty call," his mother suggested just as he took my hand and opened his mouth, no doubt to tell me how ridiculous I was being.

He shot his phone a startled look. "Mother!"

She, too, laughed.

"How do you even know such a phrase?" he asked, still looking surprised.

"I have many young friends," she said with a little toss of her carefully coiffed head. "And of course, my Caterina uses popular language when we talk each week. She says it is good for my English. But you wish to be alone with each other so that you may kiss and touch and whisper many sweet somethings, so I will leave you be. I will be out on Friday to see you all. Mind that you take care of your Bela. She looks to be a woman of discerning taste."

It was on the tip of my tongue to say that I hadn't noticed that trait, but decided that was insulting to both of them, so I simply said, "I have to admit that it's still boggling my mind that Izán and I are together, because he's so … and I'm just a former teacher … but the Netflix rom-com element aside, I am very happy to be here with him."

"Just so," she said with a nod, then sharpened her glance on Izán. "And I've taught you well how to treat a woman, so mind you do so and don't let Bela slip away like you have all the others."

"By all means, trot out my romantic history," Izán answered with a twist of his lips. His hand, which had released mine to rest on the small of my back, slid down and gave my butt a slight pinch. "When it comes to all my favorite women ganging up against me, I know it's time to withdraw so I may lick my wounds in dignity. Bela will come with me so I don't fall over and die of old age in the meantime. Come along, my delectable little squab. You can teach me the latest slang for kissing the breath right out of your lungs."

"Hoo," I said, fanning myself as he wished his mother a good evening before hanging up. "Wait … squab? Isn't that a small chicken?"

"Pigeon, not chicken, I think. I read it in a book. A romantic comedy, as a matter of fact, that Cat wanted to read when she was around twelve." He took my hand again and we strolled through the still-warm evening air to where a few curved benches sat around a small water element complete with rustic fountain splashing into a decorative pond. "I have always wanted to use it as a term of endearment, but none of the women I've been with since then have seemed like the squab sort. You strike me as a woman who enjoys things that are a little different."

"I am indeed, and I don't object to 'squab,' although now I want to read the book and find a name for you, too."

He laughed at that, and we sat together on one of the benches, listening to the soft patter of water. The silence wrapped around us, oddly comfortable as we watched night birds flit across the pastures and listened to the distant sounds of traffic.

For the moment, at least, life was looking remarkably good.

TEN

"What do you want to do about tonight?" I managed to ask five minutes later.

I had a feeling that he was not going to say anything more about a physical relationship, since he had left the terms of that to me, as well, which meant I had to be the one to bring it up. And I did so with flaming cheeks.

"Sex, you mean?" he asked, not looking at me, although his arm brushed against me as he leaned back. I fought the urge to stroke my hand down his bicep.

"This is beyond awkward," I said, losing my bravery at the situation. I stood up, and turned back toward the house. "Forget I mentioned it."

"The discussion is only awkward if you let it be so," he said, not rising to stop me, as I half expected.

I walked five steps before glancing back. Although he was in silhouette, he looked relaxed and wholly comfortable. And why shouldn't he be? He was at his home, with his people around him, and he'd all but forced me to marry him so he wouldn't have to deal with his mom.

"All right, I withdraw the term 'forced,'" I said aloud. "But you still have the home-court advantage."

He turned on the bench to look back at me. "Forced? Home court?"

"I was continuing a mental narrative," I told him, waving it away. "Disputing your statement. It's awkward not because I want it to be, but because our marriage is drawn on business lines, and you're talking about us doing intimate things when we've known each other less than a month."

"Yes, we have." He moved over to stand in front of me, taking my hands in his. Although it was dark outside, the solar lights along the path provided enough glow to see just how his eyes were glittering like a polished blue topaz. "And you're as crazy as my cousin if you don't think I've spent every night since thinking about you, wondering what pleases you, if you are ticklish, and what you taste like. All over. While you might find such thoughts awkward, I find the subject of you—particularly you in my bed—highly arousing. If you feel the same way, then perhaps we can skip over awkward and head straight for sweaty, fulfilling lovemaking."

"Hoo," I repeated, fanning myself at the intensity in his eyes. I wondered if hot flashes were common at forty-one. "I admit your way sounds better, but … it feels a bit like an employer-employee thing."

"A contented employee is a productive employee," he said.

My stomach twisted, but it was anger that burst out with my words. I pulled my hands from his and said, "And that's how you think of me?"

He retook my hands. I tried to pull them back, but he lifted each hand to be kissed. "Of course I don't think of you that way."

"Good, because I'm not having sex with my boss!" I stomped off, allowing my anger to ride me even though

I knew I was being overly dramatic. I stopped myself after about twenty feet, then turned and marched back to where he was watching me, his arms crossed. "I'm sorry."

He tipped his head ever so slightly to one side. As mannerisms went, it just kept getting more and more adorable. "For what?"

"Accusing you of being the sort of man who uses a position of power to force someone into a sexual relationship," I said, hating how stiff I sounded, but finding it difficult to come off my high horse. "You're not that sort of person."

"I hope I'm not, but I can see that what I said offended you. Bela." He kissed my hands again, sending little rivers of fire to pool in my intimate parts. "The reason I let you set the terms of our marriage was because I want you to be a willing participant in everything. I apologize if I made it seem like you are my employee—I certainly don't view you in that light. I simply wanted to point out ... oh, hell, I don't even remember what it was. All I can think of is how much I want to kiss you."

"That's part of why it's so awkward," I said, relieved that I was right in my assessment of his character. While he might be used to making decisions and getting his way with his business, he freely apologized and admitted when he was wrong. "We haven't even kissed, and you're talking about tickling, and tasting, and—"

He swooped down on me. There's just no other word for what happened; one moment I was standing with my hands in his, my body temperature having gone up a couple of degrees with the mental pictures he'd painted in my mind, and the next I was pulled up against him, his arms wrapping around me, and his breath steaming my lips. A shiver rippled down my back as I caught the scent of his aftershave, the spiciness of it pushing my libido into high.

"Bela?" The word was a question, and I knew if I gave him the permission he sought, I'd likely end up in a physical relationship that I knew had no future.

But at that moment, every hardship, every unfair act, every injustice I had to bear rose in my mind, and I grabbed his head and pulled him the fraction of an inch until his mouth was on mine, firing up all my intimate parts.

"I take it … if you wiggle against me again, I won't be able to walk … I take it this means you're over the awkwardness?" Izán managed to say in between kisses so steamy I swear my vision just about fogged over.

"You can take whatever you want, including me," I managed to say in between the waves of sexual antici-pation.

I wasn't normally one for a lot of tongue action when it came to kissing, but the way his tongue touched mine had me throwing such thoughts out the window. I stopped trying to get closer to him, my fingers tangled in his hair as I allowed his mouth to get extremely bossy with mine.

"No," he suddenly said, pushing me back just enough that I could see him without my eyes crossing.

"No? No what?" I asked in between panting breaths. "No, you don't want to kiss me anymore? No, you don't want to take me?"

"No, I don't want to make love to you right here in the garden," he said, wincing when he took my hand and started toward the house, pulling me with him. "And yes to all the rest. I want very much to kiss you and touch you and taste you, but there's half an hour until

Jacob drives Cat to her friend's house for a sleepover. I try to limit public displays of affection in front of her."

"Really? I can understand not acting inappropriately in front of her, but I've always thought mild PDAs were kind of sweet. Holding hands, kissing, that sort of thing," I said, wanting to shout with mingled joy and sexual desire. Part of my brain boggled over the fact that clearly Izán had the hots for me, while the other part was saying damn straight he wanted me, and ran through a mental review of things I wanted to do to him.

"Hand-holding is fine," he said, swinging our hands. "But the sort of kissing we were doing is not anything Cat needs to see. Not when you had me harder than I've ever been in my life after just ten seconds of rubbing yourself against me."

"I didn't rub. I wriggled," I said, my cheeks warm with both pleasure and anticipation. "But I apologize if it was inappropriate. I won't do it again—"

"The hell you won't!" He spun me around and marched us toward the house. "I'll just say good night to Cat, and get Jacob to take her to her friend's now so that I can spend the evening disputing the idea that I don't want you wriggling at every opportunity."

He yanked open one French door and marched me through a living room and straight to the stairs before releasing my hand. "I'll be right back."

He lurched up the stairs like a man in possession of an erection. I followed a bit slower, pausing to wave at Cat as she hauled a backpack out of her bedroom to deposit at Izán's feet. She waved back, but turned to face her dad as he clearly had a few things to say to her.

I took the time to go into my room and freshen up before I hesitantly opened the door to peer into the hallway.

Izán lounged against the wall opposite, his arms crossed.

"Oh, hi," I said, feeling a bit lightheaded. I would love to have blamed the champagne and chocolate, but the truth was, I felt like Cinderella at a ball. "Long time no see."

A smile flickered across his face as he held out a hand for me. "It seems like an eternity. I am pleased to inform you that Cat is on her way to her friend's, and we have the house to ourselves. Now, to our previous subject. I will highly encourage you to wriggle anytime you feel like. So long as Cat isn't with us."

"Deal," I said with a little giggle as he flung open the door to his bedroom, hauling me in after him. He released my hand, pulling me by my hips up against him, one hand fumbling behind him until I heard the lock click. "Wriggle time is private time only. Do you like this sort of move, or how about …" I hesitated a second, wanting to do so much, but another wave of awkward hit me.

"In case I didn't make it clear earlier, when my erection was attempting to attain a record-breaking level of hardness, I very much enjoy you doing whatever you want, so don't feel like you have to ask permission." He paused and squinted at me. "No ass play, though. Not for me, anyway. I'm not sure if you—"

"Nope. I'm with you on no-fly zones. I'm glad you don't mind me touching you, Izán. You're so … everywhere! And there's your hair, with the bit behind your ears that curls, and your arms are just so there. And your chest. Dear god, your chest. Can I touch you?" I asked, my hands already on his buttons.

"Touch me!" he said in a dramatic tone that had me laughing to myself.

"Anywhere! Everywhere! So long as I can reciprocate." He had been stroking his hands up my waist to my rib cage, pausing when he reached the undersides of my breasts, clearly waiting for me to give him permission.

And with that, some of the defenses that I'd built up over the years crumbled, not a lot, but enough to give me a peek at what a future might look like.

"What's good for the goose is good for the gander," I said, finally getting his shirt unbuttoned. My fingers almost tingled with happiness as I stroked my hands up from his belly to his chest. He had a hint of a six-pack, but it was the feeling of his skin that drove my need for him to an inferno surrounding me, consuming me, and starting a burn deep within that rippled outward in a manner that left me breathless.

"Oh, it's going to be very good for the goose," he said against my lips, his hands busily divesting me of my clothing. I didn't think he could make me burn any hotter, but just as I was about to tackle his zipper, I was overwhelmed with desire, need, lust, and wanting ... so many emotions, I couldn't separate them into their individual parts.

I wanted to speak, to tell him what he was doing to me, but just then his tongue slid around mine in a sinuous manner that left me staggering against him, mindless to everything but the aching need to join my body with his.

"I think this would be easier on the bed." His eyes, those beautiful blue eyes, studied me for a few seconds. "Are you sure you want to do this? I don't say that it won't come close to killing me if you change your mind now, but I want to make sure that you are good with our relationship changing."

"Yes, please," I almost begged when he pulled back enough to slide his hands up to cup my breasts. I panted, my breasts greatly enjoying being stroked by him. "I'm on birth control, but maybe we should use a condom?"

"We can if you want, but I underwent the same STD tests you did, and all is well there."

"Then I think we're go for launch," I said with a distinct hitch in my breath.

"Never let it be said I don't fulfill a lady's request. ..." He scooped me up and gently set me down in the center of the bed, immediately following me down. He lay half on me, but I wriggled around until he was more or less fully on top of me, his mouth steaming a path up my neck to the sensitive spot behind my ear.

We both still had our underwear on, but I managed to squirm around and get my bra off so my now highly needy breasts were pressed against his chest, the sensation of his chest hair on my sensitive nipples almost driving me insane.

"Christ, Bela, you're so smooth, so silky. ..." Izán released my breasts, holding my hips steady when I tried to cradle his arousal, my body desperate for completion. He groaned into my mouth, sending ripples of pure delight spiraling outward.

"I like your back. And chest. And mouth," I said, my fingers sculpting along the strong planes of his back, caressing the muscles along his rib cage before gently dragging my nails up his spine, greatly enjoying the way his breath hitched. "In fact, I like all of you."

"The feeling is more than mutual." His mouth parted from mine, leaving me empty and bereft. A sob escaped from deep in my throat at the agony of loss, and then his tongue was back, dancing around mine and enticing it into the lure that was his mouth. He tasted like chocolate and brandy, a mix that went instantly to my head.

"I want to do this slowly. I want to give you the time you need. I want—"

"Way too many words, and not enough mouth action," I protested, moaning into his mouth when one of his hands slid down my side, across my belly, and then between my legs, urging them open. I hesitated, but gave in to the desire his touch sent roaring to life.

"I am more than happy to give you as much mouth action as you like," he murmured as he started to shift lower, his mouth heading south as he kissed a fiery path to my breasts.

I didn't let him get very far, wiggling my way out of my underwear as he shucked his own before returning to kneel next to me, his hands immediately going for my boobs.

I eyed his penis, blinking once or twice before I leaned a little to the side to get a different angle.

"What are you doing? What's wrong with my cock?" Izán asked, removing his mouth from where my breast wanted it, his odd expression making me want to laugh. He looked down at himself. "Why are you frowning at it? Do you not like it? It's just an ordinary cock."

"That is anything but ordinary," I said, allowing my fingers to investigate the scenery.

"I assure you, it's perfectly normal—" Izán stopped and moaned, his penis twitching at my touch.

"You're hot and hard and smooth as a baby's bottom, all at the same time. This is a truly magnificent penis, Izán. One might almost say lordly."

He closed his eyes briefly, but they snapped open when I gently scraped my nails along his testicles.

"Christ, no! Yes! No, definitely no. Don't touch me there. … I just need a minute. …"

I released my hold on his balls and gently bit his neck. "I think you stopped breathing. Izán? Did I kill you?"

"Not quite," he said, moving down my body again, his eyes alight with something that looked a whole lot like wickedness, arousal, and revenge. "But let's see if I can't make you mindless for a few seconds."

"I have no doubt that you can do that and much more, but maybe we could have oral fun another time, because right now I don't think I can—Santa Maria, Izán!" I arched up when his fingers danced in highly sensitive flesh, my breath caught in my throat. He had one of my nipples in his mouth, the sensation almost too much for me when two of his fingers dipped into me.

With exquisite slowness, his thumb brushing against me had me on the verge of an orgasm that I knew was going to be world-changing, when he shifted again, this time wrapping my legs around his hips. "I'm happy to do whatever you like, but so long as you seem to be as ready as me—"

"TOO MANY WORDS!" I repeated, grabbing the wonderfully thick muscles of his ass and trying to pull him into me.

He growled deep in his chest, moving up while pulling my legs around him, tipping my pelvis up so that I was at the prime angle. "Such a demanding vixen. Are you ready?"

"I was ready a half hoooo—!" My voice rose an entire octave when without any further warning, he plunged into me. I flexed my legs, my body trembling on the edge of an orgasm.

"I'm going to … I want to do this slow … we should enjoy …" Izán gasped when I bit his shoulder at the same time I lightly scored his spine with my nails. He lost any sort of rhythm then, groaning loudly into my mouth, his body slamming into mine in a way that sent us both into a frenzy. My heart raced as I struggled to take him deeper, to reach that shining moment that seemed just beyond reach.

He rocked into me, speaking in Spanish, dropping words of praise and pleasure that were sweet beyond measure.

And just when I thought I would go insane with the building pressure, I crested the wave of pleasure, and let my inner muscles go crazy on him. His answering groan and short, fast thrusts told me he wasn't far behind, and in that moment, emotions and hormones and endorphins drove me into saying the words that would later make me cringe.

"That was … and you were … dear god, I could so easily fall in love with you."

He was still braced on his arms, but his head had dropped to my shoulder, his breath hot and fast on my neck. He mumbled something that I didn't understand, mostly because I was still trying to catch my breath.

"What?" I asked, instantly feeling remorse when he rolled off me, lying flat on his back, his big chest damp and heaving.

"I said that's the idea. At least, it's my idea. Christ, I'm going to have to take up swimming again. Or maybe jogging. Do you like to run?"

"I'm over forty," I told him, smiling to myself when he pulled me over to his side, tucking me in next to him before pulling up the duvet. "Of course I don't like running. You just have to look at me to tell that."

"No," he said, his eyes closing, but his arm pulled me even tighter to his side. "We are not doing body dysmorphia. I've worked hard to keep that from affecting Cat, and I won't stand for it in my wife. Your body is charming. It is full of curves—which I like—and softness—which I also like. You fit well against me. You are the perfect height for kissing, and your breasts and thighs make me hard just thinking about them."

"And you are an incredibly good father if you've managed to keep that sort of negativity from your daughter." He cracked open an eye and rolled the eyeball over to look at me. I smiled at it, and nipped his earlobe. "And thank you for the lovely compliments. I'm not overly critical of myself, if that's what you were thinking. My body is what it is. I'd prefer it to be slimmer and more coordinated, but since dieting blows, and I've long since given up having any sort of physical grace, I'm content to enjoy life as best I can. You really like all my fluffy bits?" The last sentence slipped out before I could censor myself, but I cringed at how needy I sounded.

"Fluffy?" He looked down toward my groin. "Your pubic hair? I assume since there is so little of it that you've ... er ... ladyscaped."

"I did prune, yes, but that's not what fluffy means. It's kind of a soft way of saying rotundness."

He leveled a long look at me, then turned a little so I was smooshed up against his chest and shoulder. "There is nothing about you that I find in any way displeasing. That includes the fluffy parts, the nonfluffy parts, the pruned parts, and the nonpruned parts. I like all of you. And as for what you said—"

"Would you do me a big favor and ignore that?" I asked, blushing like mad at what I'd blurted out. Although I did feel he was speaking honestly when referring to my body, I couldn't even think about what I'd said. "At least for a bit, until I stop thinking I'm going to die of embarrassment."

He laughed and gave one of my butt cheeks a fondle. "Sweetheart, there is no reason for you to feel awkward. I return the sentiment, in case you were wondering."

That was not what I was expecting him to say, and I think he noticed the flash of surprise in my eyes, but he said nothing more.

"You don't happen to have a home gym, do you?" I managed to ask eons later, when my heart rate was more reasonable, and my breathing was less of the gulping-air variety.

"I do," he answered, his eyes closed again, while his breathing had slowed and evened out. "It's on the ground floor, with a nice view of Cat's koi pond. Did you want to use it, or is this about you thinking that you are not a goddess personified? Because if it's the latter, I will reassure you again that I find every curve a delight—"

"No, no, I'm not so self-conscious that I want you to praise my body again. Well, OK, I am normally, but not now. Not when it's clear that we work really well together. I'm just glad to hear there's a gym available."

"You are welcome to use it if you like, but do not feel like you need to change anything about you in order to please me. I'm already delighted, thrilled, and aroused to the tips of my toenails," he said, still with his eyes closed.

"Thank you, but this is less about my body issues, and more about the need to not die." He did open his eyes at that and shot me a look filled with confusion.

I pinched his bicep. "Just look at me, Izán! I'm a mass of sexually satisfied woman. It's clear that if I want any hope of keeping up with the things you do to my body, not to mention all the things I want to do to yours, I need to get into a cardio program immediately."

He laughed. "Oddly enough, I was thinking much along those same lines. I don't have the same sort of stamina I had ten years ago."

The solidness of him belied the idea that he needed exercise to keep fit, but I let the comment go since his breathing slowed and deepened.

It'll be OK, I told myself as we relaxed into sleep. I relished the feeling of him next to me ... as well as a minuscule flame of hope that began to burn deep inside me.

ELEVEN

It was the cold air swirling around Izán's wet ass that gave warning.

"What—" Bela, who had just stepped out of the shower after him, stood looking like Venus arriving on a shell, but Izán had no time to admire the curves that made his hands itch to caress, stroke, and touch every bit of her delightful self. He snatched up one of the large bath towels and wrapped it around her, turning just as the door opened widely, and the tall, dark-haired man with golden eyes entered.

"—know it's early, but I figured I'd visit my favorite cousin. And, of course, you, Izán. Ha! Wait … why are you naked?" The man who stood in the doorway shifted his gaze to beyond Izán. "That's a woman!"

Bela made a horrified eeping noise and scooted behind him, then eeped again and snatched up another towel, which she held in front of him.

Izán didn't wait—he moved forward, pushing his cousin until the latter was outside the bathroom. "Stay there," he said sternly, and slammed shut the door.

"Was that—" Bela started to ask, quickly hurrying into her bathrobe.

He waited until she was fully covered before, with slightly gritted teeth, he opened the door. "It's my cousin San. You are indeed early, and yes, there is a woman here. Also yes, she's mine. Well, so far as a romantic relationship goes. Bela, this is my frequently annoying cousin, Santiago María Lopez Santos."

"It's a pleasure to meet you, Mr. Lopez. I'm so sorry that I'm not dressed—" Bela started to say, but just as Izán knew he would, Santiago interrupted, taking her hand in his only to smoosh his lips against it in what looked like a sloppy kiss.

"You must allow me to paint you," Santiago said. "Your eyes are stunning, so filled with mystery and intrigue."

The nerve of his cousin thinking he could just waltz in and start slobbering over Bela's hand before he, himself, had properly wooed her to a state where she actually wanted to be married to him. "Don't believe a word he tells you about me—he's been jealous of me since we were teens. I think you've slobbered on her knuckles enough, San." Izán took Bela's hand and made a show of brushing off the top of it with a corner of his towel.

Bela giggled.

Santiago gave him a half-lidded look that promised cousinly retribution in the future, before turning upon Bela what Izán had always thought of as San's besotted-sheep eyes. "Why did you take from me this delightful woman's hand, a hand like no other, a hand that awoke needs in me, buried deep inside, where dwelleth my soul?"

"My cousin is an artist who is under the delusion that someday he will be named poet of the year. Feel free to disregard any odes he makes to your stunning, mysterious eyes." Izán's gaze slipped to the front of her bathrobe, and lingered for a few seconds on where her glorious breasts were hidden away. "And any other part of you that might strike his fancy."

"My fancy is happy to ode away on all parts of the fair Bela." Santiago pursed his lips as he considered her. "I can say with all honesty that you would be a magnificent subject. A portrait, I think. Something traditional, and yet not. Modern but with a touch of the ethereal. Ah, but my cousin is filled with jealousy. Perhaps we will have to meet in secret, sweet Bela. So that I might paint you, of course."

San's voice was filled with amusement, but Izán ignored it, feeling very prickly and irritated. He realized it was jealousy, and was even more irritated at that. This was effectively the morning after his wedding night, and the last thing he wanted to be doing was fighting off his cousin. "Christ, San, can't you lay off charming every woman you see? Bela is very much not interested in you in a romantic way, are you, love?"

Dammit, he wanted Bela to himself for the day. He'd even arranged for Cat to go off with a friend for a shopping trip for their upcoming vacation.

"Er ..." Bela looked momentarily surprised at the endearment, but to his intense pleasure, she did that shoulder-squaring move that made him want to cheer, and said firmly, but politely, "Thank you, Mr. Lopez, but—"

"Santiago, please," he responded, trying to take her hand again. "And I will call you bella Bela. It's Italian, you see?"

"Thank you," Bela repeated. "If you would excuse me, I'll pop into my room and get into something more appropriate than a robe."

She hurried off before Izán could apologize for the interruption to what he had hoped would be sex so steamy they had to take a second shower. He cocked an eyebrow at his cousin. "Nice. It's come to you running off my lovers, eh?"

San rolled his eyes, and pulled Izán in for a bear hug. "Don't be ridiculous. Your mother said you had a woman, and I just wanted to see how serious you were about her." He narrowed his eyes, studying Izán. "You going to keep her?"

"Only if she lets me," he answered.

"Bah," San said, stalking over to look out the window. "You've always been too soft when it comes to women. You have to make the rules and explain that it's easier if they follow them."

"Spoken like a man who doesn't currently have a partner," Izán said as he got dressed. "Let alone understands what it is to have a good relationship. I suppose you plan on staying here for a bit?"

San gave him a long look that he had difficulty interpreting. "I was. I have a commission. I am to paint the wilderness of this area, and as you know, I am the best at painting wildernesses. But now I see that perhaps you will not want me with your woman. I wouldn't want you thinking you could lose her to me at any moment." The last words were spoken with humor, but Izán knew his cousin well. There was more than a hint that Santiago felt he could have Bela if he so desired.

That thought made him want to rage, but he wasn't going to go down that route. Not again.

"What Bela and I have is still new, and I'd appreciate you not ranting to her about what you think a wife should be."

"Wife?" Santiago frowned. "You married this Bela?"

"No," he lied, making sure to keep his gaze steady on San. "Not yet. I hope we can be well and truly married someday, but that will never happen if people keep trying to force Bela into a relationship."

The irony of that statement stabbed deeply into his psyche, but he ignored it.

"Uh-huh. Something's not right here, Izán." San turned toward him from the window. "How long have you known Bela? What does Cat think of her? Why does Bela have her own room? Do you not sleep together?"

"I am not answering any of those questions," he said, glancing at his phone when it pinged with a message. "Other than yes, Cat likes Bela, and vice versa. I have to go; there's a delivery that I need to receive."

It took another few minutes before he got rid of San. He quickly shaved, then peeked into Bela's room to see if she was waiting for him (she wasn't).

"I'm going to have to talk to San," he said a few minutes later, stopping by the kitchen for coffee. Jacob was sitting with a tablet, absently browsing the NPR site.

"About what?" Jacob sipped loudly from his coffee mug. "I take it he's met Bela?"

"Yes. And instantly tried to hit on her," he said grimly, his gaze shifting to a wall in the living room where Santiago had, himself, placed a self-portrait under the guise of a fortieth birthday present to Izán. "Not that Bela is the type of woman to run off with him. At least, I don't think she is."

"She isn't," Jacob said, tapping on the tablet.

"And yet," Izán said, his eyes still on the portrait, "the man could charm the socks off a nun. What hope do I have against him?"

"Have you looked in the mirror lately?" Jacob asked him, sipping loudly again.

"I'm well aware I don't make people vomit when they see me, but that doesn't mean I can stand up to San's seductive self. The bastard." He said the last word lightly, being well used to the swath his cousin cut through the hordes of women drawn to him. "I could have hordes if I wanted to," he said, verbalizing his train of thought.

"I never doubted you could," Jacob said soothingly. "But all you have is a successful business, sanity, a lovely woman, and a happy home life, while Santiago is dangerous, bad to the bone, and has dimples. Des says it's the dimples that push him over the line into irresistible to most women. I notice you don't have dimples."

"I have a cleft chin," Izán said, absently touching his chin. He swore at it every time he had to shave, and wondered what Bela would think of him in a goatee. "Women like cleft chins. Bela said she liked mine a lot. She said she wanted to bite it. I'd wager that not one of Santiago's vast herd of women has ever bitten his nonclefted chin."

Jacob took his cup to the dishwasher. "You're right, you're absolutely right. Your chin far outweighs all the other considerations that put your cousin on countless celebrity websites devoted to popular bachelors. If you're less butt-hurt now, I'll go check in with the team. I brought Cat back a half hour ago, in case you were wondering. Oh, there was some disturbance early this morning that turned out to be a drunk driver trying to force his way through the fence, but no damage was done. I will, however, be having a few words with the security team. Or did you need me to bolster your ego more?"

"You're not as indispensable as you think you are," Izán told him, feeling both disgruntled that his chin—which Bela had told him made her knees weak—wasn't considered as dashing as a couple of everyday dimples, and amused at the fact that he was even having such a ridiculous conversation. "I can get a new security head with a snap of my fingers! Faster if I gave them what I pay you."

Jacob just laughed, flipped him off with what Izán knew was real affection, then went to deal with the team that watched over the grounds and house.

His phone pinged with a text at that moment.

CAT

DAD! She's here! You have to come right now, or Bela will see! I told her I needed her to get me the bit I left in my bedroom, so you've got like seconds!

ME

On my way.

He didn't stop to find Bela in Cat's room, instead hurrying out to the stable.

"Izán!"

Behind him, he heard Bela call his name, evidently having emerged with the requested equipment, but he'd just caught sight of a white-and-blue horse trailer parked on the far side of the stable, and swerved to go around the front, hoping Bela would follow him.

"Izán?"

He stopped at the questioning note in her bellow, and turned to wave her on. "This way," he yelled back before entering the stable.

The double doors to both ends were open, making it possible to see two people unloading from the trailer a tall, somewhat stocky, dapple-gray horse. She had a crumpled ear, and he couldn't help but notice that her mane was shaggy and not at all what he connected to an eventing horse, but at that moment, Bela entered the stable behind him, puffing slightly.

"What on earth is the matter with you? Are you running away from me alread—"The words stopped on her delectable lips when she looked past him and saw the crinkle-eared horse.

"Bo?" she said, her eyes huge. She took a step forward, then stopped, looking at him. "That's Bo."

"Yes," he said, hoping he'd done the right thing. Cat, who had been overseeing the unloading, dashed toward them, causing the horse to bob her head a few times.

"Happy wedding present that isn't a wedding present because you're not married," Cat said, grinning widely, then added—no doubt because Bela was standing in an apparent daze, "We got your horse back for you. So we can ride together, because no one's supposed to ride my mule, Tara, due to her bad feet. Where would you like to put her? I cleaned out this stall because it has an outside run, but if you think she'd like to be near Dave, we can clean the other one."

Bela turned to look at him. He couldn't read her expression, and for a moment, his pleasure in giving her a present wavered. "You bought Bo from the stable I sold her to?"

"Yes," he said, wanting to touch her, to hold her, and to drown in her endless kisses. "We couldn't think of a better gift. You approve?"

Evidently she heard the thread of worry in his voice, because she flung herself on him just as he hoped she'd do, her body fitting against his in a way that instantly had his penis aroused and ready for action. "This is the nicest thing—yes, of course I approve. Thank you! Thank you both! But ... the stable ..."

"They were happy to know you would be reunited with your horse," he lied, not wanting to go into the negotiations he'd had to wrangle to get what was evidently a quite promising eventing horse from their grasp.

Cat did a couple of leaps that had the horse tossing her head again, but calmed down quickly enough.

Bela looked a bit stunned about the eyes, but Izán noticed she didn't stop smiling, not even when Cat insisted, "We can have my first lesson now. I got Dave brushed earlier after I fed him, so he's ready to go. Can I start with jumping? I already know how to go over low hurdles. Dad bought a set of real jumps that we can drag out to the arena."

"Er …" Bela, who was now murmuring sweet nothings in her horse's ear, patted her neck before leading her to the box stall that Cat and Jacob had made ready earlier.

Izán waited, ready to step in and tell Cat to give Bela some time, but wanting to see how she'd deal with his headstrong child.

"How about I make sure Bo is settled first," Bela said. "We can discuss what sort of lessons you've had in the past, and I can evaluate your level of experience riding, and then we can make plans for what you want to learn."

He beamed at Bela, realizing a bit to his surprise that she was everything he could have hoped for, both for Cat and for him. But what made him feel like bursting into song was the warm, soft feeling that he suspected was love.

It had been so long since he'd felt that emotion, he didn't believe it could be, and yet … He watched Bela, the warm feeling spreading outward along his limbs. It was love. It had to be. He had never met someone who fit so perfectly into his life and promised a future he couldn't imagine.

"OK, but I'm going to hold you to that." Cat turned to him, flashing a grin for him alone. It lit him up with another upswelling of emotion. "Although it'll have to wait until this afternoon, because Rory and I are going shopping for the Cabo trip, so I'll be gone until then. But we can work out a schedule and have my first lesson before dinner, OK?"

"We'll see," Izán said after a few moments of wrestling his inner joy until it was under control. He tried to focus on what Cat said, giving her a stern look that she completely ignored. "No, you don't have to stay and help Bela. I'll do that. Go get your things before you keep Jacob waiting."

Cat dashed off with a flurry of happy, excited promises, and he turned to face Bela as she closed the stall door, her horse immediately checking out the feed.

How did he ever think she would be only a companion, a mere mortal woman who didn't deserve to be worshipped as the sensual, enticing goddess she was? He must have been mad.

"You are so sweet—you both are—for even thinking of Bo. It's been so long … but she looks good, don't you think? I think I'll have a vet check her over just in case, though. Not that the stable was bad. I'm sure they took care of her. But just because I'm a worrier." Bela gave him another soul-searing smile.

"We will do whatever you think is needed," he agreed, content to stand there and drink in her happiness.

She chattered for a few minutes, telling him about her horse. He listened, making responses when appropriate, but for the most part, he was busy watching how animated she was, the way happiness gave a soft glow to her eyes, and the slight flush that told him she was as physically aware of him as he was of her.

Would it be wrong to whisk her off to bed without giving her time with her horse?

His thoughts were interrupted when the woman who'd delivered the horse asked him to sign a document.

"Your daughter said the horse was a wedding present?" the driver said as he gave her a tip and thanked her for her help.

"It is, yes."

She winked. "Best present ever. Congratulations!" She drove off to the sound of a few backfires, but when he turned to look into the stable, he found Bela approaching him.

"Are you—" He stopped when she took his face in her hands, studying him for a second before she kissed him, her lips seeming to flutter along his.

"Thank you," she breathed on him, her eyes shiny. "Thank you so much for bring Bo back to me. It's the most thoughtful thing anyone has ever done for me, and I will be grateful to the day I die that you did this. Izán ... I don't have words other than I really think I'm falling in love with you."

He laughed, and slid his hands around her waist, relishing the way she felt in his arms. It wasn't just a matter of them fitting together physically. ... It was as if she'd merged into his soul, as well. "I'm delighted to hear it, because earlier, when my cousin was slobbering all over your hand, I thought I might have to punch the shit out of him. Please tell me you like my chin over his dimples. I hate to admit that I'm insecure, but you make me feel like a caveman when it comes to other men enticing you."

"Your cleft chin is the best thing in the world, and I love it far more than mere dimples," Bela said, her face aglow with happiness and, yes, even a soft hint of love. "I can't believe I have to say this to you of all people, but you are infinitely more wonderful than your cousin. Irrespective of your chin, you're kind, and generous, and love your daughter the way every woman wishes she'd been loved, but most importantly, you're funny. I love your sense of humor. I love your chin."

Izán hesitated, searching her smoky green eyes for any signs of deception.

There were none.

"And do you love me?" he finally asked, his throat tight.

She smiled, and kissed his chin. "Perhaps. Just a little bit. Any man who can give me exactly what I want for a wedding present deserves to be loved a little bit."

"I knew you would want your horse over anything else." He looked past her toward the stable, feeling oddly crestfallen at her words. She loved him a little because he gave her back her horse. Of course, that made sense, but it didn't stop an ache from forming in his chest.

"Izán. We—" She stopped, her gaze searching his. To his surprise, her cheeks darkened. "We had such an odd start, and it doesn't make any sense at all—my sister is going to give me hell, I just know it—but no, it's not Bo that I wanted more than anything."

He stared at her, one foot seeming to hang over an abyss, while the other hovered over the solid ground of a woman with whom he wanted to spend every day left to him. "But ... I thought ... Cat said ..."

"Gah!" Bela yelled, then kissed his face and ears and neck. "You are the best thing to happen to me. You are what I need. You, you annoying man, are exactly what I want, not Bo. I love you for bringing her back because she means a lot to me, but I could live without her. I'm not sure I could do the same without you and Cat."

Relief was followed immediately by a joy so great he wanted to break out into a tap dance routine.

"You couldn't," he said with false bravado, fervently sending up prayers of thanks that Bela was willing to live with him. To love him. To fill his life with laughter, and silliness, and sex so hot it made him hard just looking at her. "You need me almost, but not quite, as much as I need you. Without you, I'd end up living alone with no one to eat chocolate with, and would likely end up as crazy as my cousin."

"You ending up alone is about as likely as Bo flying, but I will accept what I know you meant as a compliment, and will agree that I need you, too. I'm a bit flabbergasted how almost a month ago you came storming into my office looking like you were about to shoot lasers out of your gorgeous eyes, and now you're here, and I can touch you, and kiss you, and talk to you whenever I want."

"I love you, too," he said, his body torn between the impulse of carrying her off to his bedroom in the best romantic-hero manner, and climbing to the top floor to shout out his joy. "Lovemaking wins," he said.

"Huh—Izán!" Bela shrieked as he swung her up and started for the house, his mind going through a list of things he wanted to do to make her moan and writhe with ecstasy. "You can't carry me! And what do you mean, lovemaking wins?"

"I can and I will carry you. It is a delight to hold your lush and delectable form against me. The lovemaking was me finishing my internal narrative out loud. I liked it when you did it, so I thought I'd give it a try, as well. Thoughts?"

She laughed as they approached the house, wiggling her legs with obvious happiness. Santiago opened the door and stood watching them with an indescribable expression.

Just as they approached, he stepped back, one eyebrow cocked as he said, "Your girlfriend hurt herself?"

"Wife," Bela said to his complete shock. She plucked her wedding ring from her middle finger and placed it on the proper one. "We were married yesterday. And I'm not hurt in the least. We're just going to Izán's room so I can tell him how sexy his chin is."

"Wife?" Izán asked, stopping for a moment to look at her. He felt like he had been holding a breath for a month.

"That's your wedding present," she said, kissing the corner of his mouth. "I hope you like it."

He'd never before run up a flight of stairs carrying a woman, but he did so with joy in his heart, words of praise on his lips, and fire in his loins.

So to speak.

One month later...

CAT

Wela! We're in Cabo at last. I didn't think we'd make it, because Dad is being giddy, and Bela is giggling all over the place, despite telling me she isn't at all a giggler, but we got here all right. How did your card game thingie go at your club? Oh, I sent some pix to your photo frame.

WELA

My Caterina! I wondered why all of a sudden that

lovely electronic picture frame you gave me for Christmas was filled with photos of you and your friend in many exciting bikinis. You look charming, although I much preferred you in red to that bright shade of pink in the polka-dot suit. Are you doing more than lounging around the pool? I would have thought you'd find something to do with horses, even in Cabo.

CAT

The pink was a mistake. I know that now. I gave it to Bela, because I'm big like her, but she made kind of a weird face when I gave it to her, even though I told her I had the laundry peeps wash it. And tomorrow Rory and I are going on a daylong riding tour through the local park and onto the beach! We get to eat lunch in the park, and Dad said I could go again later in the week if we have fun. Like we're not going to have fun spending the day riding around cool places! I told him that he and Bela should come with us, but he said something about wanting to show Bela around, and then wiggled his eyebrows at her, and she blushed and tried not to giggle again. I mean, I get they're old, but to not go on an epic all-day ride just to see tourist sites? Their loss!

WELA

It sounds like your father is happy with Bela, yes?

CAT

OK, I'm going to tell you something that Dad would kill me if he knew I told you, but I know you won't tell him, because you never told him about that time I went out to see the Marvel movie after Dad said I had to wait for him to come back from California. So … Dad is really happy. Like, super happy. I said giddy, right? He's SO GIDDY, Wela!

WELA

Your father would be angry about you telling me he's so happy he's giddy?

CAT

No, that wasn't the secret part. That's … OK, big secret. Don't tell! He'll kill me if you do! Bela said they want to wait until we get back to tell everyone. Ready? Here it is! Dad and Bela got married last month! I was both Dad's best woman and Bela's maid of honor, which was cool. You can stop looking for thong women for him, because now he has Bela, and although she says she'd rather work with her mean boss again rather than wear a thong, I know she's perfect for Dad. He says she could wear the heck out of a thong, but Bela is pretty firm on the subject. And Dad keeps kissing her, and then trying to not kiss her when I come into the room, and I had to tell them that it was OK if they wanted to kiss in front of me. I mean, I'm fourteen, right? But you know how he is, such a dad. Anyway, everything is awesome! Dad and I have Bela, and although she makes me do math, we're setting up a fake stable so that I can learn how to run one when I'm older, and I have to do math to deal with ordering stuff, and bank loans, and things like that, so it's not as horrible as it could be. And then we have riding lessons afterward. So shhh! But yay! Shhh!

WELA

I will not give away your secret. Enjoy your vacation, and send me pictures from your riding tour tomorrow, and I'll get you that bridle for which you send me reviews daily.

CAT

You're the best wela ever! Love you!

CALL ME, MAYBE?

My lovely one! I hope you enjoyed reading CHER-ISH (and RESPECT and WARRIOR), all of which I handcrafted from the finest artisanal words just for you. If you want more sexy romcom fun, feel free to dive into the dishy Greek billionaire series starting with IT'S ALL GREEK TO ME.

If you just want more fun stuff, join my newsletter for exclusive reader bonuses like sneak peaks, extra scenes, shop discounts, and bonus epilogues. You can find the signup on my website at katiemacalister.com. It's free and fun. And full of weirdness. Admittedly, lots of weirdness…

ABOUT KATIE

Bird skeleton washer.

Doll's house salesperson to royalty.

King Tut tour guide.

Katie MacAlister has not just worked odd jobs, she's lived an even odder life. Luckily, she's always had a book with her to take her away from the weirdness.

Two years after she started writing novels, Katie sold her first romance, *Noble Intentions*. More than seventy books later, her novels have been translated into numerous languages, been recorded as audiobooks, received several awards, and have been regulars on the *New York Times*, *USA Today*, *Wall Street Journal*, and *Publishers Weekly* bestseller lists. Katie is a widow who lives in the Pacific Northwest with two dogs, and can often be found lurking around online.

You can also find her at katiemacalister.com

www.ingramcontent.com/pod-product-compliance
Lightning Source LLC
Chambersburg PA
CBHW032349310726
48973CB00007B/1923